DEATH'S DISCIPLE:BOOK THREE

CORRUPTION'S CLAW

EMMA L. ADAMS

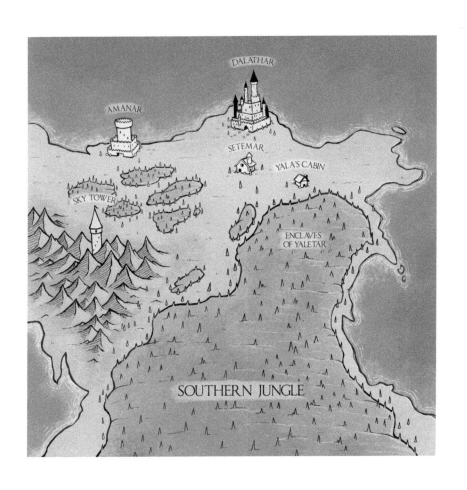

THE STORY SO FAR

Seven years ago, Captain Yala led a squad of six fellow soldiers and their armoured war drakes as part of Laria's army's flight division against the rival nation of Rafragoria. During a clash with Rafragoria over possession of an unmanned island between their nations, the monarch, King Tharen, called Yala's squad to take on a secret mission and claim the island before their rivals could gain a foothold there. Yala agreed to take on the mission before the watchful eyes of the king and his trusted allies the Disciples of the Flame, little suspecting that the island in question would contain an abandoned temple to the god of death, Mekan.

When Yala's squad landed on the island, they found Rafragoria's soldiers had already infiltrated the temple and had met their deaths at the claws and teeth of Mekan's monsters. Their actions ripped open an opening to Mekan's realm, otherwise known as the Void, and Yala and her squad found themselves fighting for their lives. Yala managed to slay the monstrous void drake and sustained a life-changing stab wound to her leg as a result, while her squad-mate Dalem begged the god of the flames to help them escape the island alive. As a former Disciple of the Flame, he was able to gain the god's attention, but he paid the price for the destruction of the island with his own life.

When they returned to the mainland, Yala and her surviving squad-mates learned that King Tharen was assassinated by Rafragorian soldiers during their absence and that he told nobody else of the mission he gave her squad. While she hoped that her squad-mate's sacrifice would help her gain the sympathy of the Disciples of the Flame, their leader Superior Datriem refused to believe Yala's reports and threatened her life if she ever shared the truth of what they saw on the island with anyone else. Shortly after, the new king disbanded the flight division of the army and Yala and her surviving squad members parted ways.

After years of living in seclusion in the deep jungle, Yala little expected anyone to disturb her early retirement, much less a war drake. The beast turned out to belong to a Disciple of Life called Niema who claimed to have been sent by her Superior to seek out Yala and to deliver a cryptic warning of danger. It emerged that Niema learned of her location from Vanat, Yala's former squad-mate with whom she'd had a brief romantic entanglement after the war, but Yala's refusal to leave her home came to an end with the arrival of a group of mercenaries vying to claim a price on her head.

Yala killed the mercenaries with the aid of a Disciple of the Sky, Kelan, who was pursuing the mercenaries for his own reasons. Distrusting his motives, Yala reluctantly joined forces with Niema instead to seek out Vanat, but found he was taken captive by a mysterious group called the Successors. Following Vanat's tail to the capital, Yala and Niema once again clashed with Kelan, who revealed that he was sent by his own Superior to investigate the rumours of someone meddling with death magic in the capital when he found the mercenaries. Niema, meanwhile, revealed that Yala appeared in a vision experienced by the Disciples of Life showing her to be a powerful ally against the rise of Mekan, the god of death.

Suspecting a connection with her experiences on the island, Yala firmly explained to Niema that she and her squad members survived through Dalem's sacrifice and not because Yala possessed any unique ability to resist Mekan. They then found Vanat's dead body on the road. Furious at the loss of her friend, Yala parted ways with her companions upon reaching the capital and went to track down her surviving squad members. While Machit was willing to listen to her, Saren refused, while Viam was safely working within the royal palace and Temik's whereabouts were unknown. Yala warned Machit of the mercenaries' seeming intention of eliminating all the survivors from their squad and he agreed to help her find the truth about the Successors' motives.

Yala and the others soon discovered that the Successors had indeed been meddling with death magic, and in the ensuing confrontation, the Successors' leader Melian revealed her face. Claiming to be a Disciple of Death, Melian attempted to sacrifice Yala and her friends to gain the favour of the god of death and overthrow the monarch. While Machit was killed in the struggle, Yala managed to fend Melian off with the help of Niema, who called upon the war drake using her abilities as a Disciple of Life and ordered it to attack the mercenaries.

In the ensuing chaos, Melian escaped, while Kelan went to rejoin his fellow Disciples of the Sky and met with the unwelcome news that some of them believed Yala to be in league with the Successors herself. It soon transpired that the source of the rumours was none other than the Temple of the Flame, which Melian had infiltrated with the help of Yala's former squad member Temik. When Yala tried to tell him the truth, Superior Datriem attempted to have Yala captured and sentenced to death.

With two groups of Disciples pursuing them and Melian's whereabouts unknown, Yala was forced to accept Kelan's offer to seek out shelter with the Disciples of the Sky. While Superior Sietra believed Yala's innocence, she also revealed that Melian was right. Anyone who glimpsed Mekan's realm had the potential to become a Disciple of Death, including Yala and her squad, whether they acted on that potential or not. As a result, Superior Sietra decided to imprison Yala as a risk factor and sent a team of her own people to the capital to deal with Melian.

Kelan disagreed with his Superior's choice, but Niema's horror at Yala's connection to Mekan led to her turning her back on both of them. With help of some of his fellow Disciples of the Sky, Kelan helped Yala her escape captivity and returned to the capital – but too late. Temik, seeking revenge on the Disciples of the Flame for their role in his squad-mate's death on the island, already killed Superior Datriem and drugged the other Disciples of the Flame, leaving the path wide open for Melian to enact her plan. With the dead swarming the city at her command, Melian had enough power to slay Yala's war drake and cut her throat.

Before Yala could bleed out, Niema had a change of heart and returned, using the power of the god of life to rescue Yala from the brink of death. During her recovery, Yala reunited with her surviving squad-mates – including Viam, now working at the royal palace, who admitted that she was the one who found the books King Tharen used to learn of the island's existence and handed them to Temik in the hopes of revealing the truth of what their squad experienced there. After Temik gave the books to Melian instead, Viam wanted to make amends by helping Yala.

Accepting that the only way to beat Melian was to call upon Mekan herself, Yala followed Viam's instructions and raised the dead war drake that Melian slew, riding upon its back to interrupt Melian's attempt to break into the palace and assassinate the king. However, Melian had already opened Mekan's realm by slaughtering some of Kelan's fellow Disciples. While Yala managed to kill Melian, she was unable to close the Void. At the last moment, Temik reappeared and gave his own life to the god of the flame in the same way Dalem did, closing Mekan's realm and ending the slaughter.

As the city made its slow recovery from the devastation of Melian's attack, Yala decided to stay with her surviving squad-mates to make sure nobody else attempted to follow in Melian's footsteps. However, several weeks later, Yala's attempts to lie low were thwarted when she learned of someone trying to raise the dead in the capital again. She was then invited to meet the Disciples of the Flame's new leader, Superior Shralin, who informed her that the book that Melian used to learn how to use Corruption was missing. He then effectively blackmailed Yala into going to find it by threatening to reveal her status as a Disciple of Death to the world.

Kelan, confined to Skytower after the events in the capital, was then sent on a mission to Setemar to find out why the Disciples of the Earth mysteriously cut off all contact with the outside world. She assigned him to travel with Laima, and neither of them was thrilled at this arrangement. After several failed attempts, the pair were eventually able to meet with the Disciples of the Earth's leader, Superior Dovial. He revealed that the reason for their isolation was that the Disciples of the Earth were inexplicably losing the ability to contact their deity or use their powers – and that the dead were rising from their subterranean graves.

Niema, meanwhile, returned home to the jungle to find one of her enclave members dying from an unknown illness. Niema came to the horrifying realisation that in saving Yala's life when Melian cut her throat, she borrowed the life force of her fellow enclave members through their bond and is now too late to undo the damage. Worse, Superior Kralia had already figured out the truth, and sentenced Niema to be imprisoned for aiding a Disciple of Death. She then ordered two powerful Disciples to hunt down Yala, too. After all, Corruption must be eradicated.

Back in the capital, Yala's search for the missing book led her to travel to Setemar. There, she joined forces with Kelan to search the tunnels underneath the city, where they unearthed a hidden Temple of Death set up by the person who took the book... Melian's younger brother Trienan. Their confrontation ended in a stalemate, but complications abounded when Yala unearthed apparent evidence that someone from among the Disciples of the Earth had been dabbling in Corruption, too, which led to its infiltration of their temple. Superior Dovial's refusal to believe her reports culminated in Yala's arrest, but she gained the support of a Disciple called Pehin who allied with Kelan and the others to help her escape.

A spate of disappearances in the village near Setemar prompted Yala and the others to return to the mines where they found the Temple of Death. There, they found that Melian's brother had already opened the void, and to avoid destruction, Yala was forced to call the undead war drake back to aid in her fight. Most of the Disciples of Death were killed in the process, including Trienan, while Yala finally got her hands on the missing book. The book turned out not to be a guide to Corruption, but a journal written by someone who visited Laria—and the island where she found the Temple of Death—long before her own people settled on the continent. And apparently the Disciples of Life and Death were both already present at the time.

Two Disciples of the Flame then showed up looking for the book, not trusting Yala not to keep it for herself. Having witnessed Yala's conjuring of the undead war drake, they figured out what she was, and their confrontation ended in Yala being forced to kill them both.

While imprisoned, Niema managed to send a warning to Yala and then went on the run from the Disciples of Life who the Superior sent to capture Yala. Having received her warning, Kelan helped her escape to Setemar, where they found that the Disciples of the Earth closed their doors again, their Superior believing that the safest way to keep out Corruption is to prevent anyone from leaving the temple at all.

Yala, knowing the rot lay within the temple itself, joined with the others to entice some of the Disciples of the Earth out into the open, where they were able to gain access to their deity again – but too late. The dead attacked the city, resulting in many casualties, including Laima.

While the city was under attack from the dead, the Disciples of Life arrived, led by Superior Kralia, who now used her abilities as a Superior to mind-control Niema into obeying her command to take Yala's life.

While the battle between the Disciples of Life and Death broke out, Yala was forced to fight a mind-controlled Niema, who managed to break free of Superior Kralia's orders. The two joined forces to close the void and defeat the dead, which led to Superior Kralia's reluctant acceptance that Yala was not on Mekan's side.

In the aftermath, Niema decided to leave her enclave for good, while Yala returned to the capital to return the stolen book to the Disciples of the Flame. However, Kelan showed up to claim it for his own Superior instead, much to Superior Shralin's annoyance, believing a dangerous book like that would be safer in Skytower.

As *Traitor's Tome* ends, Superior Shralin tells Yala of a Rafragorian soldier whose body washed up on Laria's shore, carrying note emblazoned with the following words: REMEMBER THE ISLAND.

PROLOGUE

The Disciples of the Sky descended upon the city of Amanar like a wave breaking against the shore.

To Kelan, the city resembled a blot on a page made by a person knocking over a pot of ink. Squat buildings sprawled along the coastline, without the taller structures that characterised the capital of Dalathar and no monuments to the deity who gave the city its name. Amanat, He who ruled the endless sea. The ocean was a sparkling blue mass dotted with ships whose beauty formed a stark contrast to the warren of slums that was their intended destination.

The orphanage, a squalid building of grey stone with a patchy roof, was matched by the equally bedraggled woman who met them at the door. Her gaze lingered on their well-made blue cloaks, her words punctuated by consistent dripping as the remnants of the night's storm splashed into the buckets placed at intervals on the wooden floor.

"We're looking for anyone between the age of eleven and, ah, sixteen," Kelan said, though he suspected anyone older than their mid-teens would have either enlisted in the army or fled to avoid the compulsory draft and fallen in with the local gangs as a result. "Anyone who would like to be tested by the Disciples of the Sky."

The woman beckoned, having corralled the children into the main room to wait for their visitors. A familiar tightness in Kelan's chest arose as he looked at the sea of gaunt faces, some of which had lit with hope at the Disciples' arrival. The staff, their faces as starved and weary as the children's, had to extract a few younger hopefuls who'd hidden among the others.

"Sorry, eleven or twelve is the youngest we'll take," another Disciple of the Sky told the woman. "Any younger than that and they run the risk of not passing the tests."

Or rather, not being accepted by the god of the sky. Kelan didn't blame them for trying it on; he might have been a full-ranked Disciple himself for over half a decade, but he'd never forgotten the life he'd left behind when he'd joined their ranks.

"We'll come back," Kelan told the woman when she slipped back into the room, rubbing her tired eyes on the back of her worn sleeve. "In a few years, when they're old enough."

Seven children remained, watching with the same curiosity he'd doubtless shown when he'd met the Disciples who'd come to his village so long ago. A smaller number than he'd expected, but perhaps that would heighten the odds of their acceptance.

"What will happen to us?" asked a skinny girl of around thirteen.

"You'll come to Skytower," he told them. "To be tested by Terethik, god of the skies."

As novices, they'd learn how to manipulate the air currents to fly and perform what ordinary people would call miracles. They'd never experience hunger or have to sleep in a room with a leaking roof again. Provided they passed the sky god's tests, of course, but Terethik was known for being one of the more magnanimous of the deities.

"Go on." The woman waved a hand at them. "Go and pack, quickly now."

As the children scurried out of the room, Kelan addressed her in a low voice. "I expected more. Did most of the older children enlist?"

Her lips pursed. "No, *they* took them."

"Who's 'they'?" he asked.

"The ones from the water." She didn't meet his eyes. "The other Disciples."

The Disciples of the Sea? He knew little of that branch of Disciples. While they reportedly lived off Laria's coast, they seldom ventured onto land, though logically, he knew they had to get their novices from somewhere. The Disciples of the Flame recruited primarily from amongst war orphans in Dalathar but rarely strayed outside their city's borders. The same went for the Disciples of the Earth and their own home city of Setemar. The Disciples of the Sky, who could travel further afield, picked their novices more widely, which would explain why a village orphan like Kelan had ended up training alongside the son of a respected merchant like Lakiel. As for the Disciples of the Sea, he supposed Amanar must be the closest major city to where they were rumoured to make their home. He'd never set eyes upon one before, though.

The children returned before he could ask more questions, and his fellow Disciples ushered them outside. Their small faces were already brighter at the prospect of leaving the orphanage, and they chattered amongst themselves about Skytower and the god which they hoped to serve.

"Will we get cloaks like yours?" a narrow-faced young man asked, plucking at Kelan's sleeve. "They look expensive."

"You'll be given novice uniforms when you arrive in Skytower," Kelan replied. "When you're full Disciples, you'll get a cloak."

"Are the tests hard?" The young man's voice wavered. "Do many people fail?"

"No, not at all. You'll easily pass." He caught the eye of his fellow Disciple—Lakiel—who gave him a disapproving stare for reasons he couldn't fathom. He was hardly going to tell this group of orphans that there was any risk of being kicked out of Skytower and sent back to the orphanage. "Who's ready to go?"

"Can we get something to eat first?" asked the skinny girl who'd spoken to him earlier, indicating a stall on the street's corner from which the enticing smell of fried fish drifted. "It's a long way to Skytower, isn't it?"

"We can stop somewhere on the way," Lakiel said, but the children ignored him. They swarmed the stall, casting hopeful eyes at Kelan, having correctly assumed he was more than happy to purchase lunch for them.

"I don't see any harm in waiting a little longer," he said, reaching into his pocket for his coin purse. "How much for seven of those?"

The fish had been fried to a crisp, but the orphans didn't care; this was likely the first meal they'd eaten in a while, and they fell on the food with such enthusiasm that he had to supervise to make sure that everyone got their fair share. When he saw some of them hiding extra food in their pockets, a habit he remembered too clearly, Kelan tossed another coin to the stall owner and asked him to deliver as much fried fish to the orphanage as his coin would cover.

As they ate, he joined the others where they'd gathered on a pier facing the seafront, where the ocean lapped at the wooden slats. He tried to imagine Disciples swimming to the shore in the dead of night like monsters from legend, clad in... not cloaks, surely. The fabric would become waterlogged and tangle around their legs, and he doubted their Superiors wore elaborate headgear either. His mental image morphed as he pondered on the practicalities of living in a place with so few resources. Did they subsist solely on fish and sea plants? What did they do when storms tossed the ocean's waves into a frenzy—hide under rocks?

Inevitably, Kelan's curiosity got the better of him. "Did the other Disciples ask you to join them?" he asked the nearby children, gesturing out to sea. "The Disciples who live out there?"

The skinny girl spoke through a mouthful of fried fish. "Yesh, they did. I said no 'cos I can't swim."

"Tac can't swim either," remarked the boy who'd spoken to Kelan earlier. "He's probably dead."

"Yahin!" shrieked the girl. "That's horrible."

"True, though," said another orphan. "They didn't ask if we could swim. Just if we didn't mind leaving Laria for good."

"Really?" Strange. All branches of Disciples lived apart from regular people, but the deities didn't outright forbid their followers

4

from interacting with non-Disciples, much less never setting foot upon their own shores again.

"That's right," the boy said. "I told 'em no, since my parents died at sea, in the war."

Right. Of course. Most children here would be war orphans, young victims of King Tharen's relentless campaigns against their neighbouring nation of Rafragoria. Kelan wasn't clear what had been achieved in the past few decades of conflict save for Laria and Rafragoria passing the same bits of land back and forth as one gained victory and then the other. Disciples were prohibited from participating in warfare, but now Kelan thought, he couldn't imagine it was fun for the Disciples of the Sea to have their home constantly intruded upon by boats full of Larian soldiers and Rafragoria's sea drake–riding squads. No wonder they never came ashore.

Kelan glided down the pier, eyeing the large expanse of blue with a newfound curiosity. Somewhere on the other side of the blue was the large continent dominated by the Parvan Empire. Between was the large chain of islands that formed the Rafragorian peninsula, more landmasses... and the Temple of the Sea.

He racked his memory, trying to recall whether they'd learned anything of that temple in lessons. While he'd freely admit to falling asleep in class as a novice, he wasn't convinced they *had* covered that branch of Disciples beyond the superficial details. Had his Superior ever met with their leader? Whose idea had it been to break off contact with the rest of Laria?

As his feet hovered above the pier's edge, something stirred below the water.

Kelan jerked backwards, recognising the unmistakable outline of a human hand stretching upward as though reaching to clasp his own.

"Kelan?" Lakiel's irate voice came drifting down the pier. "It's time to go."

"There's someone in the water." Unease stirred inside him. He dropped to a crouch and reached over the edge. Grimacing at the salt spray, he leaned until his sleeve was soaked to the elbow and his hand closed around the clammy skin of someone who was certainly dead and had been for a while. He tugged, lifting a lighter weight than he'd expected. A child.

"Tac!" one of the children on the docks shouted. "It's Tac!"

Screaming filled the air, mingling with the cries of seabirds. Kelan placed the small body on the wooden pier, his mind reeling. *What happened to him? Did the god of the sea reject him and leave him to drown, or did the other Disciples just leave him behind?*

Kelan was never able to adequately explain what he did next. While the others were gathered around the drowned body of the orphan boy, he found his attention back on the ocean, on the expanse of glittering blue sea. And then he stepped over the pier and glided northward, across the deceptively calm water.

At what point the waves would turn from calm to treacherous, he didn't know. Nor had he ever swum in anything larger than a river. Yet his primary thought was that he didn't believe that no Disciple of the Sky had ever been curious enough to explore the oceans beyond Laria's shore. Yes, dangers lay abroad, but Disciples had no part in King Tharen's war. Rafragoria's soldiers surely wouldn't dare strike him down and risk the wrath of every other Disciple inside Laria's borders. So why—?

Someone shouted his name. A current of air buffeted him from the side, and when he lifted his head, the sound of beating wings echoed from above.

From a war drake, saddled and armed for war, flying directly at him.

Kelan flew higher, but the beast lifted its head too. *They can't resist a moving target,* he recalled hearing, possibly during one of the many lessons in which he'd fallen asleep at Skytower. Worse, six more beasts flew behind the first, a full Larian flight squad.

The beast's rider yelled something—probably an insult—as Kelan scanned for any route of escape and found only one remaining.

He dropped out of the sky and plunged into a dive.

Hitting the water hurt more than he'd expected, his entire body recoiling as if he'd slammed headlong into a wall. At once, he was encased in all-encompassing, suffocating darkness, gasping for air that wasn't there. His cloak billowed around his legs, its weight pulling him down no matter how he kicked and flailed. His hair, thick and damp, clung to his face, further obscuring his sight.

This is how I'm going to die? Really?

He gave one last, desperate kick, and his head broke the surface. He gasped, inhaled, choked, and went under again.

A hand floated in front of him in the gloomy water. He recoiled, gasped, and the hand moved. A living hand, not dead, reaching to pull him out. Kelan grasped the hand and let its owner pull him to the surface. Surprised to see Lakiel was his rescuer, he blinked water from his eyes and sucked in air.

"Thanks." Breathing a prayer to Terethik, he drifted upward and out of the water until he reached the pier. There, he collapsed, convulsing, retching, shivering.

"What were you thinking?" Lakiel demanded. "Did you forget that you're a Disciple of the Sky, not the Sea?"

Kelan coughed. "Perhaps I was so enraptured by the beautiful ocean that I decided to get a close-up view."

"You see the ocean every time we fly over the coast." Lakiel shook his head. "You were going to the Disciples, weren't you?"

"They killed a child." His gaze went to the small body on the pier. One of the other Disciples had wrapped him in their cloak.

"They didn't kill him," Lakiel said, exasperated. "The boy drowned. Like you almost did."

"If they took him with them knowing he couldn't swim, they as good as killed him, didn't they?" he rasped. "Or their god did, which is worse."

"Not all gods are as merciful as ours."

Lucky for us. He shivered. "Is that why they left Laria? The Disciples of the Sea?"

"I haven't the faintest idea." He didn't sound as though he was interested either. That was nothing new. Kelan had enough curiosity for the pair of them, and even the orphaned children were eyeing him with a mixture of awe and incredulity.

Kelan watched the last of the war drakes disappear into the

7

distance. It took a brave soul to tame one of those beasts—though "tame" was the wrong word, as he'd seen for himself when he'd narrowly avoided being cleaved in two by those vicious teeth. They must be on their way to another skirmish with Rafragoria; another battle to turn the seawater red and leave more bodies upon Laria's shores. Another wave of orphans to wait and pray for a miracle.

Perhaps Tac had been lucky. Given the choice, Kelan would certainly have picked drowning over death in battle or starvation.

While his curiosity was far from sated, it would be many years before Kelan thought of the Disciples of the Sea again.

1

The war drake bared its teeth at Yala as she extended a gloved hand to take hold of the chain around its neck.

"Yes, very scary," she said. "Do you want to fly? Or are you going to snap at me?"

She'd taken off its muzzle, but her fingers were clothed in drakeskin gloves that would prevent its sharp teeth from severing the tendons if her attention lapsed for a heartbeat. The trick was keeping its attention on the promise of a tastier snack than her stringy human limbs. Yala tossed the war drake a piece of raw raptor meat, which it caught in its large jaws, and allowed herself a moment of pride. She'd spent years around war drakes, but this one belonged to her alone, a luxury she'd never been afforded as a soldier.

While the war drake was occupied with chewing, she sidestepped its large flank and undid the bindings around its leathery wings. She kept hold of its chain as she did so, the other hand maintaining a firm grip on the carved wooden cane that she used to compensate for the injury she'd sustained during the last mission that she'd participated in as part of the king's army.

Memories both bitter and sweet clustered in the back of her mind as she worked. The war drake strained at the chain, stretching its wings, and she reached into her pack for another piece of meat. While the beast was occupied, she fastened the other end of its chain to a post. The war drake snapped its displeasure, exhaling the stench of raw meat into her face.

"Don't look at me like that," she muttered. "We'll have a proper flight when someone's around to help, but Saren's at work, and I'm not subjecting the stableboy to your antics. Stretch your wings and quit complaining."

The chain rattled as the beast's wings flapped, gusting air at her; it didn't understand human speech, though it had grasped her meaning that she wouldn't release its chain. Not today. The paddock, designed for domestic raptors and not war drakes, offered enough space for the beast to prowl but little in the way of company save for herself.

When Yala had flown as part of a squad, they'd taken turns to help each rider mount their steed without any mishaps, and despite her extensive experience, Yala was well aware of the precarious nature of Laria's relationship with its war steeds. Years of watching her fellow riders lose limbs or worse had developed instincts that had come back sooner than she'd expected. Instincts that she'd need if she wanted to survive what might await her.

Two weeks ago, a dead Rafragorian soldier had washed ashore in a boat, clutching a note in his hand that said, *Remember the island.*

The note was unsigned, unaddressed, but as one of the few people in Laria who even knew which island the note referred to, Yala had the impression of being invited in on a secret joke that even the king wasn't privy to. In truth, she didn't know how much King Daliel had been told. According to Viam, he'd received no direct correspondence from Rafragoria either. Not a word.

After she'd fastened the wing restraints back into place, Yala tossed the war drake a last piece of meat. Wiping her greasy fingers on her drakeskin trousers, she waited for it to finish chewing then reattached its muzzle. The war drake snapped its teeth at her again from behind the thick fabric.

"Soon," she murmured. "Soon."

With its muzzle in place, Yala left the paddock. Over the

rooftops, the distant sound of cheering reached her ears, punctuated by drumbeats. Goose bumps sprang up on her arms despite the damp heat. The sound was as familiar as a war drake's cry, an echo of another time. A long-gone era of her life when she didn't have to lean on a cane for balance while she locked the gate and when she'd been surrounded by a squad in the military barracks rather than alone.

Instead, the drums and cheers struck her like a wrong note in an orchestra. King Tharen was long dead, and his son shared none of his fondness for military spectacle. That King Daliel had felt pressured to revive Laria's old traditions might be timely if Rafragoria did indeed lay the blame for their soldiers' fates at Laria's feet, but Yala had thought her nation's enmity with their neighbours had been buried with the death of their last king.

The sinking sun cast golden-red rays over the rooftops as she left the paddock, walking past a twitchy stableboy who wasn't getting paid nearly enough. She found a large, bearded man waiting for her in the street outside.

"What's wrong, Nalen?" she asked, surprised to see him in this part of the city. The burly veteran usually occupied the narrow alleyway that led to Dalathar's Undercity, guarding the streets inhabited by the capital's most unfortunate. "Not another dismembered limb in the river, I hope."

"No, it's Saren."

Yala frowned. "Isn't he supposed to be working?"

He scratched an ear with a callused hand. "I saw him on his way to the pleasure district with some off-duty guards."

Yala sighed. "Why?"

"Don't know." Nalen scuffed the cobbles with a worn boot, another remnant from his time in the king's army. Like Yala, he'd watched the king's recent recruitment endeavours with wariness; while he was theoretically within the right age range and fitness level to sign up again, he refused to give up his self-appointed role in protecting the people of the Undercity, and so far, the king's guards hadn't come knocking on his door. *Yet.*

"I'll have to wash my hands first," she told him. "I can hardly go to the pleasure district reeking of raw meat and drake dung."

Yala stopped at a nearby fountain and splashed water over her hands and boots, but there was little to do for the smell of the paddocks that always lingered these days. She didn't intend to stay in the pleasure district long enough for anyone to notice. In truth, part of her wondered if she ought to leave Saren to his own devices. She might no longer be a squad leader in the official sense, but her lingering sense of responsibility towards her former squad members remained, and so she let Nalen lead the way through the cobbled streets until they came to a gambling den.

"What's he doing in here?" Yala halted and swore under her breath. "I'm guessing it's already too late to stop him losing all his wages."

Yala pushed open the door and was immediately enveloped in a cloud of bitterleaf smoke and raucous laughter. *What's Saren doing in a place like this?* He'd been on his best behaviour recently—in fact, she'd gone as far as to conclude that he'd finally rid himself of his alcohol dependence, which was a fool's assumption, she knew. As long as the nightmares remained, so would the desire to bury those memories, if just for a short time. *Remember the island, indeed.*

Yala scanned the dingy room, where Saren sat slumped on a stool, a few dice scattered on the table in front of him. At her approach, he slumped even further until the crown of his head reached the table.

"Saren." Yala's cane beat a rhythm on the uneven floor, the wooden base sticking to the detritus of spilled drinks. "That's enough."

"I'm not done yet," he mumbled with the half-hearted defiance of someone who knew they'd been caught in the act.

"Yes, he is," said the man who sat opposite him. Despite his discarded coat, Yala would know him for a city guard from the clank of weapons at his belt when he rose to his feet. "Shit. You're Yala—"

"Don't finish that sentence." She gave the man a hard stare until he sloped away and then sat in his abandoned seat.

"Saren, aren't you supposed to be working?" She leaned over the table and nudged at a copper coin with her fingertips. "Don't tell me you bet all your wages."

She was the one who'd found him his new position as a healer's apprentice, which was a miracle, given the sheer volume of unemployed former soldiers in the capital. A number of them had joined the guards, but Saren had expressed a firm desire to have as little to do with the monarch as possible.

"No," he mumbled. "No, and I quit."

"You did *what?*" Yala flicked a coin at him, her nails scraping the table's surface. "After all the trouble I went to?"

"We had an argument." He caught the coin in a palm and cradled it to his chest. "I told him to jump in the river."

"Might I ask why?"

Saren lifted his chin, his eyes bright and defiant. "He made some comment about the war and you."

"Me." She jerked back in her seat. "*What* did he say about me?"

"Doesn't matter."

"It does if it cost you your job. You know how hard it was to find someone open to training a new apprentice in your position?"

"Yes, I fucked up, same as usual." His defiance slid away. "You don't need to remind me."

"That's not what I meant." Some of her irritation faded. Saren's habit of letting any semblance of stable employment slip through his fingers was well known at this point, and this was hardly his worst transgression. He didn't even appear to be drunk. "Tell me what he said about me."

When Saren opened his mouth to answer, someone crashed into their table, scattering the remaining coins onto the floor. As he dove to retrieve them, a gust of wind rippled through the air. Given the humid night, Yala knew the source before the person who'd crashed into the table caught his balance, and she recognised Kelan of Skytower. Disciple of the Sky, erstwhile pain in her behind, and the person who'd saved her life enough times that it would have been galling if she hadn't returned the favour in equal measures.

She climbed to her feet. "Kelan?"

Ignoring her, he lunged towards a nearby guard who held a bright-blue Disciple's cloak draped over his arm.

"Hey!" She slammed the rim of her cane down in front of him. "What are you doing?"

"We won this fairly." The guard held up the long-sleeved cloak in a hand, letting it fall to its full length. "He gambled his cloak when he ran out of coin."

"Really, Kelan?"

"No." He lifted a hand and sent a gust of wind at the guards, which missed, instead knocking over a nearby table. Wood and glass crunched, and several people shouted obscenities at him.

"Does your deity mind you using your powers for vandalism?" She stepped in front of Kelan when the guard reached for his knife with clumsy fingers. "Don't even think about drawing a weapon unless you want to see mine."

The guard's bleary eyes widened with recognition. Kelan made another attempt to sidestep Yala, but she seized his arm.

"Can't you get a new cloak?" she asked. "They have enough spares at the inn that you can afford to lose one."

"It's too early to go back to the inn." He tugged his arm free and lurched sideways. "I'll go and seek my entertainment elsewhere."

The other patrons watched with relief as Kelan staggered towards the door and out into the night. Yala debated following him, but a yelp drew her attention back to the table she'd left behind. Nalen had lifted Saren bodily from his seat by the scruff of his neck. "Where should I put him?"

"Into the war drake's pen."

"What?" Saren yelped, sobering abruptly. "I didn't do anything that bad."

"You got me caught in the middle of a fight between Disciples," she said. "Or one Disciple. What's he playing at?"

"You think I know?" Nalen carried Saren to the door and placed his feet on the cobbles outside. It had begun to rain; warm droplets slid down Yala's face and clung to her curly hair.

Kelan had already gone.

Yala blew out a breath. "Better go before we're blamed for this."

The gambling den's owner had presumably been hiding to avoid being involved in a fight involving a Disciple, but she doubted she or Saren would be welcome there again. City guards could talk their way out of almost any transgression, and Disciples—well, *they* were a force unto themselves.

They left the pleasure district, passing groups of merry individuals who paid no heed to the rain sliding down their faces and soaking the light fabric of their clothes. The sounds of laughter had replaced the cheers and drumbeats from over the wall to the upper city, but Yala's sense of unease remained.

"Fucking Disciples," she said. "You can't invite them anywhere."

———

Viam had never seen the palace so bright.

Banners and gold-and-blue flags were strewn across every edifice of the buildings within the palace complex, leaving a glare that lingered on the insides of her eyelids long after she'd left them behind for the more muted tones of the war drakes' paddocks.

Before leaving the palace grounds, she'd changed from her work uniform to a pair of drakeskin trousers—purchased out of her wages, as her old uniform no longer fit—and the gloves she'd never had the heart to throw away. With a sack of meat in one hand and a key in the other, she unlocked the paddock gate and slipped inside.

A familiar growl greeted her, the sound of a predator in wait, and Viam extracted a chunk of meat from the bag and tossed it into the open jaws of the full-grown war drake that stalked towards her on clawed feet. Several other beasts were inside the shed at the back, sheltering from the rain, but this one had both managed to get out of its hut and also somehow removed its muzzle.

"How'd you do that?" She fished the muzzle out of a puddle of rainwater and tossed it into a corner then checked to make sure the chain around the beast's neck was still secure. It was, and so were its wing restraints. Some part of her twinged in guilt at the sight of its majestic, leathery wings bound to its back, unable to stretch out, but keeping a beast of that size and strength in the middle of Laria's most populous city meant such cautionary measures were vital.

Taking the chain in one hand, Viam began to go through the basic commands. Sit, crouch, lift one leg and then the other, and duck its head so that a human rider could climb onto its back—all enforced by tugs of the chain and slithers of meat. Interacting with the beasts was a delicate dance between caution and boldness, displaying dominance without treading into foolhardiness. She'd taken to spending an hour here after work each day, with King Daliel's permission, and it was surprising how quickly she'd slipped back into her old routines. Viam might feel more at home surrounded by ink and parchment, but kneeling in the dirt, shouting hoarse commands at a large and angry reptile, was a welcome change from pretending nothing was wrong.

Pretending that Laria wasn't on the brink of war for the first time since Viam had handed in her army-issued dagger and left her old life behind.

Hence the banners, the cheering, the drums. It was all incredibly patriotic and yet somehow false at the same time. Viam knew the king to be soft-spoken and scholarly, with none of his father's desire to produce countless monuments to Laria's conquests, and until recently, the army had been a low priority. Now, new ranks of soldiers marched into the barracks every day. All volunteers. Thus far, King Daliel hadn't revived the compulsory draft, but it was surely only a matter of time.

As of yet, the Flight Division remained a distant memory, and Viam usually fed the war drakes alone each morning and evening. It was therefore a surprise when she heard footsteps outside the paddock and then the creak of the gate opening.

Viam halted, one hand on the bag of meat and the other on the war drake's chain, as King Daliel entered the paddock.

"Your Majesty." She dipped her head but didn't kneel; he'd told her she didn't need to bother with such formalities, and besides, she didn't dare take her attention off the war drake. The heavy chain prevented it from reaching the newcomer, but its pitch-dark eyes scanned the monarch's bright attire with interest all the same.

16

Even King Daliel's clothing had changed to reflect the military man his father had once been, his golden headdress less elaborate, his robes adorned with embroidery in the same gold and blue hues as the banners around the palace. His usual sandals had been replaced by solid boots that were polished to a high sheen, though that wouldn't last if he took another step into the muddy paddock.

"Viam," he said. "I'm impressed at how quickly you've gained the war drakes' trust."

"Thank you, Your Majesty." She stepped away from the war drake, retaining a firm grip on the chain. "This one should be ready to fly soon."

She assumed she'd need to ask His Majesty's direct permission to take the war drake for a flight, given that it theoretically belonged to him. While the paddock lay directly outside the back gates to the palace, she'd never expected His Majesty to come here, much less alone.

"Good," he replied. "We'll need it. I understand that your friend Yala is training a war drake too?"

At the mention of her former squad leader's name, Viam stiffened. "Yes, but it's a personal project for her."

Fool, she chided herself. It'd been hard for her to keep the king from finding out that one of the relatively few war drakes in the capital had ended up in Yala's hands, but she'd assumed that the demise of the Flight Division would prevent him from taking an interest. Naïve, of course, given their history.

"I know," he said. "However, as a former captain, it would be valuable to have her expertise in training the new recruits."

"She's never trained anyone outside of the Flight Division," Viam said, her heart plunging. "Also, it's been a long time since the war."

Yala would laugh in her face if Viam suggested she return to her former position. Her early retirement from the army had been reinforced by a payment worthy of a captain of the highest rank, which was supposed to see her through the remainder of her days without her ever having to set foot—or wing—on a battlefield again. The thought of the alternative made Viam's palms dampen with sweat.

"Yes, it has," the king agreed. "I expect it'll be a while before the war drakes are ready too. It's been difficult to recapture those who've tasted freedom."

"No." Yala often said that all drakes were wild, that humans only shared a delusion that they were in control, and Viam had to admit she agreed.

"It's a shame." His mouth turned down at the corners. "I thought— or rather hoped—that there might be a way to send an envoy to meet with Rafragoria without running afoul of those dangerous seas."

"Send an envoy?" she said. "On a war drake? They'll think they're being attacked."

Years might have passed since the war ended, but the Rafragorians would forever associate the image of Larian war drakes as a precursor to their own demise. Even King Daliel ought to know that, surely.

"Yes, my advisors told me as much, but I thought you might have a different perspective." His gaze travelled around the paddock, lingering on the war drakes sleeping within their huts. "There are other uses for these beasts than war."

"Your Majesty, I don't know that I'd entrust a wild animal to represent the nation in a fragile negotiation. Especially if you're trying to *avoid* war."

She spoke more freely than she'd intended, the image of the dead Rafragorian soldier climbing to the forefront of her mind. *Remember the island,* the note had said, but to whom? It was Viam who'd told the king the truth of their squad's last mission not three weeks ago, and until then, he hadn't known that his father's final struggle against Rafragoria had been over an island that belonged to the god of death and that Rafragorian soldiers had awakened Mekan's temple and paid the price with their lives.

If the note was to be believed, Rafragoria blamed *Laria* for those deaths, which made little sense to Viam, but who was to say what stories had reached Rafragoria's shores in the absence of any direct communication between their nations? In truth, sending an envoy wasn't the worst idea. If there was an option that didn't involve reptilian weapons of war.

The king's downcast expression prompted her to add, "I don't mean to disparage your suggestion, but I don't know that Rafragoria will ever associate war drakes with anything other than bloodshed. Certainly not peace."

"No, you're right," he said. "I'll have to think of another way. Thank you for listening to me."

He backed out of the gate, leaving Viam blinking after him in puzzlement. She wasn't entirely sure why he'd asked for her advice, but he sometimes forgot how young he'd been when he'd taken the throne. He was all of twenty-five and hadn't inherited his father's advisors, who'd been killed along with their monarch.

Killed by Rafragoria, or so everyone thought save for a handful of people, Viam included.

The war drake tugged on the chain, drawing her attention back to the present. She gave it the rest of the meat and then put its muzzle back on—securely this time—before she locked up the paddock for the evening.

Dusk painted the rooftops pink as she handed the keys to the guards outside the gates and reentered the palace grounds. To her surprise, Brenat waited for her, resting a burly arm on the low wall separating the barracks from the rest of the palace grounds.

"I thought you'd be out here," she said. "What did His Majesty want? Isn't it risky for him to visit the war drakes without his personal guards?"

"Maybe, but the rest of us can hardly lecture the monarch on safety concerns." She hoped Brenat hadn't said anything to the king. Her fellow scribe was known for her tendency to speak brashly, though her sometimes exasperating curiosity was tempered by her genuine kindness. As one of the few people in the palace who didn't indulge in whispers whenever Viam walked past—either concerning her position with the war drakes or her link to Yala—Viam treasured any chance they had to talk alone.

"True enough." Brenat strode briskly ahead, tossing a wave at a pair of passing guards. Unlike Viam, she had a natural gift for winning favour from others, and it was a constant source of bafflement that

His Majesty had elected to spend time with Viam instead. "You never said what the king wanted. To see the war drakes?"

"Yes, and... well, he wants to send an envoy to Rafragoria," she admitted. "I had to remind him that sending war drakes would have the opposite impact of what he intends."

Brenat raised a brow. "Did he not already realise that?"

"Yes, but Rafragoria isn't exactly accessible by sea." She fell into step with Brenat as they followed one of the many paths through the darkening palace grounds. Buildings housing the king's various staff flanked them on the left, while an open space on the right gave way to the tiered majesty of the palace, its gold-bedecked layers glimmering in the dying light of the sun. "If we sent a boat without any warning, their sea monsters would eat the messengers alive."

"Might be better than sending war drakes," Brenat remarked. "Best save them for the Flight Division."

Viam's steps faltered, recalling the king's interest in Yala and her war drake. She had to have known it was inevitable that the monarch would have noticed her new acquisition, but what would Yala make of the king's offer?

I suppose the worst she can do is say no, she thought, resolving to visit Yala at the first opportunity to wash both their hands of the matter.

Remember the island, a voice whispered in the back of her mind.

She remembered. Yala did too. That was precisely why they couldn't get involved in another war with Rafragoria—because the only victor in a battle waged by Corruption would be the god of death.

2

Kelan woke in a puddle of sour wine to a sharp knocking on the door.

He lifted his head, shivering, his fragmented vision assembling the pieces of his room at the Disciples' Inn. His shirt was soaked with the remnants of the wine spilled across the floor—either from the bottle or vomited up, he couldn't tell—and his chilled arms reminded him that he'd lost his cloak. Leaning on the bed, he pulled himself to his feet and winced at another aggressive thump on the other side of the door. Only one person was given to making this level of noise in the early hours of the morning.

"Lakiel," he called. "Can't you wait another hour?"

The door flew open, revealing Lakiel, whose thin lips were pulled into a frown. "The Superior wants to talk to you."

That woke him as efficiently as a bucket of water upended on his head. "She's *here?*"

"No, and she has better things to do than clean up after Disciples who ought to know better than to start brawls in public establishments."

"Her first mistake was thinking I know better." He didn't recall Lakiel witnessing the incident, but admittedly, he wasn't certain how

21

he'd got back to the inn either. His only clear memory of the previous night was the humiliation of Yala witnessing his confrontation with the guards. What she'd been doing in a gambling den, he had no idea.

Lakiel gave him a searching look down his long nose. "You might want to change clothes first."

The tall Disciple turned and stalked away, leaving Kelan to gather the shreds of his dignity.

Several hours later, Kelan stood before his Superior in the upper room of Skytower. He wore a cloak he'd obtained from the laundry room at the Disciples' Inn that was altogether too big for him and a shirt that was too short in the sleeves; while it might have been an improvement on dragging himself here from Dalathar in his alcohol-stained clothing from the previous night, it didn't make him feel any less like Dalathar's river had swallowed him up and spat him back out. The half-day flight home had cleared his head, but his mouth tasted like a cesspit, and he wished Superior Sietra would stop staring at him. She towered over him from her high-backed chair, her azure robes embroidered in gold that matched her headdress. Gold paint streaked her cheeks, and her regal demeanour was matched only by the image of the sky god on the tapestries adorning the wall on his right, whose watchful eyes seemed to judge Kelan for his misdemeanours.

"Kelan," said Superior Sietra. "I'm told you've been busy in the capital."

That's one way of putting it. "I suppose I have."

"Starting drunken fights, I hear."

He lowered his gaze, a flush creeping up his neck. What did it matter to her what he did in his spare time? He didn't recall her asking after his fellow Disciples in the same manner, and there was no law in Skytower against drunk and disorderly behaviour. Frankly, he was fairly sure Terethik would have joined in with enthusiasm had He been present in the material world.

"You need a purpose."

"I do?"

"Yes, you do," she said. "You've been drifting around like a ghost since Setemar."

The word struck a sharp chord inside him. *Setemar.* The mission had ended fatally for too many of his fellow Disciples. Who was she to judge him for seeking any means of burying that disaster in the deepest recesses of his mind?

"What do you suggest?" He swallowed nausea. "Another stint in the library?"

"No, I think we've derived all the useful information that Skytower's texts contain."

Gods, she didn't think he was being serious, did she? "If you want to look in the Disciples of the Flames' library, I doubt I'm the right person for the job."

"That *is* a consideration but not a priority." Seriousness underlaid her tone. "Our country is closer to war than it has been in many years."

"Is it?" His head had started to throb again, and his stomach churned; he wondered if he might throw up on the Superior's pristine floor.

"Really, Kelan, you haven't spent every moment buried in Dalathar's taverns for the past few weeks," she said. "You know of the body that washed up on Laria's shores after your return from Setemar and its accompanying note."

"That was weeks ago." And none of his business. The Disciples of the Flame had burned the body, hadn't they?

"Yes," she said. "Since then, no word has come from Rafragoria to explain their intentions in sending that note, and the king's attempts to contact our neighbours have resulted in no conclusive answers."

Had she been corresponding with the monarch herself? Granted, she might well have sent messengers into the palace and he wouldn't have noticed, but the notion of an imminent war was entirely too much for his wine-soaked brain to take in.

"I also spoke to Superior Shralin, and he shares my concerns," she said. "The fact of the matter is that war seems inevitable unless the king is able to have a messenger sent directly to Rafragoria."

"Is that even possible?" He delved into his admittedly patchy knowledge of Laria's prickly neighbours. "Don't they send their sea drakes to attack any unfamiliar ships that enter their water?"

"Often, yes," she replied. "And sending a group of messengers by air—using war drakes—would be a dangerous misstep."

True. He fought an unexpected smile at the image of Yala travelling to Rafragoria as a messenger on a full-grown war drake—or worse, taking her dead war drake steed instead. That would all but certainly start a war, and not necessarily one that Laria could win.

"We are in a unique position," she went on. "We're able to fly, which would get around the difficulties faced by regular messengers, and we're also a neutral force who aren't allowed to get involved with warfare."

Oh. Now he understood her interest. "You want to send in Disciples of the Sky."

"Yes, I do."

"Not me." The truth dawned on him. "You can't possibly think *I'm* qualified. I'm not a politician or ambassador. I don't even speak their language."

"Few in Laria do," she said. "In fact, that might prove advantageous. It should be obvious to Rafragoria that we pose no threat to them."

"No." He shook his head and wished he hadn't. The throbbing pain made it hard to piece together his thoughts. "They think we're responsible—Laria as a whole, that is—for the deaths of their people on the island. If we fly into their midst, they'll feed us to their sea drakes and consider it a mercy."

"I highly doubt that they'd lay the blame at the feet of the Disciples," she said. "We're a neutral entity outside of the monarchy and the government, and we've never participated in any war with Rafragoria. The same goes for their own Disciples. They would never want to risk breaking treaties that have existed for almost as long as our nations."

"That doesn't make me the right person to negotiate with them."

"You handled the situation in Setemar, didn't you?"

"I got kicked out of the Temple of the Earth. Several times." When added to his record of being banished from the Temple of the Flames, his actions in Setemar did not suggest he was the person to be chosen for a delicate political negotiation.

"For speaking the truth."

"Does Rafragoria want me to tell the truth?" His head throbbed again, but he managed to offer a smile. "I thought most politicians did the opposite."

Her mouth almost twitched into a smile. "These are dangerous times. We don't know if Rafragoria has access to Corruption, and if they do, those of you who were present during the incident in Setemar stand more of a chance of success than anyone else."

He raised a brow. "My only qualification is that I'm more likely than the average person to be able to cross the ocean into Rafragoria without being killed by the dead?"

That, at least, he did have relevant experience with, but he'd survived the mission by little more than luck. Many hadn't been that fortunate.

"That's an unlikely scenario," she added. "We've seen no proof that Rafragoria has embraced any use of Corruption, but they've accused Laria of the same. It's better for us as Disciples to absorb that blow than to let it strike the king, wouldn't you say?"

"Why not send the Disciples of the Flame?" He knew why. They couldn't fly and probably couldn't swim either. He doubted any of them had set foot on a boat in their lives, let alone in unpredictable water teeming with lethal monsters.

"Superior Shralin declined when I made the suggestion," she said. "In any case, his people will be ready to intervene should the worst happen and Rafragoria launches an attack."

"I should hope so," Kelan said. "What about the Disciples of the Earth?"

"They're recovering from the recent upheaval inside their temple," she said. "As of yet, they haven't picked a new Superior."

I hope the god of the earth makes a better choice this time. "So it's just us."

"Lakiel will be leading the mission," she said. "I've asked him to choose a team."

"He didn't choose me for this, surely." No... if she'd been alive, Laima would have been chosen for the mission instead of him, and the knowledge left a sour taste in his mouth. He'd been surrounded by people more competent than he was, and yet they'd ended up dead and he'd lived. Who was he to take her place?

He blinked hard, conscious of his Superior's too-discerning stare. "No, I did."

"And you thought I'd need convincing."

"Do you?" she asked. "Need convincing, that is?"

Objections rose to his tongue. He had none of the ideal qualities for a mission of this calibre, let alone after his recent fall from grace, but what else was there to do? Return to the capital and drown himself in taverns and pleasure houses until Laria had sleepwalked into war? Yala's face swam to the front of his mind. He could imagine what she'd say if she knew he'd had the chance to stop a repeat of the war that had wreaked such havoc upon her life and had elected to indulge his own selfish impulses instead.

"Depends on what you want me to do," he replied. "What's the intention? That we fly to Rafragoria and hope that they don't knock us out of the air with a storm of arrows?"

"Meet with our monarch first," she replied. "Once King Daliel has decided on a plan of action, he'll send word to Rafragoria. Should they accept his request, you'll proceed from there. Lakiel will tell you the rest."

He dipped his head at the dismissal in her voice. "All right."

She knew I'd say yes. He had to admit that being sent across the ocean to a deadly foreign nation was more appealing than another stint in the library, combing through ancient books in search of references to Corruption, but it sounded as though the king would have to make the final decision.

Lakiel waited for him outside the Superior's rooms. "You said yes?"

"I didn't get the impression that I was being offered much of a choice," he said. "How many of us are going?"

"I've chosen four others to accompany us to the capital." The disapproving undercurrent to his tone suggested exactly what he thought of Kelan's involvement. "They're waiting in the library."

Lakiel stepped over the edge of the platform that circled the Superior's rooms, descending gracefully to the floor below. Each of Skytower's five floors was built along the same lines, the inner portion circled by a wide stone balcony that made it easy for Disciples to move between floors without the need for stairs.

"I take it the king knows we're coming to see him?" he asked as they glided through an arched doorway and into a stone corridor. "I didn't think he made a habit of letting Disciples into the palace."

Come to think of it, hadn't the last Disciples to set foot in there murdered the king's father? *Best avoid bringing that up.*

Lakiel's mouth turned down at the corners. "He doesn't. This is new territory for all of us."

"You don't agree with our Superior?"

"I don't intend to disobey orders," he said, which was enough of an answer. "Come on."

They entered the library, a large draughty room lined with shelves. The rustle of old tomes brought reminders of the hours he'd spent combing through incomprehensible texts and trying not to doze off. Three other Disciples occupied a large table, and a worn fabric map had been stretched across its surface. Its edges curled upward, dotted with splashes of ink.

Lakiel pulled out a chair, gesturing for Kelan to join them. "Kelan, this is Kriam, Ranit, and Brikel."

He indicated each of the table's occupants in turn: an older male Disciple who barely glanced up from the map, a younger male who sat cross-legged at his side, and a woman of maybe twenty lounging in the other seat. None he'd met before; Lakiel had likely chosen people for the mission who were both more qualified than him and less likely to get distracted. All the same, his disapproval of Superior Sietra's decision made Kelan wonder how many of them were prepared for what this mission might lead to.

"We're likely to have to stay in the capital for a few days while we speak to the monarch," Lakiel said, "but I thought we should study the map so we're familiar with the route in advance."

"Is that Rafragoria?" Kelan tilted his head and saw the ocean stretching from Laria's northern shores to the islands that formed Rafragoria's empire. Various blots indicated islands that belonged to neither nation, but there was a considerable amount of blank space between.

"That's right." Lakiel pointed at a few scribbled words that Kelan had initially taken for smudges of ink. "Those islands are Larian territory, which might mean that Rafragoria will refuse to meet us there out of principle. And we *don't* want to land on one of their territories."

"What if they all look identical close up?" asked Brikel, the woman in her mid-twenties whose lanky frame and long nose made him wonder if she was related to Lakiel. "That might get awkward."

"Maybe we'll be lucky and Rafragoria will have planted a flag on every island that's theirs," Kelan said. "Otherwise, we'll hover above the ground and claim it doesn't count as trespassing."

"We most certainly won't," said Lakiel, though Brikel grinned at Kelan's words.

"They can't expect us to know the intricacies of their territorial disputes," said the younger male, Ranit. "When we were at war, the islands used to get passed back and forth every other year."

True. Yala would know. She'd been in the thick of the fighting, but he doubted Lakiel would appreciate him suggesting her as a consultant. Neither would Yala, for that matter.

"That doesn't mean we need to start out badly," said Lakiel. "His Majesty will give us instructions. Need I remind you that our aim is to stop another similar dispute from escalating into war?"

"It's not a territorial dispute, is it?" Kelan queried. "It's a threat of retribution."

For something we didn't do, he added, though in truth, he didn't know how much his fellow Disciples knew of the threats Laria had received from Rafragoria several weeks prior.

"It's baffling," said Brikel. "I assume His Majesty will want us to ask what Rafragoria meant by sending us a corpse and a threatening message without provocation?"

"Yes," said Lakiel, "but the note wasn't from Rafragoria's empress. Her government denied all involvement."

"Nobody mentioned that." What was he signing up for? Was Rafragoria's empress lying, or had one of her soldiers gone rogue behind her back?

"Our Superior believes we have a chance," Lakiel told them. "His Majesty will guide us on how to proceed."

"And how to not get ourselves killed, I hope," said Kelan. "I don't know about you, but I'm not familiar with Rafragoria's customs."

"I'm fluent in their language," Lakiel said. "And Brikel can speak a little of their language as well."

"Interesting hobby."

"Oh, I just wanted to know how to use insults accurately," said the woman, who Kelan was starting to like more with each interaction.

Lakiel narrowed his eyes at both of them. "This is no laughing matter. There are terrible risks involved, and everything we do will reflect on Laria as a whole."

"We know, we know," said Brikel. "His Majesty does too. He might even be grateful to us for taking the negotiations off his hands."

"Hardly the kind of behaviour we need for a monarch in times of war," said Kriam in grave tones. It was the first time the older Disciple had spoken.

Lakiel's lips pressed together. "I'm sure he's trying his best, but not everyone is cut out to rule."

"Rather him than me," Kelan remarked, and the two younger members of their group nodded.

"Regardless." Lakiel tugged on the end of the map and rolled up the fabric with a firm hand. "We'll leave tomorrow."

3

The forest hummed with the sound of change. Even the birdsong took on a melancholic note when Niema awoke on her final day in the enclave.

I'm leaving today. She'd delayed her departure as far as she could, for the sake of her fellow enclave members, but she'd sworn she wouldn't stay past the first rain. She tasted their sorrow through the bond that connected all five of them, and the sharp tang of loss lingered on the back of her tongue as she moved around the cabin, gathering her few belongings into a travelling pack.

Niema trod carefully past the sleeping mat where Ekim lay. Elderly and frail, she'd taken to spending most of the day in repose since Prathen died. Niema knew in her heart that however much her absence might hurt the others, staying would be worse. After all, Prathen had died because of her.

Hachim, her closest friend among the group, was the only person who truly knew what Niema stood to risk by staying in the enclave. One night, she'd confessed to him the reality of what her Superior had done, how she'd shattered the trust between Disciple and Superior and given a command that overtook Niema's will. It didn't surprise her when she found him alert and waiting for her inside their room, his long, dark hair framing his narrow face.

"I'm coming with you," he whispered.

"No." Niema shook her head. "The enclave can't afford to lose anyone else."

"They can't afford to lose you either." Tears brimmed in his dark eyes. "*I* can't afford to."

"The children need you." The younger members didn't understand her choice. Threl kept bringing animals to show Niema, as though to remind her of everything she'd miss if she left the forest, while Diaman often clung to Niema like a kekin, crying that she didn't want to lose her so soon after Prathen's death. The two of them were young enough to have few memories of life before the enclave. Before the five of them had been bonded.

"They need you too." His face crumpled. "I know I can't convince you to stay, but travelling alone is dangerous. What if you're followed? Or attacked on the road?"

What if Superior Kralia sends assassins after me again? She heard the unsaid question, but she couldn't bring herself to answer honestly. "I'll be fine."

Lifting her pack, she nudged open the door and stepped into the main room, where a small figure tackled her around the legs.

"Don't leave!" Threl sobbed.

Diaman joined him from the other side. "You can't go, Niema!"

"I'll come back." Niema put down her pack to avoid losing her balance under the combined weight of the two small children and lowered her voice, conscious of Ekim stirring on her sleeping mat. "I promise I'll visit as often as I can."

Diaman's small fist struck her kneecap. "It's unfair. Why are you abandoning us?"

"That's not what I'm doing." She took in a breath, her chest fracturing. "I'll miss you, but you'll be safer if I leave."

"Why?" Threl's high-pitched wail caused Ekim to sit upright, her wild eyes scanning the room.

"Sorry," Niema whispered to her and then addressed the children. "You can sense it, can't you? You know I don't belong here anymore."

They knew, even if they couldn't put words to the emotions like Hachim or Ekim could. She tugged Threl's arms loose from her legs and then did the same to Diaman.

"I promise it'll be easier without me here," she said. "I'll always think about you, and if you need me, send me a message. You can do that, can't you?"

She directed the last part at Hachim, who nodded without meeting her eyes. Her stomach tightened. Of all the others, Hachim was more at risk of falling astray like she had. Ekim was too old and the others too young, while Hachim alone knew what Superior Kralia had done to shatter her trust like a dropped jar.

He'll be fine, she told herself as she embraced him for the final time. He and the others hadn't broken any laws. They'd suffer no danger provided they didn't cross the same lines that she had.

If they didn't question if the Disciples of Death were as deserving of life as anyone else.

Four hearts tugged on hers as she left, and she pressed a clenched fist to the hollow of her ribs. The pain would be worse while she remained in the forest, but each step towards the boundaries of the enclave would bring clarity from the four other sets of emotions clouding her thoughts.

How did it come to this? Until recently, their enclave hadn't needed anyone but each other, and they'd known their deity would provide anything they needed. Their Superior was their protector. Not someone who would use Niema's hands to destroy another person.

Another life form reached the edge of her awareness, sending a spasm of fear through her. Her grip tightened on the pack, her head tilting towards the war drake that waited around the corner ahead of her.

Niema drew in a breath, ready to whistle and command the beast not to attack, but Superior Kralia strode to the war drake's side. She rested a hand on the crown of its scaled head, showing no fear of its sharp teeth or claws, and surveyed Niema with her usual imperiousness. Wildflowers adorned her robes and the thick layers of her hair, and the god of life's power thrummed with every step she took. Vibrant pink flowers bloomed around her bare feet, and the forest brightened in response. It was a sight that would have once filled Niema with awe, not terror, but now, her pulse raced, and her palms grew slick with sweat.

"You mean to leave now?" asked the Superior.

Niema inclined her head. "Yes."

Superior Kralia studied her for a moment, her expression a pensive mixture of judgement and resignation. "I wish I could change your mind, but I will not stop you."

I will not stop you. A shiver of fear arose at the reminder that Superior Kralia *could* make her stay. Yalet's power enabled her to coax any living creature to obey her, and as Niema had learned recently, humans were no exception. Even the god of death wasn't capable of such an atrocity; while Mekan's power forced the dead to walk around as though they lived still, He held no influence over the living.

Niema took in a shaky breath. "It's better for everyone if I leave."

A short pause ensued. "I wish you wouldn't go alone. The world outside is no friend to us."

"I'll be fine," Niema said. "I'll find my way."

"I'm sure you will," said Superior Kralia. "If you change your mind, send a message, and it'll reach me."

Was that a threat or a reassurance? Niema couldn't tell; not a word her Superior spoke would ever be the same to her again, including her reassurance that she wouldn't harm Yala or her allies. For that reason, Niema had no intention of telling her where she was going.

Niema bowed her head. Then she walked past her Superior and the war drake, away from the enclave, and away from the place that would forever be etched into her heart.

To distract herself from the throbbing pain in her chest, she ran through her intended plan. She knew all the shortcuts from the jungle to Setemar, and from there, the main road led straight to the capital of Dalathar. How she'd survive *there* was a question she'd have to address later.

As she walked, the pain began to ease more with each passing hour. When the sun's last rays slipped beyond the trees, a winged shape entered her vision, a skeletal mass of bone and scale. A shiver ran over her skin, but she didn't stop walking, knowing the monster wouldn't lay a claw on her.

Strange, that a beast that had once instilled such fear in her was now a sign of comfort.

Her understanding of why the dead war drake continued to pursue her was as lacking as her knowledge of why the beast appeared to be free of Mekan's influence that usually urged the dead to kill any living creature they came across, but the sense of familiarity remained. Yala had summoned the beast herself, and she wasn't a typical Disciple of Death. While she'd repeatedly warned Niema away from placing an undue level of faith in her abilities, Niema was no longer so naïve as to need that warning—and no longer an ordinary Disciple of Life either. She'd forged a link with Yala when she'd raised her from death, and that had inevitably changed them both. She didn't know the full extent of what they'd unleashed, but she would gain no answers in the enclave.

To learn the truth, she'd need to return to Dalathar and hope that the city didn't swallow her alive.

———

Viam found Yala in the war drake's paddock, as she'd expected, fastening a saddle to the beast's back while a trembling stableboy held its chain. A muzzle covered the war drake's sharp teeth, but its clawed feet raked at the muddy ground, and it was easy to picture them tearing through flesh on a battlefield.

Yala, by contrast, formed a strange mixture of fierceness and vulnerability as she half crouched, half leaned on her cane. The beast's wings were already half freed from their restraints, and as they stretched out, Viam recalled her own war drake with a pang of guilt at its captive state.

Yala still wanted to fly, yes, but returning to the battlefield… that was another matter altogether.

"What is it?" Yala asked. "More news from the palace?"

"Yes, of a sort." She glanced at the stableboy.

Noticing, Yala waved an impatient hand at him. "Wait over there." She took the war drake's chain from him and passed it to Viam, while the boy gladly ran out of the paddock and closed the gate.

"You want my help?" Viam gripped the chain as Yala mounted the war drake and settled into place on its back. "Wait, you're flying *now*?"

"You can hold the chain, can't you?" Yala sat back with a wince; her leg must have been bothering her again. "It's that or risk that poor stableboy losing a limb."

"I haven't done this in years." Viam gripped the chain in both hands, unsure if she had the strength to keep the beast from launching into flight and taking Yala with it.

"Lucky I trust you." Yala squeezed her legs around the war drake's neck. "Ready?"

"No!" *I need to talk to you*, she wanted to say, but instead, she had to duck to avoid one of the war drake's extended wings clipping her in the back of her head. "Wait. Yala, I've never worked with this beast before—"

"Up." Yala's command rang out, and Viam threw herself against the chain with all her strength as the war drake's feet left the ground. "Stop there."

The war drake did not stop. Viam's feet skidded in the mud as she fought to keep her grip on the chain, while Yala hissed commands into her steed's ear.

"Stop. *Down.*"

Viam skidded to a halt, her back fetching up against the wall of the paddock, but the war drake continued to strain against her grip. She'd regained her soldier's instincts in recent weeks of training, but that didn't mean she was a match for a war drake whose weight could pull her arms out of their sockets with ease.

A sack lying on the ground caught her attention. Viam reached out a foot and kicked until a piece of meat fell out.

"Down!" she called up at the war drake. "Down—"

The war drake descended as quickly as it'd taken off, its teeth snapping behind its muzzle. Viam kicked the sack again, and the war drake's heavy body hit the ground a handspan away from her. Yala spat curses from its back while Viam threw the chain around the sturdy post that anchored it to the ground. The beast continued to snap in an attempt to reach the meat, its distraction giving Viam the chance to wrap the chain tighter until the beast's wings were unable to carry it off the ground no matter how hard they beat.

"Good thinking," Yala called to Viam. "Ornery beast, this one. Might've been a bit soon to fly."

"Might've," Viam repeated, her heart thudding in her throat. "Gods, Yala."

"I'm fine." She looped her good leg over the war drake's back and slid down. Picking up her cane with one hand, she used the other to retrieve the sack of meat. "I'm not taking the muzzle off you until you promise not to bite off any fingers."

"Meaning mine," added Viam, who didn't have the benefit of her drakeskin gloves. "I didn't come here for flying practise, Yala."

"Isn't that how you spend your days? Training war drakes?"

"No, but... but the king suggested you might want to take a job training other riders." It wasn't exactly what he'd asked, but she knew better than to insinuate that he wanted Yala involved in the army.

"Did he?" Yala cocked a brow. "I hope you didn't say yes."

"I wouldn't speak on your behalf," Viam said. "I'm sure the thought has already crossed your mind."

Yala's mouth tightened. "He assumes too much. Training new riders has only one purpose."

Meaning war. Before she could speak another word, Yala lifted her head to the sky. "What are they doing here?"

Viam peered over the rooftops at the group of robed figures descending upon the city. "Is that Kelan?"

"No clue." Yala scowled. "The last time I saw him, he was drunk in a tavern."

"Was he?" She watched the group descend gracefully, angling

36

towards the wall circling the upper city. "They look like they're here for a purpose."

"Probably going to see the Disciples of the Flame." Yala's cane raked the ground, leaving a deep gouge in the mud. "Their Superior will have sent them on a mission."

"I can ask on my way back." Viam retreated from the paddock, lifting a hand in farewell, and closed the gate before Yala decided to ask her to help with another flying attempt.

Yala, of course, had no desire to set foot inside the Temple of the Flame, and in truth, Viam didn't much care for the idea either. Their history with the Disciples of the Flame was fraught with tension that had only escalated when they'd been presented with the body of the dead Rafragorian soldier and the note telling them to *remember the island.*

She and Yala hadn't discussed the note any more than necessary, but they hadn't needed to. It hadn't been addressed to anyone, but there was little doubt of the island to which it referred, and even the Disciples of the Flame surely knew of her former squad's involvement in King Tharen's last mission. It wasn't a secret anymore. Unlike King Tharen's reasons for sending them there in the first place.

Viam slowed her pace at the gates to the upper city and waited for the guards to let her through into Ceremonial Square. The group of Disciples had landed, not outside the Temple of the Flame but beside the palace's front gates.

What are they doing? Viam crossed the square, skirting the large golden statue of King Larial, and recognised Kelan amongst the four Disciples conversing with the guards at the palace gate.

"Excuse me?" She approached their group, her shoulders hunching as they turned towards her with a sweep of wind that lifted her hair from her scalp. "Can I help you?"

"Viam." Kelan gave her an ingratiating smile. "I don't suppose you can get us an audience with the king?"

"With the *king?*" She surveyed the other members of their group to discern whether he was making a joke; from their serious expressions, he wasn't. "I can try, but I'll have to wait until morning."

"I thought so," Kelan said with a meaningful glance at the guards. "They said the same."

"I wouldn't count on getting close to him." Had any Disciples of the Sky ever set foot inside the palace? Not in her lifetime, at least. "What's the occasion?"

"A delicate matter," said Kelan. "It's my understanding that the king is in contact with Rafragoria concerning how to handle the recent incident."

The tall Disciple next to Kelan cleared his throat loudly, evidently displeased at him for discussing their mission openly.

Viam straightened her shoulders. "I know what you're referring to, but I didn't think Disciples typically took an interest in such matters."

"My Superior has been in contact with the king, and she thinks the easiest way to resolve this situation is to send someone to meet with Rafragoria in person," he said. "To send Disciples of the Sky, that is. We're a neutral force, so they won't think we're declaring war if we show up. It's an unusual idea, but…"

Viam pressed her lips together. "It's not the worst idea I've heard this week."

No, that honour went to the king's suggestion that a group of ambassadors should ride war drakes to Rafragoria. After Yala's near-disastrous flight earlier, she was even less keen on that idea if possible. Would the Disciples of the Sky fare any better, though?

"If the king is willing to talk to us, it'll be easier," Kelan said. "We can explain everything in person."

"*I'll* explain," added Lakiel. "You, Kelan, would be better off staying silent."

Kelan's mouth curved into a wry smile. "You'll ask, then, Viam?"

Viam released a sigh. "I'll ask. Don't count on him saying yes, though."

He might, out of curiosity, but it struck her as a strange coincidence that Superior Sietra had come up with that idea so soon after the king's suggestion to use war drakes. If they were in contact, was it really a surprise, though? The Disciples weren't as divorced from the rest of the country as they might want others to believe, and a war would affect them too.

Viam's gaze travelled over the Temple of the Flame. Did *they* know, or had Superior Sietra come up with this plan on her own?

I shouldn't get involved with this. The king hasn't allowed Disciples into the palace since—

She cut off the thought, her stomach churning. She'd told the king the truth about his father's death, but she hadn't shared the worst detail. Namely, that Superior Datriem and several other Disciples of the Flame had conspired to murder King Tharen and that they had succeeded. Had any Disciple ever set foot in the palace since, for any reason?

I'll ask the king, she told herself. *If he says no, none of this will matter.*

4

The king will have to find someone else to train his riders, Yala thought as she coaxed the war drake back into its wing restraints. The beast's teeth snapped behind its muzzle, its claw raking at the ground.

"Don't be like that," she muttered. "You're lucky you aren't being corralled into a smaller paddock in the middle of the city and woken in the early hours by soldiers' drills."

This was undoubtedly the first independently trained war drake in years, if not the first of its kind, though that same title went to the dead war drake that theoretically belonged to her as well. For obvious reasons, she hadn't seen that beast since her return to Dalathar following the events in Setemar. People were alarmed enough when they saw a *living* giant reptile, let alone a dead one.

Really, it was no wonder that the king was desperate to find anyone in the city who might have had prior experience training new riders, but King Daliel of all people ought to know that she'd already done her part. She would not be subject to the whims of a monarch again.

Yala left the paddock, wondering if Viam had managed to catch up with the Disciples of the Sky yet. If Kelan had a new mission, it ought to at least keep him from being involved in any more drunken escapades, but Superior Sietra's ideas tended to involve putting her Disciples into the path of Corruption. Which, inevitably, led them to Yala.

Her fingertips tingled as though in response to her thoughts, and when she lifted a hand, a faint shadow leaked from beneath her gloves.

Death was nearby.

Yala turned her back on the gate. Droplets of blood led up to the stableboy's body lying in the alley alongside the paddock, his neck laid open to reveal glistening bone.

"Who did that?" She took a step forward, one hand on her cane, the other reaching for the dagger sheathed at her waist.

Two men, dressed in nondescript dark clothing, slipped out of the alcove behind the unfortunate stableboy. Each held a long knife, the worn metal caked in gore.

Yala lifted her cane and hit the first man in the kneecaps. He dropped with a thud, and she swung to intercept the other. The second man's knife grazed her glove-encased hand but didn't leave a mark. Grabbing his wrist, she twisted. "Who are you?"

The man tried to punch her with his free hand, but she drove her left knee upward into his groin. He sagged against her with a groan, and she squeezed his wrist until the knife slipped free.

A thud sounded. Her other attacker had staggered to his feet and had edged around her towards the war drake's paddock.

"What do you think you're playing at?" Releasing the groaning man's wrist, she lunged at the other, not fast enough to stop him from pushing the gate inward. "Don't touch that, fool."

Raising his knife, the man stepped back into the shadow of the gate, his teeth bared in a snarl. The sound of claws scraping the earth reached her ears from the other side of the fence. If he intended to use the war drake as a distraction, he didn't have a clue what he was messing with.

Yala jabbed his ankle with the cane again and glimpsed her second attacker reach for the knife she'd knocked out of his grip. Spinning on her heel, she drew one of the blades strapped to her waist and threw it at him.

She'd aimed for the neck, but he ducked, and the blade caught his leg instead. Blood fountained, and he dropped to one knee, moaning.

From behind, a knife pressed against her throat.

"You're dead, Disciple," the first man hissed. A growl underlaid his words from behind the paddock gate.

"You," she said, "should probably step away from there."

Another growl, louder. The blade at her throat bit into the skin, drawing blood, but the pressure abruptly eased. The knife flew from his grip as the gate hit him in the small of his back, and Yala's cane snapped up, knocking him into the path of the war drake's clawed foot.

The second man screamed. The first didn't have the chance to. The beast's claws tangled around his legs and dragged him into the paddock in the space of a blink.

The second man tried to run, but with his leg injury pumping blood, it was a simple matter for Yala to catch up to him and seize his wrist in her free hand. Ripping and tearing noises from the paddock punctuated each limping step as Yala dragged him towards the open gate.

"Let me go!" he moaned, clutching at his blood-soaked leg.

Ignoring his protests, she pushed him after his ally—or what was left of him. Chunks of flesh littered the paddock, and the war drake growled from behind its muzzle as its claw raked through the remnants of the first attacker.

"Saves me the bother of disposing of the bodies." She left the second man in a bleeding heap and reached for the war drake with her gloved hands, undoing its muzzle.

"No—no! Stop!" His howl reached a higher pitch, cut off in a gurgle as the war drake's teeth closed around his head.

Yala stepped back and let the war drake feast.

———

"What the fuck happened to you?" Saren watched Yala wipe mud and blood from her boots onto the doorstep and then close the door to the house behind her. "That's not your blood, I take it?"

"Obviously," Yala said. "Two mercenary sorts ambushed me at the paddocks."

"Shit." He ran a hand through his tangled hair. "Did they use...?"

"Corruption? No." She crossed the room to an armchair, one of two, which comprised the only furniture in the room. "No idea who they were working for."

"Pricks." He watched her peel off her gloves, revealing the faint grey tracings around the tips of her fingers. "You didn't take it with you?"

"The claw? No." She indicated the loose floorboard under which she kept the claw belonging to the void drake that had been responsible for her leg injury. "Being around any traces of Mekan is enough to terrify the war drake."

He snorted. "It'll have to get used to that. Especially if you're going to fly into battle."

"I'm not," she said. "Despite what Viam might think, I have no intention of training new riders either."

Saren draped himself over the other armchair. "Why're you training it, then?"

"For my own amusement."

That excuse might have worked coming from Saren himself but not Yala. Saren's mouth twisted as though he was debating the worth of challenging her, but he changed the subject. "The Disciples of the Sky are going to the palace, I heard."

"Who in the hells told you that?"

"Nalen heard from a guard at the upper city that they were asking for an audience with the king."

"Why would they go there?" More to the point, would the king say yes, ending his years-long habit of keeping the Disciples out of the palace grounds? Not because he knew the Disciples of the Flame had killed his father but due to their failure to prevent his death. Would one group of Disciples entering the palace lead to another?

"Your guess is as good as mine," he said. "One of them was your friend Kelan."

"And to think I hoped he'd stay out of trouble." Yala rubbed her chilled arms. *The king.* What had brought this on?

Saren lifted a flask to his mouth with a mocking smile. "As if that's possible. We're teetering on the brink of war, and this time, not even the Disciples will be able to hide away in their towers and temples and escape the carnage."

"That was almost insightful of you, Saren." She reached out her cane to prod at the flask. "What's in there?"

"Nothing."

"Really."

"Yes." He shook the flask in demonstration. "I wish it was Parvan rice wine, but you can't have it all."

"Huh." She might have expected subterfuge, but Saren had barely left the house for weeks except for his short-lived job, which was why his behaviour the previous evening had been so jarring. "Well, keep your wits about you. I fed those mercenaries to the war drake, but there might be others."

"You did what?" He dropped the flask, revulsion flitting across his pointed features. "Gods, Yala. I don't need more nightmares."

"Better than them showing up in the night to attack us."

Saren shuddered. "When that's the better option, you know you're fucked."

Yala had to say she agreed. A tidal wave hovered over the capital, and it was only a matter of time before it broke upon Dalathar and unleashed a war that made King Tharen's campaigns seem like harmless skirmishes.

She clenched her fist, felt the familiar throb in her fingers.

But would I fight as a Disciple of Death on the battlefield?

———

Entering the palace grounds was a new experience to Kelan. He'd flown *over* the palace countless times, of course, but he'd never seen the carved edifices on its walls up close, and the world beyond the towering doors remained a mystery. In truth, he was surprised at how fast his curiosity had reawakened now that he was faced with questions that his Superior couldn't answer without his help.

A messenger had arrived at the Disciples' Inn early the following morning with the news that the king had agreed to meet with Kelan and the others, and they'd made for the palace without delay.

We must be the first Disciples to set foot in here since the war, he thought, admiring the serpentine carvings on the walls as they glided up the towering staircase to the palace doors.

A cavernous hallway greeted them on the other side. A guard led their group through a series of doors and into a room lined with portraits of men and women who bore a striking resemblance to the man who sat on the ornate chair before them. The chair was carved with serpentine figures not unlike those in Kelan's Superior's office, though he didn't know which deity they represented. Banners in the colours of Laria's flags framed each portrait, garish and bright compared to the muted colours of the carvings on the ceiling and the pillars flanking the throne. The overall decor was a strange mixture of military might and ornate beauty. Kelan tilted his head back to admire the scene of a war drake in flight, which had been carved directly above their heads, and tried to avoid thinking too hard about how he hadn't the faintest idea how one was supposed to address a monarch.

While Lakiel explained their Superior's idea, a furrow appeared in the king's smooth brow. He was younger than Kelan had realised, his features soft, his dark hair neat and untouched by the wind. An ornate headdress topped his head, matching the golden embroidery on his robes. No wonder he remained seated, without turning his head. All he'd have to do was scratch his nose, and his ensemble might fall apart.

"You wish to act as ambassadors on behalf of Laria to meet with similar messengers from Rafragoria?" King Daliel said. "This is irregular, I admit."

But not the worst idea? Kelan thought. *Or better than war drakes?*

"I understand that you've tried to get in touch with Rafragoria but have been unsuccessful in setting up a meeting to discuss recent events," said Lakiel. "Our Superior thought that we would be better suited to that task than soldiers whose presence might provoke an unfavourable response. As a neutral entity, we have advantages, aside from our ability to fly. It's my understanding that Rafragoria refuses to send anyone directly to Laria in person?"

The king inclined his head. "I'll trust that you won't share the details with anyone outside of this room, but Rafragoria's Empress is reluctant to send any of her people out of the country."

"Of course," Lakiel said. "Our Superior suggested that we should put the question to Rafragoria so they can choose whether to agree, and if so, whether to send Disciples or regular ambassadors to meet with us. I know Disciples aren't typically placed in this role, but as a neutral force, we're less likely to provoke them."

"It's certainly an idea worth considering," the king agreed. "And yes, I suspect that an in-person meeting might be the only way to avoid escalation."

"Our Superior thought that this method would make more sense than sending people on a boat," said Kelan. "Travel by sea runs the risk of falling afoul of some calamity on the water, and we can move faster too."

Lakiel's posture jerked as though dislodging a bloodfly from his shoulder, though Kelan had said nothing but the truth.

Seemingly oblivious to the tension that passed between the two Disciples, the king nodded. "Yes, you make a good argument. I shall get in touch with Rafragoria's Empress, and if I receive a reply, I'll send a messenger to the inn."

"Thank you, Your Majesty," said Lakiel, dropping to his knees again.

Kelan did likewise, and with little more ceremony, their brief meeting with the monarch came to an end.

As they retraced their steps to the door, Kelan couldn't resist slowing to admire the splendour of the room. Three or four centuries' worth of artwork adorned the walls and ceiling, depicting Laria's victories over their enemies. Given the sea drakes, most of said enemies belonged to Rafragoria. On reflection, he wouldn't have wanted to set foot in Laria either, given the years of enmity between them.

He caught up to his fellow Disciples on the palace stairs, which boasted an impressive view of the grounds. Paths wound between buildings that presumably housed the other people who worked to keep the nation running, while faint shouts drifted northward from the barracks. He didn't see Viam, but she was likely at work or else training that war drake of hers. While Kelan had the impression that she spent more time around the monarch than the average person, she also had skittish tendencies that were no doubt amplified by the secrets she kept on Yala's behalf.

Such as the late king's death at the hands of the Disciples of the Flame.

King Daliel's own distrust of the Disciples stemmed from their failure to protect his father, or so Kelan gathered, but if he'd invited Kelan and the others into the palace anyway, perhaps there was some hope left after all.

When they'd reached the other side of the gates, Kelan indicated the towering shape of the Temple of the Flame across the square. "Do you think Superior Shralin should know we met with the king?"

"It's not our responsibility to keep him informed," said Lakiel. "It's our Superior's."

Kelan raised a brow. "Not a fan of him, are you?"

Lakiel's mouth pressed into a thin line. "It's uncouth to speak ill of a Superior, even from another temple."

"Oh, we all know he's a slimy bastard," said Brikal. "And he *will* want to know what we're up to, I can guarantee it."

Lakiel blew out a breath. "Kriam, Ranit, will you go to the Temple of the Flame? That ought to stop him showing up at the inn."

"He'll send his lackeys instead." Kelan fell into step with Brikal, feeling more upbeat despite the angry twitch in Lakiel's brow. "There's no harm in keeping him updated."

"That," said Lakiel, "is why I didn't ask you to go and speak to the

Superior. I would like to get through this mission without being kicked out of any more temples."

"I'm sensing a story there," Brikel said. "Is this about the Disciples of the Earth?"

"I would *rather* not speak of that." Lakiel quickened his pace, gliding across the square towards the inn. Kelan did likewise, not keen to revisit those memories.

When they reached the inn, all thoughts of Setemar fled his mind. Inside the downstairs room, Yala sat in a chair, her cane resting on one knee.

"Well?" she said.

Kelan came to a bewildered halt. "Well what?"

"Why did you need to go to the palace?" Yala asked. "I heard."

"That's none of your concern," Lakiel interjected. "Why are you in here? This is an inn for Disciples."

Yala tapped her cane on her knee. "It might interest you to know that the Disciples of the Flame have walked past at least three times."

"Told you so." Brikel gave Lakiel a smirk as she sat down, resting her feet on another chair. "You're Yala Palathar, aren't you?"

Lakiel ground his teeth. "I would like you to leave, Yala. I don't know why Yielen let you in, but this isn't the place for you."

"She didn't." Yala rose to her feet. "Fine. We'll talk outside."

"Who did let you in?" Kelan asked as the two of them approached the front door.

"A servant." She stepped outside, closed the door, and rested her cane at her feet. "So… why *were* you in the palace?"

"Our Superior wants the king to let us act as ambassadors to Rafragoria."

Yala's brow lifted. "She wants you to send messages on behalf of the king?"

"No, she wants us to go there in person," he said. "Since we can fly without the aid of a war drake, the idea has a certain appeal."

Yala grunted. "I don't think Rafragoria will go for that, somehow. It wouldn't surprise me if they assumed we'd decided to break the laws against Disciples being involved in warfare."

48

"The king's going to send them a message first," he said. "To avoid any unwelcome surprises."

"He said yes?"

"I think he's out of any better ideas." His gaze went to the Temple of the Flame, into which Kriam and Ranit had disappeared. "I wonder what Superior Shralin will think."

"I assume you haven't spoken to him recently?" Yala asked.

"Not since I stole Mavilangran's journal from under their noses, I haven't."

He doubted Superior Shralin would ever forgive him for claiming the journal that Yala had been sent to Setemar to retrieve and handing it to his Superior instead. No, he was better off leaving any future correspondence to the other Disciples.

"I assume your Superior is getting more use out of it than Superior Shralin would have," Yala said. "She's wilier than I realised, talking the king into agreeing to her plan."

"It was technically Lakiel who did the talking."

"Not you?"

He tilted his head. "I've been asked to hold my tongue."

"I have doubts that you'll manage that for long." She offered the barest smile in return and then sobered. "You can't speak Rafragorian?"

"No. Lakiel can, but that's no guarantee of a positive outcome," he said. "Honestly, I don't know how they expected us to reply."

"Reply to what?" she queried. "The message they sent with the dead body? I didn't think that was the sort of note that required a response."

"I suppose not," he said, "but we don't know who sent that message or whether they represented Rafragoria as a whole."

"No." Yala scowled. "We don't, but I think sending a group of Disciples into their midst is almost as risky as sending war drakes."

As they walked, he noticed her limp was more pronounced than usual, and there was dried blood on her boots. "Trouble in the Undercity?"

"No, but someone tried to have me killed yesterday," she said. "They ambushed me outside the paddock. Killed the stableboy."

"Who would do that?"

"I don't know." Her gaze flickered across the square. "We both know who's recently hired mercenaries, though."

"It can't be them, can it?" Did any of the Disciples of the Flame have remaining loyalties to Superior Datriem? She'd killed one of his co-conspirators in Setemar, and it was possible that more remained, but why act against Yala now?

"Well, they didn't use Corruption, at least," she said. "And if they aren't with the Disciples, who were they working for?"

That, he thought, *is a very good question.*

5

Word came back from the Rafragorians two days later, sooner than Kelan had expected. A royal messenger showed up at the inn, which was a welcome break in the monotony of yet another morning of studying maps of Laria's coastline with Lakiel glowering at him whenever he made a joke. The upside was that by this point, he could have traced the route to Rafragoria in his sleep, which lowered their odds of losing their way and ending up somewhere in the Parvan Empire instead.

"We're making an assumption that they answered yes," Kriam said when Kelan made a remark to this effect. "The messenger didn't say."

"I doubt the king told him." Kelan led the way out of the inn, Lakiel overtaking him at the door. His fellow Disciple was as taciturn as ever, and Kriam shared that trait, but Ranit and Brikel were pleasant enough to be around.

As they crossed the square, Ranit gestured towards the Temple of the Flame. "I bet Superior Shralin will want to know."

"What does it matter?" asked Brikel. "We aren't subject to the rules of another Superior."

"He wasn't pleased when we told him our mission," Ranit

reminded her. "I don't see him volunteering to cross the ocean, though."

Kelan hadn't been surprised at the others' report on Superior Shralin's reaction to their mission, though Superior Sietra had given him ample warning of their arrival. While Superior Shralin objected to them involving themselves in politics, one would think he'd have a vested interest in preventing his country from sliding into war.

"Maybe he's jealous that he can't fly," Kelan suggested.

"Don't be absurd," said Lakiel. "He's the representative of the god of the flames."

"Not much use when faced with an ocean, is it?" He exchanged a grin with Brikel; she'd been the easiest of the team to get along with, and he'd caught her eyeing him appreciatively after they'd had a few drinks the previous day. Lakiel had punctured his wayward thoughts by taking him aside and hissing, "Do you mind?"

"Do I mind what?" Kelan had replied.

"I don't appreciate you playing games with Brikel."

"What does it matter to you?"

Lakiel had leaned closer, baring his teeth. "She's my *sister*."

Oh. He'd noticed their similarities in appearance, but their opposing personalities had banished those observations from his mind. "I'm not playing games with her. You could stand to get along with the rest of the team yourself."

"This is a serious mission," he growled. "We might not survive."

"And you wonder why she'd rather talk to me than to you."

Yet his words had wormed into Kelan's head, and afterwards, he'd been assailed with nightmares of the last fatal mission he'd been involved in. If this one went the same way… no, following that thought wouldn't lead anywhere good. Certainly not if he wanted to hold his tongue throughout another meeting with the king.

Again, the guards escorted them into the palace and into the golden splendour of the king's receiving room.

Upon his throne, King Daliel greeted them with the words, "Rafragoria has agreed to meet you, with conditions."

"Conditions?" That they'd said yes was more than Kelan had

expected; he'd assumed that they'd face weeks of back-and-forth negotiations with Rafragoria if not an outright refusal.

"They refuse to meet on Larian soil," King Daliel clarified. "The Empress cited the risk to their safety as reason to avoid coming directly here."

"They expect us to go to them instead?" asked Lakiel.

"Yes, but not to Rafragoria," said the king. "They've selected an island that isn't part of either of our territories as a meeting point, in the interests of neutrality."

"The Empress wants us to meet the ambassadors in the middle of the ocean?" Kelan felt a sudden inexplicable chill; it took a moment for his thoughts to catch up to his reaction. It was within these very same palace walls that a mission involving another island in the middle of the ocean had been decided upon, and he knew with certainty that Yala would not be a fan of this idea. She'd call it a trap, and she might well be right.

"So it would seem," said the king. "Would that be a problem?"

"No," answered Lakiel. "It's irregular, but I understand why they'd want to avoid setting foot in Laria itself."

Does he really think that? Or does he just not want to say no to the king? Yes, there was no denying that they'd volunteered to speak to Rafragoria's contingent precisely because of how easily their group could traverse the ocean, but somehow, the inherent danger hadn't solidified for Kelan until now.

"When did they agree to meet?" asked Kriam.

"Tomorrow morning," said the king. "I understand that it'll take several hours for you to get there, so you might want to leave sooner rather than later."

Longer if we get lost at sea in the darkness, he surmised. "Agreed."

"We'll go at first light tomorrow," said Lakiel. "Do you have a list of terms you want us to discuss with them?"

"Yes." The king gestured to a guard on the room's other side, who handed over a piece of parchment to Lakiel. "There's also a map to the island."

At the word *island,* the image of Yala's face came into his mind. Yes, she'd be pissed off at this whole venture, but what choice did they have? She wanted to avoid war as much as the rest of them.

As they left the palace, Kelan glimpsed several pairs or groups of guards gathering in the palace grounds whisper to one another, and curious eyes followed their descent to the gates.

"Do you think they know what we're doing?" he murmured to the others. "I bet there are rumours."

"Oh, almost certainly," said Brikel. "Nobody gossips like palace servants and guards. I've learned several scandalous secrets just by walking past the gates."

"Scandalous, you say?"

"That's enough." Lakiel glided ahead of them and past the guards at the front gate. When they reached the other side, he nodded towards the Temple of the Flame. "One of us should tell them."

"Rather you than me," Brikel remarked. "Kelan?"

"Don't look at me," Kelan said. "I'm fairly sure I'm barred from the temple for life."

"Are you?" Brikel asked. "What did you do, seduce a novice?"

"No, I stole a book." At a disapproving stare from Lakiel, he added, "Technically, I took it to Skytower on the orders of our own Superior, but I'm the face of the crime."

"Harsh."

"I'll go." Lakiel passed Kriam the parchment that the king had given him. "Wait for me at the inn."

"Good luck." Kelan was almost curious enough to lurk outside and listen to Superior Shralin's response to Rafragoria's proposal, but his desire to see what the king wanted them to say won out. Rows of neat handwriting covered the parchment, along with a small map at the bottom.

"This is more detailed than the maps at Skytower," Ranit said as they sat at the table in the inn's downstairs room. "The island's also further than I thought. Can we make it in time?"

"If we leave in the middle of the night," said Brikel. "Is the fastest route directly north from the docks?"

"Not by much," Kelan observed. "You know, I'm starting to think we ought to take a boat instead. At least then we'd get some sleep."

Brikel snorted. "If we don't get eaten by a sea drake."

"The map is based on the military's routes," said Kriam in his usual serious manner. "If we follow the directions, we'll get there in good time."

Within minutes, Lakiel returned from the temple in an even shorter temper than usual. "He's not there."

"Who's not there?"

"Superior Shralin," he replied. "They say he went out. Wouldn't give details."

"I didn't know he ever left the temple." Unusual but not an unwelcome development. "At least he can't complain that we didn't inform him of tomorrow's meeting."

The evening passed quickly, and when Lakiel announced that they would be leaving before dawn, everyone retired to bed early. Since there were only four of them, Kelan didn't have to share a room with Lakiel's snoring, but the trepidation of their upcoming mission did not make for a restful night.

He woke from dreams of monsters sinking their claws into his flesh to someone knocking on the door to his room. "Wake up."

"Already awake," he said around a yawn, fumbling to retrieve his clothes from the floor. The sun had yet to rise, and he nearly sliced open a finger while trying to strap his blade to his belt in the darkness. Would Rafragoria's ambassadors take their weapons as a threat? He hoped not; travelling unarmed was out of the question, given the dangers that lurked both inside and outside of the ocean.

Lakiel paced in the hallway downstairs, but Ranit sat dozing in a corner, and Kriam kept yawning too. Brikel was the last to come downstairs, greeting her brother with a cheery, "Fuck you for dragging us out of bed two hours early."

"Rafragoria might show up early too," Lakiel said without a twinge of remorse. "We'll leave now."

Darkness swathed the streets; even the pleasure houses had closed their doors, and the docks were little more than a shadowy mass that gave way to darker water.

When they glided out over the ocean, Kelan was suddenly hit by a memory of plunging into the water and nearly drowning. He knew how to swim, but it wasn't a skill he made use of often. With his deity's power, he had no need of it, but another god held sway outside of Laria's shores, and Amanat's reach extended far beyond his knowledge.

Lakiel led the way northward, occasionally stopping to consult the map. How he could see in the darkness was a mystery to Kelan; the moon's pale light cast barely a glimmer on the ocean's depths, and the only colour was a golden strip of beach circling Laria's coastline behind them.

Had Yala's squad taken flight from a similar beach all those years ago? He hadn't spoken to her the previous day, not wanting her to add more doubts to the array that already nested in his mind, but he had to admit it'd have helped if he'd brought the journal with him so that he could ensure that their destination was nowhere near the islands that Mavilangran had visited during his travels.

"Kelan," Lakiel called, and he dragged his attention away from the beach. "Stop loitering. You don't want to get left behind."

"How do you know this isn't a trap?" He couldn't keep the apprehension out of his voice. "We're leaving Larian soil for an unknown island. It's not like anyone would know if anything happened to us."

"Did you forget Rafragoria is made up of islands?" Lakiel asked. "It's too late for second-guessing, Kelan. Come on."

As they flew, the sun began to rise like an orb disgorged from the maw of the ocean itself. Gold limned the horizon, rays stretching outward and searing the back of his neck as their path turned westward.

Shielding his eyes, Lakiel pulled out the map again. "This way. We're close."

"We're also at least two hours early," Brikel ventured. "What're we supposed to do, camp out on the island until Rafragoria's ambassadors show up?"

"Which island?" Kelan glimpsed several golden stripes ahead of them, but each was indistinguishable from the others at this distance.

"The one with the monolith." Lakiel rolled up the parchment again. "We'll get a better look when we're closer."

None of the islands bore any kind of landmark, as it turned out, but they found more similar landmasses scattered in the surrounding water. No wonder the island on which Yala and the others had encountered the Temple of Death had been undiscovered for so long. Even with daylight gilding the water in glittering blue, their surroundings were a veritable maze.

Despite his best efforts, Kelan's mind filled with Yala's descriptions of a pale mist rising from the water, and he shook his head to dislodge the thought. The day was clear, without a cloud in sight.

"There." Lakiel pointed northwest of their position. "That's the one."

The chosen island lay apart from its neighbours, marked by a narrow monolith arranged as though someone had moved a number of small rocks into a teetering pile with their own hands and placed two large boulders at the sides to hold them in place.

Brikel took one look and burst out laughing. "It looks like a prick."

So it did. "A diseased one."

Lakiel made a choked noise. "Will you take this seriously? Rafragoria's ambassadors might already be there."

"Admit it's funny," Brikel said as they flew closer. "Didn't any of them think to ask for outside opinions on their artwork?"

"Maybe it was a deliberate artistic choice," Kelan suggested. "They wanted to make an impression... but look, there's nobody there."

The island was deserted, a plain of sand where ripples washed up against the shore. Peaceful, except—

Kelan skidded to a halt in midair so abruptly that he nearly hit Lakiel from behind.

"What is *wrong* with you?" Lakiel snapped.

"Don't you see that?" He pointed at the sea just ahead of them. "There's something—"

A serpentine head emerged from the sea, spraying them all with saltwater.

"—in the water," he finished.

Nobody sat upon the beast's back, but the sea drake was equipped with an armoured saddle affixed to its scaly back in the same manner that Laria's army might outfit a war drake for battle. Its narrow reptilian face boasted two sharp horns in addition to the curved teeth protruding from its mouth.

Those same teeth clamped shut, missing Kelan's feet by a fingerspan. He lurched upward, drawing his blade from its sheath. "Is it against the law to kill one of Rafragoria's steeds?"

"Not if it has no rider," said Ranit, drawing his own weapon. "Careful!"

The beast's neck extended as its huge body crested the surface, revealing stubby wings too short to fly. Hard scales—again like a war drake's—coated its body, and clawed front feet lifted the mangled remains of a human body.

"Gods." Ranit lowered his head to peer at the body. "He's Rafragorian."

"One of the ambassadors?" With one eye on the sea drake's teeth, Kelan flew closer, noting that the body was clothed in a simple robe and not armour, and a second body lay in the shadow of the island's unfortunately shaped monument.

"That's not a good sign," said Lakiel. "We should go before we're blamed for this."

What had killed them? Not the sea drake, surely. Kelan flew around the monument, and a foul stench hit his nostrils. The second body, half-concealed by one of the large boulders, did not belong to a human at all. It resembled a raptor but with black scales rather than green and a considerably larger head. The head in question had been severed from the neck, and its clawed feet twitched, leaking shadows.

Brikel gagged. "What the fuck *is* that?"

Kelan knew. "Corruption."

Mekan's followers had been here.

———

Niema encountered few other people on the road to the capital. Given her raw emotional state, she was glad of a few days to get her head together, until the ache in her chest had faded to a dull throb and then nothing at all.

Niema hitched rides on wagons between villages until she reached Setemar, and from there, it was a straight road to the capital. She walked where she could and camped at the roadside beneath the bone-white form of the dead war drake in the sky. She feared the beast no longer; in fact, its presence struck her as more of a guardian, as though Yala had sent it to watch out for her.

When she reached the outskirts of Dalathar, an obvious problem became apparent. Yala might have changed addresses since Niema's last visit, and Niema had sent no word of her arrival due to her fear that Superior Kralia might be pursuing her. Nobody had followed her save for the dead war drake, but even the beast had receded from sight. Elsewhere, she might have been able to reach out and detect Yala's direction, but the confused mass of other humans pressed against her like the low-level noise that constantly permeated the air.

On top of the pungent smells of the market and the river and the salty tang of the sea waves, Niema's senses were muddled, and it took an hour of walking in circles before she remembered the obvious place to start looking: the Undercity.

Niema's memory of Dalathar was clear enough that in a short time, she found the narrow alleyway through which she and Yala had entered the Undercity. The man who stood at the top of the staircase leading into the gloom eyed her with suspicion. She'd worn some of the clothes she'd obtained during her last visit to Setemar rather than the usual garments she wore in the forest, but her shoes were considerably worn from her time on the road, and she was abruptly conscious of her lack of weapons. Though her deity did not permit her to use violence even in defence of her own life, at least she'd present a less helpless front.

"Can I help you?" growled the bearded man.

Niema straightened her back and prayed to Yalet that he wasn't as fierce as he looked. "I'm looking for Yala Palathar."

"Are you now?" he said. "And who are you?"

"Niema," she replied. "I've been here before. We're friends. Yala and I."

His gaze raked over her. "You look familiar, but she won't like me sending a stranger to her doorstep. She tends to get touchy about that kind of thing. Besides, you won't find her at home during the day. She'll be with the war drake."

"She's with the... war drake?" A living one, Niema assumed, though with Yala, there was no guarantee.

"That's what I said." He pointed over her shoulder. "The stables are over the river and north. Should be easy to find."

He was right, it turned out. Once she'd crossed the river and followed the winding street north, Niema heard the familiar growling of a war drake. The noise guided her to a modest-sized stable and a high-fenced paddock. Low growls issued from behind the large gate in front; Niema whistled, and the sound stopped.

The gate nudged open, and Yala's cane poked out, followed by a hand clutching a dagger.

"Who—?" Yala lowered the dagger, catching sight of Niema. "What in the gods' names are you doing here?"

"Looking for you, I'd guess." Saren peered out from behind Yala, clutching a long chain in one hand. The other end looped around the neck of the war drake, which now sat placidly in the paddock's centre. "It'll be much easier to convince this beast to behave itself with her around."

"That it will." Yala jerked her head towards the paddock. "Come in if you like."

Niema darted through the gap in the gate, holding her breath at the stench of dung and raw meat. The war drake had been equipped with a saddle, and its wings extended, with only the chain keeping it from taking flight. Yala rested a hand on her cane as she tugged the saddle tighter. A scar marked one side of her stern face, her curly hair had been tied back with a length of rope, and her drakeskin gloves prevented Niema from seeing if any scars from her encounter with Mekan in Setemar remained.

Saren gripped the chain in a similarly gloved hand, peering at Niema. "What're you here for? Another mission?"

"No," said Niema. "No, I've left the Disciples of Life."

"You *left* them?" Saren's grip on the chain slackened; at a growl from the war drake, Niema whistled, and it stilled. "Can you do that? Stop being a Disciple?"

"I'm still a Disciple," she clarified. "I'm just not part of the enclave. I can't obey Superior Kralia any longer."

"Good," Yala said. "She didn't try to follow you, did she?"

"I don't think so." Niema lowered her gaze. "I'm here to... to find out what I can do."

Now she voiced her wishes aloud, they sounded fragile, childish even. She didn't have a coin to her name nor any experience of life outside of the enclave. Dalathar was the place she'd spent the longest time, but that had been a scant few weeks, and she was woefully ill-equipped to handle the cacophony of noise and the assault on her senses.

"All right," Yala said. "You can stay with us, unless you'd prefer to go to the Disciples' Inn instead."

"I recall being tied to a bed the last time I went there." At a snort from Saren, she flushed. "Not in that way. Besides, I don't expect to be welcomed by the other Disciples."

In theory, all Disciples were allowed to stay at the inn, but the Disciples of the Sky were the ones whose Superior paid the bills to keep the place running, and their true home was Skytower. Was there a place for a Disciple without a home at all?

Yala grunted. "Neither am I, and that didn't stop me."

"You went there?" asked Niema. "Is Kelan in the capital?"

"He was," said Yala. "However, the king intended to send him and some other Disciples to meet with Rafragoria's ambassadors."

Niema's mouth fell open. "The king did *what*?"

"It was Superior Sietra's idea," she said. "I'm surprised the king went along with it, but Rafragoria didn't seem inclined to send anyone to meet with him, and he was running out of ideas."

"Why would anyone *want* to meet with them?" Niema had the distinct impression that she'd missed something vital during her absence. "What started this?"

"It's a long story."

6

Kelan glided above the island, scanning for any signs of survivors. Two more human-shaped bodies were visible below the water's surface at the edge, swathed in blood. Another monster, too, bore such wounds that could only have been inflicted by an equally large predator. Like a sea drake.

"What happened?" Ranit said. "Did they kill each other?"

A dark blur leapt out from behind the monument, resolving into a reptilian shape that resembled a raptor. Except for its teeth, which protruded larger than any raptor's he'd seen, and its dark scales, which seemed to suck in the sunlight instead of reflecting it.

"Yes and no," Kelan answered, drawing his blade. "Looks like we found the stragglers."

His fellow Disciples scrambled for their weapons, and they drew inward, forming a circle. If he'd spent any length of time in Skytower recently, he might have had more practise at fighting in formation, but none of them had ever set eyes on a beast like this.

The raptor-like creature leapt—again, higher than any real raptor he'd seen—and its teeth sank into Kelan's boot. Luckily, the thick material kept the sharp teeth from piercing his skin, but the weight dragged him down towards the water. Its spiny tail lashed upward, snagging the edge of Kelan's cloak.

"Get off." He drove the blade point-down into its skull. The beast's grip on his foot grew slack, and its scaly body plunged into the water. Shielding his eyes from the resultant splash, he shook his foot to dislodge a curved tooth that had lodged into the thick raptor leather of his boot.

"Good riddance," Brikel said with a shudder. "Where'd that thing come from?"

"Not here." *The Void isn't open nearby. They came from elsewhere.* Yes, it was possible that Mekan's followers had taken care to leave no traces of their activity on the island, but that didn't fit with their usual methods, and the god of death would surely want to maximise the number of potential corpses to feast upon.

"What're we supposed to do?" Ranit asked. "Take the bodies back to Rafragoria?"

"Absolutely not," said Lakiel. "We'll certainly be blamed."

"They'll skewer us on the spot," Brikel agreed.

"Mekan's beasts will draw more attention from His realm if we leave them here," Kelan reminded them. "We can leave the ambassadors but not the monsters."

As far as he knew, such beasts could only be destroyed by the Disciples of the Flame. *So much for avoiding Superior Shralin.*

"You can't be serious." Brikel eyed the scaly corpse. "I'm not touching that."

"I can't say I'm keen on the idea either," Kelan said. "We'll carry one each. If there are fewer than five, we'll take it in turns."

That would ensure nobody was happy, but it was better than Mekan's dead beasts remaining in the water like a beacon to the god of death and inevitably facilitating a larger attack.

Besides, part of him was curious to see Superior Shralin's reaction when he dropped a dead monster onto the doorstep of the Temple of the Flame.

When Yala had finished telling Niema of the recent turn of events, starting with the body and the note from Rafragoria, she returned her attention to the war drake. Niema, who'd had to calm the beast's impatience with whistles throughout, stared at Yala in horror.

"What did the note mean?" she whispered. "Remember the island?"

"I'm assuming it was directed at someone to whom that warning holds meaning," Yala said. "The king is not one of those people, but he took the note as a threat to the nation, and he'd been trying in vain to set up a meeting with Rafragoria for weeks when Kelan showed up and solved the problem."

While Yala hadn't ventured into the upper city herself since her brief visit to the Disciples' Inn, Viam had dropped in at Yala's house that morning to let her know that the Disciples of the Sky had left Dalathar in the early hours.

"Solved the problem?" Niema frowned. "Rafragoria wants revenge for the deaths of their soldiers, and someone thought it was a good idea to send *Disciples* to meet with them?"

"We don't know they want revenge," said Yala. "The message might have come from a single disgruntled soldier, not the government."

"Official messages aren't usually sent in the company of a corpse," Saren agreed with a slight shudder. "Hope Kelan and the others manage to solve this one."

"If he manages not to insult them." Yala placed her cane on the ground and extended both hands to pull herself onto the war drake's back.

The beast shook its head, and Niema whistled to calm it down. "What do the Disciples of the Flame think of all this?"

"I haven't spoken to them." Yala settled into position behind the war drake's neck. "Ready?"

"No." Saren cringed when the beast tugged at the chain then relaxed at another whistle from Niema. "I wish you'd been here sooner. Yala's fanged pet nearly took off my leg."

"At least I'm good for something." Niema clamped her mouth shut, perhaps aware of how self-pitying her words sounded, but Yala hardly blamed her for having a mild personal crisis after her Superior had tried to turn her into an assassin against her will and had obliterated her life in the process. She'd lost everything—her purpose, her family, even her home.

And am I to take responsibility for picking up the pieces? Yala dismissed the thought; she could hardly leave Niema on the streets of Dalathar. While Niema might have more experience than she had during her last visit to the capital—Yala noted that she'd at least worn shoes this time around—she practically had a sign on her head advertising herself as a target for thieves. Granted, she'd also never so much as handled a coin in her life. As far as Yala could work out, the Disciples of Life had no need of material possessions, as the god of life provided everything they needed.

Not that that had stopped her Superior from taking more from Niema than she was owed. And while she might have sent Niema here for the purposes of finishing the job, Yala had her doubts. If Superior Kralia had commanded her to, Niema might have set the war drake on her with little more than a whistle.

"Let's go." She squeezed the war drake's neck with her thighs, urging it into flight. The beast's docility under Niema's command made for a much less bumpy ride, though it was hardly sporting to keep the beast's free will locked away indefinitely. She kept her flight confined to the outer city, not wanting to push her luck by venturing too close to the walls circling the upper city and attracting the arrow of an overzealous guard.

"Superior Kralia still has her own war drake," Niema told Yala when she landed in the paddock again. "In the forest. She must think she'll need to travel quickly in the near future."

Yala slid from the beast's back to the ground, grimacing when the motion jarred her leg. "She's not thinking of coming here to reclaim her lost Disciple?"

"No, she let me go without a fight."

"For now." Yala moved to take off the beast's saddle with practised hands, and then Saren helped her put its wing restraints back on. Niema watched, occasionally whistling a command, but she otherwise remained quiet. Dark circles smudged her eyes, and her sleeves were frayed as though she'd been picking at them.

"What of Superior Shralin?" Niema asked, perhaps in an attempt to change the subject. "Does he know anything?"

"Does he know Kelan and the others are going to meet Rafragoria's ambassadors?" Yala guessed. "He must know. I doubt he approves, given that his predecessor let the Rafragorians take the fall for a crime the Disciples of the Flame committed with their own hands."

"Don't talk about that so loudly," Saren hissed.

"There's nobody here," Yala said. "I haven't found a new stableboy to replace the one who got killed."

"By the war drake?" Niema blanched.

"No, by mercenaries." Yala finished affixing the war drake's muzzle back into place. "Don't ask me who sent them. I haven't a clue."

Her suspicions remained unconfirmed, but she'd spent little time in the upper city, not wanting to draw unwelcome eyes. While the odds of being attacked in plain view of the palace were low, it was the king's offer of employment that urged her to keep her distance.

Niema's expression shadowed. "Mercenaries again?"

"Just like old times," Saren quipped. "She wouldn't report them to the city guard, but she told Nalen to keep an eye out for any more trouble."

"Is that why he was so suspicious when I went looking for Yala?" asked Niema as they left the paddock.

"You went to the Undercity?" Yala closed the gates. "You're lucky you didn't run into trouble."

"I have nothing for robbers to steal," Niema said with a touch of her old haughtiness. "When is Kelan due to return to the city?"

"No idea." She didn't know what time he and the others had left for Rafragoria's meeting place, but he might be back at the inn by now. "We can check, but I can't promise the Disciples of the Flame won't be sniffing around the place."

"I'll talk to them."

"Sure you want to do that?" Yala finished locking the paddock and turned towards her. "Superior Shralin isn't my biggest fan. Granted, he's even less keen on Kelan."

"Because he claimed that journal." Niema chewed on her lower lip. "Are you sure it was a good idea? Sending that book to Skytower?"

"Yes," said Yala. "Superior Sietra will keep it secured. There's no good reason for anyone in Skytower to want to call upon the god of death."

"I thought the same of the Disciples of the Flame," Niema said. "And the Disciples of the Earth too."

"And they wonder why people don't like them." Saren strode ahead down the street. "If you're going to the upper city, count me out."

"See you at home," Yala called after him. To Niema, she added, "I'm not sure Kelan *will* be back. Rafragoria is half a day's flight away, if I remember correctly, but Viam said they were meeting on an island somewhere in between."

An island. Not that unusual—Rafragoria itself was formed of a chain of islands—but she couldn't shake the feeling that Kelan and the others had flown straight into a trap.

The question was, *whose* trap? Rafragoria's or another entity's?

Yala was happy to seize on any distraction, so she and Niema made for the gates to the upper city. The guards outside eyed Niema's strange attire with their usual mixture of suspicion and confusion that vanished when Niema had declared herself as a Disciple of Life.

They were waved through into the upper city, where Niema shrank back from the square, grimacing. "I forgot how *noisy* it is here."

Yala grunted. She'd also forgotten that Niema hadn't been in the capital since the Void had split open above Ceremonial Square and reduced the bustling crowds to a pile of bloodied corpses. Not a trace of that battle remained; the crowds thronging the market stalls were as raucous as ever, and the smell of frying fish and vegetables permeated the air. Niema held her arms tightly around herself as they crossed the square, Yala using her cane liberally to clear their path to the Temple of the Flame.

There, she halted, looking up at the towering windows at the front of the second-tallest building in the city. Robed Disciples walked in and out of view between tall bookshelves and alcoves containing altars and offerings. A wide staircase led to the front door, flanked by white marble statues of past Superiors.

"Right." Yala released a breath. "Let's get this over with. I'll let you do the talking."

Niema managed a nod, looking as if she might throw up. She tottered up the stairs ahead of Yala and rapped a knuckle on the door.

A novice wearing a pale orange cloak answered, taking a startled step back. "Ah... Yala Palathar?"

"Novice Yachim." He looked even more startled that she remembered his name. "Is your Superior in?"

"He's not here," he blurted. "He's busy."

"Busy where?" Yala queried. "Is he in the temple?"

Novice Yachim faltered. "No, he's at the docks... wait. I don't think he wanted me to tell you that."

What's he doing there? "Relax, I'm not going to push him in the sea. Not unless he annoys me."

She turned her back on the startled apprentice and descended the stairs, each step punctuated by a twinge of pain in her leg. Noticing, Niema said, "I can help."

"Go ahead." Reluctantly, Yala slowed her pace, and Niema extended both hands. Green light bloomed on her palms, the light transferring to Yala's shin, and the ache faded noticeably. "Thanks."

Walking to the docks would swiftly undo the healing touch of the god of life, but it couldn't be helped. She took a side road from the square to the gates at the back of the upper city and headed north, fuelled by the improbable mental image of Superior Shralin sitting on a boat. *What is he doing?*

"How do you know where you're going?" Niema puffed out a breath, having to half run to keep up with Yala. "He might be anywhere in the docks."

"His headgear isn't exactly hard to spot." While she knew she'd pay the price in pain later, the need to know what had driven the Superior to leave the temple prevailed.

As she walked, another sensation arrived, a tingling in her fingertips that made her wish she hadn't left the void drake's claw under the floorboard at home.

Niema sucked in a breath. "You sense that too?"

"Yes." Yala's hands curled into fists. "There's some foulness afoot."

They reached the seafront, where her gaze picked out the Superior's robed figure standing upon one of the long piers extending into the ocean. It was so unlike him to be out in public that she might have taken him to be a mirage brought on by the bright sunlight glinting on the water. Three other Disciples surrounded him, holding what appeared to be a net between them.

"What in the hells are they doing?" Yala strode forward, her cane tapping against the wooden slats of the pier.

The Superior swivelled towards them. "Yala Palathar. Who sent you here?"

"Nobody did. I sent myself." Her gaze went to the net, which had slipped, revealing a distinctly reptilian shape. "What is that?"

Yala's fingers tingled again. *Mekan. It's one of his beasts.*

Niema made a choked noise. "Did you fish that out of the ocean?"

"And what killed it?" Yala took a step back when flames trailed from Superior Shralin's hand, engulfing the reptilian form. The other Disciples shook the net, scattering ashes onto the pier. No traces of whatever creature it had been remained, but the tingling sensation lingered in Yala's fingertips as she lifted her gaze to the Superior. "Who summoned that beast? Do you know where it came from?"

"No," he said. "We do not know the source."

"Did someone tip you off that it was in the water?" Suspicion prickled at her. "I didn't know your people made a habit of wandering around the docks."

"Don't be absurd," he said. "I have informants throughout the city who have been instructed to come to me with tales of anything tangentially related to Corruption."

Right. "And is this the first?"

Unlikely, after the Rafragorian's corpse had shown up in the boat. How long had he been covering up similar incidents, ones that might point to another Disciple of Death in the area? Him and his informants. Were they mercenaries, perhaps, like the ones who'd attacked her?

The Superior lifted his head as a breeze swept out from the ocean, ruffling his cloak. A group of robed figures had descended from the sky, gliding towards the coast. *The Disciples of the Sky.* Had they already met with the Rafragorians?

As they neared the seafront, Kelan veered away from the others to land upon the pier in front of them.

"Yala." He nodded to the Disciples' leader. "Superior Shralin. This is a surprise."

"I might say the same," said the Superior, an edge to his voice indicating that he still hadn't forgiven Kelan for snatching Mavilangran's journal from his grasp. "Your Superior sent you on another errand."

"Yes, we went to meet with a group of ambassadors from Rafragoria." He lifted his gaze to watch the other Disciples descend over the pier, having seen the Superior too. "Unfortunately, we found they'd been brutally murdered, so our meeting was over before it began."

Yala's heart lurched. "By whom?"

"I think 'by what' is the appropriate question." His gaze followed hers to the pile of ashes that remained of the monster. "Was that...?"

"A void beast, yes." Yala pointedly looked at the Superior, who'd flinched imperceptibly at her words. "I didn't see what kind."

"We found ours in pieces." He gestured to the other Disciples, who carried the mutilated remains of two similar beasts in their arms. "We didn't think it wise to leave them unattended, and we'd appreciate it if you were to dispose of them for us."

The other robed figures appeared equally flummoxed by the sight of Superior Shralin out in public. The Superior, for his part, scowled when the Disciples deposited the remains of Mekan's monsters in front of him, but a swift gesture conjured a flame that engulfed them in an instant.

As she watched, Yala's mind reeled like a broken door hanging off its hinges. Void beasts washing up on Laria's shores was a world apart from people dabbling in Corruption and causing skirrits or small birds to rise from death—let alone murdering ambassadors. Someone

71

had instigated this, but whom? And had they paid the price in their own blood or someone else's?

"Niema?" Kelan, spotting their companion behind Yala, did a double-take. "You're here too?"

"Shouldn't I be?" she said.

His mouth curved into a smile. "I wondered if you'd changed your mind about leaving the enclave."

"I was delayed." She lowered her head, her eyes on the water. "I just arrived."

"In time to find a dead Void beast and murdered ambassadors. You certainly have a knack for bad timing."

"So do you." Yala gripped her cane harder when the other Disciples of the Sky took flight in a billow of robes without offering so much as a greeting in her direction. The Disciples of the Flame, too, turned to leave. "Superior Shralin, aren't you going to check for any more beasts?"

"No," he replied. "It's beyond our capacity to search the entire ocean. If there's anything else out there, we'll come back."

"You'll wait for the next poor fisherman to find a piece of Mekan in their net," she surmised. "Doesn't it bother you? That someone out there must have opened the Void?"

Her body tensed when he took a step towards her, bending his head to speak in a low voice. "If you wish to set yourself at odds with hostile foreign forces, Yala Palathar, I will have no part in it."

"You think it was Rafragoria," Yala said, bewildered by his reaction. "They killed their own ambassadors?"

It wouldn't be the first time, whispered a voice in the back of her mind. On the island, her squad had found the Rafragorian soldiers dismembered, slain by their own weapons and then raised from death by Mekan's power. Those same deaths were presumably what the note had blamed Laria for—or rather, Yala and her squad.

"Who am I to comprehend those who follow the god of death?" He swept away without another word, his golden headdress glimmering in the sunlight.

"I get the impression he was trying to insult me," Yala said. "What's he playing at?"

"How long has he been hanging around the docks?" Kelan watched the Disciples of the Flame depart with a furrow in his brow. "Seems odd behaviour for a Superior."

"He claims to have informants keeping an eye out for trouble relating to Corruption," she said. "I assume this isn't the first monster that's washed up here."

"No, but what's going on in Rafragoria?" Niema asked anxiously. "Were all the ambassadors dead?"

"Yes," said Kelan, his smile slipping away. "If this is as bad as it looks, we'll have more threatening notes sent our way soon enough."

"They can't possibly think *you* killed them," Niema protested. "You're Disciples from a different temple. You can't use Corruption."

"And Rafragoria can?" Yala's body tightened like a vice. *Is it true? Did they kill their own people, or was some other party involved?* "If someone in Rafragoria is dabbling in Corruption again, it doesn't mean the authorities are aware of it. They might assume it was our doing instead."

"*Was* anyone in Rafragoria ever dabbling in Corruption?" Kelan asked. "I thought the ones who died on the island were the only team who made it to the shore."

"They were." Yala's fist clenched and unclenched, tingling radiating from the grey marks etched into her fingers. "I wouldn't be surprised if Rafragoria had access to the same texts as we do, though."

"What, Mavilangran's journal?" Kelan asked. "Someone translated it into Rafragorian?"

"It was translated into Larian from the old Parvan script in the first place," Yala reminded him. "It's not that unique, but this is all speculation anyway. Both our armies went after the island at the same time. There's no telling whose idea it was first, and Rafragoria wouldn't admit anything."

"Neither did our monarch," Kelan said. "Granted, his father died an untimely death before word got out. Now, I suppose I should tell our current king that the Rafragorian ambassadors met with an unfortunate accident."

———

They're back, Viam thought, watching the Disciples of the Sky from the upper window of the administrative building. She'd hardly been able to focus on work all day with the anticipation of their return and what news they might bring. She jumped from her seat when they flew straight *over* the gates, bypassing the king's guards altogether.

Heart sinking, she ran for the nearest exit, hoping that the other workers were too distracted by the Disciples' sudden appearance to notice her slip away.

If they returned that urgently, it must be bad news, she thought as she circled the building and spied one of the Disciples of the Sky conversing with a palace guard.

"Viam." Kelan glided to meet her, looking windswept but unhurt.

"You can't just *fly* in here," she whispered. "Do you want to give the impression that the king's guards aren't there for anything but show?"

"We're invited," Kelan said. "Besides, they know we aren't the enemy. We're Disciples."

"That's not the point," Viam protested. "What if you were Rafragorian? Their Disciples can fly too."

Not that she'd ever seen a Rafragorian Disciple herself, and she'd been under the assumption that they hadn't sent Disciples to meet with Kelan and the others either.

"The ambassadors we were supposed to meet were murdered." His words caused Viam's question to die on her tongue. "I think His Majesty wants to know right away."

"Murdered?" She swallowed, her mouth dry. "Who...?"

"Not by a human." He glanced at his fellow Disciples. "Ah, good. We can go in."

As he glided towards the palace, Viam stared after him, numb. *The ambassadors are dead. Something killed them.*

When someone caught her arm from behind, she jumped.

"Sorry I startled you." Brenat peered at her face. "You look like you've seen an apparition. What're those Disciples doing here?"

"They… they just flew over the gates." Viam scrambled to get a grip on her thoughts. "It surprised me."

"You look more than surprised," said Brenat.

Viam wished her friend wasn't quite so perceptive. "We can't have people flying in and out of the palace whenever they like."

"Doesn't seem that unusual for those Disciples," Brenat commented. "How do you know one another, anyway?"

"Through a friend." Viam took half a step forward, fighting the impulse to run up the palace steps and ask the Disciples to let her into their meeting with the king. *No. This isn't my business.* She was a scribe, for the gods' sakes. She'd chosen her position precisely to avoid being dragged into anything related to the army, to Rafragoria, to Corruption.

And just how much good did that do you the last time? a voice whispered in her head.

Brenat scrutinised her face. "You're really not all right, are you? Let me help you."

"This isn't anything you can help with." When Brenat's face fell, she added, "Don't worry about me. I'll be fine."

"Gods, what is it?" Brenat asked. "Who died?"

Viam jerked back from her. "How did you know someone was dead?"

"Nothing else would upset you this much." Brenat bumped her fist into Viam's arm. "What ambassadors? Shit, not Rafragoria's?"

"You knew—?"

"Of course I knew the Disciples were meeting with them," she said. "Nobody can keep a secret in here. I bet the entire administrative division knew within hours."

"Oh." Viam ducked her head, heat rushing to her face. "This was supposed to *stop* a war with Rafragoria, but the ambassadors were murdered before the Disciples got there."

"Shit." Brenat's usual breezy demeanour vanished. "That's not good. Should we prepare for retaliation?"

75

"I don't know." Viam faced the palace, her hands clenching and unclenching at her sides. "I'll have to ask when they've finished talking to the king. I don't know the details."

Something inhuman killed them. Like Corruption.

Brenat moved to her side, her eyes on the palace too. "I'm sure His Majesty will have a plan."

Would he? Or would he hide like he had when Melian had opened the Void in front of the palace? Treacherous thoughts pushed at her head, and the truth formed on her tongue like a confession. Not for herself but on behalf of the former king. His fascination with Corruption, his death, and now these murders, so close to where he'd met his own end.

"I have to go." Viam turned her back on Brenat and ran.

7

Niema's gaze lingered on the retreating backs of the Disciples of the Flame. The only traces of the monster they'd fished out of the ocean were the scarcely visible ashes scattered on the wooden planks, but the sour tang of the dead lingered in the salty air.

"Fools," Yala muttered. "Destroying the evidence won't make this problem go away."

"What were they supposed to do?" Niema asked. "If they hadn't, people might have—" She choked on the words. "Might have used that monster to call Mekan."

Yala's eyes narrowed. "If pieces of Mekan's beasts are washing up on Laria's shores, there's a good chance Rafragoria is having the same problem. Assuming they aren't the cause."

"You think someone in Rafragoria…"

"Used Corruption?"

Niema flinched, feeling like a fool for her instinctive reaction to the word, though part of her would always shrink away from her deity's natural enemy. "If they did, why blame Laria for... for the soldiers they lost on the island?"

"That's what I don't understand." Yala jabbed the end of her cane into the heap of ashes, scattering them across the wooden planks. "We might be dealing with more than one enemy, but if someone in Rafragoria *is* meddling with Corruption, I have a hard time believing they killed their own ambassadors to frame us. If they wanted a war, they'd have attacked us, not set us up under the guise of a peaceful meeting."

"Then who?" Niema scanned the pier as though answers might hide beneath the surface of the murky water.

"The question is," Yala began, "who stands to gain from this?"

Niema's mouth parted. "What do you mean, gain?"

Yala lifted her head, a gleam in her eyes. "If I wanted to ignite a war between Laria and Rafragoria, I'd have something to gain from that outcome. Who falls into that category?"

Niema racked her thoughts. "The god of death."

Yala let out a bark of surprised laughter. "That goes without saying, but He always needs a human to act on His behalf."

"A Disciple of Death, but that doesn't explain who...?" Niema trailed off. "Not the Successors?"

"Melian's dead, and so is Trienan," Yala acknowledged, "but their ideas reached a lot of people. I think someone who was part of a group working to overthrow the monarch would have good reason to set us up to take the fall for their crimes."

"Even if it means the whole country is dragged into war?"

"Melian wasn't one for considering all the possible outcomes of her actions." She lifted her head, her gaze skimming the row of houses along the seafront. "Come to think of it, she used to live nearby. I wonder if the Successors are still using the same base."

She strode away down the pier, and Niema hastened to catch up to her. "Do you think they'd base themselves somewhere that obvious?"

"Not many people know she used to live here." Yala indicated a row of houses. "In fact, Melian owns all those properties. Or she did."

Niema followed Yala towards the row of narrow houses, her heart racing. She hadn't known they were so close to where Melian had once lived, and although Yala had claimed the houses to be deserted, Niema cringed when Yala forced one of the doors open. She didn't sense anyone, but the constant pulsing presence of human life else-where in the city made it difficult to tell if they were being watched.

"Nobody's home." Beckoning to Niema, Yala stepped into the house.

Niema followed, the dim light revealing a room that resembled a study, containing bookshelves and a desk and little else.

Yala approached the desk, touching the wooden surface with a finger and scraping off a layer of dust. "Someone *has* been in here since I last came. The leaflets are gone."

"What leaflets?"

"Melian's attempt at recruitment." She reached for the chair behind the desk and lifted a hooded garment. "This wasn't here before either."

"If it belongs to someone, they'll know you've been in here."

"Good." She gave the cloak a shake. "I'm almost certain the men who tried to kill me were wearing these."

"The mercenaries?" Niema's mouth went dry. "But… who's in charge of the Successors now?"

"That's the question, isn't it?" Yala moved around the study, her sharp eyes roving over the almost-empty bookshelves. "Not much in the way of reading material here. Viam wouldn't approve."

"Melian wouldn't have left any clues behind, would she?" Niema licked her lips. "Like that journal."

"No," Yala said. "She wouldn't leave *that* level of proof for anyone to stumble across. I doubt her followers have anything that valuable. I'd say we're dealing with the dregs of her would-be allies."

Niema took in her words. "If they're responsible for what happened to the Rafragorian ambassadors, they're still dangerous. How'd they manage to send Mekan's beasts all the way across the ocean?"

"That's what I'd like to know." Yala's gaze travelled past the book-shelves to a faded map pinned to the wall, but it displayed only Laria's capital and not the coastline or beyond. "Mekan's creatures don't obey anyone but Him."

And me, whispered a voice in the back of her mind, reminding her of how she'd been on the brink of a grim death at the claws of a void drake when a desperate prayer had turned the creature away. How she'd managed to command the beast as though it were living was a mystery that even her Superior—her *former* Superior—hadn't been able to answer.

"Let's check the other houses." Yala left the dust-swathed office and moved on to the next house, forcing the door open as she'd done to the first.

This one was even emptier, consisting of nothing but bare floorboards and empty walls. Niema kept her senses open, alert for any hints of the god of death's presence, but none leapt out at her. Yala dug her cane into the floor, stirring up a flurry of dust.

"What a fucking waste," she muttered. "We have people in the Undercity living in shacks, and these serviceable houses lie empty."

"Someone's outside." Niema's senses alerted her to a nearby human presence. "Yala?"

"Don't worry." She returned to the door and nudged it open, peering through the crack before stepping outside. Niema followed, spying two figures dressed in the raptor-skin leathers of city guards exiting a nearby side street.

Yala swore under her breath. "What are they doing this close to the docks?"

"Looking for trouble?" Niema hastily stepped away from the house so it was less obvious they'd broken in, though any close look at the door would give them away. "We'd better go."

"The king must have sent them," Yala murmured. "At a guess, he's expecting trouble from across the ocean."

———

Whether Rafragoria intended to strike back against Laria or not, the king certainly seemed to think so if the number of guards he'd sent to the seafront was any indication. They paid little attention to Yala and Niema, who found a wagon leaving the docks and persuaded its driver to take them back to the upper city.

They passed several more patrols on their journey, more than Yala could recall seeing in this part of the capital. *The Successors want a war, and they might just get one.*

The Disciples of the Flame might not believe her, but she had an inkling that Superior Shralin wasn't entirely oblivious to the true nature of the situation. Whether he cared enough to act was another matter altogether, aside from burning any trace of Mekan that washed up in the docks.

As the wagon rattled along, Yala's thoughts churned like a tumultuous ocean. The king's request for her to train new recruits took on a grim edge now that the prospect of war loomed as close as the god of death's whisper in her ear. If the king did reinstate the old laws, would conscription extend to everyone, not just younger people who'd never seen war before? Yala's leg injury would see her more likely to be assigned to a training role, but there were no guarantees. Rafragoria hadn't outright attacked Laria's mainland for decades, the same as Laria's forces hadn't directly targeted Rafragoria's shores during any of their recent conflicts.

The two nations might have spent the past few hundred years grappling over territories surrounding both their countries, but they shared no borders and had no reason to sacrifice their people in an invasion. This was new and dangerous territory for both their sides.

The wagon dropped them off near the square, from which Yala led the way to the Disciples' Inn. Niema walked silently behind her. The young woman hadn't come to the capital expecting to be dragged into a war, but was that worse than returning to the enclave and putting herself at risk of being controlled against her will? More to the point, if Superior Kralia remained committed to her plan to eradicate Corruption, that surely didn't extend beyond Laria's borders. Most likely, she'd ensconce herself inside the enclave while the two nations ripped each other apart.

Not unlike the Disciples of the Flame, she thought as they walked past the temple on their way to the inn. During Melian's attack on the capital, the majority of them had been drugged into sleeping through the events altogether. If the Successors wanted to attempt another takeover, they must have a plan to take the Disciples out of the action, but they didn't need a sophisticated one. Superior Shralin's commitment to avoidance would be his own undoing.

The Disciples' Inn was considerably larger than Yala's lodgings, the size of several tenement buildings put together and without so much as a roof tile out of place. Yala could only assume the Superiors paid for upkeep, though Yala wasn't clear on where their money came from. The Disciples she'd seen in the capital had seemed to spend all their time idling around.

Kelan answered her knock on the door. "Yala. Good timing. We just got back from the palace."

"His Majesty didn't waste any time in sending out extra guard patrols." She followed him into the main room, where a table was occupied by the four other Disciples. Aside from Lakiel, the unfriendly man who was supposedly in charge of this mission, she didn't know the others' names.

Lakiel's arms folded across his chest as she walked in. "We're not supposed to let outsiders in here."

"I have information," Yala told him. "I think your Superior will want you to hear me out."

"You know who killed the ambassadors?" Kelan guessed.

"Exactly." Yala pulled out a chair and sat down, ignoring Lakiel's disapproving tut. "The Successors."

"*Them?*" Kelan glanced at Niema as though to discern if she agreed. "How's that possible? Even if some survived, they can't possibly be in Rafragoria."

"They might not be," Yala said. "We don't know where they're operating from, but if pieces of Mekan's beasts have been washing up in the harbour, it's got to be their doing."

"Who are the Successors?" asked one of the other Disciples, a younger man in his mid-twenties.

"Their goal is to have the monarch deposed and their own government instated in his place," Yala said. "Igniting a war between our nations would certainly give them that opportunity."

"I thought they died." The sole female member of the Disciples' group looked at Lakiel. "Didn't they rip open the Void in the middle of the city and get eaten by the dead?"

"Yes," Yala cut through Lakiel's reply. "Melian's dead, but someone's certainly using her old house, so I'll assume the Successors are far from defeated. I'd have searched the other houses, too, if the guards hadn't shown up to patrol the docks."

"Already?" Lakiel's brows rose into his hairline. "Wait—you broke into someone's house?"

"Yes." Yala ignored the sharp intake of breath from amongst the other Disciples. "Melian was a murderer and a criminal who'd have been more than happy to see Mekan Himself sitting upon the throne. What exactly did the king say when you told him about the ambassadors?"

"We didn't speak to him," Kelan replied. "Once we told the palace guards, they ordered us to leave and said they'd pass on word to the king themselves."

"And then sent people to the docks," Yala surmised. "Does he expect an attack?"

"You're asking the wrong people," Lakiel said. "Our part in this is over. We were told to go and meet the ambassadors, not chase after rogue Disciples—assuming they exist."

"Your Superior wanted to avert a war," Yala said. "If you want to do something useful, go back to Skytower and ask her to send reinforcements to the capital before Rafragoria sends their own Disciples to retaliate."

"That's what you think they'll do?" The young man leapt to his feet. "They can't possibly think *we* killed their ambassadors. We'd have no reason to."

"You're being alarmist," Lakiel told Yala. "There's nothing to connect us with their deaths."

"Except for the fact that we were invited to meet with those ambassadors, and we found the bodies," Kelan pointed out. "Our best hope is that Rafragoria finds this as suspicious as we do and blames a third party, but we'll have to wait for the king to get in touch with them first."

"Is that the plan?" asked the young woman who lounged in the seat across from Kelan. "Wait it out? We'd look even guiltier if we said nothing at all."

"Exactly." Kelan swivelled back to Yala. "Your friend in the palace. Might she be able to get an update from the king so we know what he intends to do next?"

"Who?" Lakiel's mouth thinned. "Kelan, I'm not getting involved in whatever schemes you and Yala are concocting. If you don't want to end up confined to Skytower again, I'd suggest you stay away from the palace until the king extends us another invitation."

"Or Rafragoria shows up," Yala added. "I might add that unlike you, I *live* here, directly in the path of whatever retaliatory force Rafragoria might send to the city. I don't have the luxury of hiding in a tower on the other side of the country."

A flush crept across Lakiel's face. "You're a Disciple of Death. And a soldier too."

"Yes, and as a soldier, I've seen what war with Rafragoria looks like." Yala let a tense silence ripple through the room. "If I were you, I'd do everything in my power to avoid it."

"That doesn't mean you have the right to give us orders," Lakiel said. "You might be able to convince Kelan to run around the city on your behalf looking for these supposed Disciples of Death, but we obey our Superior, not you. If she wants us to fight Rafragoria, which I every much doubt, we will."

"Then you'll be playing into the Successors' hands." Yala's remaining patience frayed. "I've faced Rafragoria, and they aren't responsible for the deaths of the ambassadors."

Nor the note. The dead body. Why hadn't she made the connection sooner? If that note had never come from Rafragoria, that explained why the king had had so much trouble convincing them to meet in person.

"What makes you think this wasn't Rafragoria?" Lakiel challenged. "They wanted to provoke us."

"No." Yala rose from her seat and began pacing. "They haven't broken the laws of combat in centuries of warfare, and there's no reason for them to start now."

The female Disciple spoke up. "Didn't Rafragoria assassinate our monarch a few years ago?"

No, they didn't. Not that any of the Disciples of the Sky knew that, aside from Kelan. He caught her gaze, and she narrowed her eyes, willing him to hold his tongue.

"They didn't use Corruption," Niema blurted. "They've never—except on the island—but that wasn't…"

Yala spoke over her mumbling. "It doesn't make sense for Rafragoria's government to send their own ambassadors into a trap. This was a third party's work, whichever nation they belonged to."

"You have no proof," Lakiel said. "Not enough for the king *or* for any Rafragorian who might seek an explanation."

"Not yet." Yala's cane rapped the floor between steps. "The Successors had a large number of supporters, and their ideas weren't unpopular. It's not implausible that some endured and continued to recruit."

"Placing the god of death on the throne is a popular idea?" The female Disciple raised an eyebrow. "That's news to me."

"They didn't come out and *say* that, but they wanted the current monarch gone and their own replacement instated," Yala said impatiently. "Either way, I think we can agree that a dead monarch is the least of what we need at the moment."

No. It was better that King Daliel knew the truth. All of it. No matter the consequences.

I think it's time to open His Majesty's eyes.

8

A brief silence followed Yala's words, punctuated by a murmur of agreement from Brikel and Ranit's direction. The pair of them didn't seem bothered by her entry to the inn, but Kriam ignored her, and Lakiel had apparently decided that he disliked her on principle.

"So," Kelan said, breaking the silence, "who's going to tell Superior Shralin? Assuming he doesn't already know the Successors are up to their old tricks?"

Yala swivelled towards the other Disciples. "Well?"

Lakiel bristled. "I told you, you're not the one giving us orders. Besides, he knows the ambassadors are dead."

He doesn't know the Successors are back. Or did he? It was plain to see that the Disciples of the Flame had been doing their level best to hide any traces of Corruption in the capital from the public. Yala's history of being blamed for crimes she hadn't committed was bound to make her reluctant to confront the Superior, but Kelan wasn't likely to have much luck either.

"Niema." Yala turned to their companion, who'd remained almost silent throughout the entire exchange. "Would you like to speak to

Superior Shralin on our behalf? He's marginally less likely to throw you out of the temple than the rest of us."

Niema dropped her gaze. "If you say so."

"Really, Yala, she only just got here." Kelan stepped to her side. "I'll go with you for moral support, Niema."

Lakiel hissed out a frustrated breath. "I'll come, too, but I still think this is a bad idea."

Kelan had to admit he agreed; there was a fair chance that Superior Shralin would close the door the instant he caught sight of Kelan outside, but he didn't have the heart to leave Niema to deal with the fiery Disciples alone. She could handle herself, of course, but who was to say how they'd react to the implication that the Successors had risen from the dead—again?

Kelan led the way out of the inn, gliding up to the edge of Ceremonial Square. The market stalls were quiet for this time of day, though the usual merchants peddled wares ranging from raptor pelts to freshly caught fish. More notably, groups of uniformed guards congregated on street corners and beside the statue of King Larial.

Yala eyed the palace gates, her mouth pressed into a thin line. "I'll see if Viam's around. I doubt the king knows that bits of Mekan's monsters have been washing up in the docks, and someone has to enlighten him."

"You don't think they told the *king*?" The Disciples of the Flame weren't in close contact with King Daliel, true, which was one of the reasons the truth about what they'd done to the king's father had yet to come out into the open. "I wonder what Superior Shralin will say when we ask."

"I'd like to know too." Yala took a step closer to Kelan and lowered her voice. "I think it's worth shaking things up. If we want to avoid war, we'll all have to make hard choices. Even the king."

Without waiting for him to reply, she walked across the square towards the palace, her cane striking the cobbles with each step.

"What was that about?" Lakiel watched her retreat through narrowed eyes. "You'd better not be thinking of insulting the Superior, Kelan."

87

"I wouldn't dream of it." He beckoned Niema to his side, and they crossed the square towards the temple.

Niema's gaze followed Yala until she vanished behind the crowd. "What did Yala imply? She wants to talk to the king?"

"I don't think she's going to get into the palace today." Kelan quickened his pace to catch up to Lakiel, who'd glided across the square with little heed to anyone forced to stumble out of his path. "Are you really that keen to see the Superior?"

"No," Lakiel said over his shoulder. "I'd advise *you* to speak as little as possible."

Kelan gestured to Niema to overtake him and knock on the door while he peered through one of the windows in search of the Superior. The wide windows offered a view of the main entrance hall, which was dominated by a colossal statue carved in Dalathik's likeness, its serpentine tail curling around an altar on which candles burned throughout day and night.

A novice answered the door with a gasp that put Kelan in mind of a raptor who'd realised mid-sprint that it was about to run off the edge of a cliff. When Niema asked for the Superior, the young man vanished, and Superior Shralin appeared in his place, looking harried; his golden embroidered headdress lay askew, revealing his thinning hair.

"You again?" His gaze slid past Niema and lingered on Kelan. "I was under the impression that you were on an urgent mission from your Superior. Some of you, anyway."

"This is part of the mission," Kelan said, to a predictable sigh from Lakiel. "We already sent word to the king that the ambassadors were murdered, but we didn't get the chance to discuss the details with you. Namely, that they were killed by Corruption."

Behind the Superior, the novice sucked in a sharp breath; Superior Shralin ushered him away with an impatient hand. "Why did you come to me rather than to your Superior? I gather that she had a specific interest in the subject."

Ah. So he does still bear a grudge over that book. "Well, you just fished a dead monster out of the ocean, so I thought you'd want to know who we think put it there."

The Superior released the faintest sigh. "You thought wrong. I'm aware of your penchant for concocting outrageous stories, Kelan, but I'll humour you. Who do you propose was responsible?"

"The Successors," he said. "They have a reason to stir up trouble between Laria and Rafragoria. It's got to be their work."

"Kelan got the idea from Yala Palathar," added Lakiel. "The rest of us don't necessarily agree with either of them."

"I agree with Kelan," Niema said. "The Successors were never completely wiped out, were they?"

"And why is a Disciple of Life in Dalathar?" Superior Shralin directed his question more at Kelan than at Niema, which struck him as unfair. "I wasn't aware that your Superior had a habit of getting involved in politics."

Niema didn't appear cowed by his rudeness. "I came here of my own accord to make sure nobody tried to repeat what the Successors did. We already know some of them survived and went to Setemar."

"And what proof do you have that the ambassadors' deaths are their doing, save for guesswork?"

"Don't make the same mistakes as your predecessor," said Kelan. "The king deserves to know someone in the capital is dabbling in Corruption. He also needs to know if those same people murdered Rafragoria's ambassadors. So does Rafragoria, come to that."

"Then by all means, share your theories with the king's guards," said Superior Shralin. "We have no part in this."

"If that's the case, what were you doing at the docks?" He knew he was overstepping, but Superior Shralin's indifference crawled under his skin like an itch. "What's your plan if Rafragoria's fleet shows up in the port? Hide in the tower and hope that your god protects you?"

Lakiel stepped in front of him, sending the faintest gust of air at Kelan that would have caused him to trip downstairs if he hadn't caught his balance. "I apologise for my fellow Disciple's bluntness," he said. "I can't fathom why my Superior chose him for this mission, but I believe that we need to be willing to cooperate with one another in the event that Rafragoria does declare war. The king seems to be preparing for that possibility."

"The king has his own advisors," said Superior Shralin. "I am not one of them, and I thank Dalathik's blessing for that."

"But—" Niema stumbled back when the door closed in her face. "He's wrong. We *can't* stay neutral."

"He's going to be in for a rude awakening," Kelan agreed. "Though I think it's safe to say the Disciples of the Flame won't be defending anyone against Rafragoria's sea monsters."

Even Lakiel had trouble arguing with that.

———

Viam stopped running when she reached the paddock. Her heart pounded against her rib cage, and she took a few calming breaths before she unlocked the gate and slipped inside. The war drake rose upright, baring its teeth behind its muzzle. Either it recognised her as the person who brought it food, or it heard her racing heartbeat and sensed prey. Luckily, she'd left her spare drakeskin gloves inside the paddock, because she hadn't thought to stop and change. Her fine clothes would soon be splashed with mud, but she couldn't face returning to the administrative offices when her country stood on the brink of toppling into war.

She loosened the war drake's muzzle and set about running through the usual commands until her heart was racing for reasons unrelated to the chaos that might be unfolding inside the palace walls. Strange, perhaps, that being in the jaws of death—in a literal sense— gave her some perspective.

It's not up to me, she told herself. The king was the one who had to make the decision for Laria's future. Viam might be his confidant, but that didn't make her privy to vital decisions like how the nation prepared for war. She focused on the war drake instead until the tapping of a cane on cobbles drew her awareness.

Yala. She secured the war drake's chain and then ran to the gate, which she pushed open. "Yala, what are you doing here?"

Yala halted, eyeing her mud-stained fine clothing with puzzlement. "Aren't you supposed to be working?"

"Yes." She didn't elaborate, and instead stepped back to let Yala enter the paddock. "What are *you* doing here?"

"I was hoping to pass a message to you. I didn't know you'd be in here." Yala's gaze flickered over to the war drakes' hut, from which several reptilian faces watched her. "How many war drakes does he have now? Enough for a squad?"

"Maybe." Her mouth went dry. "Is it true? The ambassadors are dead, and Rafragoria thinks we're to blame?"

"Apparently so," she replied. "I have an idea who did it, but I don't have access to the king."

"Neither do I." Her heart began thundering again. "Who?"

"The Successors." Yala spoke quietly but clearly. "I can't believe it never crossed my mind until now, but instigating a war between us and Rafragoria plays right into their hands."

Viam's mouth hung open. "You think they sent the note too? *Remember the island?*"

"Of course they did." Yala paced behind the gate, her hand clenching over her cane. "Melian couldn't have come up with anything better. While we're at war with Rafragoria, they'll step in and use the dead to drive all of us into submission."

Viam rested a hand on the paddock's wall as the ground tilted beneath her. "I can't tell the king that, not without proof."

"I thought not." Yala's expression tightened. "The body of one of Mekan's beasts washed up in the docks, but the Disciples of the Flame burned the evidence. I don't think it's the first time either."

"What?" Viam pushed away from the wall, her mind tripping over this new information. "They've been hiding all traces of the dead? For what purpose?"

"Maintaining order," Yala said. "The same kind of justifications that Superior Datriem used, I bet. For obvious reasons, *I* can't tell the king."

"If I tell him and he believes me, he'll want to talk to the Superior."

Yala couldn't want that, could she? Unless... "Gods, what if he figures out what they did to his fa—?" She couldn't say it.

"I'd say averting a war is our priority now," Yala said. "Regardless of the short-term costs."

Avoiding war. Would telling the king the truth do anything to stop a potential attack from Rafragoria, though? "I can try talking to him if I see him, but I don't think His Majesty is taking visitors today."

"It's worth a try." Yala turned back to the gate. "I'll see you later."

Viam watched her depart, dread cascading over her like a waterfall. *Does she really think I'm close enough to the king that he'll believe any absurd claim I make?* Yes, she'd confided in him about the island, but that hadn't implicated any of his family members in anything. Nor had she revealed any treachery on behalf of the Disciples of the Flame.

Gods, someone has to try. The consequences would reverberate far past Dalathar if war broke out. If the Successors got their way.

Of course it was them. The note made no sense to have come from Rafragoria, but the Successors had every reason to threaten the surviving members of their squad. *Remember the island.*

A growl from the war drake brought her attention back to the present. Her head wasn't in the right place for training, and if she wasn't careful, she'd suffer an injury, so she set about putting the creature's muzzle back into place. As she was locking up the gate, a shadow fell across her path, and someone came walking out of the palace grounds. Not Yala this time but none other than King Daliel himself.

"Viam," he said as she struggled to wipe the horror from her face. "There you are."

"Your Majesty." Why had he left the palace at a time like this? If he'd been here a few minutes earlier, he and Yala would have encountered one another face to face, and the mere notion made rivulets of cold sweat run down the back of her neck. "Sorry. I was just, ah, checking the war drakes."

He nodded, accepting that excuse. "I just met with the commanders, and I thought I'd look in on our clawed companions too. I didn't realise anyone was here."

I don't think he realises how much danger he's in either.

"Did you send word to Rafragoria?" she asked. "That we didn't kill their ambassadors?"

His mouth parted in surprise. "Word certainly spreads fast. Yes, I asked them to send a note of apology and my condolences."

"Oh. Good." Her pulse raced so fast that her hands tingled, and she wondered if she might faint. "Do you know who might have been responsible?"

"Me? No," he said. "My advisors have been debating the matter all morning, and the commanders are doing the same. I have to admit, I came here to avoid getting dragged into another argument."

"You did?" She glanced behind her at the closed gate. "War drakes aren't known for being good listeners."

He offered her a half smile. "Perhaps not, but they're much simpler to deal with. I'm impressed at how quickly you tamed that one."

"A wild animal is never tame, Your Majesty, but thank you." With reluctance, she lifted the key again and unlocked the paddock. "Not much has changed since your last visit."

"But you're still preparing to take the beast for its first flight?" he asked. "I hoped to have more time to prepare, but given the circumstances..."

"Prepare for what?" Then it hit her. "*You* want to ride?"

Oh. That must be why he'd been insistent on the war drakes being within the palace grounds. He wanted to learn to ride, like his father had before him.

"If needed." A pensive expression crossed his face. "My advisors are not particularly enthused by the idea, but in the event that the worst happens, I would like to be able to help my people."

Did he even have any combat experience? She could imagine the expression on Yala's face if she'd been here listening. "It's not necessary to endanger yourself, Your Majesty."

If Yala *had* been present, she'd press Viam to bring up the Successors or else tell him of the Disciples of the Flame's apparent habit of hiding Mekan's presence in the city, but she hadn't the faintest clue how to lead up to either subject. The king either didn't see her nervousness or assumed it was simply her usual awe at being around the monarch.

"True." His brow crinkled. "I just feel a sense of responsibility for this situation. Perhaps if I'd made different choices…"

"You couldn't have known this would happen." Gods. How could she offer him reassurance when her own position stood on such shaky ground? "When I was in the army, we'd been at war since before I was born. You didn't want that to be your legacy, did you?"

"I was so certain that it would be the wrong choice to declare war on Rafragoria for my father's death," he said. "If I had acted then, I might have spared us this."

"That would have only pulled us into conflict sooner." He couldn't blame himself for this. He was the *king*. Someone had to hold the country together. "Your Majesty, this wasn't them. Rafragoria didn't kill their own people, and neither did Laria. Someone is trying to—to set us against one another."

Each word hammered in her throat like the beat of a drum, and for a moment, he didn't reply. Then, understanding flickered in his eyes. "Believe me, I wish this war could be avoided too."

He doesn't believe me. "What if it is? If we found proof that it wasn't us *or* Rafragoria who were responsible for the deaths?"

"Proof?" His tone remained disbelieving, and he shook his head. "I wish it was that simple."

"It's not, but this all started with the—the Successors." She spoke quickly, forcing the words out, as if she was vomiting up a fast-acting poison before it stopped her heart. "They were the first to use Corruption. They wanted to instigate a coup against you and against Laria, and the ambassadors were killed by Corruption, weren't they?"

"Who told you that?" He glanced over in the direction of the palace gates, having apparently forgotten all about visiting the war drake. "They aren't the only people to have used those methods as far as I understand."

No. She had no proof leading back to Laria that the Disciples of the Flame hadn't burned out of existence, and if *they* set foot in the palace, their recent cover-ups were the least of what might be revealed.

Would it be worth the risk? Wouldn't it be so much simpler to let Rafragoria take the impact of both crimes? If Laria had an external foe to point its spears at, the nation was less likely to crumble from within.

Sickened with herself, she began to speak. "Your Majesty—"

A scream rang out from over the palace fence. Viam jumped, dropping the keys, and hastily retrieved them. "Did anyone leave the palace with you?"

"No, they didn't." He moved towards the palace gates while Viam quickly locked the war drake's paddock and hurried after him.

Two guards lay dead at the back gates, blood pooling around their slashed throats. Viam stared, numb, her mind spinning.

An assassin had broken into the palace, and if Viam's worst guesses were right, they were after the king.

9

---

iam ran towards the gates, overtaking King Daliel, as
more screams erupted from the other side of the wall.
Gods. It was supposed to be far safer within the palace
grounds than outside of them, but how long before the assassin
realised the king was here, entirely unprotected? The notion that
she might hold his safety in *her* unsteady hands made some shameful
part of her want to find Yala and hide behind her like she was a
novice again.

"Your Majesty." She tensed when he leaned over the bodies of the
slain guards with an expression of open horror etched on his face. "Be
careful. They might be…"

Corrupted.

The male of the two dead guards stirred, hands twitching.
Shadows swirled across his slit throat, the subtle touch of Mekan
claiming the bodies as his own. Cursing herself for not carrying a
weapon, Viam seized the official sword that the second guard kept
strapped to her waist, and she'd half pulled the weapon out of its
sheath when its owner began to stir too. Shadows brushed against
Viam's palms, and a cold whisper touched her ear.

"Come closer, Disciple."

"No!" With a cry, she ripped the sword clear of its sheath, positioning herself in front of the king.

The second guard rose upward, too, while the male guard lifted his sword with clumsy dead fingers. Viam's unpractised hand disarmed him with surprising ease, and his weapon clanged loose on the ground. Instead of picking it up, which would have been Viam's first instinct, the king didn't budge. The colour had drained from his face, and his jaw hung slack.

"Your Majesty, stay close behind me," she said. "I'll deal with them."

The dead woman lunged for Viam, her dead hands grasping. Viam swung the sword, slicing into her arm and severing the wrist. A second swing sank deep beneath her rib cage; blood and shadow spilled from the wound in a dark mass. The female guard staggered, the sword lodged in her chest, and Viam's sweaty grip broke on the hilt.

As the woman slumped, the male guard came at Viam. She reached for the dead woman again, but the sword had stuck fast, and her clumsy fingers couldn't keep their grip. Why hadn't she thought to carry a weapon of her own?

Again, Mekan's whisper urged her to take control of the dead, to stop them with only a word—but even if she'd been willing to use Corruption in front of the king, she hadn't brought her fragment of Mekan's realm that would enable her to control the dead with her own hand. Without that, her commands would be ineffective.

Instead, she sidestepped the dead man, grabbing his wrist and fighting a shudder of revulsion at the sensation of chilled flesh beneath her hand. With a firm shove, she pushed him backwards, causing him to trip over the dead woman. She risked a glance behind her at the king, who'd backed up to the war drake's pen and seized the padlock with a shaky hand.

"What are you doing?" She winced, hearing a chilling howl from within the paddock. "Your Majesty?"

"I thought—the beasts in here should be able to deal with those monsters."

"They're afraid of the dead." They were also chained up, thank the gods; a terrified war drake rampaging around the street would do nothing to improve the situation. "Let me handle this."

The male guard lurched towards the sword he'd dropped. Viam ran and snatched the weapon from his fingers before raising it in a slash that bit deep into his shins. He slumped to his knees, twitching, just as the woman rose upright, the sword still sticking out of her chest.

"Gods." The king shrank back in horror. "How do you kill them?"

"I can't, but I can incapacitate them." Cutting them to pieces was one option, but it'd take too long, and the screams within the palace had faded to an ominous silence. *Does that mean the assassins are dead?*

Viam slashed the dead woman's legs, causing her to stumble and overbalance. Then she reached into her pocket for the key to the war drakes' paddock. *Gods help us all.* "Your Majesty, can you unlock the gate?"

"Of course." He held out a hand as she tossed him the key, catching it by the fingertips. Praying that the war drakes remained secured, she resumed her attack on the two dead guards. Driving them into the war drakes' paddock was far from the ideal solution, but it would stop them from escaping into the street while Viam helped get the king to safety. She drew the line at leaving *him* in the paddock, even if being near the war drakes might well be safer than the palace grounds. If the dead were stirring without a Disciple in sight... no, she'd have to think on that one later.

With a swing of her sword, she knocked the dead woman staggering towards the opening gate. As the king stepped hastily back, Viam shoved the guard through the gate and into the paddock. *One more to go.*

The dead man was trying to stand, but she must have severed some tendons when she'd sliced his legs, and he couldn't manage more than a crouch. With swift strikes, she pushed him towards the paddock and finally kicked him through the open gate with a booted foot. Breathless, she pulled the gate shut and took the key from the king's slack grip.

"We have to get to safety." She turned the key in the lock, securing the dead inside the paddock, and then led the king towards the gates. The guards' blood had left dark smears on the ground, and her stomach lurched when another chilling scream rang out from somewhere within. "Please stay behind me."

She ran forward, past the fence cutting off the barracks from the rest of the palace grounds. Spying a group of guards moving towards the barracks, she ran over. "What's going on?"

"Assassins." The speaker, a young man with light-brown hair flopping into his eyes, pointed over Viam's shoulder. "Your Majesty! You shouldn't be walking around alone."

"Take him to safety," Viam told the guards, raising her voice. "The barracks—are they safe?"

"Yes—the assassins were trying to get into the palace." The wide-eyed guard gawped at the king, but his companions wasted no time in surrounding the dazed-looking monarch and ushering him away.

Once Viam was sure that they'd taken him into the safety of the barracks, she broke into a run again. More intermittent screams rang out from in front, and she halted at the towering staircase that led to the palace's main entrance.

Two guards lay sprawled on the steps, dead or injured. A hooded figure stood in the entryway, circled by more guards. Despite being outnumbered, the would-be intruder displayed no signs of fear, and when Viam began to climb the stairs, she glimpsed the sword sticking out of the figure's chest. *It's dead.*

"Careful!" she shouted at the guards. "It's one of Mekan's. They keep moving long after they're dead."

"It's been dead the whole time," one of the guards called back. "Watch out."

The guards shoved at the hooded figure, which tumbled down the stairs. Viam hurried upward and caught the sword that clattered loose from its hand. The hood fell back, revealing worn flesh clinging to bone and shadows in between. *They're right. It's been dead a while.* So who'd given the orders?

Viam drove the blade into the dead body's shins, severing the weakened flesh and sending it tumbling further. Certain that it could do no more harm, she ran the rest of the way upstairs. The guards crowded the open doors, where another dead intruder was strewn around the entryway.

If the attackers had been dead from the beginning, that must be why they'd made an entrance in such an overt way: they had no fear and no will of their own. The question was, who had sent them?

"Were there more?" she asked. "Just two?"

"Two did enough damage," grunted the long-haired man. "Where is His Majesty?"

"Hiding in the barracks," she replied. "He's safe. Do you know who was giving them orders?"

"There were no living assassins," said the guard. "Nobody to question."

"They killed the guards at the back gate," she said, swallowing hard. "Both guards rose from death, too, so I had to shut them in the war drakes' paddock."

"You did what?" The guard blanched. "Rather you than me."

"Someone needs to fetch..." Her mouth went dry. "The Disciples of the Flame. Only they can destroy the bodies permanently."

"Right... right." The guard moved past Viam, jogging down the steps.

Behind him, Viam glimpsed two robed figures gliding over the walls. She ran downstairs, where Kelan glided to a halt in front of her.

"You seem to share Yala's knack for trouble," he remarked. "What's going on?"

"The dead," she said, too shaken to reprimand him for trespassing. "We need to destroy the bodies."

"I'm sure Superior Shralin will be thrilled to oblige." He nodded to the second Disciple, who'd landed next to him.

"Kelan," hissed the tall male Disciple. "What did I tell you about jumping over the fence without permission?"

"I thought the circumstances called for it." He indicated Viam. "She tells me there are dead bodies that need taking care of."

"There are." Another thought hit her. "Now you're here, can you make sure there aren't any more dead assassins lurking inside the palace? I left the king in the barracks, but there might be more."

It'd be much quicker for them to search from the sky than her from the ground. Understanding, Kelan rose into the air as elegantly as a bird. His companion watched with thin-lipped disapproval and then followed.

Less than a minute later, Kelan returned. "I assume the king was the man in the fancy head-dress I saw near the side gate over at the palace's eastern side. About ten guards were with him."

Viam's shoulders slumped with relief. "Good. I couldn't watch him and fight the dead at the same time. It was pure luck that he wasn't inside the palace grounds when they attacked."

"And the person who gave them orders wasn't with them?" Kelan surmised. "Clever move. Dead assassins won't give you away."

"They killed the guards at the back gate," Viam said. "Right after— after I spoke to Yala. Where is she?"

"Far away from here if she has sense." He grimaced. "If I see her, I'll warn her to stay away. Granted, she probably already sensed someone using Corruption."

That's what I'm afraid of. Swallowing her dread, Viam swivelled back to the front gates, hoping that Yala had had the sense not to linger.

"Kelan," hissed the other Disciple. "The guards are looking at *us* like we're intruders. Which we are."

"Not if we came to remove the dead." Kelan indicated the remnants of the intruder Viam had taken apart.

As the two Disciples glided upstairs, Viam glimpsed Brenat approaching her from the direction of the administrative building.

"There you are," Brenat said. "I thought you were hiding in the paddocks... is that blood?"

Viam glanced down at her feet, which were stained in the guards' blood. "It's not mine."

A breeze lifted their hair as the two Disciples flew back downstairs, carrying the remnants of the intruders. Kelan waved at Viam as they passed, while his companion wore an expression that suggested he wished he'd stayed at the inn rather than accompanying his fellow Disciple on this whim. Glad that *she* didn't have to carry the dead, Viam called after them, "Don't forget that there are two dead bodies around the back gates as well."

"Two dead bodies?" Brenat echoed. "What's going on?"

"There was an attempt on the king's life." How hadn't she known? "Didn't they tell you?"

"No. The guards told us to go back to our quarters, but they didn't say why." Worry clouded Brenat's eyes. "No wonder. Looks like His Majesty had a close call."

He did. If he hadn't been with me, would he still be alive?

———

Niema watched the Temple of the Flame long after the door had closed in their faces and was halfway across the square when the screaming started.

As she veered towards the source, Niema caught a scent on the breeze that seemed to climb up into her nostrils and take up residence in her very soul. *Corruption.*

Heart lurching, she ran towards the palace gates. The crowds thronging the square churned like a whirlpool, and it took several breathless minutes for Niema to reach the entrance. The guards outside were peering through the gates with equal curiosity, trying to see what was going on inside, with the result that none of them saw Kelan's approach until he glided over the fence as if the guards weren't present at all. One of them exclaimed and pointed, too late, as Kelan descended on the other side.

"What's he doing?" Lakiel muttered a curse under his breath and then followed, while Niema caught a glimpse between the guards of the palace grounds. She couldn't see much from this angle, but the stench of Corruption was unmistakable.

Yala. Wherever she was, she must have sensed it too.

Backing away from the gates, she followed the wall circling the palace's exterior until she came to the street that she'd seen Yala vanish into. The screams continued, and when they were joined by the unmistakable tapping of Yala's cane, she knew she was running in the right direction.

Niema rounded a corner and called out, "Yala."

"Niema." Yala came to a halt. "You sense it too. Corruption."

Niema's heart dived sickeningly at the word. "I know. It's in the palace."

Was someone attacking the king? She turned to the wall circling the palace grounds, but the squat outline of another building blocked their view. She could only see the very top layer of the palace itself and the vibrant flowers that were the only traces of nature she'd seen in the capital so far.

"They aren't going to let anyone in." Yala swore under her breath. "Not even..."

"Kelan went in."

"Of course he did." Yala turned on her heel and began making her way down the side street again. "It'll be faster to try the back entrance again, but I don't know if Viam is still there."

They wove through the warren of side streets, while intermittent screams came from nearby. When they reached a padlocked gate, Niema realised the screaming wasn't human. "Is that what I think it is?"

"Something scared the war drakes." Yala's grim tone told Niema she knew what it was.

A sudden gust of wind lifted the hair on Niema's head, and the paddock gates sprang open. Yala jerked back with a curse when a dead woman lurched out of the paddock, a sword sticking out of her chest.

"Not to worry." Kelan glided over the fence and landed beside her, drawing his blade. "Allow me."

"Not to worry?" Yala reached for her dagger, while Niema whispered a prayer. The god of life seemed very far away from here, in the heart of the capital, but she had nothing else with which to defend herself.

"The assassins are equally dead and considerably more dismembered." Kelan swiped his blade through the woman's ankles. Niema gagged and looked away. "The king is safe."

"Never thought I'd be glad of that," Yala muttered, using her own dagger to cut off the dead woman's grasping hand. Behind, a second dead person half crouched in the paddock entrance, hands reaching out and grasping. "Who shut them in with the war drakes?"

"Viam."

"Viam?" Yala repeated, with a touch of pride in her voice. "Good thinking. She hasn't completely lost her soldier's instincts, then."

Niema didn't know what to say to that. She was no soldier, and the mere proximity of Corruption made bile creep up her throat. Swallowing hard, she said, "I can destroy them."

"We're going to leave them as a present for Superior Shralin," Kelan said. "They might be a nice reminder of the threat that awaits right outside his door."

Yala jabbed her cane into the dead woman's twitching foot. "Didn't you warn him about the Successors?"

"Unfortunately, the man's a fool." Kelan lifted the twitching remnants of the dead guard into the air, while a second Disciple of the Sky descended to help him remove the other. The war drakes must have been hiding; Niema didn't see any traces of them when she peered into the paddock, though she did hear a faint whining from the back. They feared the dead too.

Darting inside, she whistled a reassurance in the general direction of the hut that must contain the war drakes, and the noise quietened.

"Good thinking." Yala beckoned her out of the paddock. "Someone's going to have to lock this place up again."

"Yes." Kelan had knocked the padlock clean off when he'd blasted the gate open. "The war drakes will be chained up?"

"They'd better be." Yala closed the gate with a firm hand. "The Superior didn't listen to you?"

Niema shook her head, her stomach churning. The stench of the dead lingered, and blood smeared the ground in a trail leading to the palace's back gates. More blood lay in two pools; spying a guard standing on the other side, Yala waved him over and told him to lock up the paddock again with the commanding tone of someone who worked inside the palace. The guard seemed too dazed not to obey her.

With that done, they returned to Ceremonial Square, where they met a now blessedly dead body–free Kelan.

"Superior Shralin didn't appreciate the gift I gave him," he said. "I'd like to think he's rethinking his stance on the problem now that we have dead assassins running around with no clue who's giving them orders."

"Dead assassins?" Yala echoed. "The assassins were dead *before* they got into the palace?"

"Precisely." His humour faded. "It's ingenious in a way. Nobody can interrogate someone who's already dead."

"True." Niema shivered, thinking of the dead guards. "They got in through the back gate. Wasn't that where you were talking to Viam?"

"Yes," Yala said. "If I'd been there a minute longer, I might have been able to stop them."

"You didn't sense them?" Niema hadn't either, but her own senses were far from at their best in the confusion of the capital.

"I wasn't paying attention." Yala's hand dropped to her waist, and then her fingers curled inward. "Didn't have the claw with me either."

Mekan's claw. Niema didn't know if she was relieved or worried that Yala hadn't resumed her habit of carrying it everywhere. Yala's Disciple of Death abilities ought to be far from a concern for her, given everything they'd been through, but some of her old instincts remained. Enough for her to wonder what she'd been thinking in coming here.

Niema might no longer belong in the enclave, but was there a place for a Disciple of Life in a city filled with the dead?

10

———————

Yala dreamed of the first time she'd taken a life.

Her knees tightened around the war drake's back, a spear firm in her hand. Around her gathered her squad: Machit, grinning with good humour, sharp-eyed Saren looking out for threats, Viam and Dalem defending, Temik and Vanat readied to attack. The seven of them soared as a unit across the expanse of blue ocean, and from the opposite direction came a Rafragorian squad that mirrored their own, each soldier seated atop a fearsome sea drake.

A Rafragorian soldier met Yala's eyes, lifting his weapon, and her instincts kicked in. Her spear left her hand before conscious thought and pierced the soldier through the throat. Between one blink and the next, he was gone, his lifeless body toppling into the water.

That was it? she'd thought at the time. She'd heard enough tales of combat that she knew each soldier reacted differently. Some were overly keen to leap into the fray, while others panicked when they first held a weapon to an enemy's throat and faltered at the final act. Yala, though, found the result underwhelming, a moment of instinct over in the space of a breath.

The scene warped, and the dream took over. Shadows stirred

around the dead soldier in the water, and he lifted his bobbing head to face her with a lifeless gaze, blood trickling from his empty eye.

In her ear, a rasping voice spoke. *"Thank you for the sacrifice, Disciple."*

Her fingers tingled, numbing; when she lifted her hands, her gloves fell away, revealing blackened fingertips and curved, clawed hands that resembled the talons of a void drake.

"Just one more step. I am here."

Yala awakened with a tingling in her fingertips and a gasp on her lips. *Thanks, Mekan.* Why her dreams would revisit that memory now was likely more the fault of her unconscious mind than the god of death, but her life as a soldier had been simple compared to the current mess she was mired in.

She hadn't been able to ask anyone if the Disciples of the Flame had spoken to the monarch after burning the bodies, but frustration at Superior Shralin dug under her skin like a burrowing maggot. He seemed determined to repeat the very mistakes that had seen his predecessor stabbed in the back, and if he wasn't careful, she'd be the one wielding the knife this time.

A rapping on the door jolted her from her half doze; rising, Yala grabbed her cane and walked over to the window. Viam stood outside, wearing drakeskin clothes that Yala assumed were her favoured attire for working with the war drakes.

Opening the door, she said, "Why are you awake at this hour?"

"You wanted an update," Viam said. "I thought I'd draw less attention if I left the palace when most of the other staff are still sleeping."

Yala grunted and beckoned her into the house. "What's the latest?"

"The Disciples of the Flame burned the bodies," Viam whispered, glancing at the other sleeping mat, where Niema lay. "Both the assassins and the two guards who were killed."

Yala closed the door behind her. "What about finding the person responsible?"

Viam shook her head. "How? The assassins were dead from the start."

Yala strode to the nearest armchair and sat down. "I find it hard to believe that our dead assassins walked all the way from the barracks to the palace without being challenged."

"What?" Viam blinked in surprise. "There aren't usually many people around the back gates. Except in the barracks, but there are fences in the way as well as guards."

"It sounds like the assassins were unusually stealthy for dead people," Yala commented. "Maybe the person who gave them instructions was very specific, or someone was working with them on the inside."

Viam's shoulders tensed. "What makes you say that?"

"Paranoia," Yala answered without a hint of irony. "Well?"

Viam lowered her gaze. "I have a hard time believing someone inside the palace itself was involved. Not least because... well, if someone else was using Corruption, I would have noticed."

"They didn't have to *use* Corruption," Yala said. "Just letting the intruders walk past unchallenged would have done the job."

"Intruders?" Saren appeared in the stairway, rubbing his eyes on the back of his hand. "What in the gods' names are you doing here at this hour?"

"Reassuring you that the country is still in one piece?" Viam said, though her tone lacked the heat that usually preceded an argument. "Yala, do you think someone inside the palace was in on the plan?"

"It's too early in the morning for conspiracies," Saren said. "Isn't it up to the king to root out traitors inside his own ranks?"

"No, but it's not up to us either," Viam said. "Everyone's on high alert. I'm sure if there's anyone whose loyalties are in question, they'll be found soon enough."

At a faint noise from the corner, Yala glanced towards Niema, who was stirring on her sleeping mat. The Disciple of Life had been so quiet that Yala had frankly forgotten she was there.

"Anyway, if someone used Corruption elsewhere in the city, how can we possibly find them?" Viam added. "We can't search the whole of Dalathar."

"No," Yala acknowledged, "but I have some ideas as to where to start."

———

Half an hour later, Yala and Viam reached the upper city. Saren had declined to come with them, while Niema remained in a dead sleep. Not a description that she would appreciate, though she'd also have no desire to join them in searching for Corruption, so Yala and Viam made their way towards the palace grounds alone.

Shouts and thumps, the sound of a hundred pairs of boots hitting the ground, echoed from the cluster of low-roofed buildings that stood at the rear of the palace grounds, where rows of soldiers lined up for exercise drills under the punishing sun, their skin slick with sweat.

Yala didn't linger to watch, instead approaching the war drakes' paddocks and feeling a rush of gratitude towards Viam and Saren for bringing her own war drake to the outer city and not forcing her to keep it in a place as drenched in memories as this one.

"I have the key." Viam reached into her pocket. "There aren't any traces of the dead left in there, I hope."

Yala inhaled, and her nose caught a familiar smell of rot, like meat left out in the sun for too long. Her fingers sought out the pouch at her waist, where she kept the void drake's claw.

"What is it?" Viam whispered. "Do you sense something?"

"Possibly." Yala craned her neck over the fence, but the smell of war drake dung was too potent to detect anything else. "Who feeds the war drakes?"

"I do."

"Careful," Yala murmured. "Or he'll ask you to lead the new Flight Division."

Viam made a faint noise of protest. "He knows I'm not qualified, but… it's like he wants his father's army to reappear out of the past the exact way it used to be."

Yala, who'd been afraid of that, reached for the claw again. A faint whisper tickled her ear, too quiet for her to make out the words. Her gaze travelled to the narrow passage that snaked behind the paddock, with the palace's fence on the other side.

As she reached the passage entrance, someone hastily ducked out of sight around a corner "Who's there?"

Nobody answered. Yala entered the passage, grimacing at the stench of rotten meat. *The dead did come this way.*

"Yala?" Viam came up behind her. "What is it?"

Yala moved forward and came to a halt when a burly woman sheepishly edged into view.

Viam let out a gasp. "What are you doing here, Brenat?"

"What are *you* doing here?" The woman eyed Yala, her expression radiant with curiosity. "And who is this?"

———

Viam stared in horror at Brenat. Why had she been lurking between the paddock and the barracks? Pulling herself together, she said, "Brenat. This is Yala. My former captain."

Brenat's eyes widened. "*You're* Captain Yala Palathar?"

"Not a captain," Yala said. "And you are?"

"Brenat," she answered. "I work with Viam. What're you doing, visiting the war drakes?"

"Yes." Viam seized on the excuse. "We trained together in the Flight Division, you know."

"You haven't told us why you were lurking around," Yala said with considerably less friendliness. "Well?"

Brenat shrugged a laced shoulder, undeterred by Yala's sharp tone. "I was feeding the war drakes. Someone had to do it."

"I didn't know you had a key." Viam was acutely aware that Brenat's sudden appearance had triggered Yala's suspicions, but who could blame her? "You didn't go inside the paddock, did you?"

"No, I threw the meat over the fence." She grinned. "The baby war drakes are *adorable*, aren't they?"

"You haven't seen one take off a novice's finger," Yala said.

Brenat chuckled. "True, but that's because there aren't any novices yet. Unless you're coming back to train them?"

"No," Yala said.

Tension crackled in the air, and Brenat's confident demeanour slipped. "Just wondering. We could use the help."

"Not from me."

"We should get back into the palace," Viam cut in, nodding to Yala. "See you later?"

Silently, she pleaded with Yala not to argue, though her heart twinged with guilt at abandoning their search for the intruders. There was no help for it, though; she refused to put Brenat at risk, and Yala would never agree to let anyone else get involved. Especially someone who worked inside the palace. *Gods.*

Yala inclined her head in farewell and turned away, while Viam and Brenat made for the palace gates. Two guards stood in place of the ones the assassins had slain; the blood, to her relief, had been cleaned up.

"You shouldn't skulk around," one of the guards told Brenat. "It's lucky we know your face."

"Oh, come on," said Brenat. "I was only feeding the war drakes. Unless you wanted to volunteer instead?"

"Certainly not," said the guard with a shudder. "Go on in."

They did so, accompanied by the thump of the soldiers' boots on the hard ground as they practised drills on the other side of the barracks' fence.

"Your friend Yala is quite intense, isn't she?" Brenat remarked. "I can see why she's in good company with those beasts."

"She's always been like that." She walked past the barracks as swiftly as possible. "Why not tell me you were feeding the war drakes?"

"I thought someone should help you out, and nobody else is likely to volunteer."

If she'd been Yala, she might have examined Brenat's words for any trace of subterfuge, but she had a hard time believing she'd been anything other than sincere. "You... wait, you didn't follow me yesterday, did you?"

"For a bit." Her smile was laden with a hint of some other emotion. "Then I guessed you wanted to be left alone and turned back. Why?"

Maybe Yala's paranoia was rubbing off on Viam, but had Brenat seen anything near the back gates when she'd followed her? She'd never thought of her friend as particularly secretive, but Yala's pointed comments had reminded her that not everyone inside the palace grounds could be trusted. Viam had a hard time believing Brenat was in any way involved with the attack, but how much of that was her own bias? Did she really think nobody she called a friend might betray her?

Look at what happened with Temik, whispered a voice in the back of her head. *He was your friend, and he betrayed the entire squad, including you.*

Brenat was still eyeing her curiously, and Viam scrambled for an answer. "I thought... I mean, I thought you might have seen the king leaving the palace."

"No, we must have just missed one another." She frowned. "I suppose he went *through* the barracks. Strange habit for a monarch."

"Is it?" she asked. "King Tharen visited the barracks all the time."

"Yes, but he was a soldier as well as a king."

That was true enough, but King Daliel had plainly decided his father was the better monarch. She almost said as much to Brenat, but she cut herself off, knowing Yala wouldn't approve.

"He's reforming the army," Viam said instead. "I doubt he'll be taken by surprise again."

"If you say so," Brenat said. "It's hard *not* to be taken by surprise by the dead. Did Rafragoria send them, do you think?"

"Rafragoria?" Surprise leaked into her voice. "There aren't any Rafragorians here."

"No, but they're pissed off with us," Brenat said. "It'd be nice to have one enemy out there and not two, wouldn't it?"

Viam didn't manage a smile in return. Brenat's words didn't *sound* like those of someone who supported one of those enemies, but who was to say whether the Successors had had any supporters from amongst the palace staff? And who better than someone close to one of Yala's former squadmates?

She *wanted* to trust Brenat. She didn't want to interrogate her, to sever the one friendship she held within the palace, but if Yala was right...

"Why'd they choose yesterday to launch their assassination attempt?" she wondered. "The king was distracted by the news from the Disciples of the Sky, but they couldn't have known he would be."

"Unless they did that too," Brenat said. "Killed the ambassadors, I mean. It's weird that they'd kill their own people, but who's to say how Rafragorian minds work?"

Viam made a noncommittal noise. If the Successors were behind both attacks, there was still the question of how many others might be hiding within the city of Dalathar itself. Some must have controlled the dead, but there was little Viam could do to find them from her position in the palace.

All she did have control over were her own alliances and friendships, and despite her best efforts, a sliver of doubt lodged in her chest like a splinter burying deep into the skin.

Had Brenat seen the assassins?

11

Kelan arrived back at Skytower the following morning with the grim sense that their planned meeting with Rafragoria might have brought them closer to war than they'd been before they'd left the country at all.

So far, they hadn't heard any word from Rafragoria on the deaths of their ambassadors, but the attack on the palace would slow down updates for the foreseeable future as the guards focused on the more immediate threat. As a result, the five of them had chosen to return and report to their Superior. Together, they gathered in front of her desk on the rug beneath the large painting of the god of the sky, and Superior Sietra listened in tense silence to their report of the events in the capital.

"I'm glad you reported to me before acting," she said. "This is a situation that requires caution."

"Do you think the same person or people were behind both incidents?" Kelan asked. "The attack on the palace and on the ambassadors might have taken place in different locations, but both involved the dead, and certain, ah, acquaintances of mine suspect the involvement of a group called the Successors. Melian's followers went by that name, and they wanted to depose the monarch and replace him with the god of death. Inciting a war with Rafragoria would certainly further that goal."

Lakiel cast him a disgruntled look, but Superior Sietra leaned forward in her seat. "If any of the Successors survive, perhaps, but the deaths of the Rafragorian ambassadors suggest that someone is acting outside of Laria's borders as well as inside. So far, the Successors have only operated within the capital."

"They had a base on the seafront," Kelan added. "And the dead bodies of Mekan's monsters have been washing up onshore. Unfortunately, Superior Shralin's response has been to incinerate them without telling anyone else. We don't know how long this has been going on, but I'd guess it's been happening since around the time that dead Rafragorian soldier showed up."

Superior Sietra's eyes widened, and she inclined her head. "Yes, I suspect you're right. Unfortunately, it's easier for the enemy to avoid detection while outside of our shores."

"You believe some of the Successors are hiding *outside* the city?" Lakiel sounded rather put out that she'd taken Kelan's suggestion seriously. "How would they have left the country without anyone knowing?"

"Stole a boat?" Kelan offered, hearing a quiet laugh from Brikel behind him. "Or a war drake? The former is more likely, but there isn't anyone checking for Disciples of Death *leaving* the country."

The seas were undeniably treacherous, but Kelan imagined that Disciples of Death were considerably likelier to be able to survive out there than most other people.

"What of the attempt on the king's life?" asked Ranit. "If we're to believe it's the work of the same group, are the guards looking in the right place?"

"A valid question, but that is a matter for the king and his staff to investigate," said the Superior. "I have another mission for you. Namely, to expose those who killed the ambassadors."

A bewildered silence followed her words.

"You want us to go back to Rafragoria?" Lakiel asked, his tone laced with uncertainty.

"No," she replied. "I want you to visit the Disciples of the Sea."

"The Disciples of the *Sea?*" Had Kelan misheard her? "Do they even take visitors? I thought they'd exiled themselves from Laria decades ago."

"They did," she said, "but they'll almost certainly be aware of any unusual activity in the sea between Laria and Rafragoria, and they'll have a vested interest in putting a stop to Corruption encroaching on their territory."

"They also haven't set foot on Larian soil in years." With a sudden chill, he recalled his last visit to Amanar, where the Disciples of the Sea had allegedly been recruiting new Disciples, including the child whose dead body had washed up onshore. Given that the visit had ended in his near drowning, Amanar was not an auspicious place to start. "Most of them haven't, anyway. Moreover, how are we supposed to find them when their temple isn't located on any maps?"

"It should be simple to deduce their location based on the boundaries between Laria and Rafragoria," she said. "However, the ocean has a reputation for danger, and it's easy to lose one's way, which has no doubt contributed to their ability to stay hidden."

"You think we can find them, though?" he asked. "Just the five of us?"

"A bigger group might be taken as a threat," she replied. "There are enough of you to repel any danger you might find at sea."

A sea drake, maybe, but not a void drake. The Void had been opened somewhere if those monsters who'd attacked the ambassadors were any indication. Who was to say what else might have ripped its way out of Mekan's realm into this one?

"I believe this is the correct choice," Superior Sietra went on. "There are more maps in the library for you to study before you leave."

She didn't even ask if we said yes. Not that he was in any position to refuse. They had to find a solution, and who other than them would have the means of locating the most elusive group of Disciples in Laria—more so than even the Disciples of Life?

Nobody offered any argument, and they left the Superior's office.

From there, they descended into the library to find a new pile of maps on the table. Some were old enough that the edges of the pages had curled up and had a yellowish tinge from lack of use.

"When was the last time an emissary was sent to find *them?*" Brikel sat in front of the maps, her eyes gleaming. "We might be the first in a generation."

"This is absurd." Lakiel didn't sit but paced in front of the table, his cloak billowing in the breeze stirred up by his agitation. "Nobody can get into the Temple of the Sea who isn't one of them. It's rumoured to be located at the bottom of the ocean itself."

Kelan took in that information. "They can breathe underwater?"

"Did you pay *any* attention in our lessons as novices?" Lakiel grouched. "I don't know why I'm surprised. Even if there *was* a way to circumvent that problem, nobody can get near the temple when they can control the very ocean currents to drive away intruders."

"We're going to be flying, not swimming," Brikel pointed out. "What's the problem? We're being offered a chance no other Disciples of the Sky have ever been given."

"Or a death sentence."

"How is that different than meeting up with Rafragoria's ambassadors?" Kelan enquired. "This is hardly riskier than that."

"Rafragoria is a known quantity," Lakiel replied. "The Disciples of the Sea don't adhere to the rules of Laria *or* the other Disciples. They've spurned every attempt our Superior has made to contact them in the past thirty years."

"I'm willing to bet they still don't want a war," Kelan said. "Especially as they live in the path of the conflict."

"That never seemed to bother them before," Brikel said. "I don't trust them, but I *do* trust our Superior. Right, Lakiel?"

Her brother lowered his gaze and then nodded. "Yes, but I think this decision is a last resort on her part. There's nobody else to contact who might have witnessed the attack."

"Isn't it worth trying?"

If they approached the Disciples of the Sea with a peace offering, the worst response they might expect was another temple door closed in their faces.

Except their door is at the bottom of the ocean, and I can barely swim, he thought. *Let's face it, we're fucked.*

───────

Niema woke to Yala closing the door behind her, her cane beating out a rhythm on the bare floorboards as she crossed the room.

"Finally, you're awake," Yala commented. "I was starting to think you'd sleep in as long as Saren."

"I must have been more tired than I realised." She sat up on her sleeping mat, blinking the tiredness from her eyes. She didn't remember falling asleep, but the long journey to Dalathar and the emotional turmoil of leaving her enclave had taken their toll. On top of the revelation that she'd arrived in the capital just as the Successors were resuming their strikes against the king, it was no wonder she felt as limp as a wrung-out rag.

I made my choice. It's done. She repeated the words in her head as she dressed for the day in clothes already coated in a thin layer of grime. She needed new shoes, too, but she'd need to get her hands on some coin first.

As she was pulling on her worn sandals, a loud rapping on the window drew her attention. A vibrant red bird fluttered outside, carrying a note clutched in its beak.

Yala raised an eyebrow. "Someone trying to reach you?"

"I hope not." Dread skittered down her spine as she opened the door to take the note from the messenger's beak.

Niema's mouth went dry when she read the words. *Niema, I hope you had a pleasant journey to Dalathar. I would appreciate a report on anything unusual you might have encountered so far. Send your reply with this bird.*

Niema lifted her gaze to see Yala watching, her soldier's eyes assessing. "Well?"

Fear tasted sharp on her tongue. "My Superior wants me to report to her."

"Does she?" Yala said. "I thought you cut ties with her."

"I did." Niema's hand curled, crumpling the note. "I told her I wasn't going to return. I certainly didn't intend to act as an informant on the events in the city."

Is this note supposed to be a threat? Or does she genuinely want to know what's happening in the capital? After all, if the Superior's messengers could find her, it would be equally easy for Superior Kralia to do the same.

The bird made a chirping noise, a reminder that it was expecting her reply.

"Superior Kralia isn't going to take no for an answer, is she?" Yala remarked.

"I won't let her spy on us." Given the extent of her Superior's abilities, she didn't need to send a reply. Upon its return, the bird would give her a vision of exactly what she and Yala were saying to one another.

Niema took in a breath and let out a whistle of her own. The bird's wings twitched, a faint green glow alighting around its feathers. Superior Kralia couldn't influence the bird from her current location, which gave Niema a temporary advantage. Niema whistled, sharper, a command.

You obey me now, she thought, directing her will towards the bird. *Leave. Be free.*

After a short pause, the bird beat its bright wings and took flight. It soared out, over the street, becoming an indistinct red shape that vanished into the sky.

Yala watched the bird and then studied Niema for a moment. "Your abilities are still functioning here in the city. You can influence animals without a risk to yourself?"

"Of course," Niema replied. "Why?"

"Would you be able to send a spy to the docks?" She gestured to the sky. "I'd like to watch out for any more nasty surprises that might wash up on Laria's shores, and I don't trust Superior Shralin to tell me. If I spend too much time there myself, people will get suspicious."

"Good idea." That was something she could do. "If I send a bird, I can't promise it won't fly away from danger, though. Mekan's beasts terrify all natural creatures."

"It's worth a try." She shrugged. "Might give you something useful to do."

Heat crept up Niema's neck. Part of her wanted to protest at the implied pity, but Yala was right, and her abilities held an undeniable advantage.

Raising her head, she picked out a small grey bird on the rooftops. With a sharp whistle, she called it over to her outstretched hand.

"Fly to the docks," she murmured. "Watch for danger."

The bird didn't understand her words, of course, but as she whistled, she pictured the net that had been fished out of the ocean the previous day and then imagined the dead guards who'd attacked them too. If she focused hard enough, the bird would glimpse the images in her mind, and with a little luck, it would remember.

"Good job." Yala watched as the bird took flight from the window. "If you like, you can send another to the Temple of the Flame."

"They'll probably realise they're being spied on." Niema suppressed a shudder at the last time she'd called a flock of birds to cause a diversion at the temple and had felt their deaths in her very soul as the Disciples had incinerated them. "Besides, if any dead show up at the docks, the Disciples of the Flame will head there as well. Didn't you say they have spies too?"

"Yes." Yala's jaw twitched. "We'll try to beat them there. I think I'll go to the paddocks in the meantime."

She didn't ask Niema if she wanted to come, but realistically, there was little else for Niema to do. "I don't want to impose on you," she said quickly. "I haven't a coin to my name, but if I can make myself useful by helping you…"

"Volunteering to clean up after the war drake? Rather you than me." The words came from Saren, who'd appeared in the stairway without either of them noticing.

Ignoring him, Yala spoke to Niema. "If you'd rather work for a living, there are other options. You have skills. Unusual ones, granted, but ones that are sorely needed."

"Can't you bring people back from the dead?" Saren said, casually enough that Niema flinched.

"No," said Yala, guessing that Niema did not want to discuss the horrific consequences of the time she'd brought Yala back from the brink of death. "She can heal, though, and plenty of people would appreciate that."

"I can." Niema hadn't thought of the utility of that skill, much less charging for it. "Would people pay?"

"Of course," Yala said. "Saren was apprenticed to a healer, though he ended up quitting over some delightful remarks he made about me."

"You didn't have to remind me." Saren climbed the rest of the way downstairs and studied Niema. "If you want to set up as an independent healer, I can guarantee word will be around half the city by the week's end that there's a new healer who uses the power of the god of life. You'll rake in a fortune."

"Do you want that kind of attention?" Yala asked Niema. "I understand if you don't."

No, Niema's instinct said, but didn't her Superior already know exactly where she was? What better way to take a stand against Corruption than healing those whom it touched? "No, but I want to help people."

"There you have it." A slight smile touched Yala's lips. "That works. Just don't overexert yourself trying to heal *everyone* who might cross your path."

"I won't." She might have fallen into that pitfall once, but now, she knew that if she pushed too hard, her enclave members might pay the price instead of her. She'd have to be careful, but for the first time, a tendril of hope bloomed inside her chest.

Niema could survive anywhere as long as life existed. And in the city, life did exist, albeit in a different form than what she was used to.

I'll survive without my Superior. I will.

12

The war drake's wings beat, and it launched into flight with a rush that took Yala's breath away. As the wind rippled through her hair, her heart raced in her chest and her very bones rejoiced at the sensation. *This, truly, is what I was made for.*

Alone, she'd be relying upon the war drake's obedience to fly her back to the paddock in one piece, but its behaviour had been more docile since Niema had helped her with her previous flight attempt. Besides, being in the air cleared her head despite the added risk that one of the increased guard patrols might think her steed was a wild drake and throw a spear at her.

"This way." She leaned to the side, using well-practised commands to keep the war drake's path confined to the outskirts of the city. "We don't want to fly out to sea."

Not unless we have no choice, she amended, her gaze flickering over to the flat blue expanse between Laria and its neighbours. Who in that blue maze might be meddling with the dead? Or were they closer to home?

The war drake made a displeased growl as she squeezed its scaly neck with her knees and urged it to return to the paddock.

"I know," she muttered, "but we've pushed our luck already. You should be grateful that I unchained you at all."

Part of her would always yearn for the sheer limitlessness of flight, but her rational mind told her she'd never been as free as her youth-tinted memories of her earlier years might have suggested. She'd always flown at someone else's command, no freer than a war drake stretching its wings while a chain anchored it to the ground.

Don't you want to go back there? a mocking voice asked in her mind. *Didn't the king offer you a job?*

He hadn't, not directly, and she was no fool. Yala might be a former captain, but she'd be a liability in ground combat, and if they let her fly, it'd be because they had no other options.

Her thoughts returned to the present when the war drake's jaws snapped closed in a shower of feathers. "That had better not have been Niema's bird."

With reluctance, both Yala and her steed turned their flight path back towards the paddock, though the war drake growled and whined and tried to change directions several times. Yala's leg throbbed intermittently by the time they finally landed in the paddock, and the beast put up such a fuss when she was trying to put the chain back on that she didn't notice the bird until the war drake lifted its head and tried to snap it out of the air.

"Stop that." This bird was definitely Niema's spy, returned from the docks. "What is it? The dead?"

The bird chirped and beat its wings, flying in agitated circles above the paddock. Flying after it was out of the question, given the war drake's behaviour, but she almost wished she'd brought the *dead* war drake with her into the capital, even if it'd have drawn far too much unwanted attention. Yala kept an impatient eye on the bird as she bound the war drake's wings—getting clipped in the face twice for her trouble—and then retrieved her cane. From there, Yala left the paddock and followed the bird to where Niema waited inside a wagon.

"More dead?" she asked.

"I think so." Niema beckoned her into the wagon, which had no driver, though two raptors had been harnessed to it.

Yala used her cane as leverage to climb into the wagon. "Where did you get this?"

A flush spread across Niema's face. "I borrowed it from the market."

"You stole it." Yala fought an unexpected smile. "What did you do, give the raptors a command to follow you? Watch you don't piss off the wrong merchant."

"I needed to get to you," she said. "I was hardly going to borrow a war drake instead."

"Flying would save time." Yala leaned back in her seat as the raptors tugged on the wagon at Niema's command.

"Oh—I have this." Niema reached into the pack she'd brought with her and handed Yala the curved claw that had once belonged to a void drake. "Thought you might need it."

"Good thinking." Yala took the claw in a gloved hand, feeling its chill seep through the material.

As they rattled down the street, Yala kept an eye on the small grey bird fluttering ahead of them. Perhaps they ought to have picked a more conspicuous spy after all; it was hard to tell the difference between the giern and the other similar-looking birds nesting on the rooftops. Niema had certainly been quick thinking, getting hold of a wagon as soon as the bird had brought its warning, but would it be enough for them to reach their target in time?

When they reached the docks, Niema climbed to the ground and then called the bird with a whistle. Yala joined her, though the wagon and raptors might draw attention while abandoned at the dockside without a driver. At least there didn't appear to be any guards nearby, but she didn't see any signs of the dead either.

Yala jerked her head at the bird. "What did it see?"

Niema whistled, and the bird let out a shrill cry and took off in a zigzagging flight until it came to a small boat bobbing against the pier. Gripping the claw, Yala followed. A faint tingle ran up her fingertips, but no shadows leapt out at her. Instead, a person lay in the boat, its face hidden by a hooded cloak.

Yala dug her cane into the wooden pier and leaned over. "What're you doing in there?"

In one smooth motion, the figure reared up out of the boat and seized her shoulders, shoving her backwards. Yala threw out a hand to break her fall, feeling the skin break as she skidded on the bumpy wooden slats of the pier. She reached for her cane, which had clattered to the side, but the man's hands locked around her throat first.

He was *alive*. He was also damned strong, his nails digging into the skin of Yala's neck and driving her shoulders into the wooden surface beneath.

"You're Yala," he said, with a guttural voice. "Captain Yala—"

The grip on her throat loosened as Niema tackled the man from the side. She was unable to cause harm to another person without experiencing that pain herself, but she'd broken his hold on her, which gave Yala the chance to grab her cane and climb to her feet.

"That wasn't nice of you." Yala struck the man on the shoulder with her cane and sent him sprawling. He rose upward, too slow to escape another hit, and his hood fell back in a rustle of fabric.

Yala recoiled, and the claw burned against her hand with a sudden chill. His face was rotting, strips of skin peeling back to expose strips of muscle stretched across greying bone. His nose had half fallen off, and one cheek had caved in, revealing broken teeth jutting from rotting gums.

"What...?" She heard Niema retching behind her. "What kind of abomination are you?"

The dead weren't supposed to be able to speak. The man's eyes were murky, bloodshot, but regarded her with genuine alertness in a way that no dead person ever should. When he coughed, blood and bile and viscera splattered the pier.

"Who are you working for?" Yala pressed. "Who put you up to this?"

If he says Melian, I'll put his eyes out.

"Tell me." She drove her cane into his chest when he didn't reply; a cracking noise ensued. "Who sent you?"

"I am His now." The man grinned, his words turning to incoherence as his teeth crumbled out of his decaying mouth. "Mekan, I am yours."

"Not a chance." As his body sagged, Yala seized the scruff of his neck, noting that he wore the same kind of hooded garment that she'd found inside Melian's old house. And, she was willing to bet, the same as the king's would-be assassin.

Did that mean he'd been in the city the whole time, or had he come from outside, in this boat, like the body of that Rafragorian soldier?

"Speak." Yala shook him, but the brightness in his eyes faded, and the god of death's shadows filled the sockets. A garbled noise came out of his throat, mingling with the whispers that spiralled upward from the claw in her hand.

"You could be mine too. All you need to do is come home."

"Fuck that." Yala shoved the dead man, whose hands had begun to twitch towards her in the manner of the newly raised dead.

Flailing, he toppled over the edge of the pier into the sea.

"Yala!" Niema tugged on her arm from behind. "There are guards."

Tilting her head, Yala called out to the approaching guards. "Hey! We need help over here."

As the guards made their way over, she slipped the claw into the pouch at her waist to avoid unwanted questions. Yes, they'd ask the source of the dead body, but the man's rotting state showed no wound inflicted by her own hand.

He's more than the usual kind of dead, she thought, Mekan's voice an echo in the back of her mind.

What new horror had Mekan created this time?

———

Niema did not return home with Yala after they'd shaken off the city guards and sent them to dispose of the body. First, she returned the wagon and its raptors to the market from which she'd taken them, careful not to draw the attention of anyone who might report her for theft. Then, she walked to the upper city and the Disciples' Inn.

Yala had declined to come with her, wanting to avoid the Temple of the Flame, so it fell on Niema to update Kelan and the others on Mekan's new creation. She hadn't told Yala that she'd heard the god of death's words, too, the grating whisper when the man had passed beyond this world.

"You could be mine too. All you need to do is come home."

Niema knocked on the door to the inn and was relieved when it was Kelan who answered.

"Ah, Niema," he said. "You smell of the dead. I'm guessing you were with Yala?"

"Who is it this time?" asked the sour-faced Disciple of the Sky, glaring at Niema when they walked into the downstairs room.

He and the others soon began to pay attention when Niema told them what she and Yala had found at the docks.

"The man who attacked us was dying but not dead," she explained. "It's like his body was rotting while he was still breathing."

"Mekan's work?" Kelan guessed.

"Almost certainly," she said with a shudder. "He was coherent up until the last moment, when he... fell apart."

"Charming," said a female Disciple who sat in the corner. "Does this kind of thing happen to you a lot?"

"Distressingly often," Kelan answered. "Interesting. I wonder if the king's assassin was the same. He was in too many pieces to tell by the time we got to him."

Niema's stomach turned. "I don't know. I'm also not sure where he came from. He was in a boat."

"The Successors' houses are at the dockside," Kelan reminded her. "We can keep an eye out for more of Mekan's abominations while we're on our Superior's next mission. She's asked us to meet the Disciples of the Sea."

"What?" Niema glanced at the tall Disciple, Lakiel, who'd let out an audible sigh when Kelan had revealed the details of their mission. "Don't they live at the bottom of the ocean?"

Her education on that branch of Disciples had been sparse enough that she didn't remember the details, except that they were recluses who lived at sea and didn't interact with anyone, including other Disciples.

"Yes, which makes them more likely to have seen whatever killed those ambassadors," Kelan said. "I can't imagine Mekan's monsters would have escaped their attention if they've taken to swimming off Laria's coast."

"I guess not," Niema acknowledged, "but if the Disciples of the Sea have been avoiding interacting with any other Disciples for this long, there must be a reason."

"I don't blame them for avoiding the Disciples of the Flame," Kelan said. "Does Superior Shralin know about your rotting friend?"

"Yala told the guards to fish the body out of the ocean," Niema said. "They'll have taken it to the temple to be destroyed."

"I wish I could see Superior Shralin's face," Kelan said. "I thought the novice who answered the door yesterday when I showed up with those assassins was going to pass out.

"Take this seriously, Kelan," Lakiel snapped. "Need I remind you that we can ill afford to anger any other Disciples?"

"Do the Disciples of the Sea know you're coming?" Niema asked. "It seems risky for you to just show up."

"They don't have an address, and our Superior said they've refused to reply to any previous correspondence," Kelan explained. "I gather that nothing will get their attention short of marching up to their doors and demanding an audience. Unless you can ask a fish to carry a message?"

"The paper would dissolve in the water."

"That was a joke." He quirked a smile. "You *could* come with us, though."

"No, she won't," said Lakiel. "We have our orders. She has hers."

I don't. Granted, Superior Kralia assumed Niema still owed her allegiance, but she had yet to send a follow-up to her first note. Niema wasn't foolish enough to expect her to cease communications after one spurned message, but she had a hard time imagining her Superior

128

abandoning the enclave to come after her in person. Unless she sent assassins again—Niema cut off the thought. *No. I won't allow it.*

"Ignore him," Kelan said. "You can come, you know. We'd appreciate your skills."

He sounded genuine. Had he been as concerned for her suitability to survive in the city as Yala had? She might have agreed if he'd been alone, but the reactions of his companions made her conscious of her status as a Disciple without a home, without a Superior. No, she had to find her own path rather than following him or Yala.

"I'll be fine," Niema added. "Just... be careful."

"Worried about me?" Kelan lifted a brow. "I rather think the Disciples will be friendlier than Rafragoria's soldiers."

Yes, but what if there are more of those dead abominations out there?

———

Viam didn't expect to see the king again for a while. After the furore of the attempt on his life, the palace had whipped into a frenzy, with new guard patrols showing up every day and the soldiers running drills so often that the pounding of heavy boots was a constant background noise.

Even visiting the war drakes' paddock had a new layer of complication due to the increased patrols around the palace, while she found it hard even to engage in ordinary conversations with Brenat when she recalled Yala's distrust and her remarks that the assassin might have had inside help from the palace itself.

It was therefore a surprise when she returned to the palace grounds the day after the attack and saw none other than King Daliel walking towards her. Luckily, he was flanked by an armed guard on each side, but Viam's heart flipped at their proximity to the site of the attack.

"Viam." He offered a smile. "I was hoping to run into you."

"You were?" Had he learned nothing from their narrow escape the previous day? At least he'd stopped walking around alone, but two guards had been no match for the assassins, and any killed by Mekan would become His soldiers in an instant. "Ah—what is it, Your Majesty?"

He took in a breath. "Given recent events, it's clear that we need to reassure the public that we're ready to defend ourselves against any outside threat."

"Reassure the public?" She followed his gaze towards the fence circling the barracks and the rows of soldiers within. "Is that... I mean, is war with Rafragoria likely?"

Her heart stuttered. She'd forgotten Rafragoria's potential retaliation in the wake of the more imminent threat inside the palace itself, but the outside dangers had equal likelihood of bringing the nation to its knees. How could the king hope to prove that Laria had a strong defence when he'd nearly lost his life on his own doorstep?

"Not as such." He beckoned her to his side, while the guards walked slightly behind them to give the illusion of privacy. "I did receive a reply. They accepted my condolences for the loss of their ambassadors but declined to set up another meeting."

"That doesn't sound like a declaration of war." Whether they'd been honest was another matter, but the king's dismissal of her mention of the Successors made her reluctant to bring them up as possible instigators.

"No," he said. "Which gives us time to plan a show of strength for the public. A parade, I think."

"What?" Was *that* really his first priority at a time like this? "Your Majesty, are you sure this is wise?"

"Of course," he said. "And I want you to help me with the preparations, Viam."

13

Such was the nature of gossip that Kelan and the other Disciples of the Sky were already aware of the upcoming parade long before a royal messenger showed up at the Disciples' Inn the morning after their return from Skytower. Kelan answered the door to find a red-faced youth dressed in livery several sizes too big for him, who informed them that Rafragoria had declined their request to set up another meeting.

"Better than declaring war." Kelan glanced behind him at the other Disciples, who'd gathered to hear the news. "What's all this about a parade?"

The messenger blinked at him. "Yes, His Majesty is planning a grand parade for All Gods' Day, and he's busy with the preparations."

Now did not seem a spectacular time for a public display, in Kelan's view, unless His Majesty actively intended to draw out any other potential assassins lurking amid the public.

While the messenger jogged back to the palace, Kelan joined the others in the inn's downstairs room.

"If Rafragoria has declined to meet us, there's little point in delaying our visit to the Disciples of the Sea," he said. "We'll leave today."

They'd miss the parade, but that was no great loss in Kelan's view.

Another knock on the door arrived shortly after the messenger's departure. Kelan answered, expecting to find Niema or Yala on the other side, but he was instead greeted by an unfamiliar woman dressed in the red robes of the Disciples of the Flame.

"Superior Shralin would like to speak to you," said the female Disciple, whose dark hair was pleated with gold leaves and her robes adorned with a matching gold crest. "It's urgent."

"Is it now?" Superior Shralin *wanted* to speak to him? Had he gone too far when he'd dropped those dead assassins on the temple doorstep? "He doesn't plan to lock me in the dungeon, does he?"

"Kelan." Lakiel nudged him. "I'll go and see what this is about. You stay behind."

"No, it sounds like I'm the one he wants to speak to. What changed his mind?"

Curiosity piqued, Kelan followed the Disciple of the Flame across Ceremonial Square. This time, when he and Lakiel reached the temple, their companion opened the temple door and stood back to let the pair of them enter. Kelan braced himself for the sudden impact of his feet hitting the ground as his god's influence disappeared the way it always did when he entered the temple of another deity.

He and Lakiel walked through the main chamber, which was bathed in sunlight and suffused with smoke that smelled strongly of incense. Wishing he'd removed his cloak, he spied the Superior lurking in an alcove.

Superior Shralin's mouth thinned when he saw Kelan approaching. "I didn't ask for you."

"I thought you wanted to talk to us urgently." Sensing Lakiel's glare, he suppressed a less complimentary remark. "What is it?"

"I heard your Superior has ordered you to meet with the Disciples of the Sea," he said. "Is that true?"

"Who told you that?" Kelan's spoke before his thoughts could catch up. "Have you been spying on us?"

A flush darkened Superior Shralin's face. "You do intend to seek out the Disciples of the Sea?"

"It's not a crime, is it?" he said. "Our Superior did ask us to meet with them. If there's an issue with that order, I think she'd appreciate it if you enlightened us."

"The Disciples of the Sea have no allegiance to Laria nor to their fellow Disciples," said the Superior. "They are loyal only to their Superior, and they cannot be trusted."

"Is that unusual?" Weren't all Disciples bound to their leader above all else save for their deity? "Have you ever met one of them?"

"This is unprecedented," said Superior Shralin. "The Disciples of the Sea haven't made contact with any other Superiors in decades."

You didn't answer the question. "I think they'll appreciate an update on everything they missed, and our Superior thinks they can assist us."

"Your Superior, I believe, has made an error of judgement."

"Has she?" Kelan's intention to avoid provoking an argument evaporated like the contents of a jug of water placed too close to Dalathik's altar. "Maybe she's decided that we'll have more luck contacting a group of Disciples who've barely set foot in Laria for decades than reasoning with the ones on land."

Superior Shralin flushed even deeper. "You mistake me. Remember that we serve our gods and not the other way around."

What's that supposed to mean? The question lingered on his tongue, but Lakiel elbowed him out of the way. "Thank you for the warning. It's appreciated."

"Warning?" he muttered to Lakiel as they retraced their steps across the chamber after the clear dismissal. "Or threat?"

Lakiel didn't speak until they reached the doors. Annoyed though he might be at the Superior's lack of transparency, Kelan was more than happy to get out of the suffocating incense-laden warmth of the temple and out into the open air.

"*Was* he spying on us?" he said to Lakiel. "I didn't tell anyone our plan."

"Except Yala Palathar and all your other friends."

"They're not in the habit of paying visits to the Temple of the Flame," he said. "Aren't you curious as to why the Superior was so vehement that we stay put?"

If anything, Superior Shralin's warning had made Kelan even more intrigued to find out what the Disciples of the Sea had been doing throughout their decades-long absence from Laria.

"I think it's quite obvious why," said Lakiel. "They're an unknown entity allied to an unknown god."

"Amanat isn't *that* unknown." Not compared to, say, the god of death. "It's not like we're going to Mekan's island."

Remember the island. The words skittered through his mind inexplicably and brought a shiver to his skin. Along with a question. *How close did the Disciples of the Sea live to that island?*

Lakiel blew out a breath. "What if he's right?"

"You're thinking of obeying another Superior over our own?" Kelan asked, disbelieving. "One whose predecessor allied with mercenaries and unknowingly supported the Successors' plot to overthrow the king?"

Lakiel's eyes narrowed at Kelan's words. "You're allied to a Disciple of Death yourself."

"That's not the same," Kelan said. "You must know the Disciples of the Flame are serving their own agenda. Superior Shralin is a coward with a grudge against our Superior, and I can guarantee he doesn't give a shit about finding whoever killed those ambassadors."

Who else might be able to help them learn the truth? The Disciples lived within the very ocean in which the deaths had taken place, and they'd have a vested interest in keeping the god of death out of their territory, surely.

Lakiel sighed. "Fine. We'll put the decision to a vote."

And I'll speak to Yala.

————

"A *parade*." Yala paced the living room in a manner that put Niema in mind of her war drake, chained and confined to its paddock. "He's lost it."

Viam had dropped in at the house briefly to pass on the news before she'd had to run back to the upper city to help His Majesty with the preparations, so Niema and Saren had to listen to the aftermath.

"We heard you the first ten times, Yala," Saren said. "Why not go to the palace and tell him?"

Yala whirled on him with a snarl—also reminiscent of the war drake—and then her shoulders slumped. "You know why I can't. If he gets himself killed by the dead, he can't say nobody warned him."

Viam had tried, but he'd been resolute. Niema almost understood too. She'd never met the man, so she didn't know for sure, but the king wanted to prove himself worthy, if not to the people, then to the father he'd never been able to replace in their eyes.

"The Successors will be cheering him on," Saren remarked. "Maybe that's the idea. He draws out his enemies and sets the army on them."

"Except the army's a fraction of its former size and has never fought the dead before." Yala paced to the door. "This is absurd. I'm going—"

"To see the war drake, I know," Saren said. "And I'm going back to bed."

"Wait." Niema stepped towards him. "I'm taking your advice and setting up as a healer, but I wanted to make sure it wouldn't bother you if strangers started showing up at the house."

Saren paused in the stairway. "Why would it bother me? Yala's the one who owns the house."

"I thought it was polite to ask."

"Polite." He smiled and shook his head. "How *did* you end up befriending someone like Yala?"

"Circumstances." Hearing Yala scoff behind her, she swivelled to the door. "Do *you* mind strangers showing up at the house?"

She grunted. "Half the guards already know where I live. It doesn't matter."

Doesn't it? "It won't be for long. When I earn enough coin to pay for my own property, I'll leave."

"That's not necessary." Yala's frown deepened. "I did tell you that you could stay. I'm not letting you get beaten around by assassins again."

Niema's palms dampened at the thought of the main feature of her dreams the previous night. "I won't be."

"Unless you want to leave Dalathar," Yala added. "I wouldn't blame you at this point."

"No." She shook her head. "Dalathar seems to be one of the few places that a Disciple can operate alone without being looked upon as strange, at least not by everyone, and I think I need to be here."

"To keep an eye on Mekan's newest monsters," Yala surmised. "Yes. If Mekan's followers are rotting from the inside out while still alive, I have to wonder what He's offering them in exchange."

Niema's stomach flipped. "I don't know."

Yala reached for the door again. "I'm sure we'll find out when His Majesty draws them out into full view of the public like flies to a corpse."

Is that likely to happen? Niema bit back the question, knowing it was foolish. Whether the Successors would make a public appearance was debatable, but the dead had no reason to fear being exposed. They knew one command: to obey Mekan.

As the door closed behind Yala and Saren retreated upstairs, Niema was left alone with the sinking suspicion that far more than the king's life would be at risk at the parade. An attack from the dead might have consequences as far-reaching as Melian's attack on the capital, her mass sacrifice that had ripped open the Void.

Her gaze travelled towards the loose floorboard where she knew Yala kept the void drake's claw.

"Don't bother," Saren said, and she jumped, having thought he'd already gone upstairs. "I've thought of throwing that thing out a million times, but it's not worth it."

"I wasn't thinking of throwing it out," she mumbled, assuming he meant the void drake's claw. "Yala needs it."

"It's like Mekan's festering toenail," Saren said. "It does none of us any good, but there's no way of disposing of it short of asking our fiery friends, so the rest of us have to suffer the nightmares."

Niema's nightmares had revolved around her former Superior, not the god of death, but she gathered that Saren was as disturbed a sleeper as Yala. "It's a tool. Not unlike my own abilities."

"Which you intend to use upon the ungrateful public." A smile tilted his lips. "All right. I'll work under the assumption that that claw won't have any adverse effects on anyone who comes in to ask for our services as healers."

"Our?" she echoed.

"You need supplies to get started, don't you?" He vanished upstairs without waiting for a reply, while Niema battled the rising temptation to open the floorboard and see if her abilities couldn't destroy the claw after all.

No. Yala needs it, especially if the dead do attack the parade, she told herself. *It's dormant enough not to bother anyone who doesn't touch it.*

Certainly, Niema hadn't heard a word from the god of death's direction, but her misgivings remained.

You're part of His realm too, a voice whispered in her mind. *You aren't like other Disciples of Life. Even your Superior said so.*

Niema pushed the thought aside and went to help Saren gather the healing supplies.

———

Viam spent the next day in a whirlwind of preparations and questions from Brenat.

Admittedly, the latter came in batches; Viam had been relieved of her usual duties, and now, the only time they saw one another was in the dormitories at the beginning and end of the day. Instead, Viam spent most of her time watching lines of soldiers assemble outside the barracks in their uniforms. Their best gear was made for ceremony rather than open battle; their usual drakeskin trousers were adorned with impractical gold tassels, and they wore heavy black coats over their usual lightweight shirts with golden embroidery stitched into the fabric.

The heat coupled with the weighty clothing made Viam's skin itch, and the king looked even less comfortable dressed in ceremonial gold armour that made him resemble his father so much that Viam had startled when she'd first seen him.

"Ah, it suits you, Your Majesty," she'd lied. King Daliel didn't look like himself, but wasn't that supposed to be the point? People would look at him and see King Tharen instead.

The Flight Division was the one obvious absence among the assembly, but if she tilted her head, Viam could almost pretend she could see them standing at the back, their gloved hands raised to the sky and glory shining in their eyes. Her vision swam with unexpected emotion.

"Did you miss this?" The king's question brought her crashing back to the present, and she startled.

"Yes. Some of it." She licked her dry lips. "I don't miss the fighting. Are those new volunteers?"

She indicated a new group of youths dressed in the plain grey of novices and watching the rehearsal with saucer-round eyes.

"Yes, they signed up this week," he said. "They haven't been assigned yet, but it's my hope that some will choose the Flight Division."

Her heart jolted. "So soon?"

"Yes." He spoke with confidence. "Within the month, we'll have enough for a full squad."

And who will ride them? Who will lead that squad?

She bit back the question, dreading the answer. At least she hadn't been asked to give the orders; Viam had none of Yala's skill at projecting her voice or wrangling novices into obedience.

After a moment, the king said, "The Flight Division was once the centre of Laria's defence. Some might say I was a fool to disband it."

"Some might say the opposite." She clapped a hand to her mouth, mortified at her own daring. "No offence intended, Your Majesty."

"No, my mother would agree with you," he said after a short pause. "She used to say that wild animals had no business being dragged around by humans. Or that's what my father claimed she said, anyway. I was too young to remember."

Viam's mouth parted in surprise. She didn't know anything at all about his mother, she realised, except the common knowledge that King Tharen's wife had died shortly after the birth of her son. "Your father learned to ride. She must have hated that."

"Yes... yes, she did." His voice clouded. "I did too. I remember I cried as a child when he went to war. Every time."

His frankness startled her, and she was starting to understand why he'd ended the fighting as soon as he'd gained power, no matter what his father might have wanted him to do.

She faced the parade again, a lump in her throat, and another obvious absence leapt out at her.

She took in a breath. "Your Majesty... did you have any plans to invite the Disciples of the Flame? They used to walk alongside your father with his personal guard."

The king was silent for a long moment before he replied. "I sent a message with an invitation, but Superior Shralin felt attending would be inappropriate and declined."

He said no to the king? That King Daliel had asked at all might have surprised her, but then, he didn't know the depth of the Disciples' betrayal, not what he might stand to lose by placing his trust in them as his father had.

On the other hand, if the Disciples weren't present, who would intervene if another attack came from the dead, this time on a larger scale?

He's making a huge mistake.

14

Niema's first visitor was a man with a broken wrist who claimed Nalen had given him her name. Yala must have asked him to spread the word to anyone who might be able to afford her services, but she hadn't mentioned the part about Niema being a Disciple of Life. The man watched with some trepidation as she asked him to hold out his injured arm and keep still while she whispered a prayer to her deity.

When she did, green light enveloped his skin, and his eyes grew wide. "The... the pain is gone. Gone. Thank you."

"You should be fine now." She watched as he turned his hand over, awed, and she had to stop him from handing over twice the coin she'd asked for on the way out the door.

"Thank Yalet," Niema mumbled, uncomfortable at taking the praise for herself alone. "Not me."

"Why not take his money?" Saren asked as she closed the door.

"I don't want to put people off by charging too much," Niema said. "My abilities might be a novelty at first, but people will get used to them."

Saren snorted. "No, they won't. Trust me. Not many people can say they were healed by a Disciple of Life."

Several more visitors trickled in throughout the day, sent by Yala or Nalen or perhaps her initial customers telling everyone they knew. While she was grateful for the work, Niema soon ran up against the limits of her abilities. She could heal bones easily enough, but infections were more complicated, and she could only reverse the surface damage and hope that the injury didn't fester again afterwards. She could also do little for wounds that had been left untreated for more than a few hours or longer.

"I was told you were a miracle worker," yelled an old man as he backed out of the door after she'd told him she couldn't regrow his missing arm. "You're a fraud."

"I can't do the impossible." She flinched when he spat at her feet. "I'm sorry."

"Want me to break a few ribs and force him to pay you to heal him?" Saren offered, watching the man totter away.

"No." She closed the door with shaking hands. "I hope he doesn't come back and make trouble later."

"I hope he does," Saren commented. "Yala will kick his teeth in. You need to be more assertive."

"I threw him out, didn't I?"

"I think he threw himself out." Saren shook his head. "Guess even the gods have limits. Can you heal...?"

"Heal what?" She paced away from the door and began tidying everything her unhappy visitor had knocked over.

"Wounds other than physical ones," Saren said after a short pause. "Diseases of the mind and that sort of thing."

"Oh." She hadn't thought of that. "I don't think so. My healing ability is concerned with the physical."

"Right." He dropped his gaze to a worn flask he gripped tightly in both hands. "Guess the rest of us have to deal with things the normal way."

"You could be a Disciple of Death. Weren't you on the island too?"

"Strangely enough, raising the dead isn't as high in demand as healing is." He returned to the corner where he'd put the medical supplies. "I'm not letting myself get turned inside out by Mekan, thanks. I like my vital organs to stay in the right place."

Someone rapped on the door. Niema crossed the room to the window, and her heart dropped at the bright flash of an orange cloak. *A Disciple of the Flame.* Somehow, she doubted he'd come to hire her healing abilities.

Taking in a breath, she opened the door and faced the unfriendly Disciple on the other side. His clean-shaven face showed a few lines; he might be a little older than Yala, and his broad shoulders were clothed in the embroidered patterns that indicated a higher rank.

"May I help you?" she asked. "If you're looking for Yala, she's out."

Should I have told him that? If he attacked, Niema wouldn't be able to defend herself if they attacked even if she'd had a weapon to hand, but he displayed no emotion other than a faint tightening in his jaw.

"No, you're the one I was sent to find," said the Disciple. "A Disciple of Life working as a healer. Is it true?"

"Yes, it is." She couldn't tell from his tone whether he was accusing her or simply making a statement. "Do you want to hire my services?"

"No," he said. "My Superior sent me to verify if the rumours were true, nothing more."

"What rumours?" How had they found out so quickly? "It's been less than a half day."

"Your friend Yala must know that her actions have drawn a lot of attention." A flicker of an emotion she didn't recognise entered his eyes. "From all directions."

"Does that include the body we found at the docks?" A rush of unexpected daring seized her. "You must have heard from the king's guards. He was turning into Mekan's servant while still breathing. Have you seen anyone like him before?"

Disgust rippled across his face. "An abomination."

Before Niema could press further, there came the distinct sound of a cane hitting the cobbles. *Yala. Oh, no.*

———

Yala marched towards the Disciple of the Flame, unable to believe their sheer audacity. She didn't recognise the man, but his expression of outright disgust at the sight of her was familiar enough.

"Care to tell me why you're outside my house?" she asked. "Looking for me?"

"No." His gaze lifted upward, and a rush of air overhead prompted Yala to glance at the sky too.

Kelan descended in an elegant swoop, landing directly behind her unwanted visitor. "Is there a problem?"

The Disciple's jaw clenched. "I'm here to check up on the rumours of a Disciple of Life operating as a healer."

"It's a respectable profession," Yala said. "More so than yours."

"Ha." Saren sidled into view behind Niema, a smirk on his face. "I don't recall you being in charge of what people can do in their own homes either."

"That wasn't our intention," said the man. "I hope you have a pleasant evening."

"Healer?" Kelan sidestepped to let the Disciple walk past, which he did with visible reluctance. "Since when?"

"Since this morning." Niema's shoulders hunched. "He mentioned rumours, but how'd they find out that quickly?"

"Probably by spying on you," Kelan said. "Like the Disciples' Inn. They showed up earlier and dragged us to meet Superior Shralin, who warned me against visiting the Disciples of the Sea."

"What?" Yala's spine stiffened. "Why would he warn you off?"

"Supposedly out of concern for our safety." With a last glance towards the retreating Disciple, Kelan glided into the house as if he lived there. "We had a vote and decided to go anyway, but I think Lakiel's convinced we're all going to die."

What with the news of the upcoming parade, Yala had forgotten the other questionable decision of the week that she'd learned by way of Niema—namely, Superior Sietra's decision to send Kelan and the others to seek out the one branch of Disciples of whom her knowledge was nonexistent.

"I thought you already left," she replied. "That's what Niema implied."

"We're leaving this afternoon," he said with the hint of an apology in his voice. "You didn't think I'd go on a life-threatening mission without telling you, did you?"

Yala offered him an eye roll. "It wouldn't have broken my heart. At least you'll miss the parade."

"Yes, a military parade does make a watery death seem appealing in comparison," he said. "Have *you* ever met the Disciples of the Sea?"

"What do you think?" she said. "Haven't they been hiding in the ocean since before any of us was born?"

"That's what I learned." Niema eyed Kelan with concern. "If the Disciples of the Flame warned you to avoid them..."

"That says more about them than it does about the Disciples of the Sea," Kelan said, though his flippant tone didn't quite hide a hint of uncertainty. "Maybe they're concerned that we'll form an alliance with a group of fellow Disciples who aren't run by a despot or an incompetent. There aren't a lot of those going around."

"Might be asking for too much," Yala commented. "Between them, the Successors, and angry Rafragorians, I think I'll take my chances with the parade instead of the ocean."

She hadn't mentioned Mekan, but she hadn't needed to. She, Saren, and Niema all glanced in the direction of the floorboard under which she'd stored the void drake's claw. Dust motes danced in the air in the beam of sunlight streaking through the window, yet all light seemed to avoid that area of the room, leaving a patch of subtle shadow that might have been real and might have been some trickery of her mind.

"You're going to the parade?" Kelan asked with a tilt of the head that suggested their mutual gesture hadn't escaped him. "Voluntarily?"

"Never mind the fucking parade," Yala growled. "What's with the Disciples of the Flame suddenly sticking their noses into everyone's business?"

"They're in desperate need of hobbies?" Kelan suggested. "They've spent too long breathing in those incense candles of theirs?"

"Both," Saren said. "Who cares what's going through their minds?"

Yala ground her cane into the floorboard, thinking of their visitor. His attitude hadn't been unfamiliar to her, but the sheer nerve of his interest in Niema got under her skin all the same. "Unless they're working with the Successors. Again."

That didn't seem right—Temik's betrayal had been calculated, and he'd never been loyal to the Disciples of the Flame, while the others hadn't known they were playing into Melian's hands—but nothing in their actions added up to anything other than foul play.

"I suppose we'll find out," Kelan said. "They won't be able to do much to stop us leaving, given that their deity forbids them to go near the water."

He's committed, then, she thought, and in the back of her mind, the note in the dead man's hand flickered into view. *Remember the island.*

Dread clawed at her chest as though a juvenile war drake rested inside her rib cage. Her hands clenched under the gloves she wore nearly night and day now, and she said, "It's not what's in the water that bothers me. You know what else is out there."

"I didn't think you of all people would be warning me to avoid trouble," he said with a smile. "I'll be careful."

"Are you ever?" Not for the first time, Yala considered that her life would be infinitely easier if the people around her didn't insist on flinging themselves into the path of danger, but she had no way of telling how much of her paranoia was justified. Too many enemies wanted a piece of her, and if the Disciples of the Sea might be allies against a veritable ocean of enemies, who was she to stop Kelan and the others from seeking them?

"I expect not." He raised a hand in farewell, sending a gust of wind that knocked the door open. "I'll be back soon."

"You'd better." She watched him glide out of the house, fighting the urge to throw caution aside and offer to come with him. She'd have to bring the war drake, though, which was out of the question. Flying a half-tamed war drake that close to Rafragoria would get her nothing but a spear in her throat. Or worse, Corruption rotting her from the inside out while her heart still beat.

She closed the door and turned to the corner, where Saren knelt on the floor, laying coins into piles and counting them. "Is that your earnings?"

"Niema's more than mine." He laughed. "Keep this up, and we can buy a manor outside the city and be done with this grimy corner of hell."

"Don't speak too soon." Yala paced over to an armchair and sank into it. "It hasn't been a day yet, and you already have Disciples knocking on the door."

"Exactly." Saren grinned. "We'll have my last employer out of business in a week. Nobody can compete with a real miracle worker."

Yes, and how long will the people of the city tolerate that? She pushed the thought aside in favour of the more immediate problem. "You might want to stay closed tomorrow. The parade will have the whole city in a frenzy."

"If anything, we're more likely to get people stopping by with injuries from being shoved or trampled in the crowds." Saren's smile slipped away. "That wasn't a challenge, Yala. I don't want you jumping in front of the king and getting killed by a disgruntled anti-monarchist."

"I haven't a chance of getting close enough to him for that." Viam would, though, which was precisely the problem. "It'll only take one of Mekan's followers to turn the parade into a bloodbath, and I won't stay at home and let that happen."

Saren sighed. "I'm surrounded by masochists."

"Won't the king's guards be watching for trouble?" Niema asked.

"Yes, but there'll be thousands of people in Ceremonial Square alone," Yala replied. "Even if they're sharp-eyed enough to spot an assassin hiding in the crowd from up on the city walls, they won't have a hope of getting down in time to stop them."

"Unless they... shit, Yala, you aren't thinking of taking the war drake?" Saren's eyes bulged. "Never mind. Forget I said that."

"It'll be fine if I'm with her," Niema ventured. "Right, Yala?"

Yala glanced at her, surprised; she'd never put the idea forward, and even her notions of taking the war drake with her had been half formed at best. Regardless, but carnage the war drake might cause was nothing compared to what Mekan and His followers might unleash upon a crowd comprising a significant proportion of Dalathar's population. "You don't have to, but I can intervene much quicker from the air than on the ground."

"You'll still be flying a dangerous wild animal next to a huge crowd of tasty humans," Saren said. "You really think someone's going to try to get at the king?"

"Or worse," Yala said. "The Successors are going to make a play for power, and we'd better be ready."

———

Kelan and the others left for Amanar immediately following his visit to Yala's house. It was later in the day than he'd have liked, but the others had spent the morning arguing the merits of heeding Superior Shralin's warning. Ultimately, their desire to obey their Superior had won out, though Lakiel remained in a foul mood throughout the afternoon.

Their flight took them along Laria's coast, westwards from the capital. Amanar was half a day away, further than Setemar, which meant spending the night in the coastal city and waiting until morning to head out to sea. Flying across the ocean in darkness held no appeal, and Kelan's impatience was also tempered by the knowledge that they at least wouldn't be trapped behind Dalathar's walls during the parade. Admittedly, he couldn't help wondering if he or Yala had made the most unwise choice in leaving or staying—and there was a rather depressing chance that there might not *be* a monarch on Laria's throne when he returned.

Such morose thoughts aside, the journey was pleasant enough, and they reached Amanar in good time. The local Disciples' Inn was similar to the one in the capital except with the benefit of a sea view from the windows and the constant smell of fresh fish in place of the less salubrious stench of Dalathar's river. He spent the evening playing cards with Brikel and Ranit while Lakiel watched in disapproval; for once, he wasn't the most impatient among their number. Lakiel showed every sign of wanting this mission to be over as soon as possible.

Typically, he woke Kelan and the others the next morning when the sun had barely risen over the squat buildings of Amanar. Yawning, they assembled in the downstairs room to consult the maps one last time before they left the inn. He'd forgotten just how close Amanar sat to the ocean, with none of Dalathar's warehouses and other buildings obscuring the view. A vast blue expanse greeted them upon their exit from the inn, where small fishing vessels bobbed against piers, outfitted with nets to catch the swift-darting fish that swam close to shore. Few dared to venture further afield to deeper waters, where they were more likely to become the prey themselves. *Except for us poor fools, evidently.*

Lakiel wasted no time in flying outward over the open sea, angling to the west, and his fellow Disciples followed. No landmarks gave any sense of what might lie ahead, and a shiver of unease rose to Kelan's skin at the memory of his last experience with this stretch of ocean. A child's body washing up onshore to the horror of a group of orphans, possibly killed by the Disciples of the Sea.

Too late for second thoughts, he told himself, though he flew higher to ensure his feet were far enough above the water's surface to avoid the rearing head of a sea drake.

With half his attention pointed downward, he didn't see any trouble until Lakiel cried, "Watch out!"

His cry was followed by something sharp whizzing past; Kelan jerked sideways as another arrow hit Lakiel in the arm. With a startled yell, his fellow Disciple dropped several handspans in the air. *Arrows? That can't be the Disciples of the Sea.*

Saltwater stung his eyes, drawing his gaze towards a serpentine shape cutting through the water like a blade. *Sea drake.* This one had a rider, a fierce-eyed woman with flowing dark hair, her face screwed up in concentration as she fitted another arrow to the bow.

So much for Rafragoria not retaliating against us for harming their ambassadors.

Two more sea drakes joined the first, bearing riders armed with long spears. Kelan reached for his own sword, though he didn't hold out much hope for them beating a squad of trained soldiers who were as at home in the sea as his fellow Disciples were in the sky. They weren't dressed as he might have expected of soldiers, wearing cape-like garments formed of what appeared to be sea drake scales over thin shirts. Since most of Rafragoria's battles took place at sea, clothes that wouldn't weigh them down if they fell into the water would be an asset, and their fearsome steeds and weapons far outdid those of Kelan and his allies.

Another arrow whipped past, snagging his cloak. Beside him, Lakiel shouted something incomprehensible; it took a moment for Kelan to realise he was speaking Rafragorian. Blood streamed down one arm as Lakiel held his hands up to indicate he was unarmed, but the Rafragorians continued to advance through the water, their serpentine steeds circling the five of them.

Kriam spoke in Rafragorian, too, adding his voice to Lakiel's, while Kelan and the others closed in to protect their flanks. The female Rafragorian in front spoke, but Kelan didn't understand a word.

"Sorry, I don't speak Rafragorian," he called back. "We're not here to harm you. We're here to see the Disciples of the Sea."

The woman lowered her bow and spoke. "No Disciples."

"You do speak Larian." Or two words of it, anyway. "What do you mean, no Disciples? We're here to see our people, not yours."

"No." She exchanged more words with the others in rapid-paced Rafragorian and then added, "You should not be here."

"We aren't on Rafragorian soil," he said. "Technically speaking, we're closer to Laria."

"Kelan, be *quiet*," hissed Lakiel. His sleeve was soaked through with blood, trailing crimson droplets into the water. The blood would attract more sea drakes, both with and without riders, but the Rafragorians showed no signs of retreating.

"The sea does not belong to you," said another soldier in thickly accented Larian.

"If anything, it belongs to the Disciples of the Sea. It's them who we're here to see." Kelan waved a hand at the water, hoping they'd understand the gesture. "Not you. If you let us go, we won't harm you."

"No." The female soldier lifted her bow again. "You come with us."

Well, it was worth a try, he thought.

15

The Rafragorians led Kelan and the others northwest, cutting a path through the waves with the ease of those practised at navigating their way through the ocean's turbulent currents. Their sea drakes were well controlled, too, though a couple of them did raise their heads to snap at Kelan's feet when he got too close. Not that he was fool enough to attack their riders.

When they came to a rocky outcrop just above the water, the riders leapt off their steeds onto land and produced sturdy ropes with which they bound the sea drakes to the large rocks clustered upon the island.

Kelan had thought he'd feel relieved to land on solid ground, but there was barely enough space on the outcrop for the five of them to stand side by side while the Rafragorians circled them with their weapons raised. In the water, their steeds formed an outer circle around the island, their sharp teeth bared.

"This place we talk," said the female Rafragorian, which Kelan assumed equated to *this is a place we can talk freely.* Talking was better than stabbing, at least.

"About what?" Kelan watched Lakiel out of the corner of his eye;

the other Disciple had landed unsteadily, and his sleeve still drenched with blood. "Planning to apologise for attacking us?"

"Kelan," Lakiel muttered, "if you get us killed, I will seek you out in whatever afterlife you end up in to throttle you."

Kelan fought a wry smile that disappeared when the female Rafragorian pointed an arrow at his throat. "You talk."

"I'm not sure we're understanding one another." The language barrier was an impediment, but he just plain didn't understand what was happening at all. Were they being captured, or did the Rafragorians have some other agenda? "You *want* me to talk? After you attacked and injured us?"

"You kill," said the female soldier. "Kill Rafragorian."

"You think we killed the ambassadors?" Was that why they'd reacted so immediately to their appearance? "No, we didn't. That wasn't us."

"You kill," she repeated. "Larians kill. Make war."

"We definitely *don't* want a war," Kelan said. "The killers *might* have been Larian, but—"

"Kelan, quiet," Lakiel rasped. "Don't give them a reason to feed us to their sea drakes."

Kelan leaned closer to whisper, "They think Laria killed the ambassadors because the Successors *are* Larian. Can't you use your Rafragorian to explain that we're not on the side of the killers?"

"They won't know who the Successors are," Lakiel said through gritted teeth. "That's if they *are* responsible for the murders at all, and we don't have time for a debate."

"I don't care who you tell them is responsible as long as it isn't us," Brikel put in. "Tell them this is a misunderstanding."

Lakiel spoke, uttering a long string of Rafragorian that was incomprehensible to Kelan.

The woman listened then spoke an equally inexplicable reply that ended in the Larian word "Disciple."

"What Disciples?" he whispered. "What does she mean?"

Lakiel made a quiet noise of irritation. "I told them we're here to see the Disciples of the Sea, but Rafragoria has about seven words for 'sea,' and I have no idea if I used the right one. Now, stay quiet and let me listen."

Their captors began to argue amongst themselves, too fast for Kelan to follow even if he had understood the language.

"What are they saying?" Kelan asked. "That they're going to let us go, I hope."

"No." Lakiel's forehead scrunched up as he tried to listen, while Kelan racked his brain for ideas on how to make their mission clear to people who had little more grasp on the Larian language than he had on their own.

"I think they're saying, no Disciples here," Kriam said, also straining to listen. "No Disciples."

"They don't want us here?" Kelan guessed. "Or... or the Disciples of the Sea aren't here any longer?" There were myriad other meanings too, some less appealing than others. "Is the map out of date?"

"The map." Lakiel reached for his pocket with his uninjured hand. The soldiers turned their spears on him at once, and he spoke in Rafragorian, presumably to tell them he wasn't going to attack. When they lowered their spears, he finished retrieving the map and unfurled it to show them.

Now we're getting somewhere, he thought as Lakiel pointed out their location on the map and then indicated westward to show their path. Another burst of conversation between the Rafragorians followed, accompanied by a jab of a spear that made Ranit trip over his feet into Brikel.

"Ow!" he said. "What're they saying?"

The woman jabbed her spear at the map, nearly impaling Lakiel's hand in the process. "No Disciples. Kill Rafragoria."

"They—what, you think the *Disciples of the Sea* killed your ambassadors?" Kelan's mouth hung open. "Is that what she means, Lakiel?"

Lakiel's reply was drowned out by a loud splash as a wave broke against the promontory. Their captors turned to face the new threat, and Kelan's thought of escape vanished at the sight of the water churning like a boiling pot of stew. Even the sea drakes were unable to prevent themselves from being dragged away from the island; one broke free from its rope and vanished below the ocean's surface.

The Rafragorians pointed and shouted in a clear panic. They might be masters of the sea, but they couldn't control the ocean currents in which they lived. Unlike—

A tremendous wave arose, as though conjured by the hand of a god, and Kelan hardly had time to blink before the solid wall of water broke upon the island with a crash that swept them all into its wake.

———

The parade started with a fanfare of drums while rows of uniformed soldiers marched through the palace grounds. Viam watched from her position amongst the king's closest staff members at the centre of the parade, where four guards carried a litter. The king, dressed in his finest embroidery and with his head topped with a crown laden with enough adornments that it was a wonder he could keep his head upright, also wore a forced smile which turned into a genuine one when he caught Viam's eye.

"Thank you for your help," he said. "This parade is going to be glorious."

I didn't do much. The king had followed his father's template from past parades, and Viam wished she'd tried hard to convince him not to go ahead with this at all. Already, thick crowds pressed at the palace gates, and laughter and shouting thrummed as loud as the drumbeats.

Their procession carved a path through the palace grounds, past rows of other staff members who'd gathered to cheer and clap and sing. Brenat stood among them and gave her a wave before disappearing into the blue-and-gold mass of the crowd.

The front gates stood wide open, framed in billowing flags, and a path had been cleared for them through Ceremonial Square past the statue of King Larial. The rest of the square was a forest of blue and gold, amidst which the Temple of the Flame stood like a beacon. Even from a distance, Viam could make out the robed figures gathering in the windows to watch the procession, though none of them ventured closer.

Drums accompanied the soldiers' march, and shouts of "Make way for the king" and "glory to Laria!" mingled with the singing and whistling and general merriment. If there was a sign of dissent amid the cheer, Viam didn't see it. Sweat drenched her back and armpits underneath her thick coat, and she lifted her gaze to the sky in the hopes of catching a breath of air that didn't taste like other people's sweat.

An arrow arced towards her, heading straight for the king.

Reacting without thinking, Viam barrelled sideways into the guards holding the king's litter. They stumbled, tipping the king sideways, and the arrow missed, instead burying itself in a guard's thigh. His bellow was lost in a flurry of shouts from both the procession and the crowd, most of whom hadn't realised what was going on yet.

"Protect the king!" shouted the guard next to the one who'd been injured. "Over here!"

The procession closed in around the litter, but Viam held herself apart, scanning for any signs of the attacker. The arrow had come from *above*, higher than anyone in the crowd ought to be able to reach. Booted feet trod on hers, and elbows rammed into her spine as she pushed to the edge of the procession and lifted her gaze upward.

There. On the city wall stood a hooded figure clutching a bow, taking aim at the king again.

"Watch out!" She jabbed a finger at the wall and raised her voice. "The attacker is up there!"

Nobody heard her amid the furore; the guards were too busy trying to disentangle the king from his litter to listen. King Daliel's crown had half fallen off, covering one side of his face, and she elbowed her way towards him.

"Your Majesty!" she shouted. "They're on the wall. Assassins."

This time, the guards reacted, but too late. The arrow hit one of them in the throat, and he collapsed with a gurgling cry. The litter pitched sideways again, and she lost sight of the king amongst the guards hurrying towards him.

I have to stop this. From this distance, she couldn't tell if the assassin was one of the Successors or merely some disgruntled member of the public, but they shouldn't have been able to access the city wall. Every time she managed to take a step closer, the crowd drove her back in a suffocating mass of human panic. She'd worn a dagger underneath her coat, strapped to her belt, but that wouldn't do any good with the assassin so far out of her reach.

This parade was a mistake, she thought, as another arrow whizzed through the air. *I should have done a better job of talking the king out of it. I should have...*

The arrow vanished somewhere in the press of guards who blocked her view of King Daliel's litter. From what she could tell, the guards were trying to drive him backwards towards the open gates to the palace, but the procession had merged with the panicking crowd into a chaotic mass that made it impossible to tell if there were any more threats lurking within the sea of faces. The arrows would have a harder time reaching their target once he was behind the palace walls, but how many innocent people would die in the process?

What was he thinking? She winced as another boot trod on her toes, and her bulky cloak tangled around her legs, further hindering her movements. With a curse, she tugged at the buttons to give herself some breathing room, and her fingers brushed against the belt she'd worn beneath layers of heavy tassels. As well as her army-issued dagger, she'd also brought a leather pouch containing something that she'd picked up at the last minute: a piece of one of Mekan's beasts.

On impulse, she reached into the pouch. As her fingertips grazed the leathery scales of Mekan's servant, a faint rasping whisper brushed against her ear. She recoiled with a gasp.

The dead. They're close.

She withdrew her hand in a flicker of shadow coiling around her fingers, but there were no signs of the dead in her immediate vicinity. Just panicked, terrified people and guards hurrying to protect their king.

Viam joined the latter, assuming that if the dead were indeed present, the king was the intended target. As she pushed her way through the thickening crowd near the palace gates, her gaze picked out a hooded figure dressed in dark clothing who certainly didn't look like they belonged to the king's staff. The glint of a dagger in an outstretched hand made their purpose plain to Viam.

"Assassin!" she shouted.

The general noise swallowed her shouts of warning, and the hooded figure continued to push forward. Viam reached into her coat again, this time gripping her dagger by the hilt as she ploughed towards the would-be attacker. She didn't dare draw her weapon for fear of accidentally stabbing someone innocent in the fray, but when she neared the gates, a familiar stench hit her.

Mekan.

Turning towards the source, she glimpsed a second hooded figure weaving amongst the panicked revellers. The smell alone caused people to veer away, and Viam held her breath as she pulled her dagger from its sheath.

If they're truly dead, I should be able to command them to stop. With her other hand, she reached for the piece of Mekan's realm and sent a silent command to the god of death.

The figure swivelled towards her but didn't stop moving. She raised the dagger, too slow to block as he barrelled into her; the violent force would have knocked her flat if not for the press of the crowd against her back keeping her upright.

The man's hood fell back to reveal a shaved skull that had half rotted, with strips of greying flesh hanging loose from the left side. His remaining eye shone, alert with manic intensity, as he seized her arm in a surprisingly firm grip.

"Traitor!" he yelled. "You betrayed Mekan, and you will die for it."

"What?" Choking on bile, she tried to free her dagger hand from his grip, but his other hand pressed a knife to her throat.

He's alive. He might be rotting, but he's breathing too. That must be why her command hadn't worked despite his decaying state.

The blade kissed her neck, drawing blood. On impulse, Viam let her grip break on her dagger, causing it to fall blade-first; the point sliced open her attacker's already-rotting cheek. She drove her knee

157

upward, aiming at his crotch, but the crowd's momentum caused her to fall into him with a hideous crunch that suggested more than his face was crumbling as he walked.

They fell. She crashed on him as his back slammed into the ground. Spying her dagger tangled in his cloak, she ripped it free and pressed the tip to his throat. "What do you mean, I betrayed Mekan?"

Shadows danced beneath his rotting skin, and to her horror, an answering shadow wrapped around her own fingers as her blade found its mark.

Blood gushed over her fingers, and the shadows thickened, coalescing around her weapon as the light died in his remaining eye.

"Thank you for the sacrifice," whispered the god of death.

Had Mekan *thanked* her for killing one of His followers? She reeled before the shouts erupting around her filtered in. *Shit. There was another assassin.*

Viam lurched to her feet, wiping her bloodied fingers on her coat. The crowd had pulled back from her and the dead man, but she'd lost sight of both the king and the hooded figure amidst the thick contingent of guards at the palace gates.

Who are they? What bargain did they make with Mekan?

The crowd surged again, pushed in the other direction by a group of robed figures of a very different kind. Orange and red broke apart the blue-and-gold sea as the Disciples of the Flame parted the crowd with ease.

"Over here!" she shouted at them. "Here! The dead—"

Flames seared the side of her face, causing her to jump sideways to avoid being singed. White fire engulfed the dead man's body, reducing the assassin to a pile of ashes in the time it took to blink.

The Disciples didn't so much as glance at her. She might as well be another faceless member of the crowd.

"Wait." She spun and ran after the robed figures, but they continued to ignore her as they carved a path through the crowd towards the still-open gates.

They're going into the palace.

———

Yala watched the unfolding chaos from her vantage atop the war drake's back where it hovered behind one of the towers atop the city wall. Niema sat behind her, though war drakes weren't supposed to bear more than one rider, and the tight space meant her legs were uncomfortably pressed against the beast's thick neck. As this was the only way they could both see Ceremonial Square and Niema's abilities were needed to keep the beast under control, she suffered the heat and the discomfort and waited for the inevitable.

Yala's sharp eyes saw the first arrow as it flew from somewhere on their right. She lifted her head and spied the hooded figure up on one of the higher ramparts. "Niema!"

"Up there!" Niema whistled at the war drake, while Yala risked a glance down at the square. The arrow had missed its target, but the crowd dissolved into instant chaos, and a second arrow followed shortly after.

"Don't you even think about it." She urged the war drake onward, conscious of Niema clinging to her back. "Kill them."

The war drake descended upon the city wall in a sweeping glide, its claws pinning the assassin down. The man's hood fell back, exposing a bearded face and a mouth stretched in a scream that might have been either terror or ecstasy or both. Blood bubbled up as the war drake ripped his body open like a piece of groundfruit.

"Ah, fuck," she muttered. "Should've kept him alive to question."

"Yala!" Niema gasped in her ear. "There are others in the crowd... I sense them."

Yala did, too, a tingle in her fingertips that pointed her towards the square, but she wouldn't have had a hope of identifying any individual person in the crush, much less anyone who might answer to Mekan. "I can't fly the war drake down there."

Though Niema held complete control over the beast, the risks were too high that she'd lose control amid the general chaos, and they'd been spotted already. A few guards gathered on the city wall, pointing at the war drake and exclaiming. One pointed a crossbow at them.

"Look down there!" Yala yelled. "There are your assassins, not us."

As she spoke, the crowd moved in a sudden surge, parting around a spot on the ground where Viam knelt upon a hooded man. Crimson soaked her hands beneath the long sleeves of her heavy-looking coat.

"Good," she murmured in satisfaction. Viam had had her eyes open for trouble, but assassins rarely walked alone, and—"What in hells are *they* doing?"

The door to the Temple of the Flame lay wide open, and several Disciples had begun to move across the square. Everyone hastened to get out of the way as a jet of flame shot towards the body at Viam's feet, engulfing it in an instant.

"What are they playing at?" She leaned over the war drake's side, watching in disbelief as the robed figures made directly for the palace.

To reach the king, the assassins would have to get through the still-open gates to the palace, the one place she hadn't a hope of landing.

"There!" Niema extended a hand to point at a hooded figure attempting to duck out of sight amid the crowd inside the palace gates. "Yala—no, don't fly the war drake there!"

"Too late." Yala ducked as an arrow came flying past—not from the assassins but from the wall; some of the guards had clearly concluded the pair of them intended to attack the king. "Command the war drake to pick up the assassin. Preferably alive."

"What?"

"Quickly!" Yala leaned forward, and Niema muttered a curse under her breath before shifting into a whispered prayer.

They ducked into a low dive, and the crowd flung themselves flat as wind gusted from the war drake's wings. Yala kept her focus on her target, her hands twitching in tandem with the war drake's claws as it swiped at the fallen assassin.

The would-be assassin screamed, hood flying back to reveal long curls and the delicate features of a female noble, legs kicking as she was lifted into the air.

"Why'd *you* join Mekan?" Yala ducked another arrow from somewhere near the gates. "Niema!"

Another whistle, and the war drake flew higher. The woman kept squirming, heedless of the drop, so Yala urged the war drake to land in a nearby street. Too close to the palace for her liking, but almost nobody stood near the back entrance. Everyone must have gone to watch or join the parade. A banner lay strewn across the path, gold-and-blue sheen dulled by trampling footprints.

"What the—*fuck*, Yala!" Niema gasped. "You could have got someone killed."

"I trusted you to control our steed." She leaned forward over the hooded figure pinned beneath the war drake's claw. "And now, we have something more priceless than gold. A living witness."

"*Living?*" Niema recoiled when the woman looked up at them, her eyes blazing with intensity.

"You don't intimidate me," she spat. "Your simple beast is nothing compared to those Mekan has created."

"Why did you want to kill the king?" asked Yala. "No, don't bother answering that. I kind of want to kill him myself after this. Whose orders are you following?"

"I am already His," she said. "I have no fear of you, betrayer."

"Betrayer?" Yala's hands itched to close around her throat. "You might be Mekan's servant, but you can still feel pain, and He won't come to your rescue if I set my war drake upon you."

"You can never truly comprehend Him." The woman coughed, a violent spasm that almost impaled her chest on the war drake's claws. "He is remaking me into His image. I will shed all pain and disease when I join Him."

Well, that's inconvenient. "If you mean by dying, you're halfway there already."

If the hooded garment was removed, Yala was willing to bet the woman's body would be rotting like that man who'd attacked her at the docks. Yet her heart was still beating, Yala was sure. What deal had she made with Mekan? Did she have a hope of getting a word of sense out of a zealot, save perhaps for feigning interest in the hopes that the woman might think her a potential ally?

"I will be with Him soon," she said. "And you will be nothing."

"I'm a Disciple of Death." Yala calmed her tone to a level that might suggest polite curiosity. "What makes you call me a traitor? Are you and I not more alike than not?"

"You stopped Him from taking this city. He might forgive, but we do not." More coughing, violent and sharp, as though she was gargling glass.

Suddenly, Niema extended a hand from behind Yala, and a bright-green light dazzled her eyes. The light spread outward from Niema's palm and over the woman's body, settling upon her skin like a shroud.

"No!" Mekan's follower shrieked in apparent genuine distress. "Stop that, Disciple of the Traitorous One!"

"You're healing her." Yala watched, disbelieving, as Niema whispered a final prayer and withdrew her hands, while the woman writhed and sobbed on the ground.

"I thought it was worth a try," she whispered to Yala. "That should have healed her. What's wrong?"

"Apparently, she wants to rot and fall to pieces." Giving up on her brief attempt to feign accord, Yala raised her voice and addressed the assassin. "You should thank Niema. Maybe you'll live long enough to have second thoughts about pledging yourself to someone who wants to possess your rotting corpse."

"You have *no* understanding!" the woman shrieked. "I have made my peace. My body and soul will be with Mekan forever."

She might well be right, but at what cost? Did she care?

"Yala," Niema whispered. "We're being watched."

So they were. A female guard ran towards them, breathless enough to suggest that she'd followed them all the way from the square, her boots trailing the remnants of a dropped blue-and-gold flag. In her moment of distraction, Yala missed the assassin lunge upward, impaling herself upon the war drake's claws. An expression of what Yala could only describe as rapture passed over her face as the assassin choked, "I'm coming, Mekan!"

"Don't you fucking dare die." Yala leaned forward until she was perilously close to falling off the war drake's back. "You're one of the Successors, right? Who's in charge now?"

The dying woman looked her in the eyes, her mouth stretched in a manic grin. "The king."

16

When the wave hit the island, the Disciples of the Sky and soldiers alike scattered. Kelan took flight a moment too late; saltwater filled his mouth, soaking him from head to toe.

Pushing sopping hair out of his eyes, Kelan saw the Rafragorian soldiers had fared even worse. Without the ability to fly, they'd been swept off the island and were flailing in the water, while the wave must have broken the ropes securing their sea drakes. Kelan glimpsed a scaly shape vanish under the water, abandoning its rider.

Behind the Rafragorians, several figures swam towards their group, their arms and legs cutting through the tumultuous waves. Not one of them rode on a sea drake, and as they swam, the waves calmed, the ocean's surface around the island falling still.

Those are Disciples of the Sea. They weren't dressed like the Disciples he knew; each figure wore a single garment of reeds, not unlike the ones favoured by the Disciples of Life, and other adornments were woven into their long hair. They were armed with carved knives of a bone-white colour that Kelan took a moment to recognise as the spines and teeth of sea drakes. It made sense, as metal would rust in the water, but his moment of fascination turned to panic as they drew closer, and the water began to churn again.

A bluish-green glow rose to the surface, and the Rafragorian soldiers thrashed and screamed, caught in the ocean's unforgiving embrace. The rising waves engulfed the island and lapped at Kelan and the others' feet too, threatening to pull them into its midst.

"Peace," Kriam called to them. "We're Larian. We're on your side."

"We've come to pay a diplomatic visit to your Superior," Kelan added. "Also, I don't think drowning Rafragoria's soldiers will win you any favours. We were just about to come to an understanding, in fact."

Lakiel groaned. The Disciples didn't say a word in response, but the waves dropped in height, and the soldiers' struggles became less frantic as the newcomers drew closer to Kelan and the others.

"You have no appointment with our Superior." The first to speak was a hard-faced male Disciple with long hair knotted into an elaborate style that put Kelan in mind of the high-ranked Disciples of the Flame. The man spoke Larian with a strong accent that was nevertheless more understandable to Kelan's ears than the Rafragorian language. "You would not survive it."

"What—going underwater?" His gaze moved between their group, counting five—no, six hostile faces watching them from the water. "We're here on orders from our Superior. I believe she sent you a message."

"She did." The Disciple was silent for a moment, his expression unyielding. "She and you cannot hope to undo decades of betrayal, Disciples of the Sky."

"Betrayal?" Lakiel asked, his voice hoarse. "By whom?"

Behind the Disciples, Kelan glimpsed one of the Rafragorian soldiers climbing back onto his sea drake mount. As he didn't move to attack, Kelan was inclined to leave him to flee the scene with his life.

"You really can breathe underwater?" he asked the Disciple.

The man inclined his head. "As your deity gives you mastery over the sky, ours enables us to make our home here in the ocean."

Handy. Come to think of it, if he got too near to the Temple of the

Sea, would his own abilities stop working too? If so, going into the water would be a death sentence regardless of the Disciples' intentions towards their group. Perhaps that was why Superior Shralin had tried to warn them off. Yet this talk of betrayal hinted at a deeper grudge, and not one his own Superior had been aware of.

"If not in your temple, can we talk somewhere more convenient?" He kept one eye on Lakiel, whose face was leached of colour and whose cloak was plastered to his arm with blood as well as water. "You might have noticed one of us is injured."

The Disciples raised their hands—Kelan tensed, expecting an attack—but instead of advancing, they remained still and raised their voices in a wordless song. No, a prayer. The sea levels dropped, exposing the rocky promontory once more, and continued to lower until there was more than enough space for Kelan and the others to land on solid ground. The Rafragorian soldiers ceased their struggle but didn't return to the island; two had vanished, having either drowned or found their way back to their steeds. Most likely the latter; they were nearly as comfortable in the water as these newcomers were. *Not quite, though.*

When Kelan landed upon the rock, he addressed the Disciples of the Sea in a bright voice. "I think we should start over. I'm Kelan, and this is Lakiel, Brikel, Kriam, and Ranit." He pointed to the others in turn as they landed in a close-knit group.

The long-haired male Disciple swam up to the island's edge but didn't get out of the water. "I am Nanek, and this is Yalian. We're ranked second to the Superior."

The woman, dark-skinned and broad-shouldered, emerged from the water. Her pleated hair was adorned with what looked like seashells. "You need to leave. You're lucky the Rafragorians didn't kill you."

"They're a bit far from home, aren't they?" Kelan commented.

"I might say the same of you," Nanek said. "If your Superior sent you to ask us for a favour, she's wasting her time."

"We're not," Kelan and Lakiel both said at the same time; the latter's jaw tensed as though outraged that he and Kelan had had the same thought.

"We're not," Kelan added again. "We were sent to meet a group of Rafragorian ambassadors a few days ago, but we found them murdered. Not a single one survived. We came here to ask if you saw who killed them."

"You found the bodies?" said Nanek. "Then you know very well what killed them."

His companion spat into the water. "Those who speak to Mekan and call His foulness into this realm get what they deserve."

"We're in agreement." *They know.* Surely, they'd be glad of the help in driving Mekan's influence away from the water. "I don't think it was the Rafragorians who killed their own ambassadors, but Laria stands to take the blame. We need to find proof that we didn't kill them."

"What proof?" Yalian said. "Any evidence, if it exists, will have long since been washed away by the tides."

"Then can't you act as witnesses?" he asked. "You must run into the Rafragorians all the time. Can you speak the language too?"

He didn't think their request was unreasonable, but it was difficult to know what might anger these people. They'd calmed, but he would never forget the incident he'd witnessed in Amanar all those years ago. The Disciples didn't look like people who'd intentionally drowned a child—a Larian child, even—but their secrets might lie buried as deep as the oceans in which they made their home.

"So you do want a favour," said Nanek. "Our answer is no."

"Even if Laria takes the blame for the deaths and is dragged into war as a consequence?" Kelan glanced at Lakiel and the others, hoping one of them would offer a more compelling argument. "Do you really want an escalation of the sort that saw your water turn into a battle-field for so many decades?"

"You never saw war, Disciples," growled Nanek. "You lived in your tower, far away, while our home was flooded with corpses and the taste of blood lingered on our tongues for months."

"You'll get more of that if you ignore this." They must have already seen Mekan's activity offshore. Water held no boundaries, the same as the tunnels in Setemar hadn't prevented Mekan from infiltrating the Temple of the Earth. "You must have seen Mekan's beasts roaming around. It wasn't Rafragoria who called them into this realm, was it? It was someone from Laria."

"We do not involve ourselves with Mekan's followers," said Yalian. "They seek only the destruction of themselves and everyone around them."

"Like I said, we're in agreement," Kelan said. "We want these people gone too. What betrayal do you think we inflicted on you?"

"You ask too many questions." The man slid off the rock and into the water, which had risen to a much higher level; Kelan hastily glided off the ground to avoid being swept in another wave. Rather than rising into an assault, the sea lapped at the edges of the rocky outcrop, a reminder of their strength.

"Leave," said Nanek. "If you're lucky, you'll reach shore by nightfall."

What's that supposed to mean? "And if we're unlucky?"

Lakiel seized his arm and whispered in his ear. "Their meaning is plain. We have to get out of here."

"Whatever happened to fulfilling our Superior's command?" He faced Nanek again. "If war breaks out with Rafragoria, your people *will* suffer for it. Isn't it worth trying to avoid that?"

"It is not war with Rafragoria that concerns us," he said. "You'll do well to return to your tower, Disciples of the Sky."

Water splashed Kelan as the Disciples of the Sea vanished in a single smooth dive, leaving nothing behind but an expanse of still blueness.

———

"What?" Yala leaned over the war drake's back, her gaze fixed on the assassin. "What do you mean, the king?"

No response came; the woman's eyes stared up at the sky, sightless.

Her body was caked in gore from her impalement on the war drake's claws, yet a smile ghosted her pale lips.

"We need to take her somewhere else," whispered Niema. "Destroy her body before Mekan can infect anyone else."

Yala said nothing. Her thoughts roiled and tossed like ocean waves. *The king?*

"You!" shouted the female guard that Yala had quite forgotten about, who'd remained at the street's end at a safe distance from the war drake. "What are you playing at, flying that beast in the middle of the city?"

"We caught this assassin trying to get away," Yala said. "She was going after the king."

Or possibly working for him, she added silently, her mind refusing to grasp the implications.

The guard moved closer and halted, eyes widening. "You're Yala Palathar."

"Yes, and did you hear what I said? This woman was going to assassinate the king." Pulling herself together, Yala jerked her head at Niema. "I think we need to take her to the Disciples of the Flame."

Presumably, Superior Shralin wouldn't turn her away from disposing of a corpse that needed destroying. Assuming his people weren't still rampaging around the square, which was at least proof that they were capable of taking action when they wanted to.

Niema whistled a command, and the war drake lifted the dead woman's body into the air. The guard made a hasty retreat as its vast wings beat, angling towards Ceremonial Square.

The crowd had yet to disperse, but the guards had managed to corral everyone away from the gates long enough to draw them closed on the palace grounds. She hadn't a hope of getting close to the palace, and no orange or red robes leapt out at her amid the blur of blue and gold. *They already left?*

"Leave the body in front of the temple door," she told Niema. "I'll get down and speak to them."

"I won't be able to keep the war drake still for long," Niema warned. "We're too close to the crowd."

"Fine." Yala braced herself. "Take the beast to the paddock. I'll make my way back home."

When they reached the temple stairs, she swung her leg over the war drake's side. She landed awkwardly on her cramped legs, wishing she'd brought her cane. The war drake's claws released the dead woman's body, and it thudded onto the steps. Teeth gritted, Yala seized the body around the shoulders and dragged it upward to the temple doors.

She didn't need to knock. Novice Yachim answered, and at the sight of the body, he whimpered and swayed against the doorframe.

"I need your Superior," Yala ordered, breathless, between twinges of pain in her leg. "Now."

The novice fled, while Yala picked up the woman's body by the armpits again and dragged it into the entryway to wedge the door open.

"What are you doing?" demanded a voice from behind her.

Yala tilted her head. Niema had pulled the war drake into retreat, with the result that she had a clear view of the square and the Disciple crossing towards her with his face set in righteous anger. As he drew closer, she recognised him as the man who'd shown up at her house to interrogate Niema.

"Who is this?" Superior Shralin appeared, breathless, a vein popping in his forehead when he saw the body Yala had left in the doorway. "Another assassin?"

"Yes." A flickering in the corner of her eye prompted Yala to lean to the side to avoid the flames that brushed the side of her face on their way to the dead assassin's body. Pain spasmed up her leg when she put her full weight on it to avoid being burned to a crisp, but the Disciple's face showed not a hint of remorse.

"Danir." The Superior addressed her assailant. "Be more careful."

He didn't sound much like he'd have cared if she'd been incinerated. Yala readjusted her balance, again wishing she had her cane. "Do either of you want to hear what the assassin confessed to me?"

"Ravings, no doubt," said Superior Shralin. "She intended to assassinate the king."

Did she? Yes, her words might have been mere ravings, but a lie as outrageous as the one that had passed her lips snagged on the inside of Yala's mind, refusing to budge.

"She was a Disciple of Death," said Yala. "I assume your Disciples caught the others. Did you ask any questions before you burned them alive?"

Heat brushed against her neck as Danir moved in behind her. "Should I throw her out, Superior Shralin?"

"No." Superior Shralin leaned closer, his headdress slipping to expose his receding hairline. "Not yet. Yala is having trouble understanding that we are doing our best to protect the monarch and that it's not our job to interrogate assassins."

"I never said it was," she said. "It seems prudent to understand our enemy, does it not?"

Might the king not be as oblivious to Corruption as everyone had thought? Superior Shralin was not the person to ask, and neither was the hulking nuisance behind her, but to imply that he'd ordered the attack on his own parade—gods, she wished one of the other assassins had survived long enough for a proper interrogation.

When the Superior gave no reply, she added, "Speaking of enemies, why did you warn Kelan and the others against speaking to the Disciples of the Sea? That seems outside of the realm of your job too."

The Superior responded through gritted teeth. "I would have thought it would be obvious. Nobody can be trusted outside of our borders."

"Some can't be trusted *inside* our borders." The Disciple behind her seized her upper arms with the heat of a naked flame, and she bit back a yell of pain. "She got our people killed in Setemar."

Setemar. Eyes watering, Yala twisted in the Disciple's grip. "What is your problem?"

"Release her, Danir," said Superior Shralin in tones that Yala might have examined closer if she hadn't been fighting to keep herself from screaming. *Fuck,* that hurt.

The Disciple peeled his hands from her arms, leaving a trail of agony in his wake. "Trust me, she's better off dead."

"Speak for yourself." She gasped the words, arms instinctively wrapping around her chest; the heat pulsed against her skin through her thin shirt. "Do you regularly let your Disciples assault the public?"

"You're no ordinary citizen, Yala." Some regret spilled into Superior Shralin's voice, but he made no move to help her. "Tell your Disciple of Life friend to take the advice that the Disciples of the Sky ignored and keep her spies away from the docks if she doesn't want to share their fate."

"I'll do no such thing." *Share their fate?* Was that a threat? Worry for Kelan rose in the back of her mind, but her hands trembled too much even to reach for a weapon in self-defence. "Tell your Disciples to mind their fucking manners."

She held her breath, half-expecting another burst of flame as Danir brushed past her on his way into the temple. He'd done enough damage, judging by the painful tingling in her fingertips, and his words had etched themselves on her mind as though his flames had scorched more than her skin.

She got our people killed in Setemar.

Mieren. Yala had killed her... and Mieren had all but confessed to having worked with the assassins who'd murdered the king.

Had Danir too?

If so, and more of the conspirators against King Tharen had survived, it wasn't Mekan's deranged followers whom she had to worry about the most but those who'd sought to prevent His return.

Those who'd been willing to murder the king of Laria in order to ensure peace.

———

By the time the crowd had dispersed enough for the palace gates to close, the king had long since vanished amidst a retinue of guards. Viam could only hope that no more assassins had sneaked inside during the chaos, because the Disciples of the Flame had not accompanied them into the palace and had instead returned to their temple on the other side of the gate.

As for Yala... Viam had seen the war drake flying away from the upper city, but she hadn't been able to tell if Yala had been on its back. She hadn't a hope of leaving the palace grounds for a long while, so she focused her attention on watching the dispersing crowd for potential threats.

Ducking around a pair of panicking servants, Brenat came hurrying to meet her. "Gods, Viam. Isn't that twice now that you've saved His Majesty's life?"

Viam's gut twisted. "He shouldn't have been out in public. This was a mistake. I should have..."

"Should have what?" Brenat pressed. "Don't blame yourself. The king's as stubborn as his father used to be. Besides, the Disciples of the Flame were ready to act against those assassins."

"Not until it was too late." The comparison to King Tharen brought an unwelcome jolt to the heart; would anyone have dared to shoot arrows at *him* during a parade? Had his public display had the opposite effect than he'd intended, showcasing his vulnerability for the population of Dalathar to witness?

And the Disciples of the Flame? They'd come across as the saviours that day, yet they hadn't stayed to enjoy their victory. A scan of the palace grounds showed her the staff vanishing back into their respective buildings but not a single red or orange cloak to be seen.

"You don't like them, do you?" Brenat observed. "The Disciples, that is. This is about more than a few books."

"It's complicated." That was putting it mildly. "They were cruel to a friend of mine, back in the army."

"Yala?"

"Not her." Some secrets weren't hers to tell, but alluding to Dalem's history with the Disciples was safer than hinting at the crimes they'd committed against the former king.

Brenat wasn't easy to fool, but she accepted the diversion with a nod. "All right. Want to go back to the staff quarters?"

"I should check on the war drakes. Make sure the noise didn't disturb them too much." Her heart twisted when Brenat's face fell, but the notion of spending the remainder of her day off trapped inside was too much to bear. She needed to take her mind off the close call she'd had—that the *king* had had.

Away from the crowd, she could smell the burning stench of the incinerated dead on her coat. Probably, she ought to have changed into something more suitable for outdoor work, but returning to the staff quarters would mean facing questions from the others, all of whom would know about her supposed heroics after Brenat had told them everything. Instead, she walked across the rapidly emptying palace grounds. Bloody tassels swung from her coat, and her hands were sticky with dried gore, yet she felt as detached from her physical body as she did from the rumbling noise inside the barracks. Over the fence, Viam glimpsed soldiers still dressed in their finery from the parade gathering in a confused mass while senior officials moved amongst them, relaying orders and conversing in hushed voices. She ducked her head and continued to the gates, where a barrel-chested guard recognised her at once.

"You!" he gasped. "You're the one who saved the king."

Viam bit back a protest; for once, her conspicuous actions worked in her favour. "I'm here to check the war drakes weren't disturbed by the noise." Her excuse rang hollow, yet both guards gazed at her in such awe that she might have announced that she needed to borrow a weapon, and they'd have wordlessly handed over their swords.

"We're not supposed to let anyone in or out, but..." The first guard exchanged glances with his companion. "But we can make an exception for you."

Guilt and relief churned inside Viam as she hurried past the guards and around the corner to the paddock. She unlocked the gate with shaking hands, and when she reached the other side, her legs finally gave way. Gasping, she sank to the ground in the mud, her body trembling.

A hissing growl prompted her to lift her head. A war drake watched from its hut, wings beating against its restraints, teeth biting at the inside of its muzzle. *Right. I still smell of the dead.*

Watching it struggle, she was seized with the impulse to take off its restraints and let the beast soar into the sky as it deserved.

"We're both trapped," she whispered. "I almost wish you'd been invited to the parade. What's the use in having a deadly war steed at your disposal if you can't use it against assassins?"

"A valid question," came a breathless voice from the other side of the fence. "Thought I'd find you here."

"Yala." Viam jumped to her feet. "What are you doing?"

"Looking for you." When she opened the gate, Yala hobbled into the paddock. She looked ghastly, her face soaked in sweat and her arms hanging limply at her sides.

Viam reached out an uncertain hand but didn't quite dare touch Yala's arm; it was obvious she was in a great deal of pain. "What happened to you?"

"I had a run-in with the Disciples of the Flame." She leaned against the fence and closed her eyes. "I can't stay long, but I need to talk to you alone. It's about the king."

"The king?" Viam's legs were still trembling, and she rested her back against the fence beside Yala to steady herself. "The dead—are they gone? Did you take them to the Disciples of the Flame?"

She must have—but why had one of the Disciples attacked her? The man who'd burned the king's assassin had come close to catching Viam in the path of his flames, so an accident was plausible, but an uneasy pit opened in her stomach.

"Yes," Yala replied. "Before she died, one of the assassins said that the person giving her orders was the king himself."

"What?" Viam lurched away from the wall. "How can he have ordered his own assassination?"

"I can't say she was in her right mind," Yala said, "but are you *sure* that the king hasn't been meddling with Corruption?"

"It's not true." Her thoughts swam. "He wouldn't. I know he wouldn't."

"Do you know him, Viam?" Yala pushed away from the fence, sweat standing out on her forehead. "Do you really know him?"

Did she? Her mind reeled, refusing to believe Yala's words. "It doesn't make any sense for *him* to be—look, Yala, you're hurt. Who did that to you?"

"A Disciple named Danir." Her lip curled. "It was no accident, Viam. They know."

"Know what?" The war drake's growling sounded very far away, as though she was trapped on the other side of a glass wall. "Yala?"

"He knows I killed Mieren, which means there's a chance he was among the group who ordered King Tharen's assassination." Yala moved closer, enough for Viam to see the pain etched into every line of her face. "This might be my only chance to tell you. I know how little sense it makes, but the assassin told me with her last breath that the king ordered the attack, and it's up to you what you want to do with that information."

She pushed open the gate and walked out, while Viam's hands rose to cover her face. Her breath came in quick gasps. *No. It can't be true.*

It couldn't be. King Daliel wasn't his father. He'd never touched Corruption. It didn't make sense. But Yala—

Yala wouldn't lie to her.

No. I'll talk to the king. If he'll tell anyone the truth... I have to hope it'll be me.

17

Niema didn't like the idea of leaving Yala alone on the steps of the Temple of the Flame, but keeping the war drake in the upper city was out of the question with the guards shooting arrows at anyone who they saw as a potential threat. With reluctance, she flew the beast back to the paddock, part of her marvelling at how relatively silent the outskirts of the city were compared to the mass of noise she'd left behind. The air felt clear, the stench of the river almost refreshing after the foulness of Mekan's servants.

The beast landed. She didn't know how to put its muzzle or chain back on, so she whistled a complex command to sink into a deep sleep and hoped the war drake remained in slumber until Yala's return.

As she left the paddock, a bright flash drew her gaze; a large bird flew towards her at speed, holding a piece of parchment in its clawed feet.

Another letter from Superior Kralia. Niema's heart raced as she extended a hand towards the bird and retrieved the paper. The timing, she was sure, was no coincidence.

Her Superior's letter began with the ominous words, *I watch the capital with great concern.*

"Is she watching us right now?" She addressed the bird, which hovered in midair with the placidity of an animal coaxed to obey by a Disciple of Life. "If she is, she doesn't need me to tell her what's going on."

The bird said nothing, of course, and Niema turned her attention back to the letter. *Everyone at home is well, though your enclave members miss you very much, especially the younger ones. They worry about you, as do I. Dalathar is not made for people like us, and Yalet has little power where the god of the flames holds sway. I would ask you to reconsider my offer and return home.*

A rush of unexpected anger seized her. How much did Superior Kralia value Niema's life? Yes, she might claim that her decision to control Niema against her will had been justified at the time, but a cage forged by the god of life's power was a cage all the same.

Niema lowered her hands, her mind whirling. If Superior Kralia was watching the city, had she also seen the assassins, the rotting servants of Mekan who were somehow alive and dead at the same time?

"Is it you?" she asked of the bird. "Are you watching the city and reporting to her, or is she in contact with the Disciples of the Flame?"

If the latter, it wouldn't be the first time, but the little information in the note seemed calculated to stir Niema's curiosity, and it wouldn't be enough to convince Niema to abandon her hard-won freedom. She would not allow herself to become an instrument in another's hand again.

Niema whistled to the bird, uttering a command to fly as far as possible from the city and enclave alike. Then she made her way back to Yala's house, her body taut with apprehension. Every so often, she glanced up at the rooftops to reassure herself she wasn't being followed.

A commotion echoed from behind Yala's door; when she knocked, Saren answered in a state of breathless dishevelment. "Thank the gods you're back. We need you."

"Why?" Her gaze landed on Yala, who half lay against the armchair, her face taut with pain. "What's wrong?"

Yala groaned. "Fuckers burned my arms."

"Let me help you." She crossed the room and extended her hands, whispering a prayer. Green light bloomed in her palms and spread to Yala's upper arms, enveloping her skin. "Is that better?"

Yala sighed with relief and reached for her collar with a steadier hand. When she pulled her shirt down on one side, Niema recoiled. Her upper arm bore a mark in the shape of a handprint, and flakes of blackened skin peeled from the newly healed flesh.

"Who did this?" Saren knelt beside Yala.

"One of our least favourite Disciples." Yala lifted her head, her face streaked with sweat and curls clinging to her forehead. "Did it in full view of his Superior, in fact."

"Why?" Saren reached for her arm, but she shook him off.

"Why else?" Yala lurched to her feet in a movement that surely hurt her injured leg. "King Tharen's murderers figured out that I killed Mieren and that I know what they did to the former king. They sent those mercenaries, too, I'm sure of it."

Saren's attention jumped to the door as though he expected a band of sellswords to burst into the room, brandishing weapons. "Fuck."

Niema could only nod. After the brutal chaos in the upper city and the shock of her Superior's note, her nerves were frayed to ribbons like an old cloth. She crossed the room to her sleeping mat and sank onto it, drawing her knees up to her chest.

"Well." Yala sat in the armchair with a wince and stretched out her injured leg. "Ideally, we need to kill Danir the next time he shows up on our doorstep, and any other people who might know the truth. Preferably before Superior Shralin puts two and two together."

"You can't murder a bunch of Disciples," Saren said, echoing Niema's thoughts. "Yes, I know you killed that Mieren and her friend, but there weren't any witnesses, were there?"

"Exactly." Yala shifted her position, leaning forward in the chair. "It was easier to pin their deaths on another cause when I wasn't in the capital. The Disciples have the power here, but they're also held in check by their Superior. If Danir had outright incinerated me, he'd have been demoted."

"You'd be *dead*," Niema spluttered. "What if he decided it was worth the risk of punishment? And—did you mean he was the one who came to the house too?"

"Yes." Yala's curled fist rested on her knee. "He did. I'd guess the only reason he didn't torch this place is because he was outnumbered and there was a Disciple of Life present."

"You'd prefer to take him out before he gets another chance," Saren surmised. "I'm sure Nalen will be happy to get rid of the body for you."

"You can't be serious." Niema's very instincts rebelled against taking a life, even one of a murderer, and from the way Yala's eyes narrowed at her, she knew it too. Grasping for practical arguments instead, Niema went on. "There's no chance you'll get away with murdering a Disciple of the Flame in their own city. You'd be imprisoned, or..."

"Sentenced to death," Saren said. "That's assuming you don't get burned to a crisp in the process. There's got to be another way."

"Justice." Yala lifted her head, her eyes ablaze once more. "Who better to enact justice than Dalathik Himself?"

"What?" Saren said. "You can't petition the god of the flames. You're a *Disciple of Death.*"

"No, but if a Disciple disobeys their Superior, the god of the flames takes notice," Yala said. "Superior Shralin is His voice now, not Superior Datriem. The conspirators, however many survived, have to obey him. I'm not sure he even knows they killed King Tharen."

"You don't plan to *tell* him that," Saren said. "He'd never believe you."

"I know." Irritation flickered across Yala's face. "He *might* believe I killed Danir in self-defence if it comes down to it, but I'd rather not wait for that eventuality. The way Danir was acting suggests that he might come after me again at the first opportunity, but the upper city gates will be closed until morning at the least. Even Disciples will have a hard time getting in and out. That'll give us time to plan."

"Not much of it," Saren said. "Enough to flee the city... maybe."

Superior Kralia's note flitted into Niema's mind's eye. *Yalet has little power where the god of the flames holds sway.* Had she meant to hint at the threat the Disciples of the Flame posed to her and the others? There was little doubt that Danir would incinerate Niema, too, if she stood between him and Yala, but she might be misunderstanding. Superior Kralia didn't know...

Did she? Superior Kralia certainly held some awareness of Corruption's prior existence in Laria if she'd known that a temple devoted to Mekan had once existed in the place where the Temple of the Earth now stood. If she'd known about the *other* temple, on the island, had she known of King Tharen's interest? Had Superior Datriem told her?

And did she know the Disciples of the Flame planned to have him killed?

————

Viam left the paddock, the shock of Yala's claims reverberating through her skull like a drumbeat. *The king... he can't be using Corruption. Yala must be mistaken.*

The Disciples of the Flame had attacked Yala. *That* was no mistake, and if they'd worked out Yala's knowledge of their role in the last king's death, how long until they realised that Viam was also aware of their crimes?

Viam was walking past the barracks when another guard ran up to her. "Viam Tiathar? The king would like to speak with you."

"Now?" Apprehension knotted in her chest as she hurried after the guard. Few signs of the parade remained on the way to the palace save for the vibrant flags and banners littering the ground. Through the front gates, she glimpsed a few scattered individuals and groups but no sign of the crows.

She climbed the staircase to the palace doors, suddenly conscious that her uniform was dirt-stained and drenched in sweat, but she didn't have time to run back to the staff quarters to change. If the king wanted to see her so soon after the attempt on his life, he must have good reason.

The guards led her to the main receiving room, where the king waited. King Daliel had changed back into his normal attire and looked none the worse for wear for his narrow escape earlier, thank the gods, but Viam couldn't look him in the eyes after what she'd heard from Yala. Heart racing, she knelt and bowed her head.

"Rise, Viam," he said. "Didn't I tell you that you don't need to demonstrate excessive formalities with me?"

"My apologies." Yala's words had set off a whirlwind in her head and made it quite impossible to judge her own actions. "You wanted to talk to me?"

"Firstly, I wanted to apologise for not listening to your warnings," he said. "And, of course, to thank you for your efforts in saving my life."

"The Disciples of the Flame were more responsible than I was." Abruptly, she thought of Yala's face and felt sickened with herself.

"They helped, but you were more prepared," said the king. "I certainly made the right choice in asking you to stand at my side."

Viam's mind blanked. "I hope the assassins were caught. The Disciples of the Flame were here…"

Had they spoken to the king when they'd come into the palace grounds? She didn't think they had, but Yala's pained expression was hard to forget, as was her insistence that the dying assassins were taking orders from—

Are you dabbling in Corruption? The words hovered on her tongue. It'd be easy to bluff, to pretend she'd heard the words from the mouth of her own attacker—but if Yala had been mistaken, Viam was the one who'd suffer the consequences. The palace walls might be the only shield between her and the Disciples of the Flame.

"I believe they removed the attackers," said the king. "I have to admit, I didn't expect their quick actions. It seems in poor taste for me not to repay them."

"Repay them?" He couldn't be implying what she thought she was. "How?"

"For a start, I think it's time I forgave the Disciples of the Flame for banishing them from the palace after my father's death."

"No." The word came out, unbidden, and her mouth went dry. "I apologise, Your Majesty, but I don't think that's a good idea."

"You don't?" His brow furrowed. "You believe they didn't act fast enough?"

"Yes." She leapt on the excuse. "They had a better view from the temple than most people. And—and if they'd accepted your invitation to join the parade, the attackers might not have got as close to you as they did."

"That might well be true," he said. "In any case, someone else was instrumental in preventing the attack from getting any further out of control if the rumours I've heard from my staff are true."

"Rumours?"

"Concerning your friend Yala Palathar."

Yala. Her body tensed, recalling Yala's desperate, half-crazed expression. "She was here?"

Her lie sounded feeble to her own ears, but the king had been safely inside the palace grounds before Yala and her war drake had appeared within full view of Ceremonial Square. It was plausible that she might have missed the action too.

"Yes," said the king. "She played a role in saving my life and catching the assassins."

"Yala is... she's good at what she does."

"That she is," he agreed. "To that end, I think it's about time I reinstated her former position formally. Would you be able to invite her to speak to me tomorrow? I wish to present her with a great honour."

———

Yala opened the war drake's paddock gate, Niema hovering anxiously behind her. A growl told her the beast hadn't fled despite being unsecured; Niema's command had done its job well.

Yala walked inside, leaning heavily on her cane. She shouldn't be walking around while there was a Disciple out for her blood, she knew, but she didn't trust anyone else to tend to the war drake, and Saren refused to leave the house.

"We should go while we can," she murmured to the war drake as she secured the chain around its neck. "Fly south. Stay in Setemar for a while, maybe, and then go and find a new cabin in the jungle."

"No," Niema protested. "You can't—"

"Not *that* part of the jungle," Yala clarified. "I know where to avoid, don't worry."

Niema chewed on her lower lip. "I... I understand why you want to leave, but I don't think it'll stop them from coming after you."

"No. You're probably right." Besides, Danir knew where she lived, and she wouldn't put it past him to incinerate anyone who refused to tell him where she'd gone. "It's the coward's way out, I know, but lying down and waiting to die isn't my style."

"They have limitations," Niema said. "The Disciples of the Flame, that is. There are places they can't go."

"Other temples," Yala said. "Pity creating a Temple of Death isn't a simple matter, and the instructions on how to do that are likely hidden inside the Temple of the Flame's own library.

Niema made a choked noise. "That's not what I meant. Didn't you say the—the island was destroyed by fire?"

"True." She surveyed the paddock. "I suppose if I spend the night here, he'll have a harder time getting near me."

"The fences are flammable," Niema protested. "So are the stables. If they attack you here, the war drake might panic."

"What of the dead war drake?"

Niema startled. "I haven't seen it since I got here."

"Neither have I." Not that she'd given Mekan much blood lately. She didn't carry the claw around as often, not when the war drake recoiled from the mere trace of Corruption.

The dead war drake might help. It's not my worst idea.

They'd have to act under cover of darkness to avoid too much attention, so Yala finished securing the war drake and returned home with Niema. The atmosphere between them was strained, and Saren nearly stormed out of the house when Yala retrieved the void drake's claw from under the floorboard.

When darkness swathed the streets, she walked outside, gripping the claw in her hand, and faced the sky.

"Mekan." She pressed the claw to the blood-damp trousers she'd worn earlier, wondering if the war drake's kill counted as her own. "I need a favour."

Movement at the street's end. *Not* the god of death but someone hurrying towards her. Yala reached for her dagger and then recognised Viam.

"Yala." Viam halted, staring at the claw. "What are you doing with that?"

"I thought you couldn't get out of the upper city."

"It took a while to convince the guards, but I have direct permission from the king." Viam spoke in a rush. "He's asked me to invite you to the palace tomorrow. For... for a promotion. I can tell him you said no?"

"Don't." Yala lifted her head, an idea taking form. "No, I'll come to the palace. Danir will have a hard time murdering me in full view of the king."

And, she thought, *this is just the opportunity I needed.*

———

Night had fallen by the time Kelan and the others reached the shore. They hadn't a hope of getting back to the capital before nightfall, so they returned to the Disciples' Inn in Amanar. The staff provided a warm meal of stewed fish with vegetables and as much rice wine as they could drink, but what should have been a peaceful evening swiftly devolved into an argument.

"The Disciples of the Sea made their stance clear." Lakiel jabbed his eating-knife into the air emphatically. "We can't force them to contact Rafragoria and tell them that we didn't kill their ambassadors. Especially if they've also been attacking Rafragoria's soldiers."

"True," Kelan acknowledged. "But if they know what's going on out there, it might be worth persisting."

"Interrogating them isn't part of our mission." Lakiel looked to Kriam, who nodded in agreement. The stoic Disciple had remained hunched over his plate throughout the meal. "Superior Sietra asked us to talk to the Disciples of the Sea to stop a war with Rafragoria, nothing more."

"What of the Rafragorians?" he queried. "We almost convinced them that we didn't kill the ambassadors. Granted, they might not be overly keen to meet with us again after the Disciples of the Sea tried to drown them, but I think we got the message across."

Brikel snorted. "I doubt that's the part they'll remember."

"Were the Rafragorians really trying to blame the Disciples of the Sea for murdering their ambassadors?" said Kelan. "Lakiel, Kriam, you speak Rafragorian. What were they saying?"

"I couldn't make sense of it. They seemed to think we were all to blame." Lakiel pressed his uninjured hand to his forehead; his other arm was bound in a sling. "We're lucky they didn't kill us on the spot."

"Why were they so far from their home in the first place?" Kelan scanned the others, whose expressions showed tiredness and confusion rather than curiosity. "Does the king know there are Rafragorian soldiers roaming near our shores?"

"I haven't a clue." Lakiel slumped. "I'm not arguing with you any longer, Kelan. I'm going to return to Skytower tomorrow, whether the rest of you elect to come with me or not."

That signalled an end to their conversation, and the others retired to bed. Kelan did the same, but despite the soft mattress cushioning his back, he tossed and turned like he was in a boat, assailed by unanswered questions.

The Disciples of the Sea hadn't remotely been what he'd expected, but neither had the Rafragorians. Why had they been willing to risk trespassing so close to Laria's shores? Maybe they'd been avoiding the same enemy. Rafragoria, as a seafaring nation, had surely noticed something amiss in the water. Were dead monsters washing up on their shores too?

He'd scarcely dozed off when a sudden crash jolted him back to wakefulness. The window of his upstairs room shattered; Kelan rolled off the bed to avoid being sprayed with glass. The source, a large rock, hit the wooden floor with a thud.

Similar noises came from downstairs, followed by a scream. Brikel.

Kelan threw himself out from behind the bed and scrambled for his weapon. Holding up his blade, he half crawled, half glided towards the shattered window. Below, he made out several figures dressed in the reed-woven garments of the Disciples of the Sea.

What are they doing? Hadn't they wanted him and the others to *leave* the ocean? Careful not to cut himself on the shattered glass clinging to the window frame, Kelan glided out of the open window and descended.

"You know, if you wanted to talk to us, you might have knocked on the front door."

In answer, a brutish-faced Disciple raised a bone-white knife. "You'll come with us, Disciple of the Sky."

"I'll have to decline." He reached for his blade, acutely aware that he'd left his cloak upstairs, and his thin shirt would offer little protection.

Another crash resounded, a door slammed, and two more Disciples of the Sea walked into view, dragging Lakiel by the feet. His lack of reaction when his head bumped against the doorstep suggested he was unconscious, his arm hanging limply at his side.

The brutish man bared his teeth at Kelan. "If you fight, he dies."

Kelan thoroughly regretted their choice to stay at an inn so close to the water. "It's going to be like that, is it?"

18

T he night turned the ocean into a dark slab, the moon's reflection a ghostly halo on the horizon. The Disciples of the Sea must know where they were going despite the darkness, moving at a relentless pace that only slowed occasionally to make sure Kelan and the others were following.

Kelan flew alongside Ranit and Kriam, none of them daring to risk Lakiel's safety by striking back against his kidnappers. Brikel was nowhere to be seen, at least, and Kelan hoped she'd managed to escape. Nothing but flat darkness surrounded them, and he tracked their progress by watching Lakiel's unconscious body bobbing in the water, held upward by a pair of Disciples of the Sea. The others circled their group, each holding a bone-white weapon forged from the sharp spine of a sea drake. Whenever one of them fell behind, a sharp jab at their legs prompted them along.

After a long period of silence, Kelan could no longer hold his tongue. "Might I ask what this is about? I assume you took issue with us meeting with your fellow Disciples?"

They hadn't killed Lakiel right away. That suggested they had a motive other than silencing their group unless they'd brought them out to sea to ensure nobody ever found the bodies.

"Be silent," one of the Disciples of the Sea returned. "Or your friend dies."

"Is your Superior giving you orders?" A suspicion took root inside him, which intensified when the Disciple raised his bone-white knife to jab at Kelan's leg. "Who do you answer to?"

Another jab, harder. Blood dripped down Kelan's shin and into the water. *Shit*, he thought, watching the crimson swirl on the surface. That would attract sea drakes or worse.

"Who?" Kelan glided to the right, avoiding another stab from the bone knife. "You aren't following a command from your Superior or your deity. Am I right?"

The man's sea-damp face gleamed in the moonlight, his eyes narrowing. "Quiet, Disciple."

"If you kill us, you'll draw attention." He grimaced as blood slid down his shin, stinging from the saltwater. "Or is that the idea?"

Mekan was drawn to blood, to death, but surely, the Disciples of the Sea wouldn't want to forsake their connection to the ocean when they depended upon it for their own survival.

The Disciple didn't answer, which cemented Kelan's certainty that their kidnappers had no connection to the group they'd met earlier, but that didn't mean Nanek and the others would come to their rescue. They had no way of knowing how close they might be to the Disciples' home, and from Kelan's admittedly inexpert knowledge of the ocean, they were heading northeast, in the opposite direction to the area in which they'd met the other Disciples of the Sea.

Did the Disciples expect them to fly throughout the night? What was their destination? Kelan's questions multiplied as the minutes trickled by, and still, the darkness remained absolute. His only clue as to their location came from the moon, high above, reflecting on the water.

Then a blot appeared on the moon's reflection, resolving into a winged shadow. Kelan lifted his gaze and saw the same shape in the sky, bigger and clearer, as black as the surrounding night.

Was that a void drake? The beast was too far away for him to make out any more details, but that wouldn't last for long if they kept going in this direction. He knew how fast those beasts could move, and his shoulder burned with the memory of their sharp claws. Any fate was better than that. Lakiel, if he'd been conscious, would agree.

Terethik, he thought, *don't forsake me now.*

He whispered a prayer, and the air stirred at his command. Noticing, his captor grabbed Kelan's leg and pulled him downward into the water. "If you call your deity, you die."

The saltwater stung his injured leg, but the sharp pain brought clarity that gave Kelan an idea. Nudging Ranit, who was closest, he whispered, "Grab Lakiel as soon as I move."

"Quiet." The Disciple tugged harder, dragging Kelan until the water reached his waist. The bone knife pressed against his throat.

Kelan took in a deep breath. Then he kicked out, splashing water into the Disciple's eyes. With one hand, he seized his captor's wrist and squeezed until he released his weapon, and with the other, he reached out to catch the bone knife. His fingers slid against the blade, drawing blood, but he managed to grip the hilt.

Nearby, Ranit had managed to seize Lakiel by the hands, but Kriam was bleeding from a wound to the shoulder, and three more Disciples of the Sea closed in around them. Kelan moved to help, but his attacker tugged on his leg, pulling Kelan below the water's surface.

Darkness closed over his head. He held his breath and kicked out, stabbing blindly with the knife until the man's grip on his leg broke. He rose upward, but the Disciple kept pace with him, brandishing another bone knife.

"This might have been painless," said one of the other Disciples in a guttural voice. "As it is, we will make you suffer."

"Too bad you missed one of us." Brikel flew towards them, and a current of air hit the water.

Kelan closed his eyes, arms raised to shield his face, and the resulting splash scattered the Disciples of the Sea and Sky alike. Through blurred vision, he saw a very much conscious Lakiel slicing the throat of one of his captors with their own dagger. Kelan half glided, half swam towards the others, but the Disciple who'd attacked him earlier moved into his path, brandishing his knife.

Kelan drove his own blade downward and into the Disciple's arm. As he dropped the knife, blood streaming into the water, Kelan stabbed him again, this time in the neck.

The Disciple's eyes bulged. "Amanat, please…"

"Having regrets about signing yourselves over to the god of death?" He shielded his face from another splash. Ranit and Kriam managed to pull Lakiel out of the water. Two more Disciples of the Sea lay face-down and unmoving amid the waves, and Brikel's blade ploughed through the chest of another.

"Cowardly pricks." She gestured at a fleeing figure on the water. "They're running away."

"Brikel." Lakiel flew over to his sister and tried to push her behind him, but she tugged her arm free. "I'm fine. Kelan's the one who jumped into the water."

"Of course he did." Lakiel flew closer and reached out a hand. Kelan took it, hoping that Lakiel hadn't assumed he'd been willing to sacrifice him to give the others a chance at escape. When he'd seen that monster…

As they turned away, Kelan spared the sky one last glance, but the beast had vanished as though it had never existed. Only its imprint on his eyes remained: a large, winged shadow, topped with a smaller dark shape as though a person sat upon its back.

———

Something terrible is going to happen.

A sense of foreboding hovered over the palace like a raincloud when Viam entered the receiving room. It had been easy, in the end, to persuade Yala to come to the palace, almost as though she'd been waiting for such an invitation. Refusing an official summons from the king would come with consequences of its own, but she'd seemed almost relieved to be interrupted in the middle of—whatever she'd been doing with the void drake's claw. Had she intended to petition the god of death? In public?

What had Viam unleashed in inviting her to the palace?

Yala walked into the receiving room with no visible apprehension on her face. This would be her first time seeing the monarch face to face since the end of the last war, but she'd chosen to wear her old uniform. Since she'd look out of place even in her best clothes, her drakeskin trousers weren't the worst choice, and she made an unassuming sight compared to the grandeur surrounding her.

Yala knelt, leaning on her cane, but she showed no signs of pain from her injuries the previous day. Niema must have healed her, but the Disciple of Life hadn't been able to come with her to the palace, and neither had Saren. Viam knew what Yala had risked by returning to the upper city alone, but her whispered questions when they'd met at the gates had been rebuffed.

What is she planning?

When Yala rose, King Daliel smiled at her from his throne. "Thank you for accepting my invitation, Yala Palathar. It seems that I owe you my thanks for your swift actions yesterday."

Yala nodded but didn't speak. Even so, her lack of self-consciousness made Viam's stomach twist in envy.

He went on, "It's past time I reinstated your position in Laria's army. It would be my honour to allow you to oversee the rebuilding of the Flight Division."

Yala was silent. Viam tried to catch her eye, a silent plea on her lips, but even she didn't expect what Yala said next.

"Thank you, Your Majesty," said Yala. "I must decline, unless you would like a Disciple of Death to be in charge of your Flight Division."

Yala... Viam took half a step forward, but the damage was already done. King Daliel's mouth parted in surprise.

"A Disciple of Death?" he echoed. "Whatever do you mean?"

"I am a Disciple of Death." Yala spoke in calm tones. "As your father intended to be."

Shocked silence filled the room. *Oh, Yala.* Viam fought the urge to squeeze her eyes shut, to avoid watching what would follow.

"My father," said the king. "You're mistaken."

"King Tharen gave us the order to go to the island, where we faced Corruption." Yala spoke without emotion, heedless of the whispers that passed between the guards standing near Viam. "I can't speak to whether he knew what we'd find there, but it's plain that he had enough of an interest to want to claim their temple for Laria. And enough for..."

The king's brows crept higher and higher with every word Yala spoke. "Enough for what?"

"Enough for someone to want to ensure he didn't succeed."

Another ripple of shock spread amidst the guards. Viam's knees trembled, her heart thumping in her ears like echoing footsteps. *Yala. Stop.*

King Daliel sucked in a breath. "The war clearly had an impact on you. I see that now. I apologise for not considering your experiences before I invited you back here."

Still, Yala took no notice of the rising whispers behind her. "I apologise for my bluntness, but I felt it was past time that someone told you the truth. Until now, that knowledge was confined only to those of us involved in that mission and to the Disciples of the Flame."

"The Disciples of the Flame?" The king looked around the room as though hoping someone would step forward and contradict her. "What are you implying?"

"Rafragoria always denied their role in your father's death, didn't they?" she queried. "Everyone assumed they were responsible, and when I learned the truth, I didn't want to incite animosity between you and the Disciples. However, I think you have the right to know how and why your father died."

"No." King Daliel's hands gripped the sides of the throne. "What you say is impossible. My father was murdered by assassins. He was no Disciple."

"He wasn't a Disciple," Yala agreed, "but the Disciples of the Flame saw the potential threat of a Disciple of Death on the throne and decided to act first, even if it meant betraying their nation."

"Enough," a guard spoke from behind Yala. "Your Majesty, would you like us to escort her from the palace?"

"I... yes." King Daliel's eyes were dull with shock. "I think that would be best."

Yala retained her calm expression, though when she turned her head, Viam saw the tight lines at the corners of her mouth. "As you desire, your Majesty. I understand that the Disciples of the Flame defended you yesterday, but I wanted to warn you against inviting them into the palace. They wouldn't hesitate to strike if they deemed you a threat too."

"That is enough," the guard repeated, taking Yala's arm in a firm hand.

Yala made no effort to fight, letting herself be escorted from the room without meeting Viam's eyes. The king stared after her, his mouth half open. Apologies rose to Viam's tongue, all inadequate and all false.

She's right. Gods, she's right, and the king... he must know she has no reason to lie to him.

Yes, Viam knew exactly why Yala had picked this moment to make her accusation. The Disciples of the Flame had threatened her life. If the king had done as he intended and offered them any more power in exchange for their actions in his defence, there was no telling what they would have done with that responsibility.

And if he's really dabbling in Corruption? If Yala is right about that too?

Viam took a step towards the throne and stilled at the sight of tears glistening in the king's eyes.

"Leave us," he said in a choked voice. "All of you."

Viam did so, but by the time she reached the steps outside the palace, Yala was gone.

———

It's done, thought Yala. Her body felt as light as air despite the ache in her injured leg from having to climb those absurd stairs. The cold press of the void drake's claw against her upper thigh reminded her that she'd been so certain it would react when she entered the palace and point her to any nearby Disciples of Death, to save her the bother of making any accusations—but not so much as a tingling in her fingertips had stirred.

The king wasn't a Disciple of Death. He'd never touched Corruption. Neither, apparently, had anyone else behind the palace walls.

The guard escorting her down the stairs seized her arm in a meaty fist and peered at her face. "What's so funny?"

Had she been smiling? She couldn't tell. "Nothing."

"You're lucky His Majesty didn't order you to be locked away," he spat. "You dared to dismiss the honour he offered you, to say nothing of your brazen accusations."

Yala leaned away from his foul breath. Freed of the pressure of holding the truth close to her chest, her inhibitions fled. "The former king died after laying a burden on my shoulders that should never have been mine to bear. Would he not have wanted his son to know the truth?"

"You should hang for that." He tightened his grip on her arm, pressing against the spot where the Disciple had burned her. "I wonder what the Disciples of the Flame will do to you."

"What?" Through the haze of pain, fear filtered in. "You aren't taking me to *them*?"

A sneer formed on his face. "You might rethink your choices when they have you in front of their altar."

If they give me to the Disciples of the Flame, I'll be dead by dusk. "I thought the king wanted me kicked out of the palace."

"No, he left the decision to us, and I think you should have to explain yourself to them. Might make you watch your tongue in future."

Her vision swam. Grasping for her last option, she spoke through gritted teeth. "I spoke to one of those assassins at the parade yesterday. She claimed to be working for the king."

"Why, you—?" The guard let go of her as though he was the one who'd been burned. "What nonsense is this?"

Yala sucked in a breath, her arm throbbing. "I want to know what would drive her to say such a thing."

"Plainly, she was out of her mind. Like you."

"Perhaps." Yala brought her cane up and struck him in the kneecap. He collapsed, bellowing with pain, and she ran the rest of the way down the stairs with speed that sent white-hot pain lancing through her right leg.

Two more guards met her at the gates, but she'd expected them to and already had her dagger in her free hand. She raised her cane, pushing the first guard's sword hand away, and then slammed the end into his elbow. The second, she tripped, causing him to fall onto his face. A third joined them, and Yala used her cane to parry his sword. She intentionally avoided any strikes that might inflict permanent damage, but being outnumbered put her at an instant disadvantage. A blade sliced open her sleeve, drawing blood, and a guard's fist slammed into her cheek, sending a fresh wave of pain through her skull. Snarling, she twisted away from him. "Where were you during the first attempt on the king's life?"

"Fuck you." The guard's sword hilt hit her ribs, and she let the dagger fall from her hand. *I think that's quite enough.*

Gripping the cane with one hand, Yala let herself fall to her knees in surrender. Her head throbbed, and so did her ribs, while her leg protested when one of the guards snatched her cane from her and another seized her upper arm. Between them, they hauled her across the palace grounds to one of the side gates.

A mixture of relief and vindication filled her chest when they dragged her outside and northward, in the opposite direction to the Temple of the Flame. They came to a guardhouse a short distance from the palace, which must be where they put upper city folk who broke the law; the two-storey stone building was certainly a lot nicer than the ones she'd visited in the outer city.

At the door, they divested her of her weapons. Rough hands reached into the pouch at her waist. A guard held up the void beast's claw, his brow furrowing. "What in the hells is this?"

"Lucky charm."

"Some use it did you in the end, hmm?" He sneered, tucking the claw into his belt alongside Yala's confiscated dagger. She fervently hoped he'd remove it before going outside; losing her most valuable weapon to a passing Disciple of the Flame who might spy the claw sticking from the guard's belt would be more galling than Yala had wanted to admit to herself.

What a fool I am. She might have escaped death upon Dalathik's altar, but being arrested brought its own set of inconveniences. Yala didn't hear so much as a whisper from Mekan when the guards pushed her through a door into a dimly lit corridor. Bars extended from floor to ceiling, separating each cell from its neighbours, and she counted at least four prisoners behind each door. The stench of waste and neglect wasn't as pronounced as in some of the smaller prisons she'd visited, but her leg and back already ached at the sight of the hard floor.

Better than being burned alive.

At the very least, she might have prevented King Daliel from making his father's mistakes. The would-be assassin's claim made even less sense now she'd confirmed he had no contact with Corruption, but she'd have time enough to think on that during her imprisonment.

"Might I ask how long I'm going to be in here?" she asked.

"Until we decide what to do with you."

They don't hang people for brawling with guards, do they? She'd assumed not, though she'd freely admit she'd been improvising. Anything to avoid being captured by the very people who'd forced her to play her last card when she hadn't any proof to back up her word.

Eyes watched her from behind the cell doors. Her name, whispered, echoed back and forth. Inspiration lit a spark in her chest.

"What if it's true?" She raised her voice, relying on the corridor's echo to carry it to all the cells within hearing distance. "Imagine if I'm right and the Disciples of the Flame were the ones who murdered King Tharen. What then?"

In response, the guard shoved her harder. "Shut the fuck up."

"You've made your point." Her eyes watered with pain, but she kept her voice as loud as she dared. "King Tharen was murdered, though, you can't deny that. What if it was his advisors who were responsible and not Rafragoria?"

She spoke in the tones of a gossip conveying the latest rumour to a crowd of eager onlookers. Already, whispers rose from amid the cells, though the guards ignored her and began passing a ring of keys amongst themselves.

Her fingers tingled with a sudden chill, and the thickening shadows shifted, drawing her eyes to a half-empty cell on her right.

"She's right," growled a voice from within the cell, causing her heart to give a sharp jolt against her ribs. "They're the ones who drove him away. Imagine a king forced to flee his own country."

"What?" Ignoring the guards' hands on her arms, she peered into the cell and made out what appeared to be a pile of sacks in the corner. "Who are you?"

"That one's as mad as a raptor in heat." A guard laughed. "He stabbed his last cellmate's eyes out."

"Did he now?" *He's also a follower of Mekan. Where'd they catch him?*

"You two can have fun together." A key clicked in the lock, and then the guard pushed her into the cell containing the heap of sacks. Nobody else was present, but a raucous coughing laugh greeted her from the corner. She caught her balance against the wall with a hand, dampness soaking into her palm, and the door slammed shut behind her.

"Well, fuck," she murmured. To her cellmate, she added, "The name's Yala. Who're you?"

"You're Yala Palathar." The pile of sacks sat up, half laughing, half coughing. "If they locked *you* in here, they fucked themselves over."

"What's that supposed to mean?" She moved closer warily and glimpsed a pair of eyes gleaming in the darkness above the sacks. "You're Mekan's follower, aren't you?"

"I'll be at His side soon."

"Meaning you're dying." She might not be able to see him clearly, but the stench rolling over her from the corner and the rasping cough in his throat told her he was rotting from the inside out, the same as the other assassins. "What did Mekan do to you?"

"Be *quiet*," hissed someone in one of the other cells. "Else they'll punish us all."

"He rewarded me for my service." The man broke into a coughing fit again. "We're all His servants and will all return to Him in the end, whether we be peasants or kings."

Kings. "What kings? Not King Daliel. He doesn't know a thing."

"Not him." He coughed a laugh. "The foolish boy... it's no wonder his father kept him ignorant. He's not strong enough to stand side by side with Mekan."

"What?" Her lips numbed as she spoke. "You said the Disciples of the Flame were the ones who killed King Tharen."

But he hadn't said that. *They're the ones who drove him away... imagine a king forced to flee his own country.*

"Didn't say that, did I?" he muttered. "Nobody ever listens, that's the problem."

Yala leaned over her cellmate, holding her breath to avoid breathing in his stench.

"Tell me," she growled, seizing his sack-like garment in one hand. "What did you mean? Forced to flee? Who?"

"Who else?" He coughed again, and she released him in disgust. "The king. Our *rightful* king."

No. She whispered the words, half to herself. "He's *dead.* He's been dead for years."

Did that matter, though? Where Mekan held sway, nothing was certain, death least of all.

"Believe whatever you like." His coughing grew weaker. "Mekan rewards those who are most faithful to Him."

"He can't bring back the dead. Not like that." Not with their minds and senses intact. Yet this man was proof enough that He could work miracles, and if he was right...

The air fled Yala's lungs. She might have stood in a cell a thousand times smaller than this one, a suffocating space where no light could penetrate.

If he'd lived, if he'd escaped assassination... was King Tharen still a Disciple of Death?

Is he the true leader of the Successors?

19

When they reached Amanar's shore, dawn crested the horizon, and the sun's rays glittered on the broken glass in front of the Disciples' Inn's shattered windows. No other traces remained of the Disciples of the Sea's assault; inside, they found the inn's servants in the downstairs room, cleaning up the damage while the middle-aged couple who owned the property looked on, grim-faced.

"How considerate of them to only kidnap the Disciples and not the rest of the staff," Kelan remarked. "I'm glad nobody else got hurt. Brikel, how'd you avoid getting caught? I never asked."

"I hid under the bed," she replied. "I got lucky. They took my brother because he was injured."

"They weren't official Disciples of the Sea," Lakiel said in tones more subdued than usual. "They can't have been acting on their Superior's orders."

"I think we established that," Kelan said. "The question is, *whose* orders were they following?"

They dispersed to their separate rooms to retrieve their clothes and weapons and otherwise lingered only long enough to accept some food supplies for the road. Staying in Amanar any longer would endanger the inn's owners, who were perfectly nice people and didn't deserve to have their property damaged by rogue Disciples.

"Do they know?" he asked Lakiel as they left the inn. "That the Disciples who took us were working with Mekan?"

"Who, the inn's owners?" Lakiel asked. "*We* don't know if it's true."

"You didn't see the void drake." Exhaustion clouded Kelan's thoughts, but the memory of those shadowy wings etched against the moon was as sharp as ever. "That's why they didn't kill us right away. They were saving us for their master."

"I think they were trying to silence us," said Ranit. "I also think Superior Shralin knew about their feud, and that's why he warned us off."

"Good point." Was *he* aware of their alliance with the god of death? "We need to go to Dalathar."

"No, we need to go to Skytower," Lakiel argued. "To warn our Superior."

"The king needs to know too." *And Yala and Niema.* "Not least that we ran into some Rafragorians so close to the shore."

"Do as you will," Lakiel said. "If you want to go to Dalathar, you can go alone."

In truth, Kelan knew none of them would last long on the road in their current state of exhaustion. The capital was marginally closer than Skytower, but whether he'd reach there before Mekan made His next move was debatable.

Maybe He already has. We missed the parade, after all.

"All right," he told the others. "Tell Superior Sietra that I'll bring her another update from the capital when I'm done."

If I'm alive.

———

Yala's cellmate continued to rant and rave as the hours of her imprisonment wore on. She stayed on the other side of the room, but he didn't move when the guards showed up with a meal, or what passed for one in here. Yala had endured worse as a soldier, so she ate the tasteless gruel and went back to watching her cellmate for signs that the god of death had swept in to claim him.

The man's coughing grew worse as night approached. Yala's aching leg prompted her to stretch out on her sleeping mat, but she refused to let herself doze. It'd be a fine thing to escape death by flames only to end up strangled by a dying man in the king's guardhouse.

"He will come for me," the man mumbled. "Mekan will."

"Good for you," Yala said into the darkness. "Is that your hope? That He'll be waiting to embrace you at the end?"

"You might mock me, but He will soon claim you too." At the shuffle of him scrambling to his feet, she lifted her head, but he scarcely made it half a step before collapsing, coughing wetly into the pile of sacks. Soon, Mekan would indeed embrace him and then raise him from death.

Then she'd be in trouble. The guards had taken her weapons, and she had sincere doubts that they would come to her rescue when he attacked.

"You haven't told me what bargain you made," she said in the hopes of gaining a crumb of sense out of his last moments of lucidity. "How did you end up like that? What did Mekan give you in exchange for stealing your life?"

"This *is* the exchange," said the man between coughs. "I stepped into His domain, and He rewarded me greatly."

Into His domain. No human could survive setting foot in Mekan's realm, surely, but his half-dead state spoke to some grave internal damage. Had he bargained his life force in some kind of twisted version of how the god of life could transfer the energy of other living beings to Her followers?

"Where?" She lifted her head again. "Where did you go?"

"To the place where no light shines, which the god of the flames has never touched." His words dissolved into a series of spitting and crunching noises that sounded like his teeth were falling out. "Home."

"Home," she echoed. A horrible suspicion began to take shape, growing like the festering rot inside the unfortunate man, but his babbling grew more incoherent, and she could no longer get any sense out of him.

Her thoughts swirled, as black as the surface of the ocean, the lightness following her arrest replaced with the grim certainty that he wasn't talking about Mekan's realm but somewhere much closer.

Somewhere that had haunted her nightmares for years.

If King Tharen survived... why not there too?

She forced her mind to stay focused on the more obvious problem: that she was trapped in a tiny room with a dying man, with no weapons to hand. Yala half wanted to finish the job herself, but she remained still while his coughs weakened, gathering what remained of her strength.

When his coughs faded to silence, she lifted her head. In the dim light of the torch burning in the corridor outside her cell, she saw he lay in a puddle of blood and bile, his body a rotting mass that scarcely resembled anything human. Her fingers tingled, a warning, and Yala pushed to her feet. She used the wall for balance as she crossed the room to the man and pushed her foot against his body.

"He's dead," she called, but nobody responded. "Guards?"

"They don't come in here at night," mumbled a voice from the cell on the other side. "If we kill each other, it's not their problem."

I thought not. Shadows shifted before Yala's eyes, coalescing around the rotting man's wizened limbs.

He stirred. Claw-like hands scrabbled at the floor, grasped for her ankles. Yala raised her booted foot and brought it down hard, not caring which body part she crushed as long as she stopped him from getting up again. Brittle bones crunched beneath her feet; viscera clung to her boots like wet earth. Fighting the urge to gag, she stepped back from the body to take a breath away from the putrid air—and heard the faint creak of the jail door opening.

A single pair of footsteps followed, too soft to belong to a guard's heavy boots, and the soft glow of a torch illuminated a small figure hurrying towards her cell.

"Niema," Yala hissed. "Get out of here."

Reaching her cell door, Niema stifled a cough behind her hand. Her wide eyes focused on the remnants of the dead man. "Is that—?"

"Yes," Yala whispered. "He was one of Mekan's. I can't go with you. The guards will come to the house and arrest you."

"I'm not going to leave you in here," Niema whispered through the bars. "Let me help you."

How had she even got this close without being discovered? She must have caused some kind of diversion, and Yala could only assume Viam had been the one who'd told her where Yala was imprisoned. *Gods, please say she and Saren aren't planning anything foolish too.*

"Unless you're willing to sneak into the Temple of the Flame and stab Danir in his sleep, there's nothing you can do for me." Her ears picked up on rustling noises that indicated Niema's entrance had disturbed some of her fellow prisoners. If they called for the guards, Niema would be incarcerated alongside her. "I'm safer in here."

At least until someone came to get rid of the body... and the one way to truly destroy the dead was with Dalathik's flames.

"You aren't," Niema insisted. "Please."

Yala sighed inwardly. "Fine. Unlock the door. I doubt it'll do me much good. The keys will be in the same room they put my weapons in."

"Do you want me to get them?"

"The claw is more important." Yala spoke as quietly as she dared. "I fucking hope the guard left it with the weapons and didn't carry it around like a trophy. We don't need a piece of Mekan roaming the city."

Niema ducked her head and then ran out of sight, while Yala waited beside the remains of her cellmate.

"Is she coming back?" someone whispered.

"She'd better set the rest of us free too."

Great. Yala could only hope that Niema's diversion was sufficient to keep the guards away long enough for her to get to the storeroom, but she wished her well-meaning friends had stayed at home instead. There'd be no escaping the city guard except perhaps by fleeing on her war drake, which couldn't carry all three of them. If Kelan had been here... but she didn't know if he was even alive or if he'd run afoul of the enemies that lurked off Laria's shores.

Like the former king.

No, she had to survive just to confirm if the dead man's ravings were true.

When Niema returned, Yala muttered, "How many people heard my claim that the king was murdered by the Disciples of the Flame? How far has the rumour spread?"

"I—don't know. Should I?"

"I guess not." She listened to the clink of keys as Niema unlocked the cell, and her tingling fingertips reached for the war drake's claw. As her hand curled around its too-familiar shape, Mekan's whisper filled her ears, and the pile of bones in the corner began to twitch once more. Niema passed her the pouch and her belt next, which Yala wrapped around her waist and returned the claw to its rightful place. The whispers quietened but didn't cease.

"Are you coming?" Niema whispered. "The diversion won't last long."

"No." She grimaced. "Let the others out too."

The ensuing distraction wouldn't stop the guards from blaming her for instigating the breakout, but the resulting confusion might slow down the consequences long enough to spare her friends.

As Niema moved to the next cell, a new set of footsteps sounded at the end of the corridor.

"What's this?" said a voice that sent a thrill of dread through Yala's veins.

Danir.

———

Niema froze in the middle of unlocking the cell as the robed figure walked into view. Even if she hadn't recognised him as the Disciple who'd visited Yala's house, the tight-lipped expression on Yala's face told her everything she needed to know.

"What's this?" he repeated. "A jailbreak?"

205

Niema's mind blanked; she tripped over her words. "You aren't part of the city guard. Are you supposed to be in here?"

"Yala Palathar." The Disciple—Danir—looked straight past Niema. "I heard you'd been arrested. Did you think you could escape justice?"

"Justice is for the gods alone to enact," Yala retorted. "Not you."

"Dalathik is my guide." Flames danced in his eyes, and the air thickened with heat. "You can't avoid Him, Yala."

"Did you say the same to the former king?" Yala's expression was drawn, pained, but her eyes gleamed. "Everyone in here knows what you did, Danir. Your reputation is already damaged enough."

With a snarl, he lunged forward. Yala reacted first, shoving the door open from the inside, and the edge caught the Disciple in the chest and sent him staggering back. As he caught his balance, Niema whispered a frantic prayer to the god of life.

No response came, but there was nothing living in here to react, and the rodents she'd unleashed as a distraction on the other side of Ceremonial Square were too far to reach.

Instead, she stuck out a foot and tripped him. The Disciple stumbled against the cell door opposite Yala's and recoiled when the prisoner on the other side spat at him.

"King killer?" growled the prisoner. "Is it true?"

Niema caught Yala's eye. Yala looked startled for an instant, then her mouth twisted into a grin. "Yes, it's true. Right, Danir?"

"Enough!" He lunged but missed, stumbling forward with a grunt as a heavy object collided with the back of his skull.

Grinning, Saren moved in, wielding Yala's cane like a club. *There he is.* He and Niema had both been at home when Viam showed up, dishevelled and breathless, to tell them that Yala had been taken captive, and they'd wasted no time in putting together a plan.

"Always wanted to do that." His eyes gleamed with satisfaction that mirrored Yala's. "What do you say to the rumours that you conspired with Superior Datriem to kill King Tharen?"

"That is a poisonous lie." Danir straightened upright, pressing one hand to the back of his head, but the flames in his pupils burned as bright as ever.

"There's one source of poison here, and I'm looking right at him." Saren tossed the cane to Yala, who caught it in one hand.

Fire licked the side of Niema's cheek, and she bit back a gasp at the sharp pain. Yala swore, having dodged by throwing herself behind the open cell door.

"What's going on in here?" The unfamiliar voice echoed from the corridor's end and brought all four of them to a halt, even Danir, though his eyes still burned with white fire.

"One of your prisoners is trying to escape," Danir called to the approaching guard. "With help."

Saren swore under his breath. Yala flashed him an urgent look and then caught Niema's eye, communicating a silent plea to leave that she couldn't bring herself to obey.

Saren leaned over to Niema. "She'll be fine. I'd be more worried for the guards than her. Let's go."

Danir moved to grab Saren, but he ducked, slipping out of the Disciple's grasp. Heart sinking in her chest, Niema ran after him around the corner, praying to all the gods that Yala had a plan that didn't involve being locked back in that cell. The exit was still mercifully free of guards for the time being, but Niema's heart tugged her back towards the corridor where she'd left Yala.

"This is a mistake," she whispered.

"So is getting ourselves arrested," Saren returned. "Trust me—or rather, trust Yala. Danir won't burn her in full view of the guards, not without proving her right."

A short distance away, Ceremonial Square was already bustling with noise. While the market stalls had yet to open, a crowd had congregated around the palace gates. Strange.

"You didn't put rodents in the palace, too, did you?" Saren peered at the crowd.

"No." As they moved closer, Niema heard the words "King Tharen" and "murder" and "Disciples" tossed amid the crowd like sparks from a kindling flame.

Saren grabbed her arm. "It's happening. Yala is a fucking genius."

"She asked me how many people heard the rumour that the Disciples killed the king," Niema murmured back. "Is that what she meant? Has she been telling... everyone?"

"She's wanted to tell the king who killed his father for years, and he left the door wide open for her." Saren wore the boyish grin of a novice who'd received high praise from their Superior for the first time. "Hells, *I've* wanted to see those Disciples squirm for what they did to us."

"Most of them will still be asleep." She cast a worried glance towards the temple. "Saren?"

"What?" His face lit up like the sun. "Don't ruin this for me. The gods rarely smile on the likes of us."

"Saren!" She gestured to the side street, from which Yala had emerged flanked by two guards. Slightly ahead of her walked Danir. Dirt scuffed his bright cloak and smudged one cheek, remnants of their fight in the cells. "Are you *sure* she has a plan? What if she thinks that now the truth is out there...?"

"...it doesn't matter if she dies?" The mirth faded from Saren's face. "Shit."

"Exactly." The guards might temper Danir's fury, but that would only last until they reached the home of the Disciples. "I broke her out of the Temple of the Flame once before, but that... well, that required a war drake."

Saren groaned. "Let's save that for a last resort."

We might need that, Niema thought as she watched Yala and the Disciple enter the temple.

The door closed behind them.

———

Yala had hoped in vain that at least one guard might believe her story of Danir's assault. Unfortunately, when they saw the state of her cell-mate, they were all too happy to get rid of her.

"If I may," Danir had said with an air of sanctimony that made her want to gag, "Superior Shralin would like to speak directly to her. He expressed an interest in hearing her account of her false accusations levelled at the king."

"What, you mean how I accused you and Superior Datriem of conspiring to murder King Tharen?" Yala projected her voice, and whispers sprang up amid the surrounding cells like weeds. Doubtless, there wasn't a person in the jail who hadn't heard the rumour by now.

"You have a great deal of nerve," Danir said. "But no sense."

"Ah, but I don't hear you denying it." Between the guards at the palace and the prisoners, the Disciples of the Flame would be hard-pressed to silence all potential witnesses to the rumour. *It's over for them. Danir knows it, and if any of his fellow conspirators survive, they'll know too.*

Danir addressed the guard with exaggerated patience. "She won't cause you any trouble if I take her to my Superior."

Won't I? Yala's cellmate's claims had awakened a new angle of questioning, another reason to survive long enough to pry a confession from the conspirators. And an apology from Superior Shralin, too, perhaps.

"Right." The guard beckoned, eyeing Yala warily. "We'll escort her there."

Danir's jaw tightened with irritation, but he didn't argue. "Let's go."

Jeers followed as they left the cells behind. The guard hadn't taken away Yala's belt—perhaps not noticing the pouch containing the void drake's claw—but when she tried to grab her cane, he snatched it out of reach. "You'll get this back when you're at the temple."

"How generous of you." Yala's leg throbbed—the beating she'd taken the day before coupled with a night in a cell had left her bruised all over like a piece of fruit left out in the sun—but that was nothing compared to the agony of Dalathik's flames.

They emerged into daylight, angling towards the Temple of the Flame. Yala knew better than to think she'd have an easy way out once she was behind those doors, but all the streets leading out of Ceremonial Square were blocked by guards too.

"What's going on?" she asked her armed companions. "Seems early for patrolling."

"Skirrits," one of the guards said. "All over the southern side of the square."

Niema, it seemed, had revived her effective plan to create a diversion with a swarm of rodents, on a slightly larger scale this time. She probably hadn't intended to get Yala trapped in the square in the process, but both she and Saren were nowhere to be seen. With a little luck, they'd got away without the guards being any the wiser.

Oddly, a crowd had assembled outside the palace gates, too, but they were too far away to hear the content of their shouts. Her guard escorts halted partway up the temple stairs, but Danir shadowed her as she climbed, preventing her from stopping to rest her aching leg. Her fist struck the door once, twice.

A tired-eyed novice answered, and when she asked for the Superior, he blurted, "The Superior is asleep."

"Believe me, this wasn't my idea." She twisted around to glare at her captors. "Can I have my cane back?"

A guard tossed the cane to her, which Yala hefted in one hand. Danir didn't budge despite the temple door being open; half his attention was on the crowd near the palace gates instead of on her.

The door opened wider, and the novice beckoned her to enter. Yala's instincts told her that she'd have no chance of escape once inside, but what choice did she have? Danir wanted her dead. Superior Shralin, as far as she knew, did not.

She entered. A number of curious Disciples watched; she glimpsed novices in long night-garments peering down from balconies as she crossed the main hall to an alcove.

"Wait here," the novice told her. "He'll see you soon."

When the novice departed, Danir lingered, his lip curling. "You're wasting your time avoiding your fate, Yala. Dalathik's fire will cleanse your soul, and I will be there to watch when He claims you."

Soon after he vanished, Superior Shralin appeared. He wore his cloak but not his ceremonial headdress, his balding scalp on display for all to see.

"My apologies," she said. "Danir decided to drag me here from the guardhouse instead of waiting for a more appropriate hour."

"You were imprisoned for starting a fight in the palace and insulting the king, were you not?" he said. "If you expect me to be kinder to you than the city guards were, you're mistaken."

"Danir tried to kill me," she replied. "He's not even doing a very good job of denying it."

"Danir is devoted to his deity."

"Let me guess, he was close to Superior Datriem too," she said. "I'm working under the assumption that you were in ignorance of your predecessor's order to have King Tharen assassinated before he became a Disciple of Death?"

"I refuse to let you spread such lies within this temple," he said. "Whatever your grievances with my predecessor, I am not him."

"That's why I'm trying to be honest with you." Her head throbbed as well as her body, and she wished there was a seat for her to rest her leg. "I have no intention of becoming a sacrifice upon Dalathik's altar. What's the usual punishment if a Disciple murders a member of the public? Let alone a king?"

"That," he said, "would depend upon whether the action was provoked."

Dread curdled in her stomach like sour milk. *Danir will seize on that excuse, make no mistake. This is far from over.*

Which left her with one option: the full truth.

"I'm sure you'll have heard the rumours," she said. "The palace guards are all talking about whether your people were involved in King Tharen's murder. If King Daliel decides to pursue this further, I think it'd be in your best interests if the Disciples who *were* part of the conspiracy put themselves forward and confessed to spare the rest of you."

"King Tharen was assassinated by Rafragorians," said Superior Shralin. "Everyone knows that."

"Your predecessor played a part in spreading that lie, but it was never true. He had the king killed for dabbling in Corruption."

"Meddling with Corruption has damaged your mind, clearly," he said. "I won't listen to another word of this."

"You don't have to believe me," Yala said. "I'm on your side, believe it or not. I have nothing against you personally, and I don't want another war either. I don't think hiding the truth is going to do anything but see to your own doom, and I have no desire to see the rest of Laria fall into chaos."

His jaw clenched, and his gaze flickered over to a spot just behind her. Yala didn't need to turn around to know that Danir had returned to watch her punishment play out.

"In that case," he said, "you are to leave here and never set foot in this temple again."

"Gladly." That was all? No. The blood surged in her veins as she turned away, gripping her cane, her other hand reaching into the pouch at her waist.

When she stepped out into the main chamber, Danir waited for her. "You aren't leaving."

"Your Superior told me to leave." She walked, her uneven steps no match for his swift stride. "He didn't give you any orders to stop me."

No. He'd washed his hands of the responsibility, turned his back so that he wouldn't see her fate should Danir decide to bathe her in Dalathik's flame. The heat from the altar brushed against her side, and Danir's eyes reflected the flickering candles.

"Give it up," she added. "You can turn me to dust on the spot and not make any difference to your fate. The wheels are in motion now, Danir."

Her death didn't matter now that the truth was out, and neither did his. They were both pieces in a bigger game, and she had a sinking feeling she knew exactly who sat at the head of the table.

"You're wrong." He stepped into her path. "If I burn you out of existence, few will mourn."

"You'd be doing yourself no favours." Her surreptitious glance around the temple revealed no witnesses; the curious onlookers had melted away like candle wax. Dismissed on his orders, no doubt. "Confessing to your crimes would set you free of the burden. Isn't that what Dalathik would want?"

"You don't understand what's at stake here, do you?" With each word, the temperature increased, and her arms began to throb with the reminder of her injury. "You're a dull-witted soldier, nothing more. Unlike my Superior, I have no intention of letting our enemy take us by surprise. That's why you have to die."

"Pity," she said. "It sounds like we should have been on the same side."

She drew the claw from the pouch and let Mekan's shadows seep through her fingertips. Danir's prayer cut off in a choked noise when she drove the claw into his thigh, hard. Blood spurted; a fresh streak of fire singed her already battered clothes, but Yala was already running for the door.

When she burst out into daylight, Saren and Niema came hurrying up the stairs.

"Yala." Saren caught her arm, his face ashen. "You're alive."

"Anyone would have thought I'd been sentenced to death." She dragged her arm out of his and hobbled downstairs without looking back to see if anyone had followed. Danir's blood splashed on the stone, leaving a trail of crimson droplets.

"How did you get out of there alive?" Niema choked.

"I made it clear to the Superior where they stand." She held up the claw, soaked in blood, before returning it to the pouch. "And I may have stabbed Danir."

"In his own temple?" Saren blanched. "How long will it be before he comes after you for revenge?"

"A few hours, I hope." Yala's legs trembled with exhaustion. "I need some fucking sleep."

20

V iam woke in the early hours to such a clamour that she at first thought she'd missed another assassination attempt. She leapt to her feet and ran across the staff dormitory, where she found Brenat and several others gathering in the doorway. Some were fully dressed, while others still wore their nightclothes, blinking in the bright sun streaming through the open door.

"What's going on?" she asked.

"There's some kind of protest at the gates," Brenat said. "No idea what."

"Someone mentioned a rodent outbreak," added another staff member. "Sounds fake."

"Rodents?" A suspicion seized her. *Is it Yala?* Viam had been sick with worry for her, especially when she'd confirmed that Yala had been locked up in the guardhouse, but Yala would have been in far more trouble if the Disciples of the Flame had hauled her off to their temple instead.

Viam quickly dressed and hurried out of the staff quarters. Guards and other staff members alike gathered in groups or stood to watch the commotion on the other side of the front gates. There were smaller groups near the side entrances, too, and she suspected the same was true of the back gate near the war drakes' paddock.

"They've blocked the roads." Brenat waved her over. "The guards have. There *is* a skirrit outbreak, and some people think it's a cover for another attempt on the king's life."

"Isn't the king asleep?" Then the first part of Brenat's words sank in. "There's no way to get out of the upper city?"

"Does it matter?" Her eyes widened. "Your friend Yala is locked up in the guardhouse, isn't she? Did *she* set a plague of rodents loose as a diversion?"

"Of course not." Viam's heartbeat quickened. "That's beyond her power."

I think. The rumours of *why* Yala had been arrested had varied, but everyone agreed that she'd started a brawl after accusing the king's father of a crime and that she'd made some similar accusation against the Disciples of the Flame.

With each step Viam took towards the front gates, whispers crackled like embers, interspersed with the occasional shout.

"She's out of her mind," said a deep voice that Viam tracked down as belonging to one of the guards. "After her arrest, she nearly started a riot in the guardhouse."

"But is what she claimed true?" someone called to him. "The Disciples of the Flame killed King Tharen?"

"I don't see anyone denying it," chimed in a second voice. "Didn't the king throw the Disciples out of the palace years ago?"

"I never trusted them," put in a third. "I bet they did it."

Oh, Yala. This had been her plan, Viam was sure. She'd been backed into a corner and had struck back with the only weapon that Dalathik's flames couldn't devour: her voice.

"Viam?" Brenat caught up to her. "Did I hear that right? Did Yala accuse the Disciples—?"

"Of murder?" The words tasted coppery in her mouth. All her instincts told her to bite her tongue and keep the truth close to her chest, but she forced herself to speak. "Yes. She did."

"And... it's true?"

Viam's throat locked. There wasn't enough air. "I—"

Her breath stopped as though her head had been pushed underwater, a blue haze creeping at the edges of her vision. Brenat noticed; without a word, she seized Viam's hand and pulled her away from the gathering crowd.

Viam was too shaken to fight back. Her heart pounded in her ears, her skin went clammy, and once they were alone, she sank to the ground. A sob choked her throat, her body trembling violently until Brenat's arms might have been the only thing holding her together.

When the sobs racking her chest subsided, she lowered her hands from her face. "I'm sorry."

"Don't be," Brenat said with concern. "You have good reason to fall apart. If you've been holding onto this for years—"

"I didn't say it was true."

"You didn't need to," Brenat said. "It's obvious. The Disciples killed King Tharen—you know, that explains a lot about Yala too."

"Yala." Viam rubbed her eyes on her sleeve. "Gods, she'll kill me."

"Why?" Brenat's tone was layered with suspicion. "Did she order you not to tell anyone?"

"No. She told me not to *trust* anyone, that there might be traitors here inside the palace."

"Oh." Brenat made a quiet noise of understanding. "I caught her attention when I followed you to the war drakes' paddock, didn't I?"

Viam didn't reply, but Brenat groaned. "Oh. She thinks I'm a Disciple of Death?"

"No, of course not." She lifted her head to the clear sky, focusing on the clear blue to regain some semblance of calm. "She's suspicious of everyone. She thought the assassins had help on the inside."

"She can't possibly think I want the king dead. He's the only person keeping both of us employed. For now, anyway."

Viam tried to smile. "*I* know that. Yala has bigger concerns."

"She's still locked up?"

"Yes, and the Disciples of the Flame want her dead. Well, some of them do."

"Can't you report them?"

She jerked her head to the side. "To whom? The guards think she's unstable, like that man we heard. She also accused them of murder, and... and with Superior Datriem dead, it's not like they're going to confess."

"Right, of course he is," said Brenat. "I don't know if it'll help, but I'll tell anyone who'll listen that Yala is right, and the Disciples are the ones spreading lies."

This time, Viam managed a shaky smile. "Thanks. I can't control what anyone else says, and neither can Yala, but she was backed into a corner when she told the king the truth."

"Well, if those fuckers come in here and threaten *you*, they'll have to go through me."

Viam's face flamed. "Please don't."

"Worried about me?" Brenat's voice gained a mischievous edge. "You do realise I followed you around because I *like* you, Viam, don't you? If you want me to back off, you can tell me, but I don't think you do."

Viam's mouth parted. *This* was a development she hadn't planned for. "I..."

"Or you can keep moping over Yala from afar," Brenat added. "It's your choice."

Viam was spared having to reply when a guard walked up to them. "You're Viam?" he said to her. "The king wants to talk to you."

"Now?" Her mouth went dry. Did he intend to punish her for Yala's accusations?

"Alone?" Brenat asked. "If not, I'll go with her."

"No—it's fine." Viam lurched to her feet. "I'll speak to him."

While he might not be able to prevent the Disciples of the Flame from further pursuing her, this might be her only chance to talk the king into sparing Yala any further punishment. Between losing the king's trust and ensuring Yala's survival, her choice was clear.

Gods forgive me.

———

217

Yala woke several hours after her return home from the Temple of the Flames, her eyes gummed together with sleep, to the sound of a whispered argument between Saren and Niema on the other side of the room.

She lifted her head blearily, and their argument quietened. Though she'd changed out of the clothes she'd been imprisoned in, the smell of the Temple of the Flame lingered on her skin. So did the stench of the dead, despite her having left her boots outside to avoid treading bits of her unfortunate cellmate into the floorboards.

"No unwanted visitors?" She sat upright, squinting in suspicion at the flask Saren handed her. "What's in there?"

"Groundfruit juice," he said. "If you want something stronger, you'll have to get it yourself."

Niema held out a plate. "I bought food from the market, but I don't know what you wanted."

"Anything that isn't gruel." She reached for the plate and picked up a ball of fried dough seasoned with spices. "What?"

"Nothing."

Her appetite fled at the way Niema watched her guardedly, almost like she had when they'd first met and Yala had killed two mercenaries in front of her. Saren avoided her eyes too. He returned to the armchair, holding the flask, though he didn't drink from it.

"What is it?" she finally asked, putting her plate aside. "If you want to know why I got myself arrested, it was that or let Danir incinerate me."

"It looks like he tried to do that anyway." Saren jumped to his feet. "Gods, Yala. Is that what you wanted? To die?"

"What?" She rose upright, too, her body protesting with a new array of aches. "Didn't you notice that I've spent the past day and a half doing my best to avoid exactly that?"

"You accused the king's father of being a Disciple of Death. That's not an act of someone who wants to stay alive."

"I had to explain *why* the Disciples of the Flame tried to kill his father. He'd never have believed me otherwise." She limped to the other armchair, glad that she'd manage to get her cane back from the guardhouse. Not to mention the void drake's claw. "And I started a fight with the guards so that they'd lock me up in the regular jail, not the Disciples' dungeon. Of course, Danir didn't let that stop him from trying again."

"They locked you in the same cell as a Disciple of Death," Niema said. "Didn't they?"

"Yes." Did they really think she wanted to die? Yala hadn't felt this alive in years, but her relief at setting the burden of silence aside was somewhat dampened by her cellmate's other revelation. "The Successors. I'm almost certain that their leader is King Tharen."

The ensuing silence was broken by Saren choking on a laugh. "Fuck, Yala. Maybe you need more sleep."

"I thought you'd say that." She rubbed her eyes on the back of her hand. "Doesn't it explain why that assassin claimed to be taking orders from the king, though? I didn't sense any Corruption in the palace, I can tell you that much."

"Sure," said Saren. "These people are out of their minds. They probably think Mekan Himself is their leader."

"That might be true," Niema ventured. "They aren't exactly stable."

"I'm aware," Yala said. "I also know we don't need any more enemies—"

"You don't say?" Saren shook his head. "The king was confirmed dead by witnesses. I'll never fucking forget that day, and neither will you."

"They said his body was never recovered," Yala reminded him. "And wasn't there only one survivor, who died shortly after telling everyone the king was dead?"

"I think we'd know if our old king was out there, Yala." Saren shook his head. "Gods, this is absurd. The king is *dead*. Why wouldn't King Tharen tell anyone he survived?"

"Well, there is the fact that the Disciples of the Flame tried to have him killed," Yala said. "And until recently, the person who gave the order was their Superior and one of the most powerful people in the city."

Saren rolled his eyes. "When King Tharen heard of Superior

Datriem's death, he decided it was time to remind Laria of his existence, did he?"

"Quite possibly yes."

Saren sank back into his armchair. "Fuck, Yala, you're making this sound plausible. And you wonder why I have a hard time telling the difference between reality and a nightmare?"

Yala rested her head against the back of her own chair. "I'm not saying it all makes sense. We're still missing some pieces, but if he's leading the Successors, that explains why they're still active after Melian's death."

"What does he plan to do, unseat his own son from the throne?" Niema asked. "Or rule alongside him?"

Saren gave her an incredulous look. "You believe her?"

Niema glanced at Yala. "It does sound plausible. If you never saw a body..."

"Don't assume the person ever died," Yala finished. "We know that now. We didn't then."

"He's not one of Mekan's monsters, is he?" Saren asked. "It's been years. He'd have turned to dust by now."

"I know." Yala clenched and unclenched her fist, surveying the thin grey lines spreading from her fingertips. "When the Disciples of the Flame sent assassins after him, what better way to avoid them than to fake his death and go into hiding? I've been tempted to do the same myself."

"Wait," Niema said. "If King Tharen *did* survive, why would they need to silence you?"

"That's true." Saren's expression brightened and then faded again. "They still want you dead. We're not safe here."

"I know." Yala had won herself some time, but Danir wouldn't let the wound she'd dealt slow him down for long. "I haven't thought this over, I'll freely admit, but now that the rumours are sparking, there'll be unrest that I don't think the two of you want to get involved in. I'm worried about Viam, too, but the palace is marginally safer than outside."

"Assuming King Tharen doesn't come back." Saren laughed humourlessly. "After all the trouble you went to to expose his killers."

Yala scowled. "You don't have to remind me."

"*You* don't have to take responsibility for everything," he said. "Don't deny it. You want us to leave the city so you can stay behind and throw yourself into the path of whatever assassin comes for the king next."

"No, I want you to leave the city so I can make sure the Disciples of the Flame face the consequences of their actions," she said. "It won't hurt if King Daliel sends an apology to Rafragoria for accusing them of murdering his father too."

That wouldn't stop them from retaliating for the deaths of their ambassadors—and if King Tharen had been responsible for sending Mekan's monsters after them, Rafragoria had all the more reason to blame Laria after all.

"And if King Tharen did survive?" asked Niema. "What then?"

"If he survived, we have to ask another question," Yala said. "Did the Disciples of the Flame know he escaped?"

21

Viam approached the palace with a renewed sense of trepidation. She couldn't imagine why the king would want to see her now if not to discuss Yala, and it was anyone's guess as to whether he'd accepted any truth might exist in her words.

When the palace doors closed, Viam took in a steadying breath and wiped her face with her sleeve to disperse any lingering tears. Brenat hadn't followed—or if she had, the guards hadn't let her in—and Viam entered the receiving room alone.

She found the king seated on his throne, wearing an expression of contemplation. Not anger at least, but there was none of the usual friendliness in his gaze, and when she knelt, he didn't tell her not to bother with formalities.

"I apologise for what happened yesterday, Your Majesty," she said into the awkward silence. "I shouldn't have expected Yala to accept your offer."

"No, it was I who made an error in inviting her here." Up close, he looked as though he hadn't slept all night, and his eyes were underscored with thick shadows. "The wounds my father's wars inflicted upon her ran deeper than I thought."

"I hope that you can forgive Yala for her rash words." She might have said that Yala hadn't been thinking clearly, but that would have been an obvious lie. "She's been... troubled."

"By the Disciples of the Flame, or so it sounds." A pause. "I am not quite the fool that some may believe me to be, Viam."

Viam drew her arms to her sides, her fingers curling into her palms. "They refused to believe her account of the incident we faced on the island. That... that's the reason we stayed silent for so long."

"She also accused them of ordering my father's death."

Viam flinched. If she were capable of speech, she didn't know what would be worse—denial or confirmation.

"Do you believe this too?" His voice was quiet, but each word lingered in the air like the smoky smell after a fire. "The Disciples of the Flame were my father's trusted advisors. I was never able to believe that they'd failed him so terribly."

Viam lifted her head, encouraged. "I believe they did fail him. Especially Superior Datriem."

"Superior Datriem was killed by one of his own." The king was silent for a moment. "Factions within factions. I cannot even trust those in my confidence. Nobody in the palace would tell me why the Disciples failed to save his life from the Rafragorians."

"Your father's close advisors were all killed too," she said. "There weren't any witnesses who might have given you an eyewitness account."

"No." A sigh entered his voice. "It's clear what I must do."

Viam's heart missed a beat. "What is that?"

"I want to hear the truth from the mouths of the Disciples of the Flame themselves."

———

Kelan's plan to reach the capital within a day was too optimistic. Even a Disciple of the Sky had limits on how far they could fly, and he and his fellow Disciples had surpassed theirs. When they parted ways outside Amanar and the others made for Skytower, Kelan hadn't made it further than the next village before he found himself being more battered around by the wind than gliding gracefully. With his abilities hampered by exhaustion, Kelan was left with the more mundane manner of convincing local farmers or merchants to let him ride on their wagons between villages. Several times, they had to wake him from a doze, and as evening approached, he stopped at an inn for the night and found the place jammed with mercenaries.

He ordered a bowl of hot stew and joined a group of rough-looking men at an already packed table. Some eyed his cloak distrustfully, but the majority were drunk enough not to care if a Disciple joined them.

"What's the occasion?" He blew on his bowl to cool the stewed meats and vegetables. "Trouble in the capital?"

Did anything happen at the parade? That was his prevailing question, though his absence from Dalathar felt long enough that anything might have occurred without him knowing.

"You might say that," one of the mercenaries slurred. "They say there's a plague of giant rodents in the upper city."

Kelan frowned. "Giant rodents?"

"That's right," said the man. "If we help drive them off, they'll reward us, you watch."

"Right." Kelan had his doubts, so he finished his stew and went in search of someone who looked more sober.

In one corner stood a group of people who wore raptor-skin leathers and short swords that painted them as city guards. *They're a long way from Dalathar.* When he neared their group, a bearded man gave him such a glare that he decided against joining them, instead seating himself at a nearby table with another group of mercenaries playing cards.

He declined to join in the game and instead angled himself to eavesdrop on the guards, catching a few sentences that made little sense out of context.

"Complete madness."

"They said the Disciples of the Flame killed the king."

Kelan gripped his mug. *No. It can't be.* He'd know if the king was dead, right? Word would have made it to Amanar, messengers would have dispersed throughout every surrounding village, and the whole country would had been plunged into instant mourning. When King Tharen had died, everyone in Skytower had known by that evening.

Summoning his remaining patience, Kelan waited for one of the guards to peel away from their group and then waylaid him. "Excuse me—"

"Fuck off, Disciple."

"Delightful to see you too." Shaking his head, he looked for another likely person to question and met a number of hostile stares in return.

They really are pissed off with the Disciples. He spied the tavern's owner lurking in a corner and went to speak to him instead.

"What's going on?" he asked. "Everyone's looking at me as if they caught me in bed with their lover."

"You've not been around, have you?" The owner, an elderly plump man with a thick grey beard, lowered his voice conspiratorially. "The Disciples of the Flame are in trouble with the king."

"Wait, so he's alive?" Kelan glanced behind him then back at the owner. "Why're they in trouble?"

"No idea." He shrugged, wiping down a table with a dirty rag. "Who's to say how monarchs think?"

"You don't mind my being here?"

"You're wearing blue, not red or orange. People're idiots." He shook his head and spat into the same rag he was using to clean the table.

Kelan put down his mug and declined a refill. Spying a group of guards who were more inebriated than the others, he made his way to their table and sat beside the one who was still conscious. "Did you hear any rumours about the king?"

"Huh?" the man grunted.

"The king and the Disciples of the Flame," Kelan went on. "Hear anything?"

The man's unfocused gaze took him in. "Aren't *you* a Disciple?"

"Not that sort." He held up a hand and whispered a quick prayer.

The god of the sky responded with a brief stirring of air. "The Disciples of the Flame. What're the rumours?"

The man leaned closer, half falling out of his seat. "They say the Disciples killed the king."

Kelan frowned. "Not what I heard. King Daliel's still alive and mad at them."

"No. King *Tharen*."

Kelan's head snapped upward. *King Tharen?* "Are you sure?"

"Sure, that's why we left," he slurred. "Not gonna stand in the middle of a feud between the king and the Disciples."

If he was right, this had Yala's name written all over it. *Did she finally get the Disciples of the Flame to confess to their crimes?*

———

Kelan spent another frustrating day on the road before he was able to fly. This gave him time to pick up on a few more updates from mercenary bands—the "giant rodents" rumour turned out to be false, but there was a general agreement that someone had made an accusation against the Disciples of the Flame. And he heard King Tharen's name enough times to confirm that some people, at least, believed the rumour.

Kelan reached Dalathar as the sky began to darken. He glided over the city wall and promptly found several spears pointed at his throat.

"Is there a problem?" He hovered before the row of guards—more than were usually on the wall—and deduced that the king's parade had *not* gone as planned. "I need to get to the Disciples' Inn."

"Then go through the gate like everyone else," a guard said. "King's orders."

That's new. Kelan dropped a handspan in the air, but curiosity got the better of him. "What's going on? I've heard all kinds of outlandish rumours on the road. Something about the Disciples of the Flame?"

"You don't know?" Another guard spoke up. "This ex-soldier accused them of murder. Got herself locked up."

Yala. "Locked up where?"

"Guardhouse at first. Then, the Disciples showed up and took her into their temple."

The Disciples of the Flame arrested Yala. Shit. They hadn't killed her, had they? For that matter, what had driven her to make an accusation against a group of people who could incinerate her in a snap of their fingers?

Thoughts whirling, he descended to the upper city gate, where he was treated to yet another questioning from the guards. He had no way to confirm if they all believed Yala's story, but they'd certainly heard the rumours, and each told a different version of Yala's arrest.

Once through the gates, he headed straight for the Temple of the Flame. He wouldn't be able to see the inside of their prison from the window—he knew its location due to an unpleasant experience inside their dungeon himself—but surely, if they'd arrested her, Niema or Viam would have tried to help.

The front door opened, though he hadn't knocked, and a Disciple whom he vaguely recognised limped out. One of his legs was heavily bandaged, and his eyes narrowed at Kelan. "Might I ask why you're lurking outside our temple at this hour?"

"I need to talk to your Superior," he said. "My apologies for the late hour. I just got back from Amanar."

"I know your face," said the Disciple. "You're a friend of that Yala Palathar's."

Yala. Wait, he *had* seen this man before: when he'd come to Yala's house to check up on Niema. "Was she really arrested? Is she still in there?"

An expression of calculation crossed the Disciple's face. "Is that what this is about?"

"I really did have news for your Superior." He tried to peer around the Disciple, but the man's hand ignited. Kelan jumped back, bemused, and raised his own palm. A torrent of air blasted the flames aside before they reached his face, but the heat seared his skin. *What's wrong with him?*

"What are you doing?" He held up both hands, deflecting the next fireball and sending it spiralling into the air. "Is using Dalathik's flames to attack members of the public acceptable now?"

The Disciple's face screwed up in concentration, but Kelan struck first, a gust of air lifting the Disciple off his feet and sending him tumbling down the stairs. He landed awkwardly, spitting curses.

"Kelan." Superior Shralin appeared in the doorway, looking down at the pair of them with thin-lipped disbelief. "What is going on?"

"Believe it or not, I didn't start this fight," Kelan said. "He attacked me."

"He came here to cause trouble." The Disciple pushed, his face taut with pain. "He's as much a traitor as that Yala."

"Danir," said Superior Shralin. "Didn't I tell you to stay in the temple? We don't need more rumours."

Rumours. Kelan's curiosity sparked. "Was Yala really arrested?"

Danir's mouth twisted at her name, but Superior Shralin ignored both of them and beckoned to his Disciple. "Come."

Still glaring at Kelan, Danir climbed the stairs and entered the temple behind his Superior.

Kelan stepped forward before the door closed. "As you may have gathered, I survived meeting the Disciples of the Sea. Did you know some of them have turned on their deity and their fellow Disciples and allied themselves with Mekan?"

Superior Shralin's eyes widened. "You should report to your own Superior, not me."

"That's what my fellow Disciples are doing," said Kelan. "You tried to warn us off. Did you know?"

"No." He didn't meet Kelan's eyes. "No, and your friend isn't here. I'd advise you to return to Skytower and not return to the capital for a long while."

"Why's that?" he said. "I heard some interesting tales on my way to the capital. Is the king—?"

The door slammed in his face. Kelan, having expected that reaction, glided back to the ground, his heart lifting marginally. *Yala isn't here.* He *hoped* Superior Shralin was telling the truth, but getting out of the upper city to visit her house would mean another argument with the guards on the way back in, and she wouldn't thank him for disturbing her at night.

Knowing she's alive is enough. I'll have to find her tomorrow.

———

Danir did not show up at Yala's house that evening, but she and Saren remained tense enough that Niema eventually offered to feed the war drake just to get away for a while. There was little she could do to defend any of them against a furious Disciple of the Flame, though feeding raw meat to a giant reptile wasn't her idea of a pleasant leisure activity either. Handling slippery raptor meat made her gag, and she nearly missed the bright bird flying towards the paddock in her distraction.

The war drake's claw shot out, nearly spearing the bird and causing its claw to release a scrap of paper. *Not again.* Niema ran to pick up the note and tried to read the words, but the lack of daylight made it hard to make out her Superior's handwriting. She crumpled the note and whistled to calm the beast before putting its muzzle back on.

Niema left the paddock, unfurling the note when she reached a streetlamp and peering at the words on the page.

Niema, I heard the king has taken steps against the Disciples. If you aren't careful, you'll be caught in the aftermath. I understand that you have reason not to trust me, but I ask that you give me the chance to speak to you in person.

Come to the docks at dawn tomorrow. Alone.

"She's here," Niema murmured into the night. *She's really here. In Dalathar.* If she expected to meet Niema at the docks by dawn, she must have already flown her war drake close enough to reach the capital.

She ran the rest of the way back to Yala's house without stopping and knocked breathlessly on the door.

When she answered, Yala's sharp eyes caught on the note in

229

Niema's hands immediately. "Not another message from your Superior. Is she *still* demanding that you return to the enclave?"

"No, she's coming *here.*" Niema crumpled the note in her fist. "Or she's already in Dalathar."

Yala's eyes widened. "Shit. She left the enclave?"

Niema folded the note over again and again as though by creasing Superior Kralia's words, she might erase them from existence. "She must think that it's worth the risk."

"That or she's desperate for you to be back under her control." Yala's eyes bored into hers. "Don't, Niema. It's not worth it."

Isn't it? Her Superior might be able to fill in the gaps in their knowledge surrounding the events of the past few weeks. She and Yala might have their suspicions as to the nature of their enemy, but they remained nothing but that. Suspicions.

"Did *she* know the Disciples of the Flame ordered King Tharen's death?" Saren asked. "Fuck, I bet she did."

"Without a doubt," Yala said. "She's been aware of the island long before the rest of us knew too."

But does she know the former king might have survived?

If Superior Kralia had been aware of Superior Datriem's intention to assassinate the king, did she also know if that plan had failed? Nobody but Niema would stand a chance of convincing her to share the truth. Assuming, of course, that Superior Kralia didn't have an ulterior motive.

The others would never believe she didn't. Niema knew they'd see her as naïve for believing her Superior's promise not to take away Niema's will after her prior betrayal too.

Would it be worth the risk?

Yes. I have to find out the truth. For Yala's sake, she had to place her faith in Yalet and trust that her Superior kept her word this time.

22

For the second time in a week, Viam stood at the back of the king's receiving room with the sense of a noose tightening around her neck.

Though this wasn't a formal trial, some of the guards jeered and muttered when the small group of Disciples of the Flame walked in. She'd never seen them show such disrespect to Disciples before. King Daliel had asked for his father's former advisors and the high-ranked Disciples who'd worked closely with Superior Datriem, and only seven Disciples had answered the summons, including a man named Danir who wore a bandage around one leg and such a furious expression that Viam would have suspected he was amongst the conspirators even if she hadn't already known him to have attacked Yala.

"Thank you for coming," King Daliel addressed the Disciples. "You were close to my father, and for that reason, I hope you'll be honest with me today."

He might have been hoping for too much, given the murderous expression on Danir's face. The others were more subdued though visibly discomfited. They must have known from the moment they received the king's invitation that they'd been found out, if they hadn't already heard the rumours. Viam found herself both wishing Yala was here to see and glad that she wasn't.

The king continued. "You might remember the last time we spoke was at the previous king's funeral, when you offered condolences on my father's death. I have regrets about how I handled the matter and banished you from the palace, though I was young at the time and grieving."

Oh. She'd forgotten that they would have spoken immediately following King Tharen's death. Viam recalled seeing the Disciples at the funeral, but she hadn't paid attention to any interactions they might have had with the new monarch.

"However," he went on. "New information has come to light from the individuals who participated in the last mission that my father ordered before his death."

"Are you referring to the disgraced former captain Yala Palathar?" said the bandaged man. "She's violent and unpredictable. She attacked some of your guards, didn't she?"

"We're not here to discuss the captain." The king's tone was as close to sharp as Viam had ever heard it. "Whatever she may have done, it's your own actions that concern me. My father trusted you with his safety, as did his personal guards."

Nobody spoke for a moment. The Disciples' expressions gave nothing away, but Viam held her breath, fighting the urge to flee the room to avoid the inevitable flames.

"Rafragoria never claimed responsibility for his death," he went on. "Since then, I've been informed by a reliable source that the mission was no ordinary skirmish over territory but one centred on a site dedicated to the god of death, Mekan. This information was not conveyed in any official reports, nor were any of the soldiers directly involved in the mission allowed to put forward their experience, by order of your former leader, Superior Datriem.

Viam's vision tunnelled; she took in deep breaths, knowing that she needed to stay conscious in the moment to witness this, not just for herself but for Yala and Saren and for the other squad members who'd lost their lives before seeing their experiences on the island validated as truth.

"Yala Palathar is a liar," said Danir. "Your father was murdered by Rafragorian assassins. One of his own personal guards confirmed it before his own death."

"Yes," said King Daliel. "Certainly, that is the story. However, when I asked questions of my own staff, there are some obvious discrepancies between their accounts of events. More critically, the person who passed on the sole survivor's last words to the commanders and the staff at the palace was Superior Datriem."

The other Disciples didn't speak, but some exchanged glances or fidgeted. They must know this was their last chance to admit the truth before it was drawn from their mouths but that once they'd made a confession, they'd never be able to take it back.

"Superior Datriem died before I was ever able to discuss the matter with him directly," said the king. "That is why I have asked you to come here. I would like to hear your own accounts of the events surrounding my father's death. Some of you were, I believe, present at the preparations for the battle."

"Yes," said an older male Disciple. "We waited for the king's return and were sent back to the temple when he was declared dead."

"And did you know what was upon the island that my father sought?"

This time, nobody answered. Tension laced the air, and the temperature climbed higher, unless it was merely Viam's imagination.

"Did any of you know the island contained a source of Corruption?"

"Yala Palathar accused your *father* of dabbling in Corruption," said Danir. "Why believe anything she claimed?"

"I never claimed to believe Yala or the others who may have backed up her account." He didn't look at Viam, but her shoulders tensed all the same. "It's you whom I want to hear an answer from. Did you know anything of the island my father sought?"

"No." The Disciple who spoke shifted on his feet as though considering making a run for it, but the guards blocking the exit banished the notion from Viam's mind too.

"I have been made aware of a book that contains a detailed map of the island that my father had access to," King Daliel added. "This information came to me by way of Superior Sietra of Skytower."

Viam stiffened. *Superior Sietra?* Did Kelan and the others know she'd been in touch with the king?

"The book in question once belonged to your former Superior," he went on. "It's hard to assume that he, at least, was unaware of what my father sought."

Gods. Even Danir couldn't argue his way out of this one.

"With that in mind," said the king, "it's easy to conclude that your former Superior sought to keep that information from me and from the army and that he went to some considerable lengths to silence those who knew the truth. Those are not the actions of someone who had my father's best interests in mind—nor those of Laria as a whole."

"You're mistaken," said Danir, though without his former confidence. "Our Superior wanted what was best for Laria. He gave his life for his country."

"Regardless, I would appreciate an answer." King Daliel faced the Disciples. "Did your Superior order my father's death?"

All the air fled the room. Rivulets of sweat ran down Viam's back. The Disciples wavered before her; she didn't know if she wanted to hear them deny the accusations or throw themselves at the king's feet and plead for mercy.

A female Disciple stepped forward. "Superior Datriem gave the order. As he represents Dalathik Himself, the rest of us have no choice but to obey him."

King Daliel was silent for a moment, planes of emotion flickering across his face like the Disciples' own flames. "Superior Datriem ordered you to kill my father?"

"Yes." She spoke in a choked voice. "If he had been allowed to bring Corruption back to Laria, you saw for yourself what terrible consequences would have resulted. The decision haunted us, but it was the correct choice."

"I see." He swallowed, closed his eyes briefly. "All of you were involved in his death?"

"This is ridiculous," Danir burst out. "Yala Palathar is a Disciple of Death herself. She's slaughtered hundreds."

"She is a soldier," he said. "And irrelevant. You were assigned to protect my father and failed, and for that, you will face trial." His voice gained a hint of steel, and even the Disciple fell silent at the display of a kind of power that even their deity couldn't give them.

The guards moved at the king's command, drawing their swords, and one of the male Disciples panicked. "It's a lie! It's all a lie!"

"Be still, Disciple." A guard pointed his short sword at the Disciple's back. "You already confessed."

"King Tharen isn't dead!" His voice rose, high, echoing off the walls. "He's not dead!"

Viam stared, transfixed. So did the king, though the guard continued to point his short sword at the terrified Disciple.

"You can spin all the lies you want, but you'll face the penalty one way or another," growled the palace guard. "Now, still your tongue."

"I'm not lying." He looked to the others, his eyes wide and pleading. "We killed the guards, but he escaped on his war drake. We never killed him. I swear in the name of Dalathik—"

"Get them out of here," the king ordered. "All of them."

As the guards rounded up the Disciples and herded them from the room, the man's terrified words lingered in the air like smoke, burning through Viam's skin. *He's not dead.*

He must be lying. He *must* be. King Tharen's death was absolute. An undeniable fact. Like the conspiracy amongst the Disciples, headed by Superior Datriem.

He wasn't there. The Superior wasn't. The others carried out the order.
Or did they?

———

Niema was gone.

Yala had woken refreshed that morning despite another night of trading shifts with Niema and Saren to keep watch in case Danir tried to burn down the house while they were sleeping. She vaguely recalled Niema taking over the watch at midnight, arguing that Yala needed rest after her imprisonment and escape, but now, there was no sign of her anywhere.

Had she gone out on some errand? Yala pulled on her clothes and splashed cold water on her face from a bucket that Niema must have brought in, but her sleeping mat was unoccupied, and her coin purse lay with her other meagre belongings in the corner.

"Saren." She peered up the stairs, one hand on her cane. "Saren?"

"What?" Saren appeared in the stairway, dishevelled but alert. "Niema's keeping watch until dawn, I thought."

"It *is* dawn, and she isn't here." Uneasy, she crossed the room to Niema's sleeping mat and gave it a nudge with her cane. The crumpled remains of one of the notes Niema had received from her Superior caught her eye. "Shit."

"She hasn't gone to meet *her*, has she?" Saren asked. "Her Superior?"

"There's a possibility." Yala scooped up the note and skimmed the words. *Meet me at the docks at dawn.*

Niema had been subdued after she'd come back from the paddocks the previous evening, though that wasn't unusual for her, and they all had enough to occupy their thoughts. Yet the note's revelation that Superior Kralia was in Dalathar might have prompted Niema to seek her out, to prevent her from coming after Yala.

Why does nobody ever do as I ask them to?

Sighing, she paced to the door to retrieve her shoes. "I'd better check she hasn't taken the war drake."

If not, she'd have either left on foot or by wagon, which might give Yala a chance of catching up to her if she flew on the war drake herself. Of course, landing that beast near the docks was a risk in itself, but didn't Superior Kralia own a war drake of her very own?

Hoping she wasn't making a mistake by leaving Saren alone at home, she walked to the paddock and found the war drake chained up where she'd left it. *Good.* Not that she'd really believed Niema would have taken the beast without Yala's knowledge, but when she opened the paddock, the war drake let out such a howl that Yala backed up a step.

Ah, shit. I brought the claw. She'd put on her belt that still contained the void drake's claw, and the mere trace of Corruption's presence had scared the living hells out of the beast.

"It's only me," she murmured to the war drake. "Stop that."

The beast remained ill at ease, though she managed to distract it with a handful of raw meat for long enough to let her strap on its saddle. She left the muzzle on just in case, though she removed its wing restraints.

"You and I are going for a flight," she said. "A proper one this time."

The war drake growled in response.

"Yes, I know Niema isn't here," she said. "She's the one you like best, but it's because she uses her magic to calm you. Mine doesn't work on the living. Be glad of that."

What if Superior Kralia has bound Niema to her will again? whispered a voice in her mind. *If she sends her to kill me, I'll need to be ready to fight back.*

Why, though, had Niema decided to meet her in the first place? If she'd believed Superior Kralia had information that might help them find a way to avoid the nation collapsing, she might have thought it was worth gambling her own autonomy, but Yala would not allow her friend's will to be stolen. Not again.

———

Niema rode in a wagon to the docks, having coaxed its raptors away from the market as its owner was setting up their stall. She'd debated borrowing the war drake instead in case she needed to get away fast, but if things went badly, Yala would need an easy route of escape.

Please don't let this be a mistake.

The wagon stank of raw meat; Niema hadn't checked what the merchant had been selling before she'd climbed in. She whistled, and the raptors drew to a halt. As she climbed out of the wagon, it was easy to spot the large reptilian shape in the sky above the docks. Niema's heart leapt into her throat at the sight of Superior Kralia sitting atop its back as they gracefully came to land.

Niema walked fast until she came to an open space in front of a row of warehouses where the war drake crouched. Superior Kralia wore gear more suited for battle than her usual attire, not unlike the clothing she'd worn during the fight in Setemar. It felt like a lot more than mere weeks since they'd seen one another last, yet simultaneously, they might never have been apart. Her pulse thrummed with longing and fear in equal measures.

"Superior Kralia." Niema half dropped to her knees out of habit but caught herself and rose upright. "Why are you here? I thought the enclave needed you."

"Some matters cannot be trusted to anyone but myself."

"Then why were you so desperate for me to reply to your messages?" Her hands clenched into fists. "What was the point?"

"Is it hard to believe that I feared for your safety?" she queried. "You'd be safer with your enclave members. They miss you a lot."

Niema's nails bit into her palms. She knew her Superior—her *former* Superior—was trying to muddle her thoughts and make her doubt herself, but knowing didn't mean that her tactics were ineffective.

"Your friend Hachim has been suggesting he might come to the city too," Superior Kralia added. "The others are worried about him."

"Hachim." Of the others, he was the one most likely to follow her despite her warnings. "You can't be that concerned if you left him behind. Why *are* you here? You didn't come for my sake."

"I'm here to protect the enclave from Corruption," she said. "That, above all, is my purpose."

"Even if it means turning on your own Disciples." Niema's fists clenched tighter as she fought to keep eye contact with her Superior. "I haven't forgotten."

"Yet you came here to meet me despite knowing the risks. Why?"

"I only agreed to this meeting because I wanted to ask you a question," said Niema. "Concerning King Tharen."

Superior Kralia's face remained impassive. "The former king?"

"He was killed by the Disciples of the Flame," Niema said in a rush. "On Superior Datriem's orders. Did you know?"

The faintest flicker of emotion stirred in Superior Kralia's eyes. "Now, what would give you that idea?"

"If you've been watching the city, you'll know that Yala told the king the truth about his father's death," she said. "Superior Datriem was willing to murder the king to stop Corruption. That's a goal you both shared. Isn't it?"

"You thought I would conspire to kill the monarch?" She shook her head. "I have never been involved in politics, Niema. The schemes of kings and emperors have no interest for me."

"You just *said* that stopping Corruption is your purpose above all else." Niema would not allow her to talk around the subject and turn Niema's own words against her. "I'm not accusing you of directly being involved. I'm asking if you knew."

"If I did, would it make any difference to you?" she asked. "You already believe me to be a villain."

"You tried to kill Yala for being a Disciple of Death. You tried to kill *me* for allying with her."

"And yet you came here behind her back." Her tone was knowing, too much so. "Niema, I understand you well. For instance, you see your personal safety as placed below the need to protect those you love, and you had more than one question to ask me."

Niema's hands uncurled. In the end, despite it all, she couldn't keep any secrets from her Superior. Her face was laid open like a flower in bloom.

"I have another question." Niema swallowed. "I heard some claims that the Disciples of the Flame failed in their attempt to kill King Tharen. That he—"

"Is alive."

"You knew," Niema whispered. "Didn't you?"

"Yes," she said. "And that, Niema, is why I am here."

Niema closed her eyes, her legs unsteady, as though the ground itself might give way and send her plummeting into the ocean. "You think he's coming back. To Laria."

"I would prefer to avoid that," she said. "However, events have progressed far quicker than I anticipated, and I have little doubt that word of King Tharen's survival will begin to spread as quickly as that of his murder at the hands of his own advisors."

"What—what makes you think that?" He was hiding, wasn't he? Only Yala and a handful of people suspected he was anywhere other than in the depths of the ocean.

"Do you really think," said Superior Kralia, "that your friend Yala will stand by and let the man who cost her everything return to Laria?"

No. She won't. Gods, Yala...

"Mark my words, she'll seek him out first," she went on. "And I hope that when the time comes, you'll remember my warning."

23

Kelan might not have seen the war drake if he hadn't happened to be looking out of the window of his room at the inn at that precise moment. He'd woken to dawn's light piercing his eyes, and when he saw the large, winged shape soaring above the city, Yala immediately came to mind. He'd have thought she'd be trying to avoid attention after her recent arrest, and while few people would be awake at this hour, the city guards certainly would.

He dressed quickly and headed downstairs, but the war drake had long since vanished beyond the rooftops by the time he'd left the inn. He tried to shortcut over the wall to the outer city but found himself again faced with a row of spear-wielding guards.

"Surely, you don't mind people *leaving* the upper city," he protested, but to no avail.

Sighing, he glided back downward and made his way to the front gate instead. When he'd talked his way past the guards, another winged shadow passed overhead, this one much closer than the first—and heading northward.

This one had to be Yala, surely, but who was the other? Kelan glided north, skirting the upper city, and closed in behind the beast.

Yala tilted her head; relief and surprise flickered across her face before she tamed her expression. "Thank the gods you're alive."

"I'm honoured." He glided to her side, and the war drake growled in annoyance when a current of air buffeted its wings. "I heard you got arrested."

"I'll have to tell you the full story when we're on the ground." She gestured north with a hand. "Niema went to meet her Superior."

"She didn't, did she?" He'd have thought Niema would have more sense than to go back to the person who'd controlled her against her will. What was Superior Kralia even doing this far from the enclave? "Shit. Was that the other war drake I saw?"

Yala squeezed her knees around the war drake's neck to urge it to continue flying onward. "Yes. I know that flying a war drake without her is risky, but this was the quickest way to reach the docks."

"That's where she went?" He swivelled north, where he could make out the glittering expanse of the ocean beyond the city. "Why would Superior Kralia leave the enclave in the first place?"

"Long story." Yala leaned forward as her war drake gained speed, its huge wings propelling it over the rooftops. "I'll tell you when we're on the ground."

Once they were past the upper city, Kelan spied the second war drake's massive form crouched in the open space in front of a row of warehouses near the docks. Yala's steed did, too, and it dropped into a sudden dive. A growl rumbled in its throat, as though to challenge its fellow beast.

"Stop that," Yala told the war drake. "Stop. *Stop.*"

From the second war drake's back, Superior Kralia let out a shrill whistle. Yala's steed abruptly stopped mid-dive, gliding to a halt. From where she stood in front of Superior Kralia, Niema stared up at Yala and then Kelan.

"Niema." Kelan descended to land at her side. "Need help?"

"Kelan." Niema's mouth parted. "When did you get back?"

"Yesterday." He nodded to her Superior. "Just in time."

"I am no threat to Niema," Superior Kralia said. "She came to me willingly."

"It wouldn't be the first time you manipulated her into doing your bidding." Yala leaned over the now-placid war drake's side. "Leave her alone."

"I believe our conversation is over." Superior Kralia whistled, and her steed rose upward in a graceful wingbeat. "I'd advise all of you to consider your allegiances."

Her war drake continued to rise upward over the docks. Kelan could only imagine the confusion of anyone who happened to look out the window to see two giant winged beasts roaming the area. The actual seafront was all but deserted; he might have blamed the early hour, or the possibility of an imminent attack from Rafragoria was to blame, but a stillness hung in the air that he'd never experienced in the capital beforehand.

"You didn't have to come to my rescue." Niema lifted her gaze when Yala's war drake descended to take Superior Kralia's place. "I'm sorry I didn't tell you I was leaving. I thought—"

"You thought I'd try to stop you. You were right." Yala watched her through narrowed eyes. "Did she try to control you again?"

"No." Niema turned to Kelan. "I'm glad you're back. Are the others all right?"

"Yes, mostly." He had the distinct impression that Niema was trying to divert attention from her own narrow escape, but if her Superior had ordered her to attack Yala, she would have already struck. "They're on their way back to Skytower. I came here to—"

The war drake interrupted by trying to take a bite out of his leg; Niema whistled, and the beast went still once more.

"We can't stay here." Yala extended a hand to Niema. "How'd you get here?"

"By wagon. I'll tell the raptors to return to the market."

"You'll tell the what?" said Kelan.

Yala made a noise halfway between a sigh and a groan. "Really, it hardly matters."

"It does matter," she protested, backing away from the warehouse. "I'll be right back."

"She took a ride in someone's wagon by convincing their raptors to obey her," Yala said in explanation. "She'd make a fine thief if she let go of that conscience of hers."

Kelan grinned. "Adjusting to Dalathar, is she? I assume *she* didn't get arrested like you did?"

"Right, of course you heard the rumours." She pursed her lips. "Might be easier to start there. What did you hear?"

He thought back. "Firstly, something about a plague of rodents. Then, that the Disciples of the Flame were accused of murdering..."

"King Tharen." Niema was already back. "That's what Superior Kralia wanted to discuss with me. She wants me to find him."

Kelan blinked. "To find King *Tharen?*"

"Well, he's not a king anymore." Niema paced over to Yala, who extended a hand to help her climb onto the war drake's back. "But yes."

"He was also dead, last I heard." Kelan looked between them, half expecting them to share a laugh at the joke, though he didn't think Niema was capable of that level of deceit. "Did the Disciples of the Flame get any kind of punishment?"

"Not yet." Yala shuffled forward as Niema settled in behind her on the war drake's back. "Depends on if they confess and if the king believes them."

"I'm lost." He darted sideways when the war drake lifted a claw. "Why'd *you* get arrested?"

Niema calmed the steed with a whistle. "She started a public brawl to stop the Disciples of the Flame from killing her in retaliation for accusing them of murder."

Kelan raised a brow at Yala. "Is that how it went?"

"Pretty much." Yala leaned forward on her war drake's back. "I'll tell you the rest on the way back home. And then Niema can tell us why she decided to risk being made into an instrument of death in her Superior's hands again."

"I'm sorry." Niema lowered her gaze, her face flushing. "I suspected Superior Kralia might know something we didn't and that she'd only share that information with me."

"Something concerning King Tharen's assassination?" Some of the pieces slid together in his mind. "Was she involved in the conspiracy?"

"Not directly." Niema addressed the war drake's back as they rose into the air. "She was in correspondence with Superior Datriem, though, so he kept her updated. Including... including when the plan failed."

Yala's whole body tensed. "Are you sure you believe her?"

"Why else would she have come to the capital alone?" Niema spoke in a whisper. "She knows that if he's alive, it means he might return, which means Corruption on a scale we've never seen before."

"And by 'he,' you mean the former king?" Kelan's blood went ice-cold, and he recalled the Rafragorians' inexplicable accusations and the Disciples of the Sea's strange warnings. "Tell me more."

Kelan listened, half-incredulous, as Yala recounted the attack on the parade and the threats from the Disciples of the Flame, her invitation to the palace, and her subsequent arrest and encounter with Mekan's servant in the guardhouse.

"After everything, King Tharen truly survived?" Kelan spoke after a moment had passed. *"He's* behind this?"

"I wouldn't normally give credence to the ravings of one of Mekan's followers," said Yala, "but if Superior Kralia confirmed it was true..."

The war drake took a steep dive, descending over the roofs of the outer city. Kelan watched her guide the beast towards the paddock, his mind churning. King Tharen's survival *did* make sense when he examined the pieces closer. He'd died at sea. His body was never recovered. Everyone knew that, but in the intervening years, those facts had solidified until nobody could ever conceive of any alternative. If anyone had known of his survival, it would have been the Disciples of the Sea, but they kept little contact with Laria.

As for Rafragoria...

"It's no wonder Superior Shralin tried to warn you off going to see the Disciples of the Sea." Yala straightened in her seat when the war drake's large claws touched down in the paddock. "How *did* that go? Not as badly as it could have, I assume, if you're still alive."

"Oh, it was a disaster," he said. "First, we got kidnapped by Rafragorian soldiers, and then two separate groups of Disciples of the Sea tried to kill us."

Yala listened while she redid the war drake's restraints and fed it chunks of raw meat as a distraction as she bound up its wings. Niema, too, listened without asking many questions, at least until he reached the part when they'd been kidnapped in the dead of night.

"Some Disciples of the Sea joined forces with Mekan?" Niema asked. "Why would they do that?"

"Same as those Disciples of the Earth, I imagine," Kelan said. "Dissatisfaction with their own Superior. Lust for power. If it was King Tharen himself giving orders, that lends legitimacy too."

The Disciples of the Sea wouldn't bow to any other authority unless they had a very good reason. There might even have been threats involved. How were they supposed to defend against the forces of the dead infiltrating their own temple? They'd have nowhere to run if Mekan's beasts swam into their midst in a similar manner to how they'd tunnelled through the walls of Setemar.

"I almost feel sorry for the Rafragorians," Yala added. "They didn't ask for our former king to summon Mekan's monsters near their shore."

"The Disciples of the Sea resolutely refused to back up our accounts," Kelan said. "As far as diplomatic missions went, I wouldn't call it a resounding success."

"Do they still blame us for the ambassadors' deaths?" Yala's jaw tensed. "That must have been King Tharen too. Clever, manufacturing a distraction from his own survival. I'll bet he'll use it as an excuse to declare war again upon his return to power."

Would he? If he was in charge of the Successors, he didn't need to show his face to elicit terror throughout Laria and Rafragoria alike.

"After being absent for that long?" Kelan left the paddock ahead of her. "I thought the army was a shadow of what it used to be."

"That doesn't matter if he brings a force of Mekan's monsters to supplement his forces." Her voice was quiet but thrummed with tension. "He's had years to plan. How many of us can honestly say we're prepared?"

"Not enough" was the honest answer. "If the Disciples of the Flame who knew of his survival end up being locked up for murder, that leaves... us."

"What about Superior Shralin?" Niema asked. "I forgot to ask Superior Kralia."

"Oh, *he* won't have known," Yala said. "Almost certainly, he wasn't in on the plan. That's why Mieren and Danir bristled against his authority."

"Yes, I spoke to him yesterday," said Kelan. "Your charming friend tried to burn my face off."

"Danir?" Yala's brows rose. "You're lucky. He did the same to me, and I barely got out alive."

"What if—" Niema tripped over her feet on the cobbles. "Shit. If King Tharen survived, there's no reason to punish any of the Disciples of the Flame. The conspirators will walk free."

"Not if I have anything to do with it." Yala's cane hit the ground with each step. "The attempted murder of a monarch is still punishable by death."

Yes, he thought, *but they're still among the few people in Dalathar who might be both willing and able to take a stand against King Tharen in the event that he does return.*

Unbidden, an image rose in his mind from the night of their capture. A man sitting on a void drake's back, stark against the moon.

Might that have been the former king?

———

Yala's leg was displeased with her for the morning's flight, but she'd escaped lightly, considering. She and the others stopped at a nearby market to buy breakfast—Niema making a sudden disappearance when she saw the merchant whose wagon she'd borrowed—and she also bought her new shoes while she was at it, as Niema's were worn to ribbons after only a few short days.

247

"You can pay me when we're at home," Yala said through a mouthful of fried fish. "I saw you left your money behind. And your weapons."

"I don't have any weapons." Niema nibbled at a piece of flatbread, reluctant to meet Yala's eyes, perhaps out of guilt at visiting her Superior behind her back. "I can't even use them."

"I have more than enough to spare, and yes, you can, if you get creative." She nodded to Kelan, whose face was lined with tiredness from the long days he'd spent on the road, but he didn't appear to have suffered any lasting injuries in his escape from the Disciples of the Sea. "When did you say you were going to Skytower?"

"I didn't, but I am intrigued to see if the Disciples of the Flame face any consequences after your accusation," he said. "Some of the guards have already assumed their guilt. And mine too. At least the ones who can't tell the difference between one Disciple and another."

Already? Her surprise was tempered by suspicion, especially knowing how swiftly the guards had turned against her. "I suppose we'll find out when Viam can next get away from the palace."

They didn't have to wait long. When Yala opened the door to the house, Saren jumped at them, wielding two of Yala's daggers, though he dropped the weapons when he realised who they were.

"Good, you're both alive." His gaze fell on Kelan. "And so is he. Have fun swimming with the Disciples of the Sea, did you?"

"I've had better holidays." Kelan glided to one of the armchairs and would have sat in it if Yala hadn't pointedly lifted her cane. Shrugging, he positioned himself against the wall instead. "You need more furniture."

"Not until those Disciples are locked up," said Saren. "We don't need more flammable material in here."

"No." Yala's hand dropped to the pouch at her waist. "I'm glad they didn't attack while I was gone."

Within an hour, a tentative knock came from the front. Again, Saren seized a dagger and then dropped it when Yala opened the door and Viam sidled into the room. She wore her best clothes this time, suggesting that she'd come from the palace and not the paddocks, and she did a double-take when she spotted Kelan.

"You're alive." She swivelled to Yala, her eyes red around the edges as if she'd been crying. "I came here as soon as I could. The Disciples…"

Yala's pulse surged. "What of them?"

"They confessed?" Saren spoke before Viam did and then whooped when she nodded. "Finally, some justice."

"Not yet." Viam tugged at her lacy sleeve. "They'll be put on trial individually later. They were questioned as a group initially so His Majesty could assess if there was any truth to the accusation. They came out with the usual story of the king's body being lost at sea, but I don't think they ever expected to have to relive the experience again"

Despite the whirlwind kicking up in her head, Yala forced the words out in calm tones. "How'd King Daliel convince them to admit the truth?"

"He mentioned seeing pages of a journal his father read. From—Skytower."

"What?" Kelan's mouth dropped open. "My Superior sent him the journal?"

"I don't know how much of it he read, but it was enough for him to believe that his father knew what was on the island and that Superior Datriem did too," she said. "The Disciples tried to claim they didn't have a choice but to obey because their Superior's commands came from Dalathik Himself."

"Those self-righteous pricks dug their own graves," Saren said. "I wish I'd seen their faces, especially that Danir."

Danir. If he came after her again, he'd be committing treason against the crown. That might not stop him, of course, but it was something, a slither of a consequence where she'd never thought one would exist.

"Danir…" Viam choked on his name. "He tried to argue, but one of the Disciples panicked in the end. Said the king wasn't dead and that he escaped on his war drake."

Yala's whirling thoughts came to a dead stop. "What did King Daliel say to that?"

"Nothing. He ordered them to be locked up until they face a proper trial."

"Few prisons will hold Disciples of the Flame indefinitely." Yala kept her tone free of emotion. "The king must be confident they'll stay put."

"Yala." A pleading note entered Viam's voice. "Yala, you'd tell me if you thought it was true, wouldn't you? If he—survived?"

"Yes." The word was uttered without inflection, yet Viam stumbled back as though Yala had struck her across the face.

Swaying, Viam caught her balance against the wall and gasped, "*How?*"

"We don't know," Saren said. "Yala thinks so, and the others have gone along with her, but—"

"Superior Kralia is here," Yala told Viam. "She thinks King Tharen is going to return to Laria. With Mekan's army, I assume."

Niema, who'd shrunk into the far corner of the room as though she hoped the others would forget she was present, flinched. "She didn't say that directly."

"No, because it isn't true." Saren spoke loudly, as though by emphasising each word, he might will the truth into existence. "We've seen no proof."

"I saw someone riding a void drake at sea," Kelan said. "I did wonder who'd have the nerve."

"Fuck!" Launching out of the armchair, Saren seized one of the daggers lying on the floor and flung it at the wall with such force that the hilt snapped clean off.

"When you've quite finished destroying my weapons," Yala said, "we have some decisions to make."

"You aren't going after him." Saren spun on his heel, pointing at her with a shaking hand. "Please tell me you aren't going after him."

"We don't know *where* the Successors are hiding." Even Kelan eyed Yala warily, as though he thought she might call the war drake there and then and order the others to follow her straight to King Tharen's hideout.

Yes. She knew exactly where to look. She'd known, on some level, since that dying man had told her to come home.

To Mekan.

To the island.

"It makes no sense!" Viam threw up her hands. "Why would King Tharen make no effort to contact his son in over half a decade? To let him know he survived?"

"That would have alerted the Disciples of the Flame," Yala said. "Superior Datriem wouldn't have hesitated to send more Disciples to finish the job, given the chance. Without him, the other conspirators are outnumbered, and now they're in jail, they're no longer a threat."

In a way, *she* had helped facilitate his return. The realisation galled her, but it was the truth.

"What will he do to King Daliel?" Viam whispered. "He won't harm his own son, will he?"

"Probably not," Yala said. "How did King Daliel react to the Disciples' confession?"

"How else? He's in shock," said Viam. "He didn't believe their claim that his father survived, I don't think."

No, thought Yala. *He wouldn't... but he will.*

24

With Kelan's curiosity about the outcome of the Disciples' trial satisfied, he had little excuse to stay in the capital. His Superior would expect him to show up and explain why he hadn't returned to Skytower immediately—and moreover, she owed *him* an explanation of why she'd sent the journal he'd entrusted her with to the *monarch* of all people.

He left Yala's house without returning to the Disciples' Inn, heading south and then west. At least his enforced rest had restored his ability to fly, and he didn't need to take any more detours on the way back to Skytower. Part of him wondered if he might run into the other Disciples on the way, but he encountered nobody else in the air as he made his way over Laria's flattened expanse of fields dotted with farms and villages.

The sun had begun its descent when Skytower came into view, gilding its stone edges and creating the illusion of a flaming torch on the mountainside. He glided to the upmost level and knocked on his Superior's office door. She'd doubtless be displeased with him for separating from the others, but the news of the former king's survival would distract her. With luck, she'd also have a plan as to how to stop the country being dragged into war, because Kelan was sorely lacking in ideas.

"Enter," Superior Sietra called from the other side of the door.

He did so, kneeling before her on the prayer mat. "My apologies for the delay in my return."

He assumed, at least, that the others were already here. When she didn't respond, he took that to imply that he'd guessed right and that she expected a good reason for his late arrival.

"Lakiel accounted your experiences in Amanar extensively," she said. "He mentioned you went to Dalathar to warn the king of a possible attack from Rafragoria."

Oh. Right. He hadn't been near the palace at all in the end, but he could hardly be blamed for letting his original plan slip away, given the circumstances. "Yes, but I learned something, ah, rather pertinent. Something I think you'll want to know."

"Oh?" she said, impassive.

"He's alive," he said. "King Tharen. He also might be the Successors' leader."

"Explain." The word sliced through the air with all the force of a command from the god of the sky Himself, and it never would have occurred to Kelan to refuse.

As the others had already told her of their disastrous encounters with the Disciples of the Sea and with the Rafragorian soldiers, he skipped straight to his entry to the capital and the outlandish rumours that had solidified into even more improbable fact.

"I'm inclined to accept it's him," he finished. "The Disciples of the Flame might have been lying in order to avoid a death sentence, but Superior Kralia wouldn't have left her enclave without cause."

"No," Superior Sietra said. "She would not, and I long suspected her and Superior Datriem of being in secret correspondence. Nevertheless, if their plan to dispose of King Tharen *didn't* succeed, why would he not make himself known to his son or his former allies?"

"I can't imagine it's easy hiding at sea while surrounded by Disciples and hostile soldiers," said Kelan. "He must have been afraid enough of Superior Datriem to decide it was worth keeping his distance. He wasn't a Disciple himself. Not then."

"You think he is now," she surmised. "And that he intends to use Corruption to reclaim his throne."

"That's conjecture on my part, I admit," he said, "but Yala, Niema, and the others believe the same. The Successors have certainly been targeting the current monarch, though I don't know that King Tharen necessarily wants him *dead*. He's testing to see if Laria is ready for his return."

"And allying with the Disciples of the Sea." Her lips pursed. "Kelan, if you're wrong, the consequences will be severe. I'd keep this to yourself for the time being."

At least she believes me. Until he'd met the other Superiors, he'd never truly appreciated the value of having a leader who was both competent and believed her Disciples above all else.

"Whoever their leader is, the Successors almost certainly killed the Rafragorian ambassadors," he said. "I thought the Rafragorians we ran into were trying to blame the Disciples of the Sea—which they might have been if the ones who betrayed the others were responsible."

"That might well be the case." Her gaze travelled over to the desk, which was laden with papers and pots of ink. "I spoke to the others about our potential options, but we mutually decided to wait for your return before we made a decision. I won't ask you to risk your life by going back to the Disciples of the Sea again, though it would have helped if they had agreed to assist you with preventing conflict with the Rafragorians."

"I can't imagine it'd be easy to explain that some of their fellow Disciples turned against their own deity to someone who doesn't speak the same language."

When her attention fell on the desk again, he made out the upside-down shape of Mavilangran's journal.

"Yes, the journal has been enlightening," she said. "Thank you for bringing it to me."

"I thought..." He squinted in the dim light. "I heard the journal's contents were instrumental in the king's decision to prosecute the Disciples of the Flame."

Her attention sharpened. "He did?"

"Well, he's putting them on trial," he amended. "I thought you wanted to keep the journal here. What did you send him?"

"I've spent the last few weeks making several copies to ensure the information survives in the event that the journal goes astray again," she said. "I sent one of those copies to him, with a letter explaining the journal certainly depicts the same island his father sought."

"Did you know...?"

"That he was going to put the Disciples of the Flame on trial for murder?" she said. "No, I did not. Have you read the journal yourself?"

"Not cover to cover. The translation is difficult to understand in places." He lowered his gaze; he knew she was aware of his struggles with reading, but that didn't mean he wanted to mention them aloud. "Yala told me the main parts. Mavilangran travelled to the island and then came to Laria, or whatever existed on this continent before King Larial's arrival."

"And he met the Disciples of Life," she said. "I do have to wonder if Superior Kralia is aware of that history."

He'd wondered the same. "She might be. She did know the king was interested in Corruption, through Superior Datriem, and it's reasonable to assume she saw the journal as well. Now she's claiming to be on our side and that she wants to help."

"I wouldn't trust her," said Superior Sietra. "Do not forget the abilities she possesses are not restricted by the bounds of a temple."

Just like Mekan's.

"What of the Disciples of the Flame?" he asked. "Superior Shralin warned us away from the Disciples of the Sea. I'm not convinced he was unaware of their treachery, though his Disciples already have their hands full with the king's accusation of murdering his father."

"I am not in contact with them." She picked up the journal and closed the pages. "Hence why I wrote the monarch instead. That, and I doubt Superior Shralin will easily forgive me for taking the journal."

"No, he's not best pleased with me either." When she beckoned,

Kelan glided to the desk, where she presented him with the journal. "What should I do with this?"

"I think Yala will have more use for this than I will if she intends to seek out the former king herself."

His mouth parted. "How on earth did you know that?"

"I met Yala long enough to gain her measure," she said. "I can't imagine she'd be content to stay idly in the capital now that she knows the true nature of her enemy."

"No." Taking the journal was risky in itself, though it didn't contain any instructions on how to summon the dead. Moreover, Mavilangran's account might offer some clues as to the former king's location. "But she can't beat the Successors alone. Even if Superior Kralia is on our side, there aren't enough of us."

"That's why I'm intending to send a force of Disciples of the Sky with you to the capital," she said. "I'd like to think that the Disciples of the Flame will rouse themselves to act if the city does come under attack from Corruption, but given the last time…"

"They might just stay hidden in their temple, I know."

Granted, if the Disciples of the Sea assisted in the attack, the god of the flames was no match for the ocean.

What about us, though? Or are we all signing up to die?

———

Viam waited for news of the Disciples' trial with almost as much apprehension as the Disciples themselves must feel. The king did not call her back to his side, nor was she invited to the questionings, for which she was grateful. After Yala's apparent confirmation of King Tharen's survival, she didn't trust herself to maintain her composure in front of his son. The news of the Disciples' betrayal had already shaken him beyond measure, and she didn't need to let it slip that she believed their claims that the assassination attempt had failed.

And if the rest was true? If his father was the Successors' leader? Viam didn't believe that King Tharen would have sent followers of Mekan to murder his son, but with no news forthcoming, she spent the day in the war drakes' paddock to avoid having to answer the others' questions. The rest of the staff knew she'd attended the initial questioning for the same reason news of the trial itself had spread throughout the palace: in Dalathar, rumours flowed as fast as the river and picked up equally as much debris along the way. She had no desire to spend her day putting down the more outlandish claims she'd heard, such as that King Daliel intended to personally execute his father's killers with the same blade that his father had taken with him to the bottom of the ocean. Supposedly.

Mercifully, the war drakes had little to say aside from snarls, and handling them was a job that required her to be alert enough not to dwell on recent events—including her recent conversation with Brenat. They'd scarcely exchanged two words since, and Brenat hadn't followed her to the paddocks either.

She's giving me space. To decide how to respond.

When Viam did leave the paddock at the day's end, she was greeted by someone else entirely walking out of the army barracks.

"Oh, Your Majesty." Her heart stuttered to a halt. "I didn't expect to see you here."

"I needed a change of scenery." King Daliel sounded as tired as he looked, as though the Disciples' betrayal had stripped away the remnants of his youthful optimism. "I've been meeting with the commanders."

She nodded, spying two guards standing behind him. He travelled nowhere alone now, and her heart twinged. She'd never considered him to be a friend—the gulf between their positions was too deep—but she was surprised at how much she regretted that their closeness had been replaced with a distance as deep as a crevasse.

"I cannot forgive them." He spoke in a murmur.

She didn't need to ask who he meant. "I wouldn't expect you to."

He released a sigh. "They acted on the orders of their Superior, for entirely valid reasons."

"And... Yala?" She licked her lips. "Would you forgive Yala, at least? She did no wrong."

"Yes, I'll pardon Yala Palathar," he said. "She will face no punishment at my hands."

That wasn't the same as forgiveness, but Viam doubted Yala would care for the distinction. Just as long as—

"And my offer remains open," he added. "If she wishes to join the Flight Division again. For now, I would like to offer you the position of commander instead."

"Me?" Viam took a step back. "I can't lead the Flight Division. I'm not qualified. I've never been a captain."

"You're qualified," he said. "Moreso than almost anyone else at the present time."

Viam shook her head. "There *isn't* a Flight Division yet. There's nobody to give orders to."

"Not yet, but we have a team of volunteers waiting to be trained." He gestured towards the barracks. "With some instruction, I'm sure they'll be more than capable."

"I don't mind teaching them to fly," she said, realising that that was true, "but it'll take some time, and they won't be ready for any missions for a long while."

Was there truly nobody better qualified? She'd never led a squad before, much less an army. Even Yala hadn't.

And if she's right? If it's King Tharen who's sending the dead to attack his own son?

What kind of a war were they really preparing for?

———

King Daliel, thought Yala, had more of a backbone than she'd given him credit for. With the Disciples of the Flame jailed, there was considerably less chance of Danir showing up to enact revenge on her, and while he and the others could theoretically use their powers to escape with ease, they wouldn't be able to run from the consequences of what they'd done.

Victory didn't taste as sweet as she might have once expected, but it had a certain spice to it, and she had to talk Saren out of throwing a party to celebrate.

"I'm not inviting a bunch of strangers to my home," she told him the morning after the Disciples' arrest. "We've spent enough time thinking the Disciples would burn the house down in the night."

"Speaking of Disciples." Niema, who'd been even quieter than usual since her encounter with her Superior, gestured towards the window. "Kelan's back."

"Already?" Yala watched his cloaked figure land in front of the house; seeing her, he waved.

"The others went straight to the inn," he explained when she opened the door. "I decided to come here first, since the guards are being such a nuisance about letting people in and out of the upper city."

"By 'the others,' how many do you mean?" Yala sensed some tension in his voice, though maybe it was her own imagination. "Enough to stand a chance against an oncoming army?"

"None of that," Saren said. "We're not going to fucking war."

We might be. From the expression on Kelan's face, the answer was no. "And did you tell your Superior everything?"

"Yes." He took in a breath. "She told me not to share the possibility of the former king's survival with anyone else, but I think she believes me. She also told me not to trust Superior Kralia."

"We can agree on that," Yala said. "What's her plan? To stay here and wait for Mekan's followers to strike first?"

"That's one option," he said. "The other is to take them by surprise."

"How?" Niema said. "We don't know where they're hiding."

We do. As the thought flitted through her mind, Kelan reached into his pocket and pulled out Mavilangran's journal. "This might help."

Yala's heart missed a beat. "What the fuck did you bring that back to Dalathar for?"

"Superior Sietra made several copies before she gave me this, don't worry," he added. "She reasoned that it would be easier to find where our wayward king is hiding with a map."

"What map?" Niema blanched. "You can't seriously be considering this."

"Oh, I'm not the only one." Kelan waved the journal in Yala's general direction. "My Superior seemed pretty certain you'd already be making plans, so I wanted to make sure you had company."

Yala tilted her head. "Your Superior thinks I'd go looking for the king's hiding place alone?"

She's not wrong. Nevertheless, Yala was unnerved that Kelan's Superior had figured her out that deeply during their brief meeting.

"If you knew where to find him." Saren squinted at her. "Fucking hells. You know, don't you?"

"I have suspicions." She indicated the journal. "But no, I didn't plan to go alone. At least not without a plan."

"You can't," Niema protested. "There aren't enough of us to fight an army, even with Kelan and the other Disciples of the Sky."

"I don't see the Disciples of the Flame stepping forward," Kelan agreed, "but I wondered if we might convince the other Disciples of the Sea—the ones who didn't betray their order—to help us."

"Didn't you just get captured by the same people?" Yala enquired.

"A misunderstanding," Kelan said. "Brought on by Rafragoria's soldiers, who, I'm sure, will be grateful for our efforts in ridding their home of Mekan's pestilence."

"Grateful?" Yala snorted. "I hope they have the sense to avoid the area where the king is hiding, considering how many of them were killed in the war."

"When you've quite finished planning your imminent deaths," Saren said testily, "can someone please tell me where you're even going?"

"The one place nobody would ever go looking for a king in exile," was Yala's reply. "And for a Disciple of Death."

The colour drained from Saren's face. "No… not there."

"Yes." She spoke without emotion despite the furnace inside her chest. "The island."

"I thought…" Niema gasped. "I thought it was destroyed."

"So did I." If King Tharen had survived, a Temple of Death was infinitely more resilient than a mortal king, Disciple of Death or not. "If he's not there, it's a place to start looking. And we know the way."

"I'm coming with you," Niema said. "I won't let you go alone."

Yala had expected as much, though the odds of a Disciple of Life surviving a direct encounter with Mekan's own temple were not heavily in her favour. Regardless, Yala would not wait for King Tharen to arrive in Dalathar. She'd hunt him down first.

25

Niema could hardly believe Yala would speak so calmly of returning to the island that had wrought such a heavy impact on her life, but if she knew anything about Yala, it was that inaction wasn't in her nature. Within the hour, she'd convinced both Kelan and Niema to accompany her to the Disciples' Inn to talk to the others, though Saren stayed behind, declaring that they'd all lost their minds and that the guards would never let them in. Yala merely rolled her eyes in response, though they encountered their first guard patrol before they'd even reached the gates.

"What's your business?" asked a scarred woman with a missing ear. "Where're you going?"

"We're going to the Disciples' Inn," Kelan replied. "Is it illegal to walk out on the streets?"

"You're all Disciples, are you?" Her attention lingered on Yala. "You aren't."

"This isn't a discussion you want to have with me right now," Yala said. "Trust me."

"I know you." The guard's male companion pointed at Yala's face. "You were arrested."

"I was pardoned," she said. "Ask Superior Shralin if you must."

A discontented mutter passed between the guard and his companion, and then the female guard shook her head. "You certainly won't be welcome in the upper city."

"And you aren't welcome out here," retaliated a loud masculine voice. "Yet here you are anyway."

Nalen stepped into view with his arms folded over his broad chest. The guards' mutters suggested they recognised him, and Niema had never thought she'd be glad of his intimidating appearance.

"Careful," said the male guard who'd pointed at Yala. "There's going to be a tightening of the laws in this city. Any sign of trouble will be met with steel and iron."

"Good for you." Nalen glowered, while the guards glanced at one another as though weighing up the odds of their small group winning against Yala's. After a short pause, they left, and Niema breathed out.

"Thanks," Yala said to Nalen. "Good timing."

"Did you really piss off the king?"

"I turned down his offer to lead the new Flight Division," Yala answered. "Wouldn't you have done the same?"

"He offered you that?" He grimaced. "He ought to have known you didn't want to get back in the saddle."

Yala shrugged. "It's done now. Why are the guards acting like walking down the street is a crime now?"

"No fucking clue," he said. "They haven't started that drakeshit in the Undercity yet, thank the gods, but His Majesty has given them a free pass to throw their authority around wherever they like, and they're using that command to its full extent."

Yala swore. "They should be watching for trouble from outside the city instead of from the likes of us."

"That so?" he grunted. "Trouble outside of the city? Anything I should know about?"

"I don't know where to start, frankly," she said. "You heard there might be a war, right?"

"With Rafragoria?"

"Possibly." Yala lowered her voice. "Or with Corruption. I'll tell you the rest later. We need to get to the upper city."

"I'll hold you to that." He stood back and watched them leave, while Niema braced herself for another confrontation when they reached the gates, this time without Nalen to stop them.

Sure enough, Kelan's attempt to glide straight through the gates was met by several spears pointing at their group, followed by the guards' prompt recognition of Yala as the former captain who'd recently been arrested.

"Ask Superior Shralin, and he'll tell you I was pardoned," Yala told the guards, raising her voice. "And then tell any other guard you encounter so I don't have to go through this drakeshit every time I want to walk into the upper city."

"Come on, let them in," a scarred man called from near the guard tower up on the wall. "It's not worth it."

"Glad we can agree on one thing," Yala muttered as their group passed through the gates. "This is going to get very old very fast."

"They won't let you fly over the wall?" Niema asked Kelan. "Are they policing all Disciples?"

"And everyone else, apparently," Yala said. "Whatever instructions the king gave them, I gather they were waiting for an excuse to exert authority over us outer-city rabble."

Yala walked onward to Ceremonial Square, which was less crowded than during Niema's previous visit. The market stalls were rather threadbare, and Niema would have had considerably more difficulty borrowing an unattended wagon from near the close-knit huddle of merchants on one side of the square.

The Disciples' Inn, by contrast, was packed with Disciples of the Sky, most of whom Niema didn't recognise. When their group entered the downstairs room, all eyes landed on Yala.

"Kelan," said Lakiel, the tall Disciple who wore a thick bandage on one arm that must be a souvenir from the events in Amanar. "Why exactly did you bring *them* here?"

"Give it a rest," said a female Disciple who Niema recognised from her last visit to the inn. "If we're going up against the dead, I want Yala Palathar with us."

"*You* aren't going anywhere, Brikel," said Lakiel. "I told you not to come with me."

"And you aren't the Superior," Brikel retaliated. "We all volunteered to come here to fight the dead."

"I have an alternative." Kelan pulled the journal out of his pocket. "Namely, that we hunt down the source."

Yala tensed. "I don't remember volunteering to take all of you with me."

"Where?" Lakiel looked at Kelan as though he'd lost his wits. "What are you talking about?"

The island. Is that truly where the former king is hiding? Niema felt a shiver of anticipatory dread, though it must be a thousand times worse for Yala. Niema might have seen the island in the vision she'd experienced through her Superior's eyes, but it was Yala herself who'd fought the dead, who'd watched her friend die, and who had faced the possibility that she'd never escape that cursed place alive.

"Where?" Yala echoed. "To the Temple of Death, of course."

A brief silence ensued. Someone laughed then stifled their reaction when nobody else joined in.

Lakiel swivelled to Kelan. "This was not in our orders. We're to help defend the city, not fly out to sea in search of mythical islands."

"Oh, you know it's an island," Yala interjected. "That's a great start. Is there a chair I can sit in? I'm not explaining all this while standing in the doorway."

Niema half expected the Disciples to push the three of them out of the room, but someone produced a chair and offered a second one to Niema. She sat, conscious of the others' curious stares, though most of their attention was levelled on Yala.

"This is absurd," Lakiel muttered. "We're not listening to the wild claims of someone who got arrested by the king a few days ago."

"Want to listen to me instead?" Kelan held up the journal. "I can explain some of it but not all, and Yala's one of the few people who's ever set foot on the island in question."

"Shut *up*, Lakiel." Brikel tugged on his sleeve. "Let her talk."

EMMA L. ADAMS

Glaring, Lakiel sat down again. Whispers flickered across the room and then ceased when Yala tapped the cane against her chair leg.

"I'm only explaining this once," she said. "The last mission King Tharen gave to my squad sent us to an island that contains a Temple of Death—abandoned centuries ago—and we thought we'd destroyed it. My suspicion is that it somehow survived and became the Successors' current hiding place, though I'll freely admit I'm making an educated guess, and none of us has been to the island since the mission. Regardless, destroying a small island strikes me as considerably easier than driving an army of the dead out of the city, especially if they're aided by some of the Disciples of the Sea."

"Easier?" Lakiel barked out a laugh. "If you go there without a single Disciple of the Flame, there'll be no hope of getting rid of Mekan's beasts, let alone a temple."

"We have a Disciple of Life," Kelan said, gesturing at Niema.

"I'm not volunteering to close the Void single-handedly," Niema objected. "I don't think I *can,* frankly."

Superior Kralia might, but Niema couldn't afford to trust in her coming to their aid, and besides, the Superior throwing her own life away would mean the death of the enclave.

"There it is," said Lakiel. "This debate is over. We're staying."

"Why not ask the Disciples of the Flame for volunteers?" one of the other Disciples suggested. "They can't want to stay here and wait for the Disciples of the Sea to flood the city until they drown in their own home."

"That isn't going to happen," Lakiel said as a flurry of whispers rose from the others. "One small group of dissident Disciples can't overcome the entire capital."

"They did nearly kill us," Kelan reminded him. "Now, if the Disciples of the Flame had to choose between an unpleasant death and helping us instead, they might make the sensible choice."

"I'll ask them," Niema offered. "I might not annoy them as much as the rest of you."

Kelan shot her a sideways grin. "Sure about that?"

No. If she had to choose between putting her faith in Superior

266

Kralia and persuading the Disciples of the Flame to help, she wasn't entirely sure which was least likely to end in disaster.

"Well, *I'm* certainly not going to talk to them," Yala said. "I'll tell Viam, and it's up to her if she wants to inform the king."

"Best not to," Kelan remarked. "Let him focus on preparing the city's defences. What are we missing?"

Niema racked her thoughts. "If by some miracle the Disciples of the Flame say yes, how will they get across the ocean? I doubt they'll consent to being carried. Or flying on war drakes either."

"No." Yala snorted. "Also, it'll be easier if you and I fly on separate steeds, Niema. You have better control over the war drake than I do."

Niema stiffened. "What will you use?"

Yala's mouth curved in a smile. "I think it's about time I found my dead steed again."

———

Yala and Niema parted ways outside the inn, and while the latter approached the Temple of the Flame, Yala went in search of Viam. She circled the palace grounds from the side, following the sound of growling war drakes, and was unprepared to find the paddock occupied by a cluster of wide-eyed novices. Through a crack in the gate, she glimpsed Viam standing at the front of the group with a war drake's chain in her hand, and she appeared to be instructing the novices on how to approach the beast and handle it without getting bitten.

Yala nudged the gate inward with her cane, and a chorus of gasps came from the novices when she shuffled in. Ignoring them, she addressed Viam. "I'd like to talk to you alone."

"One moment." Viam turned to one of the novices, a strong-jawed man in his early twenties who looked marginally less dazed at the sight of Yala than the others did. "Can you hold this? I'll be right back."

After she handed him the war drake's chain, Viam hurried out of the paddock to join Yala. "What is it?"

Yala moved along the front of the fence, ducking out of hearing distance of the novices. "I thought you should know I'm going to look for the former king."

"No," Viam whispered. "Why?"

"It's that or wait for him to show up here," Yala said. "With an army of the dead, in all likelihood."

"You can't beat an army single-handedly, Yala."

"I won't be alone." She'd expected more of an objection, but from Viam's defeated stance, she knew that Yala had made up her mind already. "Niema and Kelan will be with me, and there are thirty or so Disciples of the Sky here in the city as well. Some will stay behind, no doubt, but I'm hoping at least one of them will survive to come back and warn the king if the rest of us don't make it."

"Don't say that."

"Just being realistic." Hadn't they shared the same sentiment before each mission they flew on? If Viam was training novices to fly on war drakes, she'd have reason enough to recall the many close calls they'd had as a squad. "I'm not going to ask you to come with me, but I thought you should know."

"Yala." Viam's eyes glittered. "Please don't die. We need you."

"I think you are needed here more than me." She gestured towards the paddock. "Good luck."

She'll need it. Training a group of novices wasn't for the faint of heart under the best of circumstances, and the king might have already waited too late to revive the Flight Division. If Yala and the others provoked Mekan's forces into an attack when they hadn't yet intended to strike, Viam's fate would be on her conscience, make no mistake. Was Yala ready for that? She didn't know, but for all they knew, the former king was already on his way to the capital.

As she turned down a side street, a bolt of flame shot past, skimming against Yala's side and singeing the edge of her cane.

Danir.

The disgraced Disciple stood at the street's end, one leg still bandaged and almost unrecognisable dressed in plain clothes and not his usual bright cloak. Yet the flames dancing above his palm showed that imprisonment hadn't diminished his resolve for revenge.

"You've doomed us," he said. "You will regret your choices before you burn."

"This isn't a good time." She reached for her weapons belt and drew out her dagger, stepping to the side to avoid another fireball.

The blaze left a scorch mark on a nearby building; Yala threw her arms over her face and gritted her teeth as the smell of burned hair filled her nostrils. *Bastard.* Danir must know he didn't stand a chance against her in hand-to-hand combat, so he kept his distance, throwing handfuls of fire down the narrow street and giving her little option but to retreat. A blaze stung her ear and the side of her face, and her eyes watered with pain.

"Too much of a coward to get any closer?" she called, goading him. "Or are you scared Dalathik will abandon you and leave you to die at my hands?"

"My deity will never forsake me." He lifted a hand, sending a fresh wave of fire towards Yala. She released her cane and dropped to her front, pain flaring up her leg—but before the fire reached her, a sudden gust of wind sent the Disciple's fireball spinning upward into the air.

Kelan landed behind Yala "Need help? I knew we shouldn't have let you wander off alone."

"Keep his fire off me." Yala pushed upward, gripping her cane. "I'll finish this."

She reached for her dagger with her free hand. Danir responded with a ball of fire that Kelan knocked aside with ease, and Yala flung the knife at her opponent's throat. He fell back with a gurgling cry, the flames dying to an ember. Satisfaction surged inside Yala; despite the renewed pain in her leg, she limped to his side and reached for Mekan's claw. Already, tendrils of shadow snaked out from the pouch at her waist, reaching for the dying Disciple.

"Take this sacrifice," she murmured, "and bring me my steed."

"Yala!" The shout came from Niema, who ran into the street behind Kelan. "Are you all right?"

"I've been worse." She retrieved her dagger from Danir's throat and returned it to its sheath. Her ear and face stung, but she'd got away lightly.

"I can help." Niema extended her hands, whispering a prayer. At once, the pain in her face dulled, and her leg stopped throbbing as intensely. Good. She'd need to be at her best if she wanted to make it to the island that day.

And now, there's one less Disciple who might have helped us destroy it, she thought with a glance at Danir. *Not that he'd have ever consented to fight on my side.*

"What did he do, get out of jail at the first opportunity?" Kelan guessed. "I hope the others didn't do the same."

"I think he decided that finishing me off was worth the risk of being caught," Yala commented. "How'd it go with the other Disciples, Niema?"

"Terrible," Niema replied. "Superior Shralin didn't want to know."

"I thought so," said Yala. "Now that's taken care of, I have a dead war drake to find."

"How do you know the creature is even in the area?" Kelan asked.

"I don't," Yala replied, "but it's usually not far away from me or Niema."

Kelan tilted his head. "Most people would find being stalked by a dead war drake unnerving."

"Most people don't make a habit of talking to the god of death either."

He grinned. "True. I'll go and make sure Lakiel hasn't talked all the other Disciples of the Sky out of coming with us."

Yala didn't hold out much hope that Kelan would be able to convince all the Disciples of the Sky to come with them, especially Lakiel. After all, they'd come here expecting to defend the city against an attack from the dead rather than intentionally seeking them out.

That would be the more sensible choice, she admitted to herself. *Then again, there's no stopping an army of the dead without closing the Void.*

"Yala, you didn't call the dead war drake *here*, did you?" Niema asked as they crossed the square. "I thought you didn't want everyone to know we were leaving."

"At this point, it hardly matters," Yala said. "We should go to the war drake's paddock before we leave, though. You'll need my other steed."

Luckily, talking their way out of the upper city was considerably easier than getting in, and they reached the paddock long before the dead war drake had made an appearance. Yala kept an eye on the sky while she saddled the living war drake and got the beast to fly with Niema's assistance.

"Where *is* that dead war drake?" Yala reached for the claw, and the living war drake growled in displeasure. "We made a bargain, Mekan."

The claw's new coating of blood gleamed as she held it up to the sunlight, and shadows coalesced around its edges. Her skin tingled beneath her gloves, and a cold rasping voice rubbed against her ear. *"Not enough."*

Not enough, was it? "I killed a Disciple, Mekan. Isn't that enough for one favour?"

No answer came. Did the god of death know that she intended to return to the island, not to join Him but to destroy His army before they reached Dalathar? No, He might be able to communicate with her in a limited manner, but He didn't know what she was thinking or saying when she didn't hold the claw.

This wouldn't be the first time she'd tricked Him.

"I'm coming home," she told Mekan. "To get there, I need to be able to fly."

"Yala." Niema, who'd retreated into the living war drake's shadow, pointed a shaking finger.

There came the beating of wings, and the war drake appeared as a skeletal silhouette flying towards her, ever the loyal steed.

A shiver rose to Yala's skin. *This is it.*

26

Opting not to linger in Dalathar and potentially draw untoward attention, Yala mounted the dead war drake and took flight, while Niema did the same on her living steed. Yala had to admit that Niema was probably more comfortable, as even the abrasion of the war drake's scales was an improvement on the spiny bones digging into Yala's legs beneath the drakeskin trousers, but the beast's effortless obedience was worth the pain.

When Kelan came gliding out of the upper city, only three Disciples of the Sky followed, though a moment later, a fourth Disciple joined them. Lakiel was not among them. Spying Yala and Niema, Kelan angled his flight path over the rooftops and presented them with a large sack containing several spears.

"Where did you get those?" Yala asked.

"I may have swiped them from an inattentive guard on the city wall."

"I should have asked Viam." Yala took the sack from him, wishing she'd brought one of the sturdier raptor-skin bags which she and her squad-mates had strapped to the side of their war drakes for ease of access in battle. As it was, she had to wedge the sack awkwardly between the dead war drake's ribs and hope that the spears didn't fall out. "Which of your people volunteered?"

"Ranit, Sothen, Charen, and… Brikel." He paused when naming the last Disciple to join their group, a young woman Yala recognised from the inn. "Does Lakiel know you're here?"

"Oh, he's spitting fire," said Brikel. "I promised him I'd come back at the first sign of trouble, but we both know that's drakeshit."

"I hope you're ready," Yala warned them. "I'll be honest and say I don't know what we'll find out there. If we're attacked, we're likely to be outnumbered by far."

Niema's reticence to get involved in battle directly wouldn't help either, though Yala hoped the war drakes' teeth and claws would make the enemy think twice about singling her out. Regardless, their small group would be at a disadvantage even before they reached the island.

"Stop trying to put us off," Brikel told her. "We know the risks. Some of us almost got sacrificed to the god of death the other day, remember?"

"Will the Disciples of the Sea be on the island too?" Ranit asked. "Will they fight alongside Mekan?"

"They might," Kelan said. "The Disciples of the Sea who turned traitor aren't directly working for Mekan as far as I know. They still serve their own deity. If they didn't, Amanat would have drowned them."

"Didn't stop them from trying to hand us over to the enemy," Brikel said. "Be prepared for anything. Got it."

"Right." Yala turned her steed northward, facing the gleaming expanse of the ocean beyond the city. "Follow me."

Niema flew alongside her, occasionally whistling to calm her war drake whenever it got unnerved at being too close to Yala's dead steed. The dead war drake didn't require much prompting; the shadows holding its bones together responded to the slightest touch of Yala's hands.

Kelan glided to her other side. "You remember the way? I did bring the map… and the journal."

"Yes, I remember," she said, though her heart shuddered when the ground gave way to vast ocean. "It's Viam and her group of clueless novices I'm more concerned about. One of them will lose a limb by the day's end, I guarantee it."

"I can see why you didn't volunteer to train them yourself."

Yala grunted. "Best hope we don't need them as backup."

She willed her heartbeat to slow, but her body knew what her mind refused to accept. Even a Disciple of Death was no match for the vastness of the ocean, an expanse as deep as the Void itself.

An hour or so passed in silent flight. Before long, Yala's legs began to cramp, and her shoulders ached from leaning forward, on constant alert in case an enemy came at them from the water.

Her sharp eyesight picked out a reptilian head above the surface, and she slowed her flight. "Sea drake."

"Is it Rafragorian?" Kelan flew ahead of her. "I don't see anyone on its back."

"It's alone too." *I think.* If Rafragoria's soldiers lay in wait to ambush them, she could only hope that the dead war drake's unnatural presence would make them think twice about engaging them in a fight. She could hardly hide her conspicuously bone-white steed behind the others, and Niema's living war drake would make them assume her to be a Larian soldier.

"I don't sense anyone," Niema said. "I... I don't think that's a sea drake either."

Her war drake let out a growl that made the hairs on Yala's arms stand up. *It's afraid.*

"Careful," she called. "Something's rotten here."

The beast might resemble a sea drake from a distance, but closer, she saw its scales were jet-black in colour, and the eyes with which it watched their approach were dark pits that put her in mind of a void drake.

"Some monster of Mekan's, is it?" Kelan asked. "Did He decide to make a twisted variety of a sea drake to go with his void drakes and monstrous raptors?"

"You're joking, aren't you?" said one of the other Disciples of the Sky. "Please tell me you're joking."

The smell of the dead rolled over the water, and the beast extended its long neck, its mouth opening to reveal sharp teeth. Yala reached into the dead war drake's ribs for a spear, scanning the beast for weak spots. It'd be hard to aim with most of its body underwater, and its smooth scales looked as hard as rock.

"Niema." She pulled out a spear. "Now would be a fine time to demonstrate that handy skill of yours."

Niema flinched. "What skill?"

"You know what." Yala hefted her weapon, though she didn't hold out much hope for its flimsy wood to stand up to those scales. "It'd be a shame to waste all my weapons on a single beast before we reach our destination."

Niema's expression was conflicted, but she took in a breath and whistled. The sea drake-like beast turned its head towards her, and to the astonishment of the Disciples of the Sky, it plunged below the water again.

"I can't do the same to more than one at a time," Niema whispered to Yala. "I doubt it's alone."

No. The stench remained, and when Yala peered ahead, a large shadow blotted the water. It looked, at first glance, like the reflection of a storm cloud, but the sky above was clear save for the thin layer of mist encroaching on her vision.

That's not the island.

Yala slowed her flight, addressing the group with grim certainty. "They're already on the move. Mekan's army is coming to Laria."

———

Kelan watched the shadows move across the sea with a familiar rush of dread. The blot of darkness was too far off for him to make out individual shapes within, but it didn't appear to be moving towards Dalathar.

"Where are they going?" He gestured towards the dark smear on the water and the haze of mist gathering above.

"No clue." Yala continued to fly without changing course, while the darkness above the water widened and extended and merged with the mist coalescing overhead.

"You aren't thinking of flying *through* that, are you?" If the island lay on the other side, they might have little choice in the matter, but the dead were flying in the opposite direction to the capital. The dark mass skimming the water undoubtedly moved west, not south. As though heading for…

"Amanar." Brikel pointed left with a shaking hand. "Aren't they heading for Amanar?"

"Shit." That did seem the most likely option. "Or are they trying to create a diversion so Dalathar's forces will head that way instead and leave the capital undefended?"

"They might be." Yala's attention was riveted on the dark patch on the water, one gloved hand gripping her spear. "Amanar, though? Are there any soldiers stationed there? I'm guessing not."

There was an uneasy silence. Already, the shadow had covered such a distance that it might equal a small town or bigger. How long did they have before the beasts within that darkness reached land? To say nothing of any unlucky souls who might be out at sea?

"Anyone want to volunteer to come and warn the king?" said Sothen, one of the Disciples of the Sky who'd offered to join them. "Or should we turn around and fly back to the capital?"

"And leave the people in Amanar undefended?" Kelan's heart twinged, thinking of the Disciples' Inn and then of the orphanage from all those years ago. "Someone needs to warn them too."

"I don't see us overtaking that army," Brikel said, an apologetic note to her voice. "Tell you what, I'll fly back to the capital. Maybe I can talk Lakiel and some of the others into changing their minds. They might be keener to fight on land than on an island in the middle of the ocean, and they'll get to Amanar faster than the army."

Not fast enough. The darkness skimming the water was close enough for him to make out the individual forms within it: writhing limbs, beating wings, a frenzy of horrors moving towards Laria's shore. He didn't see any void drakes amid the haze, though, let alone ones with humans upon their backs.

"Their leader isn't with them," he murmured to Yala. "Unless you can see him?"

"No." Tension underlaid her voice. "I think he's still on the island."

"He's attacking his own country and doesn't even have the nerve to come in person?" If this was a distraction, they might be falling for the very trick the Successors intended, but reaching the island without colliding with the army seemed increasingly unlikely. Thick mist swept over the surface of the ocean, entirely blocking their view of the other side. Such was the density of the shadows that nobody noticed the smaller shadow in the water until Niema cried, "Watch out!"

The ocean exploded into life, and a wave arose like a giant hand to seize them all and drag them down into the deep.

———

Niema saw the rising wave first and urged her steed to fly higher, but even the war drake couldn't outrace the sea. Yala's warning shout was cut off when the wave crashed over their heads. Leaning forward, Niema clung to the war drake's back with both hands; drenched and gasping, she tried to whistle but couldn't draw breath.

The beast shook itself violently, and her grip broke. With a hoarse cry, she tumbled off her steed and plunged downward into the ocean.

The sea hit like a slap, disorientating her for a few moments. Niema coughed, gasped, arms flailing as she fought to bring her head above the surface. Niema could swim, but she'd never been out in a stretch of water this vast and this deep, and the others had vanished in the blur of foam and salt and unforgiving darkness.

Raw terror gripped her as a firm grip locked around her legs, pulling her downward again. She squirmed, fighting for breath, but the grip held fast. As her lungs screamed for air, she prayed to her deity.

Yalet, help me. Help!

Through the panic, green light bloomed. Life existed, even here in

EMMA L. ADAMS

the water. Yalet was with her, and with her last breath, Niema pleaded with her deity to come to her aid.

The grip on her legs loosened. She kicked hard, and her head broke the surface of the water. Air rushed into her lungs, and then she was falling, tumbling downward as the water lowered as swiftly as it had risen.

Throwing out her hands to break her fall, she crashed onto a stretch of sand that she was certain hadn't existed a moment before-hand. She lay stupefied on her front, gasping like a fish stranded onshore. Several moments passed before she thought to look for her rescuers. Certainly, Yalet Herself hadn't thrown her out of the water, and the sand around her formed a perfect circle. Too perfect.

As she pushed to her knees, from the water emerged two people who could only be Disciples of the Sea. Their seaweed-woven clothing bore a surprising resemblance to her own attire at home, and they carried curved knives made of bone. Sea drake, she assumed.

One, a man with what appeared to be the teeth of a longfish woven into his hair, surveyed her with obvious surprise. "You are a Disciple of Life. Why do you fight alongside the dead?"

She coughed, spitting out saltwater. "I thought *you* were with Mekan."

"We're not on their side," said the Disciple of the Sea. "You were flying with one of Mekan's dead creatures."

"That's Yala's, and she's not on their side either." She knelt upright, her fingers carving deep grooves into the sand. "We were going to *stop* the dead. Until you tried to drown us."

"Impossible," said the Disciple. "Even your deity cannot overcome the might of Mekan."

How do they know that? Indignation rose, unexpected, and she lifted her chin. "You don't know anything about me. Have you ever met a Disciple of Life before?"

"She has a point," said his companion, a female Disciple with her hair styled to resemble the spines of a sea drake. To Niema, she added, "I'm Yalian. And you?"

"Niema."

"Nanek," said the male Disciple. He'd turned sideways, his gaze upon the dark mist passing above the water. "It was the Disciples of the Sky who drew Mekan's attention. They caused this."

"Excuse me?" Niema could imagine how Kelan would react to that accusation. "What were they supposed to do, let the enemy get away with killing those Rafragorian ambassadors and allow Laria to take the blame? Ignore the attempts on the king's life?"

She didn't know if the Disciples were all aware of the Successors' location, but she wouldn't have a hope of reaching the island *or* finding her allies when she was stuck down here, without her war drake or any other means of escape.

"A sole assassin is nothing compared to an army," said Nanek. "Thousands of people are going to die."

"And you're just going to watch it happen?" Niema rose to her feet, her hands clenching at her sides. "I know Disciples are supposed to be impartial, but I thought you'd have *some* sense of loyalty towards the rest of Laria. At least as much as any other Disciple."

"No." His tone was as sharp as the wave that had swept Niema off her steed. "We are not Larian."

"Why?" Niema asked. "You serve Amanat foremost, yes, but weren't you born on land before you were recruited as children? Did your Superior forbid you from ever returning on pain of a severe punishment?" *That,* she understood on an intimate level, and she knew she'd hit a nerve when the water around the island surged inward, knocking Niema's feet out from underneath her. Her back hit the sand, the breath jolted from her lungs.

"Don't provoke the ocean, Disciple of Life," growled Nanek. "The tides do not forgive, nor do we."

"Then explain." Niema scrambled back to her feet, breathing hard. "I might be a Disciple of Life, but I left my enclave and my Superior because they no longer matched my own values. I might not understand why some of your fellow Disciples chose to ally with Mekan, but I do understand what it feels like to have one's loyalties divided."

The two Disciples exchanged glances.

"It wasn't our Superior who exiled us from Laria," Yalian said. "It was Superior Datriem of the Disciples of the Flame."

————

Viam's first training session was not going well. The novices were eager, but twice, she almost missed a war drake get close enough to bite someone and had to swiftly intervene before they lost a finger. Her distraction was in no way helped when Brenat came to watch, remaining on the side until the session ended and the novices returned to the barracks. Several were dripping blood from scratches, but they'd avoided any more serious injuries.

"They're slow, aren't they?" Brenat watched her put the muzzle back on the war drake they'd been training. "Are you all right?"

"Yala." She ducked her head. "She and her friends are doing something foolish, and she might get killed."

"Isn't that a daily event for her?"

"It's bad this time." Viam stepped back from the war drake, her hands trembling. Once, not so long ago, she'd have changed the subject, but with her renewed trust in Brenat came a reluctance to keep any more secrets from her, even ones with world-shaking implications. "She's going after the former king,"

"What?" Brenat dropped the sack of raw meat she'd been carrying. "*What?*"

Viam winced. "I know it sounds implausible, but you must have heard the rumours."

"Yes, that the Disciples of the Flame tried to pretend they failed to kill the king in order to save themselves from being hanged for murder."

"I wish that's all it was." Viam closed her eyes. "I don't know for sure, but I trust Yala, and if she thinks the former king is alive, he probably is."

Brenat went quiet. Then she lifted her head. "Who's that?"

Viam lifted her head, spying a Disciple of the Sky soaring towards the palace at speed. Without stopping, the figure glided directly over the palace wall to an eruption of shouts from the guards.

"That's not Kelan." Viam checked the war drakes were all securely chained up and then ran past the paddock to the gate, Brenat on her heels. The guards, distracted by the new arrival, waved her in without asking questions, and as she broke into a sprint, another Disciple of the Sky joined the first.

"Brikel, what are you doing?" The newcomer, a male Disciple who wore a bandage on one arm, called to the Disciple who'd arrived first. "You can't fly in here without permission."

"I'm here to warn the king," returned his companion, who appeared unfazed by the number of guards who ran to surround the pair of them. Raising her voice, she called out, "There's an army of the dead coming for Laria. We think they're going to target Amanar first, but they'll be here soon, I don't doubt."

All the guards within hearing distance broke out in exclamations, but Viam didn't wait to see the rest. She launched into another sprint, past the Disciples, this time heading for the palace. Once in front, she climbed the stairs, scarcely pausing to take a breath until she reached the top.

"Need to warn the king," she gasped to the guards outside the door. "I have information. Urgent."

Recognising her, the guards parted to let her in. She entered and made straight for the receiving room, where she skidded to a halt in front of the throne.

"Your Majesty," she wheezed. "The dead are coming from across the ocean. They're going to attack Amanar."

"Amanar?" He half rose from his seat. "Who told you that?"

"The Disciples of the Sky." She pointed vaguely at the door. "They're outside, but the guards…"

"Thank you for coming to me," he said. "Amanar? Are they sure?"

"I'm sorry." She sucked in air, her head spinning. "I should have told you. Some of the Disciples already left the city to find the Successors. With Yala."

"Yala Palathar." A hint of betrayal flickered in his eyes. "She refused to fight for me, yet she schemed with the Disciples behind my back?"

"I think Yala wanted to stop the enemy before they reached Laria," she said. "She didn't know the army would already be on their way. If they're going to Amanar—there aren't any soldiers in the city, are there?"

One of King Daliel's more controversial acts, after disbanding the Flight Division, had been to withdraw soldiers from each of Laria's major cities except for the capital. There'd been an outcry at the time, she remembered, from people convinced that Rafragoria would launch an attack on the coast while it remained undefended.

"No." He drew in a breath. "I'll speak to the commanders. You, fetch your squad."

"My squad isn't trained." He couldn't possibly expect her to take a team of unprepared novices to war, could he?

"The war drakes are faster than any soldier," he said. "If you fly ahead of the main army, we might be able to avoid some casualties."

He can't be serious. "They aren't ready. The war drakes haven't had more than a day of proper training."

"You won't be alone long," he said. "If Yala's out there, she can help too."

Objections rose to her tongue. He wasn't thinking clearly, it was obvious, but who was to say she wouldn't have done the same in his place?

"The dead can't be stopped," she said. "They can only be destroyed by..."

"By what?"

"Fire." She dropped her gaze to the marble floor. "I'm sorry, Your Majesty, but we'll have to ask the Disciples of the Flame."

The king surveyed her in a moment of painful, condemning silence. "You would ask me to forgive them?"

"No, Your Majesty," she said. "I worry that we won't survive without them."

27

"Superior Datriem?" Niema repeated. That he'd been responsible for the Disciples of the Sea's decades-long exile shocked her but not as much as she might have once expected. "How could he have stopped you from coming back to Laria? He wasn't your Superior."

"He held authority," said Nanek, "as the one Superior who lived close to Laria's coast and as the only one who worked hand in hand with the king."

"The king's—" *Dead,* she almost said, but that wasn't true, and mentioning so would send them down a route of discussion she wasn't ready for. She didn't yet know how aware they were of the Disciples of the Flame's attempt on his life—though if Superior Datriem had deployed his threats against the Disciples of the Sea, too, they'd be all too familiar with his methods. "Why would another Superior even *want* to exile another group of Disciples from the country? What would he have to gain?"

Yalian spat onto the sand. "He claimed that our position as neighbours to Rafragoria made us untrustworthy."

"Why does it matter that you live close to Rafragoria?" Niema frowned. "Disciples aren't allowed to be involved in warfare. It's been that way for centuries."

"He wanted an excuse, nothing more," Yalian said. "It wasn't Rafragoria that he saw as the real threat."

"Not...?" Her voice dropped to a whisper. "The island?"

Recognition flickered in their eyes.

"Exactly," said Nanek.

"But it's been uninhabited for decades," Niema protested. "What did he think? That you were using the—the temple yourselves?"

"You know more than you should," Nanek accused. "Are you *sure* you aren't working with Mekan?"

"I'm a Disciple of Life. I *can't* work with Mekan." Not that they'd know that if they'd never met someone like her before. "Besides, my Superior knows all about the island. It's been known among our people for years, maybe as long as it's existed. Is it the same for you?"

Nanek eyed her, thin-lipped with suspicion. "We don't talk openly of the island, least of all with outsiders."

I thought not. "My ally... she was sent to the island during the war. She told me it was destroyed by fire."

"That was her?" Nanek's eyes narrowed. "No... the island was never destroyed. The Void's roots reach deep below, far deeper than the physical world."

Niema's heart dropped. The meaning was plain: as long as the island existed, the Void would remain open no matter how many of Mekan's monsters they destroyed. Yala must suspect the same, and that was why she was so adamant she had to be the one who eradicated the island for good this time.

But she can't. Not alone.

"Why did the Disciples of the Flame think you'd ally with Mekan?" she asked the Disciples of the Sea. "Wouldn't their same logic apply to the whole nation of Rafragoria, given that they live close to the island?"

"Obviously," said Yalian. "For all we know, that might be where the distrust between Laria and Rafragoria originated."

"Nobody's *used* Corruption until recently, though," said Niema. "If you knew of the island all along, why not—?"

"Why not warn the king?" guessed Yalian. "What would be the point? When he did learn of the island's existence, he wasn't to be deterred from his plan, and the Disciples of the Flame would never have allowed him to pursue his interest to its natural conclusion."

They know it all. Everything. Did that include...? "Then you knew someone started using the temple on the island again recently."

"There's no need to play coy," Yalian said. "You wouldn't have come out here unless you knew King Tharen was the one commanding that army."

Niema's heart skipped a beat. "How long—?"

"Long enough," growled Nanek. "Spare us your accusations, Disciple. We owe you nothing."

"I didn't mean..." She trailed off. "You could have warned *someone*. You must know not every person in Laria was on Superior Datriem's side."

"The former king was far too weak to be a threat to anyone for a long time," said Nanek. "Most of us assumed he would swiftly expire, like other exiles cast out into these waters. He's far from the first."

"But he didn't," she said. "Some of your people have joined him, haven't they?"

"Traitors," said Nanek. "They believe their faith in Amanat doesn't require them to obey their Superior."

That's true, she almost said before she caught herself. She didn't have time to explain her fraught relationship with her own Superior. "Mekan won't allow any other deity to coexist with Him. Including yours."

"You should worry for your own people, not mine," he said. "Tharen is a poison infecting our ocean, but Laria was his home, and he intends to take it back, along with his crown."

"You're just going to stay here and let the army of the dead attack Laria?" She cast a gaze over the water and was alarmed at how much larger the shadow above had grown in the past few minutes. "You aren't even going to try to fight back?"

Yalian lowered her head as if ashamed, but Nanek was resolute. "We've lost too many of our people already."

"So have the Disciples of the Sky, and they're still fighting—or they were before you attacked us." The dark blot on the water wavered before her eyes. "I need to find them."

"All right," said Yalian. "We'll help you find your allies."

"What?" Nanek looked scandalised. "What are you talking about?"

"Some of us don't believe in afflicting blame for past sins upon those who weren't responsible for them." Yalian slipped Niema a wink. "Besides, I admire her nerve. I think she *can* close the Void and destroy the island."

"Nonsense." A muscle ticced in Nanek's jaw. "That said, we're not barbarians. We will help you find your allies, Disciple of Life, provided none of them is allied with Mekan."

"They aren't."

Except that Yala is in a dangerous position, given her shaky agreement with Mekan. Niema needed to find Yala first, and she had a sinking suspicion that an island that had resisted the flames of Dalathik would fight equally hard against the power of the god of life. No surprise, when Mekan rested inside its very bones.

Yalet help us all.

———

War drums sounded in the capital. The vibration thrummed under Viam's feet as she paced outside the barracks, waiting for the commanders to call her inside. They were rounding up the novices, assigning them to units. And, she assumed, asking which ones were willing to die in a war drake's saddle.

She'd run back to the dormitory to change into her uniform—her real uniform, not the ceremonial coat she'd worn at the parade—and was tugging on her gloves when a bewildered Brenat caught her arm. "What *is* going on?"

"The dead are coming to attack Laria." She fumbled her glove, biting her lip. "He wants me to fly. We're all going to get killed."

"Fly where?" Brenat asked. "Wait, is this to do with whatever you said Yala was doing?"

"Yes," she said. "She went to find the enemy, but they're already on the move."

"I thought you said she was looking for... for the former king." She spoke in a low voice.

"He's with them." If King Tharen did indeed lead the army, it wouldn't remain a secret for much longer. "The former king is a Disciple of Death."

"Viam!" A harried captain beckoned her into the building. "We need you."

She left Brenat gawping at her and ran into the barracks, following the captain to the grounds where the novices had assembled. The commanders stood at the front, each at the head of their unit, but Viam's group of new novices were scattered in a disorganised mass.

"Here." She moved to the front and corralled them into line, praying to whatever deity might be listening that they wouldn't have to fly today after all. "I'm not sure who the new Flight Division commander is..."

"Viam." Commander Sranak approached her, his moustache and hair considerably greyer than the last time she'd seen him.

"Commander." She bowed. "I thought you retired."

"I'm here as a favour to the king." His eyes, more wrinkled around the edges than before, passed over the novices. "You're the new squad leader."

"As of this morning." Gods. She'd thought, naively, that she might feel easier about her new position if someone older and more experienced than she came to take command, but even the old commander's presence didn't change the fact that her new recruits were little more than children who'd rarely interacted with a war drake in their short lives. "Commander, I don't think we're ready for this."

"I expect not." He beckoned. "That's why I called in the volunteer reserves."

"The reserves?" She spied a number of newcomers at the back of her line of novices. Some were strangers to her, but she did recognise a few faces among the uniformed figures.

"Yes, from the old Flight Division."

Her heart lifted, but that wasn't enough to suppress the sickening pit in her stomach. *They might have more experience, but none of them have flown in years, and our current war drakes have never flown with riders at all. Will they fare any better than the novices?*

The head commander called everyone to attention and spoke loudly. "The king has ordered us to send troops by both land and sea to Amanar, while others will stay to protect our capital. You will be distributed as followed."

He pointed to each squad and unit, offering instructions to each. Viam's remained ignored until the very end, before the commander announced "Viam Tiathar will lead the Flight Division, and each of you will be assigned a squad leader. You'll travel ahead of the rest of the army, straight to Amanar."

A murmur ran through the line, but nobody dared to raise their voice in argument.

This is it. Odds were, their unit would fight alone until the rest of the army had caught them up, however long that took. The certainty of her own demise choked Viam's breath from her lungs, and it was all she could do to keep herself together in front of the novices.

Commander Sranak moved down the line to count the recruits and then whispered, "You can select your own squad first, and then I'll divide the rest into groups of seven."

She ducked her head, numb. Seven per squad, each with a nominal role, but flying as a unit. All were equally ill-prepared, so it didn't matter who she chose. The experienced fliers would all be assigned as squad leaders, and the novices outnumbered them.

Viam scanned the terrified group, and her gaze snagged on a recruit at the very back of the line, her uniform lopsided as though she'd pulled it on at the last minute and her hair curling loose to her shoulders rather than tied neatly at the nape of her neck. Brenat.

"Come on, Captain," Brenat called. "Pick your squad."

Viam's head spun. For a moment, she considered throwing caution aside, grabbing Brenat's hand, and running for her life, but it wouldn't be of any use. Aside from the inevitable punishment that would result, her replacement would be someone with even less recent experience. At the very least, the current group of war drakes would recognise her as the one who fed them.

Focus. With a shaking hand, she picked out five other novices and then chose Brenat last, mostly so that she'd be able to talk to her somewhere that wasn't in full view of the army.

"If you picked me so that you can send me packing, you're mistaken," Brenat said as they walked out of the barracks. "I'm coming with you."

"You *can't*," Viam hissed. "You've never flown on a war drake in your life."

"Neither have this sorry lot." She spoke in a low voice. "I'll take my chances."

"Why?" Her breath caught on the word. "Why sign up to die?"

"You have to ask?" Brenat gave her an eye roll. "I know you might not feel the same way, but I have the strange desire for you *not* to die in battle. So, you're stuck with me."

"That's… now is not the time to have this conversation." The war drums beat again, louder. "Please don't do this. I can't lose anyone else."

The drumbeats drowned out her reply, and Viam's heartbeat hammered. Commander Sranak waited outside the grounds to take them to the paddock, where the war drakes would be saddled for battle.

Ready to fly to certain death.

———

Yala blinked salty water out of her eyes, her dripping hair clinging to her shoulders. The dead war drake had survived the hit, but the Disciples had scattered, and Niema had fallen from her steed and vanished below the surface of the water. Would her Disciple of Life abilities enable her to survive the fall and prevent her from drowning? Yala didn't know, but the shock of the water must have broken her spell on the living war drake. The beast abruptly changed direction, wings clipping Yala's side and nearly sending her pitching off her own steed.

"Shit." She clung to the dead war drake for balance, gripping the spear by her fingertips. *"Niema!"*

She'd gone, swallowed by the deep, while the dark mass above the ocean appeared to have grown in size in the past few minutes alone. Each beat of her dead war drake's wings brought Yala closer to the cloud of darkness that streamed forth like a legion from Mekan's hell itself.

A dark shape detached itself from the army and resolved into the form of a giant bird, its skeletal wings shedding decaying flesh.

Yala lifted her spear but hesitated to waste a weapon on a single beast when an entire army wasn't far behind. Instead, she forced herself to wait until her steed drew closer to the beast's cruel beak, and its claws ripped through the flimsy flesh of the monster's wings. *One down, a thousand to go.*

How many had already reached Amanar, where nobody would have ever fought the dead before? At least Dalathar had past experience in that area, though that didn't mean they'd be any more equipped to deal with an invasion on this scale. Regardless, the army was entirely stationed in the capital, and King Daliel had abandoned the other coastal cities.

"What was he thinking?" she snarled, driving her spear through the wing of another beast. Below the winged mass was an equally large shadow on the water, formed of monstrous sea drakes and the gods knew what else. Like their living counterparts, the latter might not be able to leave the water, but there were still too fucking many.

Withdrawing her spear, she turned her steed away from the endless swarm of wings and claws. *I need to find Niema if we're to have a chance in hell of surviving this.*

When the wave hit, sending Kelan and the other Disciples scattering into flight, he momentarily lost sight of Yala and the others. He flew through blurred vision, his cloak trailing water, too focused on keeping his balance in the air to notice which direction he was going in.

At least until a winged shape descended upon him, its cruel beak snapping a fingerspan from his face.

"Hey!" He reached for the sword at his belt, gliding backwards and shedding water as he did so. His blade plunged into the beast's eye; black goo exploded like oil, and its body fell into the water with scarcely a splash, swallowed up by the mass of other beasts in the darkness below.

He blinked his vision clear, alarmed at the size of the army he'd almost flown into. A dark swathe above the water merged with an equally dense blur of darkness on the ocean's surface. *Gods.* He dragged his attention away, scanning for any flashes of blue cloak that would point to his fellow Disciples, and within the endless darkness, a bone-white gleam drew his vision. A dead war drake, weaving in and out of the shadowy army.

"Yala!" he shouted. "Over here!"

She didn't intend to take on the entire army alone, did she? The dead war drake vanished from sight and then reappeared, closer, while a shadow detached itself from the mass and followed her.

"Yala!" he shouted again. "Behind you."

Her war drake's bony claws shot out, trailing shadows, and pierced the monster through the throat, ripping its belly open. Ribbons of rotting guts spilled out into the water.

"The Disciples of the Sea won't like that." Kelan took in shallow breaths in a futile attempt to avoid breathing in the stench as he flew towards her. "And I thought the Disciples of the Earth had a rough time with their temple being invaded. At least they had doors, when Superior Dovial deigned to let anyone use them."

Yala spun on another monster and drove her spear through the beast's neck. "Kelan, have you seen Niema?"

"No." The water was impenetrable. He couldn't see past the darkness churning under the surface. "Gods, I hope she's alive."

"I know." She paused, her steed's skeletal wings somehow balancing on the air without anything more substantial than shadows to hold them upright. "I saw her fall in, but she's a Disciple of Life, and for all I know, she can survive underwater as well as a Disciple of the Sea can."

"You don't know that for sure," he said. "Amanar rules the sea, not Yalet."

"Niema can use her power anywhere, even in other gods' temples, remember?"

That might have been a reassurance if he didn't know Mekan could do exactly the same, and He might have already taken up residence inside the Temple of the Sea. "Wherever she is, she can't have gone that far."

In truth, he'd completely lost track of his surroundings when he'd been blown off course by the tidal wave, and more concerningly, his fellow Disciples were nowhere to be seen. If any of them had fallen into the water, they wouldn't fare any better than Niema. Worse, if anything.

"I can see why that island was undiscovered for so many years," he said to Yala as she resumed her flight, tilting slightly so that Mekan's army wasn't entirely out of her line of sight. "I can hardly tell north from south out here."

Yala scowled. "Me neither. I'd suspect the Disciples of the Sea were messing with us if I didn't know better."

"They might be." Like how the Disciples of the Earth had manipulated the tunnels under Setemar to suit their needs, the Disciples of the Sea were able to shape the ocean's currents to their will—but this was all Mekan's work, he was sure. "Though I wouldn't want to be in the water near Mekan's rotting corpses."

The mist obscuring his vision made it hard to tell if anyone was in the water. Calling on the god of the sky for aid, he lifted his palm and sent a gust of air into the mist. The view cleared momentarily, and he glimpsed a reptilian head in the distance, topped with a blur that might have been a human figure.

"Is that a sea drake?" He raised a palm and cleared the mist again, but he'd need to move farther from the army to be able to properly see.

"I doubt it," Yala told him. "No living creature would come this close to the dead."

As she spoke, the reptilian shape changed directions, undeniably heading their way. Kelan flew forward a few handspans, confirming that the creature was indeed within the water and that it also had a human rider.

"There's someone on its back." Someone small and unarmed. "Niema."

She's alive. His heart lifted, and he picked up speed, cloak billowing behind him.

"Careful," Yala warned. "She isn't alone."

Two other figures swam through the waves, one on either side of Niema, their expert strokes making their identities undeniable. "I'm guessing they're from among the Disciples of the Sea who didn't try to kill us."

"I should hope so." Yala overtook him, and when they saw her winged steed, the Disciples ceased to swim. With shouts, they raised their spiny weapons, the ocean stirring around them in a warning tremor.

"Niema!" he called. "It's us."

Up close, he recognised the Disciples as Nanek and Yalian, two of the number who'd declined to help him and the others. While Niema didn't appear to be their captive—in fact, they moved more like allies —both Disciples of the Sea wore expressions of distrustful hostility when faced with Yala's dead war drake.

Kelan flew past Yala, positioning himself in front of her and waving at the newcomers. "Niema, how'd you survive that fall?"

"The grace of the god of life," she replied. "And... well, the Disciples of the Sea."

"Weren't they the ones who almost drowned us?" He raised his voice for the Disciples to hear. "Don't tell me you befriended them."

"They thought we were with the enemy," Niema said. "We talked it over."

"Ah. Easy mistake to make." He approached the Disciples, careful to keep at least a few handspans between his feet and the water. "You're a long way from home, aren't you?"

"Your friend is playing a dangerous game." Nanek jerked his head at Yala, whose war drake had stopped mid-flight with its wings spread in its unnervingly still manner. "If she intends to double-cross the god of death, there will be only one outcome."

"You're welcome to tell her that yourself. It might be entertaining." He grinned down at Niema. "Those spines can't be comfortable to sit on."

"I needed to get out of the water," Niema said. "I lost my steed. Where are the other Disciples of the Sky?"

"I don't know. We got lost in there." He gestured towards the writhing mass above the water. "I don't suppose your new friends are willing to help?"

"We won't sacrifice our lives unnecessarily," said Nanek. "Least of all for you."

"Is there anyone leading the army?" Niema asked, directing her question at Yala. "Any humans?"

"Any Disciples of Death?" Yala surmised. "Not that I saw."

"They know," Niema added, with a nod to her companions. "They know it's the former king who's giving orders to the Successors."

"Do they?" Kelan supposed that it was difficult for a man in exile at sea to hide his existence from people who knew every fingerspan of the surrounding water, though it would have been nice if they had shared that information outside of their own circle. "I expect he'll be at the head of the army if anywhere."

Yala's only reaction was a tightening in her jaw. "Niema, we need to find your war drake. Your new friends can stay with us or leave. It's all the same to me."

"It's not their fault they weren't able to warn us," Niema said. "They were exiled from Laria—by Superior Datriem."

"What?" Kelan blinked in surprise. "He exiled another branch of Disciples? Is that allowed?"

"He was paranoid about people finding out that the island existed," Niema explained. "He claimed they were in league with Rafragoria so they'd be banned from the mainland."

"Superior Datriem." Yala ground her teeth. "That sounds like him."

"Is that why some of your people sided with Mekan?" If they wanted to take out the Disciples of the Flame as revenge for what they'd done, Kelan understood why some had joined forces with the god of death.

"Yes," growled Nanek. "Now, we've brought Niema to you. I wish you the best of luck in the upcoming fight."

"Excuse me?" Yala resumed her flight, her war drake's bony wings carrying her closer to the Disciples of the Sea. "You attacked us, but you wouldn't lift a finger against that army? You're just here to watch Laria burn for your own amusement, are you?"

"Mekan has poisoned our very oceans," said Nanek. "We're here to ensure the threat doesn't reach its claws inside our temple, Disciple of Death. We have no love of Laria, but we will not celebrate its destruction either. Our concern, however, must always lie with our own."

"You do realise Superior Datriem has been dead for months?" Kelan said. "Also, the other people who exiled the former king are dead or in jail. They confessed to their crimes in front of his son too."

"Is that right?" Yalian asked.

"Yes," Yala confirmed. "I can't speak for all the Disciples of the Flame, but his replacement isn't running the temple in the same manner as his predecessor."

That's one way of putting it. It seemed unwise to mention that Superior Shralin was making some rather glaring mistakes of his own, but he wouldn't have gone as far as to exile another branch of Disciples from the mainland, would he?

"It's impossible to expect forgiveness," Nanek said. "Our Superior will never allow it."

"You don't have to forgive them," said Kelan. "What of the innocent people who didn't ask to be caught up in a struggle with the god of death?"

Without offering an answer, the pair vanished below the water's surface, leaving scarcely a ripple behind.

"I did try asking them to help," said Niema. "They said the army is too big, which... well, it's true."

"Unfortunately." He didn't need to turn around to see the shadow over the water growing larger with each passing moment. "The king's army will take days to reach Amanar. They don't have a Flight Division, do they?"

"Not yet." Yala gripped her spear. "But they have Viam."

"The king wouldn't..." He stopped. Kelan didn't know the king, not really, and he knew King Tharen even less well. Really, sending an army of the dead to attack his own nation—and his own son—was hardly sporting behaviour for a monarch.

"I wouldn't speak for what the king will or won't do to protect Laria," Yala said. "Besides, Viam herself won't sit back and wait while the capital is invaded by the dead. When it comes down to it, she'll fight back to protect the ones she cares about. I know that about her."

Shit. "What should we do?"

"Find the others," Niema said. "And find my war drake."

28

Riding a sea drake wasn't quite as comfortable as flying—the spines dug into Niema's legs, and each movement of the beast's sinuous neck threatened to unbalance her—but Niema had to admit it was much faster than swimming to shore on her own.

"How near are we to the coast?" she asked Kelan, who had a much better view from up in the air. "The others might have gone to find solid ground."

"They might." Kelan glided over to her, his cloak swirling around his ankles, "but that's also the direction the army is going in."

Niema shivered. From her current vantage point, she couldn't see most of Mekan's army, especially with the mist that obscured the horizon on one side. If the other Disciples of the Sky had flown into the midst of that chaos, they were as good as dead.

"I'll call the war drake first." She lifted her head, perched on the sea drake's back, and whistled her prayer to the god of life. "I'm not sure if it's close enough to hear me, but it's worth trying."

She whistled again, urging her current steed to swim in the opposite direction to the army of the dead so that their insidious presence wouldn't frighten the war drake into immediately fleeing again. Yala wore an expression of scepticism, as did Kelan, but there were so few living beings out here that tracking one beast wouldn't be impossible, and the war drake ought to recognise her call after they'd flown together for hours.

Several moments passed. Yala and Kelan exchanged glances then raised their brows when the beating of wings reached their ears. Soon, the war drake's reptilian form appeared in the sky, gaining speed.

"I knew it hadn't gone far." She straightened, but the awkward angle of the sea drake's head meant that letting go with her knees would risk her falling backwards into the water.

Kelan reached out a hand. "I'll carry you. I think you've spent enough time in the water."

"Thanks." Niema let him lift her off the sea drake, feeling a twinge of guilt for leaving the beast stranded in a sea teeming with Mekan's monsters. Would any living creatures survive the onslaught? Every one of them was at risk of being wiped out, including the Disciples of the Sea.

Kelan carried her to her steed and helped her climb back onto its back. To her great relief, the war drake hadn't suffered any damage from the attack, and a few whistles calmed it to placid silence. She then uttered another longer whistle, a command to seek out the missing Disciples of the Sky. She didn't know if it would recognise them by scent or appearance, but a few human-sized figures in the sky would be easier for the beast's larger eyes to spot than her own.

"Where are you going?" Kelan watched Niema's steed change directions, angling away from the army of the dead.

"I asked it to find the other Disciples," she explained. "Neither of us will have a hope of seeing anyone if we fly into the mist again."

With her high vantage point restored, the extent of Mekan's forces was even more apparent. The surging darkness to their north extended across her entire line of sight, from east to west.

"How can there be that many?" Kelan said. "Even in Setemar, Mekan's forces weren't that extensive, and there was a Temple of Death underneath the city."

"The Void has probably been open for weeks if not longer," Yala said. "The enemy has been holding back for this moment. That, or it's a trick of the mist to make the army look bigger than it is."

"It's big enough," Kelan murmured. "I don't like our odds of overtaking them."

"No." Niema whistled a command. "We should head for the shore."

With their backs to the army, the impression of being pursued by a faceless enemy intensified, and every breath of the wind on her heels might have been a claw reaching to pull Niema from her steed and into the abyss. When the coast's jagged outline appeared in the distance, she turned her path westward towards where she knew Amanar lay, as if they might have a chance of reaching the doomed city before the army did.

The coast neared, uneven cliffs jutting above wide beaches, and Kelan took the lead. "There's someone over there."

"Shit." Yala lifted her spear again. "Those aren't Disciples."

"No." Niema peered at the cliffs, upon which a small group of stone houses were clustered above a narrow beach. A flurry of activity stirred; within moments, they drew close enough to see the ruptured bodies of villagers strewn across the beach, rivulets of blood soaking into the sand.

"We're too late," she choked. "The dead must have come ashore."

With a curse, Yala flew into the lead as a reptilian shape rose above the houses. Her dead war drake's teeth closed over the smaller beast's foot, dragging it into the path of her spear. She drove the weapon into its eye with a burst of gore that made Niema gag.

A second beast met its end at Kelan's blade. Its decapitated body toppled downward to join the bodies on the beach, and the stench of rot filled the sea air.

"If there are survivors, we have to get them out of here." Kelan gestured to the houses on the clifftop, though Niema didn't see a single living human up there. "Before Mekan claims their dead."

"How is this possible?" Niema's soul shrank away from the violence, the sheer meaninglessness of the lives taken away. "Why would the army attack a harmless village like this one? If it's the king giving orders—"

"I doubt they care if they kill anyone else on the way to Amanar," Yala spat. "I don't think anyone *is* leading them. At least, I didn't see anyone at the front of the army."

Is that true? Niema was too dazed to take in the implications. Her hands trembled against her war drake's back, her palms damp with sweat.

"What are *they* doing back here?" Kelan gestured across the water, where two heads had popped up. Nanek and Yalian must have followed them after all.

"Come to gloat, maybe." Yala descended on her bone-white steed as the bodies on the sand began to stir. "Shit. That was fast."

Kelan's blade severed the head of a man who rose upward, eyes blank and unseeing. "I don't think they're here to gloat. There are more than two of them."

"Are there?" Niema saw Nanek leading the way, arms cutting through the water as he swam towards their beach. Behind him were three, four, five other Disciples. "You're right. They must have found others."

At least ten, Niema counted, though they reached the shore without getting out of the water. Instead, they watched as Yala and Kelan took down the rising dead, reducing them to piles of twitching flesh. Niema gagged and spat bile over the war drake's side.

"What?" Yala called to the Disciples of the Sea, shaking a piece of intestine off her spear. "If you're here to help, you're too late. All the people in that village are dead, and I bet the same is true all the way up the coast to Amanar."

"We might be able to save some of them if we move fast enough," Kelan added. "*Are* you volunteering to help us? Is that why you came back?"

"No." Nanek eyed Yala. "There is no stopping this army without cutting off the source."

"The island," Yala said. "The temple."

Niema twisted to stare at her. "You want to go there *now?*"

"We know how to get you to the island without going through the middle of that army," said Yalian. "I can take you there myself. Nanek and the others have volunteered to go to Amanar. We're going to fight."

Niema's heart lifted and then sank. Amanar's people would face the same fate as the villagers, and a handful of Disciples hadn't a hope of defending them against Mekan's forces without losing their own lives. They must know that, surely.

"Niema." Yala eyed her. "Your call."

She swallowed. "All right. We'll go with them."

Yala eyed the Disciples. "Fine. You'd better not intend to lead us astray."

———

Kelan hadn't expected the Disciples of the Sea to return, much less agree to help in the fight. Yalian's promise to lead the others to the island was even more surprising, though their odds of closing the Void before Mekan's army destroyed Amanar were all but nonexistent.

"What changed your mind?" he asked Nanek. "Niema, right? She's endearing enough to make you want to be a better person."

"Kelan," Niema hissed at him. "Quiet."

"Just curious." Or rather, trying to distract himself from the lack of any good options before them. They'd face the army whether they went to Amanar or abandoned them to a grim death, and while the Disciples of the Sea would add to their number, they were scarcely a splash in the ocean compared to the tidal wave of Mekan's forces. "I thought you didn't care for the fates of the people of Laria."

"The dead aren't just attacking nobles or Disciples," said Nanek. "They're targeting innocents."

"Don't you do the same when you recruit new Disciples?" A question that had been buried since their first encounter reared in his mind with inconvenient timing. "I was under the impression that the ones who aren't strong enough to swim to your temple are left to drown."

"What?" Niema sucked in a breath, and even Yala twisted to stare at him.

"Who told you that?" Yalian said, an edge to her voice.

"I saw," Kelan told her. "In Amanar. You expect us to trust you when you killed a child?"

"The water contains many dangers," said Nanek. "If we were permitted to recruit openly rather than coming ashore in the night and leaving by dawn, we might have a better chance of guaranteeing our novices' survival."

"So that's the fault of the Disciples of the Flame too?"

"They do far worse to their novices," Nanek retaliated. "It's up to you. If you'd rather we returned home…"

"It would help if you apologised for trying to drown us," he said. "My fellow Disciples of the Sky are still missing. Perhaps dead."

"One of them went back towards the capital," Yalian said. "I saw."

"Really." Kelan didn't entirely trust her word, but he hoped someone *had* gone to warn the king. Not to mention the other Disciples of the Sky who'd stayed behind at the inn.

"They aren't in the ocean," Nanek said without so much as a hint of remorse. "We'd know if they were."

"Would you?" He glanced at Yala and Niema. "You're sure you want to trust them to take you to the island?"

"It's that or fly straight through the army," Yalian told them. "Don't forget that we're in the same water as Mekan's rotting beasts, which means we're taking more of a risk than you are."

"Fine." Yala swerved her dead war drake around mid-flight. "Let's go before I change my mind."

"Good luck." Kelan nodded to her then to Niema, who looked less than certain about this turn of events. As the one person who *could* close the Void, she must feel the pressure worse than Yala did. Yala, by contrast, seemed almost resigned to her fate.

I hope she knows what she's doing.

Yalian turned away from the shore and began to swim eastward;

after a short pause, Yala and Niema flew after her. Now alone on the coast, Kelan left the ruined village behind and flew outward over the water, conscious that positioning himself between a group of Disciples of the Sea and an army of the dead was not a recipe for a long and happy life.

"If the others aren't in the water, where are they?" he asked Nanek. "You can sense anyone who enters the sea, can you?"

"Anyone living," he corrected. "We didn't aim to kill you."

"Maybe not, but that army might have finished the job." He watched the Disciples of the Sea cut ahead of him, moving so swiftly that he might almost have believed they had a chance of catching up to the army before they reached Amanar.

Would that help, though? He let them overtake him and turned back, uttering a prayer to the god of the sky to help him track the others. Without the haze masking his view, the air was clear, at least when he turned towards the shore. Another prayer left his lips.

"Help me find them."

The air caught his arms, propelling him like the wingbeats of a war drake. He let himself fall into the sky god's hands, and to his great relief, Terethik carried him down the shore until he caught sight of a robed figure hovering above a distant cliff.

"Ranit." He resumed control over his flight and soared onward to meet his fellow Disciple. "You're alive."

"Kelan!" Ranit nearly fell out of the air. "We thought you drowned."

"Not quite." He caught Sothen's eye as his fellow Disciple approached them. "Is everyone here?"

Charen joined them too. "Brikel went back to the capital to warn the king and ask the other Disciples of the Sky for help, but the three of us got away. We thought you were dead."

"Lakiel will be happy." Admittedly, he'd be livid that Brikel had left in the first place, but her survival was some consolation to him, even weighed against the knowledge that the army would not leave Dalathar alone for long.

"Where were you?" Sothen asked. "Did you get lost at sea?"

"In a way," he replied. "The Disciples of the Sea have generously decided to help us fight. They're on their way to Amanar."

"You want to keep going?" Ranit's eyes widened. "We're outnumbered."

"Imagine how Amanar's citizens feel." It would help if Brikel sent reinforcements, but there were no guarantees that the other Disciples of the Sky would sign up to die. Even Sothen and Charen looked appalled at the mere thought of continuing. "It's that or fight the dead in the capital, without the help of the Disciples of the Sea. It's safe to say that's where they'll end up when they've finished razing Amanar to the ground."

"There's the king's army." Ranit sounded unsure, though. "Fuck it. If we're going to die, might as well drown some of those monsters on the way out."

"Precisely my thinking." With the others behind him, Kelan flew north along the shore until the Disciples of the Sea reached their line of sight. They'd slowed, perhaps assuming he'd fled, and Nanek offered the others a nod that might have been an apology.

"Shit, what happened over there?" Ranit had spotted the ruined village behind them.

"The dead," Kelan replied. "Amanar's not the exclusive target. We might stand a better chance if we divide up the army and fight our foes in smaller groups, in fact."

They continued, cutting westward alongside the coast towards Amanar. They hadn't been flying long before a screeching cry came from ahead of them. One of those ghastly birds with rotting wings flew towards them from the ruin of another village, the leg of some unfortunate person sticking out of its beak.

Kelan sliced the monster's feathered chest with his blade and gagged at the stench when its rotting innards spilled out. Farther ahead, another descended upon a fleeing man, ripping him in two like a blade slicing through a groundfruit.

As Kelan flew at the beast, he glimpsed the Disciples of the Sea fighting some scaly monstrosities in the water. They moved swiftly but efficiently, and the water was soon thick with scales and viscera.

His blade severed the bird-creature's head, and its screeches grew silent.

Kelan shook pieces of dead monster off his sword and checked on his fellow Disciples. All alive, uninjured, but it wouldn't last if the entire coast was in a similar state.

It's going to be a long day and a longer night.

———

While the bulk of the army went to the docks, Viam and the rest of the Flight Division would fly from the paddocks to avoid causing too much chaos when transporting the war drakes out of the city. She helped each of her new squad members climb onto their steeds before she mounted her own, unable to shake the feeling that she was knowingly leading them to their deaths.

Of the group, Brenat alone showed little fear. She insisted on helping Viam aid the quaking novices before mounting her own war drake with the confidence of someone with a decade of experience.

"I'll fly in the lead," Viam told the squad. "Watch what I do, and only unfasten your war drakes' chains when I say so."

Her hands were clumsy, as if they belonged to someone else, and it took her three attempts to undo the padlock and let the chain fall to the ground. When no barriers remained between the war drake and the air, she tried for a reassuring smile. "Now it's your turn."

The clank of chains filled the paddock. Viam watched each fall to the ground, and when all the war drakes were freed, she raised a gloved hand and called, loudly enough for the entire paddock to hear. "Fly."

The others repeated her command with less confidence, but their war drakes needed no encouragement. Seven sets of wings beat, and air buffeted her in all directions. Together, they rose into a sky that was soon thick with beating wings as the other squad leaders joined her. As she'd expected, each squad was led by a veteran and otherwise formed of uncertain novices. Already, two had almost fallen off their steeds and had to be rescued by their companions. Another was throwing up. Sensing her own novices losing their nerve, she gave them a nod of reassurance.

"Fly west." She squeezed her war drake's neck with her knees, applying pressure on its left side, and was relieved when its flight path angled westward over the city wall without resistance. "West!"

Six voices repeated her command, with varying results. Their lopsided formation was less important than everyone reaching the coast in one piece, so once everyone was flying in the same direction, Viam focused on making sure she stayed in the lead and assumed a stance of command. A part of her rebelled against flying in the position that Yala ought to be in, but there was no time to dwell on the circumstances that had landed her here. Soon, the docks lay below them, where the king's army assembled on their ships. Some boats were already out in the open sea, but nothing compared to a war drake in flight for sheer speed, and she'd soon left them in the dust.

"Left!" she shouted as her war drake's path veered to the east. "Fly left!"

"Left! Left!" Urgent cries prompted her to turn in her seat.

One of her companions was having considerably more difficulty getting his steed to turn in the right direction. The war drake soared northward, caught up in the euphoria of flight, and Viam's own steed turned its head to watch with interest.

"No." She squeezed her thighs around its neck and rapped its neck with her left palm. "Left. This way!"

The beast responded, but a frantic scream from behind her prompted her to slow her pace. To her horror, one of the riders toppled off his steed, arms flailing, into the waiting ocean. *No.*

"Wait for me!" she shouted. "Down. *Down.*"

Her war drake obeyed, sweeping into a dive, but not before the man hit the water and sank into the waves.

Gods. Could she pull off a mid-flight rescue? She'd done it before, but not on an unreliable beast unused to carrying a rider, and not with a group of untrained novices behind her. To her alarm, their war drakes began to descend, following her lead.

"No!" she called back at them. "Stay. Wait for me. Stay—"

Her war drake came out of its dive so abruptly that Viam nearly went flying over its head and into the sea. She held on, gasping, scanning the water for the fallen rider and instead spying a dark shape. Something with a scaly head, and sharp teeth, and bone-white spines covering its neck. It reared up, out of the water, revealing a body coated in jet-black scales like shadows made solid. *It's like a sea drake but wrong, twisted.*

The beast was Mekan's. They shouldn't be this close to the dead, not with the army halfway to Amanar.

"Down!" She urged her war drake to change its path, but her steed let out a shriek of displeasure and veered sideways, nearly tipping her off again.

"Hey—stop that!" She repeated her commands, but the monster had spooked the other war drakes, not just hers. Their cries rang in her ears, and her squad broke apart in collective panic.

With a curse, she reached for the spears strapped to the war drake's side. She didn't have full confidence in her ability to aim from this height, but maybe the beasts would stop panicking if she demonstrated that it was possible to kill one of Mekan's creatures. *At least, I hope it is.* She'd never seen a beast like this before.

"Aim for the eyes!" she shouted, but her words were lost amid the cries of the war drakes and the screams of their human passengers.

She took aim, but the spear missed, breaking against the water's surface. Her heart further plunged when she saw the fallen novice frantically trying to swim away from the monster.

"Down. *Down.*"

The war drake ignored her; below, the monster's teeth closed on the soldier's heels and dragged him like a fisherman reeling in a catch.

"Hey!" She grabbed and hurled another spear, and this one glanced off the beast's back. Blood bloomed in the water around the soldier's body as the monster's teeth crunched over his legs.

"Viam!" Brenat's cry came from above. "Duck!"

"What—?" Viam lifted her head and saw Brenat descend, hurling her own spear with more power than Viam possessed. She obeyed, belatedly ducking, and the void drake's eye exploded in a shower of gore.

How did she figure that out?

"One eye down, one to go." Brenat reached for another spear as though she wasn't as new to flying as the novice who lay dismembered in the water. "Want to take this one?"

"How'd you get that beast to listen?"

"Easy." She waved a sack of meat with one hand and hefted a spear with the other. "Coming?"

Brenat's war drake had already dropped into a dive; Viam reached for another spear, urging her war drake to fly for the weakened target. She wished she'd brought a sack of meat with her too, though Brenat was incredibly lucky that her steed hadn't tried to grab the sack from her hands mid-flight and dislodged her in the process.

Before she could reach her target, the sea drake-like beast's head plunged underwater, spraying both of them with salt.

"Hey!" Brenat called down to the spot where the beast had vanished. "Are you going to hide instead of fighting me?"

"Brenat!"

The monster's head reared up again, teeth clamping around Brenat's war drake's legs. With a yell, Brenat flung herself sideways, straight into the water.

No. Viam's arm moved as though it didn't belong to her, and she scarcely felt the spear leaving her hand. Nor did she feel the impact as its slammed into the beast's other eye, bursting through the back of its head.

"Down. *Down.*" Her voice cracked, her gaze fixed on Brenat waving her arms from the water. *Please don't let there be more dead beasts in there. Please.*

Brenat's war drake spun away, its injured claws trailing blood. Viam gasped orders at her own steed, her knees clamped around its neck. "Down!"

"Viam!" Brenat held up her arms. "I need a hand."

"Down!" Relief flooded her when the war drake finally dropped low enough for her to extend her hands towards Brenat's. "Come on!"

As Viam took Brenat's hands, another head broke the surface behind her. With a jolt, she recognised the soldier who'd fallen from his mount, his arms cutting through the water of their own accord, his eyes wide and sightless.

She tugged on Brenat's arms, but the war drake tilted sideways beneath her as it changed directions, spooked by the dead soldier.

Toppling sideways, Viam fell from the war drake's back and into the ocean's waiting maw.

29

Viam hardly had time to hold her breath before she hit the water. Despite the short distance, the impact slammed into her bones, and darkness closed in, tasting of salt and something unpleasantly rotten. She kicked twice, and when her head broke the surface, the first thing she saw was Brenat swimming to her side, her hair plastered to her face.

Behind her, the dead man reached for her with outstretched hands, his waterlogged body held aloft by the water.

"And to think I assumed dead people couldn't swim," Brenat gasped. "At least this is a memorable way to die."

Viam scrabbled to free her dagger from its sheath at her belt, but her hands moved slowly, encumbered by the weightlessness of floating. Too slowly. The dead man's hands seized Brenat's arms, pulling her into his clammy embrace.

"Leave her alone!" She kicked and splashed, fingers fumbling the sheath, and Brenat's scream drove a knife into her own chest.

"No!" Water flooded her mouth, and she ripped the dagger free of its sheath. With a desperate lunge, she threw herself at the dead man. His hands had locked around her friend's head, and there was blood in the water. So much blood.

Viam stabbed wildly, her blade sinking into dead flesh over and over, but the man's grip remained unincumbered. *It's hopeless. He's dead. I can't do anything.*

Wait.

He's dead. And I'm a...

Reversing her aim, she drove the dagger towards her own arm. When the blade met flesh, she screamed the god of death's name.

"Mekan!" The cry tore from her lungs, and pain exploded from her arm. "Leave her alone!"

Shadows filled the water, merging with the blood. Brenat screamed again, and Viam tried to reach for her, but her bleeding arm refused to move.

Through the haze of blood and shadow, a hand extended towards hers—*Brenat*—but the shadows thickened and swallowed the world.

———

Yala flew slightly ahead of Niema, and Yalian swam below, occasionally vanishing below the water's surface. Dalathar soon reappeared as a dark mass on Laria's coast, and she glimpsed a number of ships heading out over the water.

"The king's army." Yala's attention sharpened at the distinct cry of a war drake. "They did send the Flight Division."

"I thought there wasn't a..." Niema trailed off, horror dawning on her face. "Oh, no."

Exactly. "Nobody except Viam is trained, and she's never taken that war drake for an open flight before. King Daliel has sent those people to their deaths."

"Why would the king send untrained soldiers into battle?"

"Desperation?" That was part of it, but not all. "Or the same reason he held that parade. To show the public he can act decisively, like his father did, even if the decisions he makes are fucking atrocious."

Yala's flight path veered in the direction from which she'd heard the war drake's cry. Yes, they'd delay their arrival on the island if they took a detour, but there was no help for it. If Viam died because of the king's foolishness, Yala would never forgive herself.

The Fight Division must have already overtaken the ships; while Yala didn't see any reptilian forms among their number, several were visible to the north and west. She angled her flight away from the shore, following the sound of another cry.

A war drake flew towards her, tongue lolling in fear. No rider sat on its back; either they were dead or had been thrown off, which essentially meant the same outcome. Chills racing down her spine, Yala continued to fly.

"Watch out!" Niema yelled not at Yala but at the Disciple of the Sea in the water below.

A reptilian head broke the surface, rearing upward like a sea drake. Its pitch-dark scales and shadowy eyes marked it as one of Mekan's beasts.

Around Yalian, waves began to churn, forming a barrier between herself and the monster. She lifted her spiny weapon, but her figure was a small dot on the water compared to the sea-drake-like creature's towering neck.

Dropping into a dive, Yala reached for a spear too, aiming at the creature's pit-like eye. "Straggler, are you?"

She hurled the spear, but she'd misjudged, and it glanced off the monster's side. She reached between the war drake's ribs into the sack to grab another, but the beast lunged upward in time with her descent, and its teeth closed over Yala's next spear before it left her hand. Startled, she released the weapon before the momentum carried her out of her seat.

Niema's whistle turned the beast's head sideways, giving Yala the chance to grab another weapon and drive it into one of those pit-like eyes. The beast roared and thrashed its tail, but Yala ignored it, withdrawing her spear and stabbing the other eye.

The beast's serpentine body crashed into the water. Yala held up her spear hand to shield her face from the salt spray, and Niema made a choked noise behind her. "Oh, gods."

Yala lowered her hand. "Shit."

The beast was no straggler. More reptilian heads reared up from the water, too many to count. In the sky, winged forms flew towards them at speed, too small to be war drakes, and heading right for Laria's oncoming army.

"Mekan's army... weren't they heading for Amanar?"

"I thought so too." An army of that size, though, could break into several pieces without losing ground.

The Flight Division, by contrast, had scattered. She spotted a few more war drakes—some with riders, some without—but not enough to form a squad. Her heart sank even further when she saw the soldiers' bodies in the water. They floated without uttering a sound, arms flailing as though pleading for help. One was missing half his face.

Niema made a quiet noise of horror. "They're... He turned them into the dead. How?"

"I doubt Mekan cares for the method of death. All bodies are the same to Him." She tensed, seeing another reptilian form bobbing in the water, but the beast was undeniably dead. Its serpentine body coiled amid Mekan's newly created soldiers; somewhere within, a hoarse, quiet cry sounded.

"Yala!" Niema shrieked. "There's someone alive in there. I sense them."

On the other side of the beast's tail, one of the bodies waved an arm, rather more forcefully than the rest. Yala's mouth went dry when she recognised Brenat's blood-caked face among her fellow soldiers, waving one arm, the other propping someone else up above the water.

"Viam." She flew down, her war drake's claws brushing away the dead's grasping hands. Brenat had put some distance between herself and the other corpses, but holding Viam upright must be costing her what little strength she had.

"Hurry," Brenat gasped. "I can't hold on much longer."

"I'll take her." Yala leaned over the war drake's side. "Is she breathing?"

"Yes—yes, she is." Niema uttered the words that momentarily calmed the tempest in Yala's head. "I'll help."

Green light bloomed in Niema's palm and streamed over Viam's unconscious face. Her eyelids flickered then widened. *"Yala?"*

"Good, you're awake." Brenat half-pushed Viam up into Yala's arms; she tightened her knees around the war drake's neck to keep her balance. The pain in her leg was nothing to the ghastly state of Brenat's face. Viam looked better; her left sleeve was soaked in blood, but now she'd regained consciousness, she managed to climb up with Yala's help, and the two of them scrambled to reposition themselves on the dead war drake's back.

"Hang on tight," Yala told her. "I'll get you to dry ground."

"Oh—*Brenat!*" Viam sobbed, seeing her companion's crimson-drenched face. "Help her too. Please."

"Here." Niema, too, reached over the war drake's side. Brenat was easily twice her size, but she was luckily conscious enough to pull herself up onto the war drake's back behind Niema with little assistance.

"Thank the gods." Viam held on behind Yala with her one good hand, the other hanging limply at her side. "I thought you were going to..."

"As if I'd leave you to die for His Majesty's misjudgement." Yala turned her path southward, though she maintained a slight angle so she would see any flying beasts that might catch up to them. "Didn't you try to talk him out of it?"

"I did," Viam whispered. "Brenat wasn't supposed to fly either. She came to help me."

"It looks like she was one of the lucky ones." The king must have known the plan wouldn't end in anything other than disaster, but desperation had overruled common sense.

Not that the rest of the army was faring any better. Winged beasts flew at the ships and swiped at the soldiers on the decks, whose arrows and spears made little impact on their enemies. She'd lost sight of Yalian, too, but there was no help for it—reaching the island would have to wait until she'd got her friend to safety.

"Aim for the eyes!" Yala yelled at everyone, but she didn't slow down.

The dead had yet to reach the city, but that wouldn't last with the way those winged beasts had broken apart from the main army. The capital might have more protections, but its defences primarily covered the upper city and the docks, not the outer city. She did see a couple more war drakes with living riders, but they were too busy fighting the airborne beasts to notice Yala.

The guards certainly did. When they flew towards the wall around the upper city, Yala was unsurprised when the guards pointed their spears in their direction.

"We have some of your soldiers!" Yala called to them. "They need urgent medical attention."

Yala let Niema overtake her, since her living war drake was less likely to elicit a violent response than her dead steed, and they descended into the paddock. Not a single war drake had been left behind. *On top of everything else, he's lost any chance of reviving the Flight Division again after this.*

When they landed, the king's guards came rushing in through the gates to surround them. Viam slid off the war drake's back first, stumbling when she hit the ground. "Wait. It's me."

The guards, recognising her, lowered their weapons a little but didn't budge. Half their attention was still on Yala.

"Did you not hear me?" Yala said to them. "We need urgent medical attention."

Niema clambered off her own steed and helped Brenat climb down too. The other soldier was trembling, and her face looked even worse close up. Gouge marks scraped one side of her face, straight through her left eye socket. Viam let out a sob when she saw her.

Yala dismounted, her leg twinging when she put weight on it. "Don't just stand there. What part of 'urgent medical attention' do you not understand?"

The guards finally moved, ushering their group through the gates towards the barracks. It'd been years since the last time Yala had set foot in the infirmary, but the sight of injured soldiers lying on sleeping mats brought an unpleasantly familiar jolt.

"Let me help." Niema pleaded. "I can heal injuries. Some, not all of them, but please give me the chance to try."

Viam already looked better, the wound in her arm bleeding less obviously than before, but her face had drained of colour, and she refused to move from Brenat's side. The other woman had fallen unconscious, her face seeping blood that refused to stop despite Niema's efforts.

"This is my fault," Viam rasped. "Brenat shouldn't have been there. She signed up because I did."

That answers the question as to whether she's trustworthy, Yala thought, but she refrained from saying so aloud. Niema finally stepped back, her eyes shining with tears. "I—sealed the surface wounds, but I don't think I can heal her eye."

"Don't push yourself too hard."

The tears spilled over. "There are others out there who need my help too," Niema choked. "How can I abandon them?"

"If we don't cut this off at the source..." Yala paused.

"What?" Viam sat upright to listen to her. "What are you planning?"

"We're going to close the Void," said Yala. "It's in Mekan's temple. On the island."

Viam jumped to her feet. "No."

"You know that's where this started." Yala took in a breath. "You know that's where *he's* hiding. He's not with the army."

Viam sank back onto her sleeping mat. "Please don't die."

I can't make any guarantees there. Yala moved towards the door, slower without her cane, and beckoned to Niema to join her.

"Viam." Brenat stirred, her good eye half opening. "What've you done?"

"Me?" Viam protested. *"How could you follow me like that? You could have died?"*

Sensing the need to give them privacy, Yala beckoned again, and Niema followed her out of the infirmary.

"What a fucking disaster." Her leg twinged with each step. Noticing, Niema extended her hands, and a green glow ignited over Yala's shin, soothing the ache.

The despair in her chest would not so easily be dispelled, nor would her dread at the slaughter they would have to abandon the army to face while they flew to the island.

King Daliel is a fool. Did he really think this plan of his would end in any other way?

The guards at the back gate took one look at Yala's scowling face and moved hastily aside to let her out of the palace grounds, but instead of going to the paddock, Yala made for Ceremonial Square.

Niema hurried behind her. "Where are you going?"

"The Disciples' Inn," Yala said. "To see if any of the Disciples of the Sky have changed their minds."

Upon reaching the inn, she knocked once and then pushed open the door. Several Disciples came running to waylay her, one of whom was Lakiel.

"What are you playing at?" he demanded.

"Don't push me," Yala returned. "I just saved two of the king's soldiers' lives, and I doubt anyone's coming here to arrest me."

"Are you sure about that?" Lakiel took a step back, his arm bandaged but otherwise in better shape than the soldiers she'd left near the docks. "Did you see Kelan? Is he alive?"

"Last I saw, yes," Yala said. "He and the others are on their way to Amanar. Niema and I were going to deal with the source, but we got diverted when His Majesty sent a squad of untrained fliers to certain death."

Lakiel's eyes widened. "I thought I heard war drakes. What was he...?"

"Thinking?" Yala finished. "I'm wondering the same myself. Where are your fellow Disciples?" The room at the inn was emptier than she remembered, and while four Disciples had accompanied Kelan when they'd left the city earlier that day, not everyone was accounted for.

"Some of them went to catch up with Kelan and the others." Brikel walked into view from the stairs, strapping a blade to her waist. "Others are going to help the army and protect the city."

317

"*You* aren't going anywhere," Lakiel told her. "You're staying here, where it's safer."

"I'm not waiting for them to come here. And they will, you know." Her hands twitched towards her weapon. "It's a matter of choosing where and when we want to die, and I'm not hiding under a bed this time."

"Would anyone else like to come with me?" Yala addressed everyone in the main room, raising her voice in case anyone else was upstairs. "I'll kill as many fuckers as possible on my way out of the city, but I'm not staying. I'm going to close the Void."

"Sounds like my chances are better with you," Brikel said. "Don't look at me like that, Lakiel. You know it's true."

Several other Disciples stepped forward too. She might have been surprised if not for the fact that they'd volunteered to help defend the city in the first place, even if they hadn't planned for the battle to take place in these circumstances and on this scale. Even Lakiel grudgingly joined his sister at the back of their group when she made to leave the inn.

"Nothing from the Temple of the Flame?" she guessed.

"Not a word." Brikel sent a violent gesture in that direction. "Pricks."

"If Mekan's forces enter the city, they're doomed along with everyone else." Yala reached for the void drake's claw, preparing to call her steed and enter the fight again.

———

The water was thick with the dead. Scaled sea drakes rose upward, their long necks reaching towards anyone fleeing along the beaches along Laria's coast. Others fled southward, but avoiding the sea did nothing to protect them against Mekan's airborne monsters.

Both kept coming, the dark tide breaking against the shore and spewing horrors with each heave of the water.

Blade in hand, Kelan flew at a nearby winged monster, spearing it through the eyeball. Its body dropped from his sight, but another immediately took its place. Even when Kelan and the others had been joined by a second group of Disciples of the Sky, Mekan's forces far outnumbered them.

He glimpsed the Disciples of the Sea in the water, indicating they hadn't fled, but it couldn't be pleasant to fight amid the chaotic soup of Mekan's creations. Not just monsters but dead bodies of slain humans occasionally rose waterlogged to the surface, perhaps locals who'd jumped into boats in hopes of escaping the carnage in their homes. *Poor fools.*

Hours blurred together until Kelan had lost all sense of time. If not for the constant presence of the ocean on his right-hand side, he wouldn't have known they'd drawn any closer to Amanar, and it came as a disorientating surprise to see the sudden sprawl of buildings ahead of him.

"We're here." Ranit spoke hoarsely, his blade dripping blood, his hair plastered to his face with sweat. "Amanar. Shit, it's bad."

It's bad enough out here. They'd lost two Disciples on the way and had been lucky it hadn't been worse. They hadn't seen any of Mekan's larger beasts yet, but a familiar winged silhouette greeted their arrival in Amanar. *Void drake.*

Two, in fact, vast winged shapes circling above the rooftops. Gods. Their bedraggled group was too exhausted to fight *one* of them.

Screams filtered through the roar of the ocean. Kelan gritted his teeth and picked up speed, praying to Terethik to give him strength enough to survive this.

In the ocean, he glimpsed several Disciples of the Sea fighting the dead with spear and knife, but using their abilities to their fullest extent would involve submerging the city in the same ocean that Mekan had claimed.

The piers and docks were already underwater. His heart swooped sickeningly, remembering the orphanage from which he and his fellow Disciples had recruited novices all those years ago. He hoped everyone inside the building had managed to get out before the place was submerged.

The high wall around Amanar's centre would prevent the water

319

from reaching the interior, but while the wall resembled a smaller version of the one that encircled Dalathar's upper city, no soldiers patrolled, and anyone who fled through the gates to find protection would instead find themselves boxed in as the void drakes attacked from the sky.

"Watch out!" Air gusted from his hand, knocking a winged reptilian beast out of the path of a fleeing family with young children.

The void beast recovered its balance and dove again, but Kelan was ready with his blade. He and Ranit stabbed it through the eyes, giving the children the chance to run.

"This way." He beckoned to the family and pointed down a side street that was free of the dead. "Avoid the inner city."

From above, it was easier to direct the fleeing citizens to escape routes, but Mekan's beasts took every chance to dive at any unwary humans they saw, and the bodies of those slain rose upward too, turning upon their fellow citizens.

One of the void drakes noticed their approach and changed its flight path towards them, claws outstretched. Kelan's shoulder twinged with the memory of their sharpness, but he took his blade in hand and thrust upward into one of the beast's eyes.

The beast roared, its claws gouging Sothen in midair. The Disciple fell with a gurgling cry.

"Shit." Kelan aimed for the other eye. He missed, and the beast's tail swung at his ribs, knocking the breath from his lungs.

He caught his balance, half upside down, and Ranit came to his rescue, slicing through the beast's wing.

Kelan regained ground and slashed at the other wing until the beast was unable to keep its balance in the air. On the way down, he drove the blade into its other eye until it hit bone.

The second beast had left his line of sight; when he scanned the city, he saw fewer monsters in the sky than beforehand. At the seafront, the ocean had crept back, exposing the piers and docks that had formerly been submerged. *That's a good sign, right?*

"Regroup!" he called. "Everyone over here."

Ranit landed, one arm seeping blood, while Kelan checked on the

Disciples' Inn. The building was barely standing, and he hadn't dared check on the orphanage. He looked for the Disciples of the Sea instead, but while numerous dead sea drakes and similar beasts floated on the surface of the water, he didn't see Nanek or the others.

"Where are the Disciples of the Sea?" Ranit asked, echoing his thoughts. "Have they abandoned us?"

"Some of them are over there." Charen pointed to a sea drake that lay in the water, thrashing and bleeding, surrounded by figures wielding spine-shaped weapons.

Kelan drifted out over the water to see if they needed a hand and recognised one of them from amongst the group who'd captured Lakiel. Stopping mid-flight, he swivelled to Ranit. "Are you seeing what I'm seeing?"

"Did they have a change of heart?" Ranit asked. "I thought they were working for... him."

"So did I." *They did try to sacrifice us, didn't they?*

As Kelan stared in confusion, movement on the water pointed him to the surprising sight of a large wooden boat moving towards them.

"Who's sailing in these conditions?" He was more baffled to see the boat was the right way up and appeared undamaged, at least as far as he could see. The sun had begun its descent over the ocean, and its dying rays gleamed on the boat's polished hull as it approached.

"I think they're with the Disciples." Ranit gestured to the ocean, whose churning waves had calmed to a gentle stirring that pushed the vessel towards the shore. More Disciples of the Sea swam on either side of the boat. They, too, were from among the Disciples who'd tried to sacrifice them to the god of death.

"This must be some new trickery of Mekan's," he murmured to Ranit. "The same Disciples who captured Lakiel are out there, which suggests whoever's on that boat is not on our side."

"They're fighting the dead, though." Ranit indicated the floating body of the dead sea drake. "What're they doing?"

Some of the citizens had begun hesitantly moving towards the seafront, perhaps drawn by the calming water and the sight of the boat's steady approach.

"Look, the boat's flying Laria's flag," someone said. "They're here to save us!"

Really? The boat might be small, but it moved with the demeanour of a much larger vessel. The flag was indeed Laria's, and the person standing at the front...

"It's the king!" The cry came from farther down the pier. "It's King Tharen!"

The words were swiftly echoed, back and forth, until the air was redolent with shouts.

King Tharen had returned to Laria.

30

Yala caught up with the army at the coast. Her dead steed joined the living ones, most of which had no riders, though some did, and she recognised the faces of some she'd fought alongside in the Flight Division.

"Valthias!" she shouted to a long-haired man who sat atop a war drake some distance below her.

The man lifted his head. "Yala?"

"Yala?" Another rider cried in triumph. "Yala Palathar is here!"

Stop that, she thought. They ought to know that her presence didn't make any difference. A good soldier was still just that. A weapon in the hands of... well, Yala didn't know whose hands held the weapon anymore. Wasn't that just the fucking problem?

"Yala!" Niema's shout drew her attention to one of Mekan's mockeries of a sea drake, which reared up out of the water in front of one of the king's boats. The soldiers on the deck used spears and arrows to repel it, but few weapons made an impact on its rock-hard scales and getting too close to its teeth risked being cleaved in two.

"Aim for the eyes!" Yala shouted for what felt like the thousandth time. "Niema?"

Niema whistled, and the sea drake stopped partway through dragging a soldier off the deck. Spears dug into its eyes, and the beast's tail thrashed, sending several soldiers stumbling over the edge into the water.

Yala flew down to help, her dead beast's claws seizing her quarry and dragging it away from the boat. The soldiers watched, some wary of her steed, but all arguments were cast aside in favour of a mutual cause. When her war drake's claws dealt the final blow, one of them even cheered.

Yala let the monster fall into the water and flew upward, where Valthias battled a void drake in midair. He fought competently but would have a hard time without a squad around him, so Yala flew into the left flank position and aimed her spear at the void drake's eyes.

"Watch the spines," she warned. "That's what got me, years ago."

"Why in the gods' names didn't you *tell* us what you saw on that island?" he grunted, knocking the void drake's claw aside with his own spear.

"Be honest," she said between breaths, "would you have been willing to listen? The king was dead. The Flight Division was in a state of collapse."

And I fled the city for the jungle.

Did she regret that choice? It was hard to say. Yala had never had much time for regret. When she'd spent so long living from one moment to the next, with survival a luxury, how could she look back at the years of hard-won freedom and wish she'd spent them locked in a futile struggle to prove her own truth?

No... there was no path that wouldn't have led to this moment in the end. Similarly, there was no path that didn't lead her back to the island.

"Niema!" she shouted. "We need to find... shit. Where's Yalian?"

In the chaos of rescuing Viam and Brenat from the ocean, they'd left Yalian behind, and no Disciples of the Sea appeared within the churning water. Mekan had infected the very ocean, and scaly beasts rose to attack the soldiers alongside the bodies of their own slain comrades.

Yala flew on above the carnage. There were so *many* bodies that it was impossible to identify any individuals or to tell if anyone was alive amongst the dead. Niema flew at Yala's side like her shadow, her gaze haunted.

"I can't sense anyone living down there," she whispered. "I… oh, gods."

She pointed. Yalian lay tangled amid the corpse of a dead serpentine beast, her body slumped over its tail and her hand locked around her weapon. Her teeth were bared in a final snarl of defiance.

"Fuck." Yala's gaze lifted to Valthias, who'd half blinded the void drake but had sustained a cut to the face similar to the one that had left her scarred.

Flying upward to join him, she jabbed her spear at the void drake's clawed foot. The beast ignored her; its tail whipped around into Valthias's steed, and the war drake screeched in pain. Valthias clung on with one hand, the other held awkwardly as if his arm was broken.

He lifted a spear with his free hand, but the end had bent sideways, perhaps from impact with the void drake's armoured scales.

"Come on," Yala snarled at her steed, her fingers trailing shadow. "Get the bastard."

The dead war drake grabbed the beast by its clawed feet, tugging it downward. Its wings beat, fighting to gain height to reach its prey.

Valthias took aim with his spear in his one good hand, holding on with just his legs. As the spear left his grip, the void drake's claws pierced him through the chest.

Blood bubbled to his lips.

Yala let out a howl of anger and despair when her comrade, her friend, tumbled sideways from his seat. She clenched her fist, shadows pulsing between her fingers, and the war drake's fist clenched, too, its claws closing around the void drake's neck and snapping through skin, sinew and bone.

Slowly, she unfolded her fingers. The dead war drake did the same, trailing shadow from each claw and releasing the dead beast into the water.

Oh, she thought. *That's new.*

She lifted a hand, and the dead war drake's claw moved in unison, responding to her silent commands. She was both rider and steed, and the distance from herself made her exhaustion melt away until the fight became all that existed.

———

Niema could hardly breathe.

The ocean, once teeming with life, heaved with death. Her hands were numb on the spear she couldn't use, instead waving it in defence at any of Mekan's monsters that might come too close.

She healed anyone she could get near, but that wasn't often. The water spared nobody, and the victims were often drawn under the waves or ripped to shreds before Niema had a hope of reaching them.

There was little life to draw from either. If she wasn't careful, she'd exhaust herself long before they could put an end to the horror. After Yalian's death, Yala had had the idea of following the path the other Disciples of the Sea had taken, but they were long gone. They'd have reached Amanar by now or met their deaths at the claws of Mekan's monsters farther up the coastline.

"I notice Superior Kralia hasn't joined in the fight," Yala said over her shoulder. Her face was streaked with blood, but most of it wasn't hers. "She'll be hiding, I guess."

Niema bit her lip. "She'll probably say her own death means the end of the enclave, which might be true."

"You seem to be doing fine without her."

I'm not. Niema's very being rebelled against involving herself in a war, even if she wasn't actively fighting. Yala, though… she fought in a way Niema had never seen before. At each violent gesture of her hands, the dead war drake's claws ripped and tore through the dead as though it could somehow *hear* her through the shadows linking them together. She didn't even look tired but exhilarated.

Niema had to look away. She focused instead on healing, on distracting any of Mekan's creatures who might be able to hear her whistled commands, and on not giving in to despair and letting the ocean's waves claim her too.

Despite her exhausted state, she noticed before Yala did that the fighting had stopped. Below, a few people had gathered on the docks, while one of the arm's ships had turned back.

"Yala?" she called.

Yala didn't react. Her steed released the ruined body of a void beast into the water, and her hands twitched in front of her as though she was in a trance.

The second time Niema called her name, Yala lifted her head. "What?"

Niema gestured at the water with a shaking hand. "They're retreating."

"It's over," a passing rider called. "The king's scouts from Amanar said that the army has gone. The dead aren't attacking any longer."

"That can't be possible."

The dead couldn't have disappeared. Yes, Dalathar had escaped lightly compared to Amanar, but how could an army of that size vanish into nothingness?

"They aren't gone," Yala said. Her voice sounded slurred, as though she was drunk. "Can't be."

"Yala!" Niema leaned forward, alarmed, as Yala slumped in her seat. "Are you all right?"

"Might've... overdone it."

She toppled sideways off the dead war drake's back.

———

Kelan and the other Disciples joined the growing crowd on the seafront, watching the boat approach the shore. The former king had a few companions outside of the Disciples, dressed in the plain clothing of soldiers or civilians. They didn't appear to be dead, at least as far as Kelan could tell.

Mekan's army had evaporated, as though the thick cloud of darkness on the water had been a mere illusion.

"Are you sure it's him?" Ranit whispered to Kelan. "He doesn't look like a king."

"I'm sure." *I think.* If not for Yala's absolute certainty that the former king was the Successors' leader, he might not have known this was King Tharen. The man was dressed in the simple garb of a sailor and didn't wear the characteristic crown or embroidered cloak that Kelan remembered, but he'd only ever watched the parades from a distance. He'd never seen the man's face up close like his soldiers or staff had.

"The Disciples of the Sea are still there," Ranit muttered. "If they spot us…"

"They might try to sacrifice us again?" Kelan guessed. "I'm not sure that's their plan any longer."

When the boat was secured to a pier, the former king disembarked. Cheers and applause erupted from the crowd, and as he moved towards the waiting people of Amanar, they knelt before him with their heads bowed as they might have knelt in front of an altar.

In a way, he was exactly the same to them. Proof of the gods' justice.

Just not the god they expect.

The bitter voice in his head reminded him of Yala. *Someone has to tell her…* but both the island and the capital were a long way from Amanar. Even if he'd had energy enough to endure the flight, a whisper in his mind urged him that it was vital to stay here to witness this impossible sight with his own eyes. Kelan had little doubt that King Tharen had sent the army of the dead and had somehow made them vanish at the last minute, but nobody else reacted to his appearance with anything other than joy and awe.

The king reached the pier's end and walked to an open space on the seafront, around which there was room for a crowd to gather.

"I return to Laria with grave news," he told them. "Yes, I survived the attempt on my life, but I see that my country is not better off from my absence. The opposite, rather."

"Your Majesty!" someone shouted. "How did you survive? Didn't Rafragoria kill you?"

"No," he said. "It was not Rafragoria who attempted to take my life.

I was betrayed by those closest to me. I barely escaped. Now, I return to Laria at great personal risk to myself."

Shocked exclamations broke out amid the rapidly growing crowd. He hadn't mentioned the Disciples of the Flame by name, but he'd certainly received the intended reaction. If Kelan didn't already know the truth, he might've fallen for the act too.

"Why did you return?" someone else called from the back of the crowd.

"Why else?" he said. "To save my country from ruin at the hands of hostile forces."

"I think we ought to leave," Kelan murmured to Ranit and the others. "If he levels the blame for his exile on *all* the Disciples, that includes us."

Nobody argued. They retreated, taking care not to fly too high and draw attention to their abilities, and found an empty street in which to regroup.

"What the fuck is going on?" Ranit whispered. "You don't think he'll blame us for this?"

"Didn't you see how the guards were already reacting to us in Dalathar?" Kelan muttered back. "If I had to guess, that'll be his next stop. The capital."

"He's not going to destroy his own city," another Disciple said. "Or execute his son."

"I doubt anyone thought he'd send an army of the dead either." Kelan surveyed their exhausted faces. "It's not ideal, but I'm going back to Dalathar as soon as I can. You can vote on whether to come with me."

He left them to discuss their options and drifted upward to listen to the king continue his speech. He didn't hear every word, but *Dalathar* came up several times. That would be his next destination.

Unless Kelan was able to beat him there.

The impulse to sneak up on the crowd and whisper the truth in their ears arose, but he squashed it down. What was he supposed to do, tell the people who'd lost everything in today's attack that their beloved leader was no saviour at all? Even if one or two might listen, Kelan would probably be hanged for treason on the spot.

He descended to join the other Disciples again, who'd voted to come back to Dalathar, but not by flight.

"It'll take too long if we travel on the road," he warned. "Also, I don't see anyone volunteering to take us by wagon, do you?"

"It's nearly dusk," Ranit protested. "I know we can't stay at the inn, since it was underwater until a few minutes ago, but flying through the night is suicide."

"I know." Spying a couple of men ducking out of a side alley, he glided in their direction without quite knowing what he planned to say.

One of them halted when he saw Kelan. "Is it true that King Tharen survived?"

"Yes, but it's not good news." Kelan took in a breath. "King Tharen survived, but he's a Disciple of Death."

The man laughed. "What are you talking about?"

"He sent this army." He gestured to a reptilian body that lay sprawled across the nearby rooftops, dripping gore into the street. "Then he sent them away and staged his return so that we'd celebrate him as a hero."

The second man snorted. "You've been in the air too long, Disciple."

It was worth a try. King Tharen—whether he was truly a king or not—had everyone cupped in the palm of his hand. None would challenge him.

Whatever happened next might well depend upon how fast the Disciples of the Sky were able to get back to the capital.

31

Yala dreamed of the island, of flying above the gaping void waiting to welcome her into its embrace. Her dreams merged with memories, both recent and older, and she woke with the taste of blood on her tongue.

The bed she lay on was softer than she was used to, and while the room wasn't familiar to her, Niema lay on a sleeping mat beside the bed. A glance at the window showed a street she knew. *Right. I'm at the Disciples' Inn.*

Someone had removed her boots, but she was dressed in the same gore-stained clothes she'd worn the previous day, and her drakeskin gloves were plastered to her hands with dried blood. She didn't remember falling asleep. In fact, she didn't remember anything past the point when the battle had ceased and the spell that bound her to the dead war drake had finally faded.

"Yala," Niema said. "You're awake."

"Yes." Her leg protested when she rose upright, her body reminding her of how she'd pushed herself beyond her limits. She held onto the wall with one hand to climb off the bed. "You didn't have to sleep on the floor."

"You needed the bed more than I did," said Niema. "I barely got under you in time to catch you when you fell. Do you remember?"

"No." She remembered being swept away in the rush of the battle, moving the dead war drake's claws as if they belonged to herself, but everything beyond that was as black as the Void. "Where's my war drake?"

"I don't know." Niema crouched on the sleeping mat, her eyes dull and glassy. "I was more focused on getting you in here. I tried to convince the commanders to let me into the barracks to heal the injured, too, but they wouldn't let me."

"Bastards." It might not have made any difference, given that Niema's healing abilities didn't work on every wound, and there'd been so much injury out there. So much death. "Hang on. Is the battle over? What of Amanar?"

"The soldiers said it was over," Niema mumbled. "They said... they said the army near Amanar disappeared."

"That's not possible." Memories of the battle's end came filtering back in. The bodies in the water, the beasts in the sky. "The king's messengers must have been mistaken."

To start, Yala peeled off her gloves and washed in the basin that someone had left in the room's corner, using a cloth to wipe the blood from her face and arms. Fresh clothes had been left out, too, a plain shirt and trousers that resembled the attire the Disciples of the Sky wore under their cloaks. Lightweight enough not to impede movement but not designed for battle. She'd have to visit either her home or the barracks if she wanted to fly that day, though she kept on her weapons belt and the pouch containing the void drake's claw as a precaution.

Yala had left her cane behind in the paddock, too, which was a more immediate annoyance. Niema had healed some of her aches, but climbing downstairs stole much of her remaining energy, and her leg cramped when she reached the lower floor.

A few subdued-looking Disciples of the Sky sat at tables in the downstairs room. None spoke, even to object to her presence, though Lakiel glared at her across the room.

Yala ignored him and picked out a seat at an empty table, trying not to think about Kelan's obvious absence and the unknown fate of those who'd gone to Amanar.

"Sorry," whispered Niema, joining her. "We could have gone to the barracks instead, but I didn't know if you'd be safe there."

"They have enough injured to treat." Like Viam and Brenat. They'd both been hurt, but they were amongst the lucky ones. Undeniably, His Majesty's first campaign had been an unprecedented disaster, and she was glad not to be inside the palace grounds to witness the aftermath.

The inn's owner glowered at her, too, but she agreed to serve Yala and Niema breakfast—for a fee. As she'd expected, the Disciples' meals were prepaid along with their rooms. *Must be nice to always have comforts at your command,* she thought, fingering the sleeve of her finely made shirt. Rather than here, she wanted to be at home on her sleeping mat.

She wanted to be in her jungle cabin, resting in a hammock, far away from the blood and death.

Yala's hand clenched, her fingers tingling with the memory of the shadows she'd wielded. *No. It's too late for that now.*

She'd never made it to the island the previous day, but if the Void remained open, the soldiers' sacrifices would be for nothing.

The plates of flaky fish pastry, crisp flatbread, and sliced fruit were a world away from the dismal fare she'd have been fed at the barracks, but Yala hardly tasted a thing. As they were finishing breakfast, the inn's door swung open, and Kelan stumbled in. He looked as though he'd flown through the night, which must be the case, given the timing. His bloodstained cloak was wrinkled as if it had been soaked and dried several times, and his face was leached of colour.

"Good, we're all here," he said to the room at large. "I have good news and bad news. The bad news is that King Tharen is back. The good news is that he got rid of Mekan's army and spared the people of Amanar."

Yala half-rose from her seat. "You're joking."

"I wish I was." He crossed the room, holding the wall for balance, and sank into a vacant chair. "I owe a significant sum of money to the man who let me borrow his wagon overnight. I had to leave it outside of the city."

Yala did some mental calculations. "That doesn't work. Raptors can't move that fast."

He flashed her a weary smile. "I may have made a deal with the god of the sky. He loaned me some speed."

For a price. He looked ghastly, not unlike those poor corpses in the water. "The others...?"

His smile faded. "The others are a few hours behind me. The ones who survived."

"Who?" Brikel spoke up, her mouth twisting. "Who died?"

"Sothen... Yorel and Tolin." He slumped in his seat. "We'd have lost more if the army hadn't vanished mid-battle, but I have a feeling we're going to see the downside of that soon enough."

"Where'd they go?" King Tharen might have survived the impossible, but even a Disciple of Death couldn't make an army of the dead vanish into nothingness. "And where's—?"

"King Tharen?" Kelan finished. "At a guess, he's on his way here."

Shocked murmurs filled the room. Lakiel began to speak, perhaps to argue, but Brikel grabbed his arm and yanked him back into his seat.

Yala blew out a breath. "How long do we have?"

"Not long enough," Kelan said. "He'll be travelling by boat, and he has those Disciples of the Sea aiding him."

"Of course he does." Yala's mouth twisted. "Did he state his intentions?"

"I left in the middle of his speech," Kelan said, "but he blamed a betrayal from those closest to him for his exile, so it's safe to say Superior Shralin is going to have to rethink his approach of denial and avoidance if he wants to survive the week."

"I have no sympathy." Yala pushed out of her seat. "How big is his army?"

Kelan shook his head. "His Disciples don't outnumber ours. He had other companions, but they mostly looked like regular people.

Soldiers or sailors, perhaps. He sounded like he was trying to recruit people in Amanar, too, and I can imagine he'll pick up more along the way."

"What are we going to do?" Niema whispered. "We can't fight the king, can we?"

"We might not have to if he's painting himself as a hero." Yala gripped the table's edge in a hand, wishing again that she had her cane. "Whatever he's up to, he can't have banished the dead altogether, though. That's not possible even for a Disciple of Death."

I think. Who was she to know what secrets Mekan had whispered in King Tharen's ears during his years of exile?

"I didn't see him controlling the dead," Kelan added. "He didn't show any outward sign of his link to Mekan."

"And he wasn't leading the army after all." They'd misjudged, assuming he intended to use his army of the dead to pressure Laria into submission and force his son to give up his throne. *Maybe that is still his plan. When he gets to the capital.*

King Daliel deserved some warning either way, and while she doubted that she'd get near him today, she knew where to find Viam.

Kelan's gaze followed her across the room to the door. "Where are you going?"

"The palace," she said. "I'll try to send word to the king. The army's in no shape for another clash with the dead, but it's partly his own damned fault."

Kelan inclined his head. "Then we'd better hope that wherever that army is, it's not coming back."

———

Viam was half awake when she heard a commotion at the door to the infirmary.

"Let me in." Yala's voice banished all traces of sleepiness. "Did you not see me fight alongside your army yesterday? If I wanted you dead, I wouldn't have bothered to announce myself first."

Viam pushed herself into a sitting position. Her arm throbbed, but

Niema's healing abilities had helped alleviate the pain, though she'd been unable to save Brenat's eye.

Brenat. Viam turned to the sleeping mat next to hers where Brenat slept soundly, undisturbed by the noise in the doorway. Not wanting to wake her, Viam tried to stand but half fell back, her legs refusing to obey.

Yala swept into the room, her mouth taut with annoyance. Several people sat up to watch her; every soldier who was still conscious would know Yala Palathar.

"Stop staring," she reprimanded one particularly awed novice who'd stopped to gawp at her. "If you want to make yourself useful, fetch me a cane I can borrow. I'm sure you have a spare lying around somewhere."

"Yala." Viam rubbed tiredness from her eyes. "Is what they're saying true? The battle is over?"

"Not exactly." Yala reached her sleeping mat and murmured, "King Tharen seems to have shown up to save everyone."

The soft words brought Viam into full wakefulness. "No."

"Kelan and the Disciples of the Sky saw him with their own eyes," Yala said, her lips barely moving. "I don't believe that I'm back in King Daliel's good graces enough to give him that information without another stint in jail, but I thought you should know."

Dizziness swept over Viam. "Where is he? The—former king?"

"Amanar," she replied. "According to Kelan, he was in the process of gathering allies from among the public after he so generously banished the dead for them. He already seems to have a few soldiers on his side, along with some Disciples of the Sea."

He banished the dead. Did that mean he wasn't openly declaring himself as a Disciple of Death? Had nobody made the connection between his arrival by sea and the army of the dead's assault from the same direction?

A novice held out a cane towards Yala, breaking the tense silence. She snatched the cane and glared until the novice scurried away, leaving them alone again.

"What of the island?" Viam whispered. "You never made it there, did you?"

"Not yet." Yala's tone was calm, but emotion glimmered in her eyes. "I think it's safe to say that's where the Void opened, and I might stand a better chance of getting there without an army in the way."

"Are you sure...?"

"Oh, I doubt the army has gone for good," Yala said. "It's just inconvenient for His Majesty's attempts to paint himself as a hero, so he'll have hidden it away."

"Then he must be on his way to Dalathar," Viam whispered. "Now."

"Yes." Yala glanced behind her at the doorway, near which had gathered several soldiers who were making little effort to hide the fact that they were trying to eavesdrop. "You can tell the king as much or as little as you like, but I thought you should hear directly from me."

As she retreated, Brenat stirred beside Viam. "Was that a dream, or was Yala in here?"

"Not a dream." Viam climbed off her sleeping mat and managed to stay upright this time. "I have to talk to the king."

Changing into clean clothes was difficult with one arm all but useless, and washing was even harder, but looking presentable was the least of her concerns. Doubtless the king knew she'd been injured, and he'd be preoccupied enough with the aftermath of yesterday's disastrous conflict.

The rest of the barracks was eerily quiet, and Viam didn't attract much attention from the soldiers nor from the guards huddled in tense groups in the palace grounds. She could only assume the administrative staff had been asked to stay at home for their own safety unless their roles were pertinent to the army.

Yet the dead had never come here. They'd vanished as though they'd never existed at all.

Viam climbed the stairs to the palace and spoke to the guards outside. "I need to talk to the king."

The guards passed her message to someone inside, and far quicker than she'd expected, she was ushered into the receiving room.

The king didn't sit on his throne, instead pacing in front of the tapestried walls. He wore his usual fine attire, but his headdress was in disarray, as though he'd been tugging at the hair beneath.

"Viam," he said. "I am sorry. I shouldn't have sent you to fight."

"It wasn't..." *your fault?* That would be a lie, though she had no room in her heart to offer him more blame than he deserved. This was his father's doing in the end. "Your Majesty, I have something else I need to tell you. Urgently."

"Yes?" He didn't turn around. His hands clenched and unclenched at his sides, his gaze fixed somewhere in the distance, and she had the sinking suspicion he'd be in no state to give orders today.

"King Tharen... your father..." she faltered. "He's back. He's in Amanar."

King Daliel halted. His wild-eyed stare landed on her. "What?"

"An eyewitness saw him, Your Majesty," she said. "He landed in Amanar last night, around the same time as the army, ah... disappeared."

"He was responsible for thwarting Mekan's army?" His eyes grew wide. "Truly?"

"Yes, but—no." She stumbled on her words. "A single person can't stop the dead unless—unless they're the one who sent them in the first place."

Her body tensed, waiting for a blow to fall, but the king's lips moved silently, and then he began to pace again, whispering, "My father... alive."

Didn't he hear the rest?

"He's dangerous," Viam said. "I don't know what his intentions are, but he'll be in the capital within a day."

"My father doesn't mean me harm, I'm sure."

He still might replace you. Though it wasn't the worst outcome, by far, and possibly the best for his own survival.

"You're probably right," she said, "but... if he intends to take back his crown, what will you do?"

The king did not answer for a long moment. "I shall think on it, Viam... thank you for telling me."

She left the room with a whirlwind tossing her thoughts like debris. King Daliel had only half listened to her, though she couldn't think what she would have done in his place. After all, he'd done his best to undo what his father had built, and his recent attempts to mitigate the damage had only wrought more harm.

Would King Tharen forgive him? Or would he even cut down his own son in his bid to revenge himself upon those who'd tried to have him destroyed?

———

After Yala left the inn, Kelan joined Niema's table and picked up an abandoned piece of flatbread from her plate. "I assume you didn't want this?"

Niema shook her head. "Maybe I should have gone with Yala."

"If she fought in the battle yesterday, I would hope the king's guards would think twice about challenging her."

True. She'd shown herself to be on their side, and if the guards took issue with her entering the palace grounds, Niema would fare no better.

"I doubt warning him will help," Kelan added. "I hope he's ready to hand over his crown as soon as his father shows up."

Niema started to speak, choked on the words, and shook her head again. A *Disciple of Death* couldn't become the monarch of Laria. How could anyone allow that?

"You look as bad as I feel." Kelan bit into the flatbread. "Did you fight yesterday?"

"You know I can't harm other living creatures." The words tasted bitter on her tongue. "I'm a healer. I only flew out there because—"

"Yala persuaded you?" He finished eating and absently brushed crumbs off his bloodstained cloak. "Yes. I have to admit it was her I had in mind when I decided to make an ill-advised attempt to fly across the coast overnight. She has this way of getting into your head."

"You're lucky you didn't drop dead." He looked awful. The colour had drained from his face as though the god of the sky Himself had leached the life out of him in exchange for His aid. "You're in no shape to fight. Go to bed."

"That was the plan." He rose to his feet and stumbled on his way to the stairs. "I do hope they have a spare room."

"I'll wait for Yala," she called.

She didn't have to wait long. Yala soon returned, leaning on a wooden stick that she must have got from the barracks. Upon seeing her outside, Niema hastened to meet her at the inn's door.

"That was easy," she remarked. "I think the guards know better than to refuse me entry to the palace after yesterday."

"You didn't speak directly to the king?" Niema asked.

"Of course not," she said. "I told Viam. She'll pass on word to him, and it's his decision as to whether to act on that information."

"There's not much he can do to stop his father, is there?" She lowered her voice, though none of the Disciples of the Sky were paying much attention. Of the few who'd made it downstairs, many were injured, and doubtless the other Disciples on their way back from Amanar would be in an even worse state.

Nobody was in any condition to fight another battle, but they might not have to if the dead had truly gone and King Tharen was here with the intention of reclaiming his throne peacefully and not conquering the country by force.

He's a Disciple of Death, a voice screamed in the back of her mind. Did Superior Kralia know of his return? Did she know what he intended to do next?

"I don't envy King Daliel's position," Yala said. "After how badly he fucked everything up yesterday, I wouldn't be surprised if he simply handed his crown over on the spot. He'll escape lightly compared to the people who tried to have his father assassinated. I don't envy the Disciples of the Flame."

Niema's skin chilled. "The ones responsible for trying to kill the king are in jail. The others…"

Yala made a dismissive noise. "Probably, someone should warn Superior Shralin, but I have other priorities. I need to get home and see Saren for a start."

"I need to..." *Find my Superior.* "Check on the war drake."

She'd ordered the beast to return to its paddock, but she didn't know if her command had lasted through the night, and Yala's own war drake's whereabouts were unknown. Yet it was Superior Kralia's war drake that had been a notable absence during yesterday's battle. If she was still in the area... if she didn't already know of King Tharen's return, Niema would have to give her the news.

What then? Would Superior Kralia break her lifelong promise not to intervene in Larian politics or put her own safety on the line to remove a Disciple of Death from the throne? No... there was a third option, far more likely, and the reason she omitted telling Yala her intentions. Namely, that Superior Kralia would order Niema to act in her place.

I'll have to take the risk. If she knows a way to stop him, this is my only option.

As they left the inn, another question hit her. "Yala... do you want to go back to the island?"

"Do I *want* to, or do I think we *should* go back?" Yala closed the door behind her, resting her other hand on her borrowed cane. "If the army truly has vanished, which I very much doubt, the Void was never closed. The island remains a danger."

"But—can't the king open the Void anywhere?"

"With enough sacrifices, yes." Yala's tone turned bleak. "I don't want to contemplate what he's willing to do to the rest of us to reclaim power, frankly."

Niema shuddered. "And if the army *is* still lurking at sea?"

"He'll use it as leverage," Yala said. "At a guess, he somehow directed the dead back into the Void to wait for more instructions. That would explain how swiftly they vanished."

But that means... that means closing the Void on the island might not matter. He'll open it again, this time in Laria itself.

"No." Yala spoke with such certainty that Niema gasped. "Your face is as transparent as glass, Niema," she added. "Yes, he might open the Void again when he reaches the mainland, but that island is a Temple of Death. Mekan is far more powerful there than anyone else. Destroying the temple will sever a vital link to his forces."

If it's even possible. Niema ducked her head, though she knew Yala would have read her expression again regardless. "Then let's go."

The guards let them out of the upper city with surprisingly little resistance, and on the other side, she spied a winged shape circling the outer city.

"There it is." Yala's tone was tinged with relief. "I knew my steed hadn't gone far."

"What—what happened between you?" Niema whispered. "In the battle, you were controlling the war drake, but not like... not like before." She didn't have the words to describe the eerie manner in which Yala's hands had moved in synchrony with the beast's claws.

"No." Yala's lips compressed. "I've been fighting alongside the beast for long enough that our bond must have become instinctual."

"Are you sure that's all it is?" Niema's mind conjured images of Yala's hands trailing shadow, puppeteering the war drake's corpse. "You don't feel... closer to Mekan?"

"I didn't hear the god of death," said Yala. "The war drake and I were linked, yes, but it can't think for itself, and I can."

That's not very reassuring. If every movement of the beast had been Yala ... but had Niema expected any less? Yala was a soldier to the core. She fought as naturally as she breathed. In any case, from Yala's drawn expression, the battle the previous day had taken its toll on her. Were either of them strong enough to fight again that day, let alone fly to the island and ensure Mekan's army wouldn't return to attack Laria?

She needed to find Superior Kralia first. While Yala headed home, Niema walked to the paddock. Shuffling noises from behind the gates told her the beast hadn't fled in the night. She unlocked the gate and then startled.

Superior Kralia herself stood inside the paddock, next to the placidly sleeping war drake. *Two* war drakes, the second of which was eating something from her hand.

"Superior Kralia!" Niema halted in the entryway. "Have you been waiting for me all this time?"

"No," she answered. "I came back to the city in the hopes of finding you, yes, but I flew here from a village further up the coast. I spoke to some Disciples of the Sky there in the hopes of gaining an accurate picture of yesterday's events."

"Then you know that he's back?" Niema asked. "King Tharen?"

"Yes."

"And?" Niema's panic bubbled up in her throat. "He's going to reclaim his throne, and then Mekan—*Mekan*—will rule the nation."

"Not entirely true," said Superior Kralia. "I doubt Mekan cares much for mortal thrones. That said, King Tharen is likely to usurp his son upon his arrival."

"He's a Disciple of Death." She could hardly believe her Superior's nonchalant tone. "You know what he is. Isn't that why you and Superior Datriem wanted him dead?"

"You overstate my role in the plan, Niema," she said. "The Disciples of the Flame were always more in favour of taking his life rather than exiling him as I suggested. In the end, we both got what we wanted."

"And now you're fine with him coming back?" No. Protecting the enclave would always be her priority, but wasn't King Tharen a bigger threat to the enclave than anything else?

"Absolutely not," she replied, "but I recognise when events are not within my control and are instead the domain of the gods."

"Yalet doesn't want this either," said Niema. "I thought you just said that Mekan doesn't care about thrones. This is all the king—it's all him. He wants the throne, he wants revenge, and he'll drag us into war with Rafragoria as soon as he's done punishing the Disciples for what they did to him."

"Yes," she said. "I expect he will."

Her hands curled into fists. "Aren't you going to *do* anything?"

"What do you suggest?" Superior Kralia's serene tone battered at Niema's remaining patience; she'd almost forgotten who she was talking to.

"You're a Superior." At one time, she might have thrown herself to

343

her knees and begged forgiveness, but what would be the point? If Superior Kralia punished her for insolence now, it was hardly worse than what Mekan was about to unleash on them all. "You can command him to leave the country, the same way you ordered me to kill Yala. Or you can drain his life as an offering to Yalet. Can't you?"

"Again, you overestimate my abilities," Superior Kralia said. "Away from the enclave, my connection to Yalet is far weaker than I'd prefer. Why do you think I was so reluctant to let you leave? We aren't made to survive in a place like this."

Tears burned Niema's eyes. "He'll burn our forest too. You know he will."

"In that eventuality," she said, "yes. I will act. But not before then."

When it's already too late.

"He's summoned an army from the Void," Niema said. "It's still out there, isn't it? What if he sends it to the forest, or...?"

"We won't be his first target," said Superior Kralia. "We have time to prepare."

"You do. I don't." Niema's last hope fled. "I'm going to the temple on Mekan's island. That's where he initially opened the Void."

"Destroying the temple is impossible." Superior Kralia's lips pursed. "I doubt one Disciple of Life can close the Void within Mekan's island with their own hands. Even you, Niema. There is no life left on that island."

"There won't be any life left in Laria either." The pity in her Superior's eyes made her want to scream. Had she been naïve in thinking that Superior Kralia would ever help against Mekan's forces if there was no immediate threat to the enclave? She'd been nowhere in sight during the battle the previous day, and yet... she'd hoped.

I should have known better.

Superior Kralia climbed onto her war drake's back, and in a steady beat of its wings, she was gone.

32

Saren took the news about as well as Yala had expected.

"His Majesty sure knows how to make an entrance, doesn't he?" he said after letting loose a stream of expletives. "*That* hasn't changed."

"No." Yala finished putting on her belt, having discarded the borrowed clothing from the inn and changed back into her drakeskin trousers and army-issued shirt. "To be honest, I'm not sure what kind of reception he's expecting here in Dalathar. I don't *think* he'll send another army of the dead ahead of him, but I'd never have expected him to do the same in Amanar either."

"Who would?" said Saren. "King Daliel's got to be shitting himself at the moment. Does he know?"

"I told Viam." Yala retrieved her cane, propping the one she'd borrowed from the barracks against the wall; it didn't fit comfortably into her hand like her own did but would do as a spare. "She'll tell the king. His father won't harm him, I assume, but the same can't be said for the rest of us."

"Then what?" His shoulders hunched. "Gods. Is he going to reform the army and force us back into service?"

"How should I know?" She tried to smooth the annoyance from

her voice, but he shrank away all the same. Regardless, now was not the time to spare his feelings. "The Disciples of the Flame will be his first targets, but as the survivors from his last mission, we're witnesses. If he's hiding his Disciple of Death status, we're the ones most likely to be able to give him away."

The colour drained from Saren's face. He kicked the armchair and then swore, clutching his foot. "Please tell me you have a plan."

"I'm going to talk to Nalen," she decided. "If the king sends someone to find us, you'll be able to hide in the Undercity. Nalen'll protect you."

I hope. Nalen was trustworthy, but he had the burden of protecting the rest of the Undercity on his shoulders as well. As he was a former soldier, too, he'd be on the list if the king *did* call upon everyone who'd served to rejoin the army. Same as her and Saren.

After grabbing her spare drakeskin gloves and a couple of extra knives, Yala left for the Undercity without delay. Her body reminded her of the previous day's exertions with every step, but she couldn't rest when King Tharen was on his way to the city. That knowledge pushed her upright, taking one step and then another until she reached the Undercity entrance.

Nalen listened in grim silence to her pronouncement. "Fuck, Yala. King Tharen..."

"I know," she said.

"He's a..."

"Yes."

He swore. Dug the heel of his boot into the step. "If you're right, do you want me to spread word through the Undercity?"

"Best keep it quiet for now," Yala said. "There'll be a panic and arguments and speculation that'll only cause more harm. When he returns, you won't be his priority."

"I doubt anyone down there gives two shits who's on the throne," he agreed. "We might as well have had no king for the past half decade."

"It's not going to be like that for long," she warned. "I don't know what King Tharen will do at first, but it's safe to say rebuilding the army will be among his top priorities."

"Plenty of people can't go back," he said. "They're injured. They have families."

"I know." Gods, she knew, but how could she protect anyone else when she scarcely knew how to spare her surviving squadmates from suffering the same fate? Nalen himself was the self-appointed protector of the Undercity, but nothing in that job description entailed defending them from unpredictable monarchs who also happened to be Disciples of Death. Yes, they'd survived one attack from the dead, but it was for that reason that Yala knew hiding in the Undercity was no guarantee of safety.

Time was running low, and she hadn't checked on the war drake yet. She left the Undercity behind and met Niema halfway back from the paddocks.

"What is it?" Yala rested her cane on the ground at her feet. "Is the war drake still missing?"

"No." Niema lifted her gaze, her mouth trembling. "I ran into my Superior."

"Did you?" Yala studied her face. "You aren't going to attack me?"

"That's better than doing nothing," Niema burst out. "My Superior said she's not going to fight against the king or his army unless they land on the enclave's doorstep. She's given up."

Yala couldn't say she was surprised. "Has she already left?"

"Don't *you* care?" Niema's eyes glittered with tears, her hands clenching and unclenching. "We can't *give up*. If Mekan takes over the throne of Laria—yes, the god of death doesn't care about mortal thrones, but it's not a *good* thing, is it?"

"I never said it was." Had Niema expected Superior Kralia to extend an offer of help? Yala had all but forgotten the leader was present in the city at all. "What else did she have to say for herself?"

"Nothing," Niema whispered. "She confirmed the island is the source—that the Void is open there—but said it can't be closed by a single Disciple of Life. And that army of his…"

"She stayed behind just to discourage and berate you?" That was entirely characteristic of Superior Kralia, but Yala wanted to chase her down and throttle her. "Fuck her. We're better off without her."

"She said I'm not strong enough." Niema took in a shuddering breath. "It doesn't matter, does it? None of this *matters*. If we destroy the island—even if that could be done—Mekan will still be on the throne, won't he?"

"I wouldn't go that far," said Yala. "I wouldn't be making plans to get my friends out of the city if it didn't matter."

Niema's eyes gleamed with tears. "And what, leave the rest of Laria to suffer?"

"Has it ever been within my power to do more?"

"I..." Niema lowered her gaze. "It's not you I'm angry with. Superior Kralia claims her power is weakened away from the enclave, which might be true, but that means my abilities are weaker too. I can't destroy the island. She said the temple is impossible to destroy."

"Anything can be destroyed." Could it, though? Yala had guessed that the reason for the sheer size of King Tharen's army of the dead was due to him using a true Temple of Death as the source. Like in Setemar—and there, it'd taken the collective efforts of the Disciples of Life and the Disciples of the Earth combined to close the Void. Of course, there was one branch of Disciples that they hadn't had access to. "Unfortunately, I think the only person who might be able to achieve that is Superior Shralin."

Niema's eyes grew round. "You think he can destroy it?"

"I think he'll have to be dragged kicking and screaming," she said. "I also think he might choose death on the island over punishment for his predecessor's actions against the king, though I've been wrong before."

While the surviving conspirators were imprisoned, the other Disciples of the Flame would also have to face the brunt of the former king's wrath. Convincing him of the impending danger would be another matter altogether, of course.

"It might not take a Superior," Niema said. "He's the most powerful, but the other Disciples have Dalathik's favour too. If we could convince some of them..."

"Behind his back? Good luck with that."

Niema's teeth ran over her lower lip. "The conspirators were willing to act without his knowledge, but they're locked up."

Yes, they are. Yala was aware of the irony of her regret for their fates, considering that they'd happily have burned her along with the king. If she tried to set them free, they might still.

And yet.

"Niema," she said, "if I wanted to break someone out of the guard-house, would I need as big a distraction as setting a plague of rodents loose? Or something more subtle?"

"You want to—?" Niema stopped. "I can try something more subtle, but it depends how many guards are there."

"Fewer than before," Yala said. "The king will have assigned most of them to defend the city instead. I can't promise this will work, but with Danir gone, the others are marginally less likely to turn me to ashes when I walk in there. They were considered strong enough to take out the king, and that's good enough for me."

Niema's expression was conflicted, but she nodded. "I'll create a distraction."

"And I'll refrain from telling Saren until it's over." *If I'm alive.*

Getting back into the upper city was easier than before, since word had spread amongst the guards of her actions during the previous day's battle, and she reached Ceremonial Square without opposition. Few people were around, and Yala avoided the palace gates as she crossed to the side street leading to the guardhouse.

She made for the back entrance through which she'd been rescued, but Niema caught her arm. "Wait. My diversion..."

"There are at least two war drakes in the paddock," Yala muttered. "I saw them when I visited Viam earlier."

"Oh." Niema went quiet again. "All right."

They continued down the side street, seeing no one and hearing little except the murmur of conversation from the other side of the palace fence. When they neared the guardhouse, Yala ducked into an alley and waited for Niema's diversion. While the back entrance to the jail was seemingly unguarded from the outside, the keys to the cells would be in the front, and besides, she didn't know how many guards remained inside.

A war drake's cry sounded. Then another. Shouts rang from the palace grounds, and as Yala watched, a guard ran out of the jail. A second followed. She waited, listening for more footsteps, but none followed. *Time to go.*

Yala made for the jail's back door and entered. The smell of sour sweat and urine brought back unpleasant memories of her capture, but the stench of the dead had gone. Burned away.

Her gaze panned across the corridor until she laid eyes on a subdued-looking man whose face was vaguely familiar. He jumped to his feet when she walked into his line of sight. "You're Yala—"

"Quiet," she hissed. "I don't have long, but I'm going to let you out of here. In return, you're going to do something for me."

"What?" A female Disciple stepped into view in the cell next to his. "You're *letting us out?* Wasn't it your stories that got us locked up?"

"It's more complicated than that." At the echoing howls of war drakes from outside, more Disciples moved to the front of their cells, their attention fixated on Yala. "In short, the man you tried and failed to kill years ago is coming back to Laria with an army summoned from the island that he's spent his exile on. He'll be here within the day."

Shocked whispers erupted.

"If it's true, why set us free?" asked the man she'd first spoken to. "You're trying to trick us. Didn't you kill Danir? His body was found mutilated, the guards said."

"He tried to kill me. It was justified." She was done arguing. "I need you to help destroy the source of that army. You know what I'm talking about. If you can't do that, you're of no use to me."

"The island," the female Disciple said. "You want to destroy it? Is that possible?"

"Not for me," said Yala. "Unfortunately, I need a Disciple of the Flame, or as many as possible, so I want to make a deal. Here are my conditions. Help me destroy the island and I'll set you free. Refuse and

King Tharen will put you to death by the day's end. I know which option I'd choose, but I'm not you."

Flames danced in the woman's eyes. "Fine. I accept."

Yala jerked back as the temperature rose too fast. Her hand was on her dagger, but the flames hit the inside of the door instead of her. A sizzling noise sounded then the crunch of a lock breaking.

The woman stepped out of the cell with a touch too much smugness for Yala's liking. *They have to remind me they can still turn me to ashes if they choose.*

Such was the risk she took. Yala bared her teeth in a smile. "It's lucky I didn't bother picking up the keys. I'll meet you at the docks in an hour."

Given the volume of the war drakes' cries, Niema's diversion was at risk of causing more harm than she intended. Yala left the Disciples to make their own way out, figuring that if they let the other prisoners out in the process, at least it'd deflect the blame from herself.

That left her with one more stop to make... the Temple of the Flame.

Yala found Niema lurking in the narrow passage between the paddock and the palace grounds. When Yala beckoned, Niema whistled to calm the war drakes as she made her way to Yala's side.

"Where are you going?" Niema hurried behind Yala as she retraced her steps to the square. "I thought you went to the jail to *avoid* the temple."

"The more people we have, the better." Yala's hopes were as slim as the odds of King Daliel keeping his crown, but the success of their jailbreak had given her a rush of reckless determination that she grabbed onto, knowing she'd need all the nerve she could get. "At least Superior Shralin won't be able to claim I didn't warn him."

When she reached the temple, Yala climbed the stairs and hammered on the door with her free hand. A startled novice answered, flinching away from her clenched fist. "What... Yala Palathar?"

"I need to pass on a message to your Superior," Yala told him. "Immediately."

"What message?" Superior Shralin appeared, sweeping the novice behind him as though he was nothing more than an ornament. "I thought I told you never to come back, Yala Palathar."

"And I thought your people deserved warning that the former monarch is on his way to Dalathar," Yala retaliated. "He blames your people for his exile, and he has the support of a group of rogue Disciples of the Sea."

His mouth hung open. "What nonsense."

"She's right," said Niema. "You knew some of the Disciples of the Sea were working with the Successors already. He's their leader."

"Traitors." Anger rippled across his face. "They betrayed us."

"Your predecessor exiled them for a crime they never committed," Yala said. "I don't want you to pay the price for his mistake."

"Was that a threat, Yala Palathar?"

"No, a warning." Yala took a step back, her shoulders itching with the memory of Danir's flames. He must have learned of his Disciple's fate, and while Danir had been in disgrace, had he worked out who was responsible? "I might not be here to help you when he does show up."

"No." An ugly expression crossed his face. "You might not, at that."

The smell of burning filled the air, stifled a moment later. Niema let out a soft noise, and the Superior took a step back as the shadow of a war drake fell over the steps.

Yala swivelled around and locked eyes with Superior Kralia, who was seated upon its back. The beast landed sprawling on its claws at the foot of the temple stairs, while onlookers in the square gawped and shouted.

"Superior Kralia?" Niema said. "What are you doing here?"

Ignoring her former Disciple, Superior Kralia addressed Superior Shralin. "You're making a grave error, Shralin."

He shook his head as he fought to displace the shock of her sudden arrival. "Who are you to judge? Shouldn't you be with your enclave?"

"The Successors are a threat to all of us, Shralin," she went on. "If the former king is indeed on his way here, hiding won't save your people from the consequences."

"How dare you insinuate that I won't defend my people," he said.

Niema took Yala's arm and whispered, "I think we should go."

Yala was inclined to agree.

———

Niema's mind rebelled against what her eyes were seeing: Superior Kralia, facing the Temple of the Flame from atop her war drake without a care for the attention she'd drawn. Superior Shralin wore an expression more furious than she'd ever seen on him. *He's not going to attack her, is he?*

Her instincts told her to creep away while both were distracted, but Superior Kralia's behaviour ran so counter to the warning she'd given Niema earlier that she wanted to know what had changed her mind. Hadn't she told Niema it was futile to fight back? She couldn't know that Yala had freed the imprisoned conspirators, but she must think it was worth trying to talk to their leader.

Out of the corner of her eye, Niema watched Yala descend the stairs but didn't follow. Heart torn, she caught her Superior's eye when she twisted in her seat, and green light bloomed from Superior Kralia's palm. A burst of energy rushed into Niema's veins, and she staggered, mouth gaping open in shock.

Did she just... heal me?

"Go to the island," she told Niema. "Find the source of this and end it."

"I..." What had she done? Loaned Niema some of her power?

"You aren't alone," said Superior Kralia. "Trust in Yalet."

"Get away from my temple!" Superior Shralin bellowed.

"Definitely time to go," Yala murmured, reaching for her belt and the pouch that contained the void drake's claw. Her fingers twitched, her mouth moved, and within heartbeats, a shadow descended over the square.

Niema descended several steps and let out a whistle. She'd left the war drake unchained, ready to answer her command, and its winged shape ascended over the rooftops shortly after Yala's steed. The few people around the square who'd remained after Superior Kralia's arrival fled from its approach, leaving plenty of space for the beast to land.

After she'd mounted, Niema's steed took flight at another whistle. Yala joined her, angling northward over the rooftops, but Niema's attention lingered on her Superior until the towering form of the Temple of the Flame blocked the other war drake from view.

"I told the Disciples of the Flame we'd meet them in an hour," Yala said. "Of course, that leaves us with the question of how they'll travel to the island without their own war drakes. Did any beasts escape during your distraction?"

"No," said Niema. "I asked them to cause a disturbance, but they can't break the chains without help, and I didn't go into the paddock itself."

"Inconvenient." A war drake could carry two people at most, and Yala had no intention of sharing her steed. If any Disciple had been willing to fly with her, she wouldn't have trusted them not to turn the beast to ashes beneath her. "Did your Superior have a change of heart?"

"I have no idea." Niema glanced over her shoulder, but the palace and the surrounding buildings blocked their view of the scene outside the Temple of the Flames. "She... she confuses me."

"You and me both," Yala said. "I despise her, but I dislike Superior Shralin more at the moment, frankly. He's going to get his people killed."

"He doesn't know you freed the prisoners." Niema's stomach churned. "They might be the only ones who'll escape the city without being hanged."

"I doubt it," Yala said. "They have nowhere to go after this, assuming they walk away from the island alive."

We might not walk away either. Niema squashed the thought down and asked, "Do you think they're actually going to fight? Superior Kralia and Superior Shralin?"

"No," Yala said. "If what you said about your Superior is true, she'll be weaker than he is. He's in his own temple, don't forget."

True. Little could stand against the incinerating power of Dalathik, but Superior Kralia might have intended to create a diversion so that she and Yala could escape the city without being harassed by the guards or dragged back to the palace.

As for what she'd given to Niema? She couldn't call it healing power, exactly, but the pulse of light continued to burn beneath her skin, as tangible as her own heartbeat.

She's right... Yalet is with me, she thought. *Even when my own Superior turned against me, my god always answered to my will. However dire the odds, I have to trust that Yalet will help us defeat Mekan.*

———

Kelan felt as if he'd barely closed his eyes when he was woken by a cacophony of noise. War drakes—more than one—and the kind of panicked furore that preceded another battle. *Gods, no. Not again.*

The room tilted sideways as he rose blearily from the bed—he hadn't even had the energy to undress—and stumbled to the stairs. Everyone had gathered in the main room to look out the window. While the inn didn't face Ceremonial Square, he had a clear enough view of two war drakes rising from the square on the left-hand side, one of which was undoubtedly the bone-white steed that belonged to Yala.

"Are we being attacked again?" he asked.

"I don't have a clue," Lakiel snapped. "What's all this drakeshit about the king coming back from the dead?"

Kelan, who'd assumed that Lakiel had heard his announcement earlier along with everyone else, blinked at him. "King Tharen is coming back. Whether he's dead or not is debatable."

"That doesn't even make sense!" Lakiel ran a hand through his hair —his arm was no longer bandaged, which had to be Niema's doing— and jabbed a finger at Kelan. "I notice the others haven't come back yet."

"That's because they're sensible and stopped at an inn for the night," he retaliated. "What are you insinuating, that I killed them and dumped their bodies in the sea?"

"I'm saying your memory might be unreliable," said Lakiel. "And people tend to die around you."

"*Lakiel.*" Brikel hit her brother in the arm. "What kind of thing to say is that?"

Kelan's mouth parted, but no words came. The rational part of his mind knew that Lakiel was searching for someone to blame, and he was the obvious choice, but too many people *had* died around him, and there was no good reason for him to have survived instead of them.

Tiredness forgotten, he made for the door. He heard Brikel calling his name, but Kelan didn't turn back. He didn't dare to call upon the sky god's power and instead rounded a corner into the square.

There, he forgot all about the sting of Lakiel's comment in the face of the scene taking place in front of the Temple of the Flame. Superior Shralin stood at the top of the stairs, facing a war drake that carried a passenger who Kelan took a moment to recognise as Superior Kralia.

Am I dreaming? He didn't see any signs of Yala's war drake, but the one Superior Kralia rode was undeniably alive, its claws splayed upon the ground.

Kelan approached warily, confirming that the scene was not an incredibly detailed sleeplessness-induced hallucination when Superior Shralin spotted him and shouted, "Get away. I'll not have you causing trouble too."

"I assume Yala already told you that King Tharen has returned to Amanar with an army of the dead and some Disciples of the Sea who aren't pleased with you either?" Kelan spoke before his mind could catch up with his mouth. "And that they're on their way to the capital?"

"You're lying."

"I'm not." He addressed Superior Kralia next. "Did you know?"

"Yes." She indicated the sky. "Yala and Niema went to find and stop the source of Corruption before Mekan's army returns."

They went to the island.

"They *left?*" At a time like this? If King Tharen brought more dead with him when he returned to the capital, nobody would be able to stop them except—*oh.* His gaze landed on Superior Shralin. "Was she trying to persuade you to help fight the dead? If so, you might want to consider your chances of survival if you shut your doors. They'll be here within the day regardless of your choice."

"That is enough," said Superior Shralin. "I won't be threatened in my own temple."

He closed the door. Superior Kralia's war drake's wings gave a sudden beat, narrowly missing Kelan's face; he ducked around in front of the beast to catch her eye. "You sent them to the island?"

"They chose to go, and I assisted them in the only way I could." She rose higher into the air. "I must return to my enclave, Disciple. I'd advise you to rejoin your people, too, while you can."

Kelan moved out of the way as the beast ascended in a long beat of its wings, air gusting in its wake. *Assisted them?* What did that mean?

No answers came. He faced the temple's closed door, at a loss as to what to do next. King Tharen might arrive at any moment, but how much danger they were in depended on the closeness of his army and how many new followers he collected along the way. While Kelan's exhaustion was far from dispelled, the notion of spending any longer at the inn with Lakiel's judgemental presence was more than he could bear.

Kelan followed a side street, walking instead of gliding to avoid taxing his depleted resources. He'd reached the end of the street running parallel to the palace grounds when he saw someone had followed. A novice Disciple of the Flame. What was his name, Yachim?

"Kelan, right?" Yachim said. "I... I heard that Yala talking to the Superior before she left. I listened."

"You should go back," he told the novice. "The temple is the safest place for you."

"I want to know what's going on," Yachim insisted. "I know our Superior isn't telling us the truth. Yala said King *Tharen* is coming here? And that he blames us for...?"

"Trying and failing to kill him?" Kelan said. "That's about right.

357

This is all Superior Datriem's fault, not your current leader, but he's certainly not helping matters."

The colour drained from Yachim's face. "What's the king going to do to us?"

"I don't know." He felt sorry for the novice, but he hadn't the heart to conjure up a comforting lie that would sting the worse in the long term. "You'll be safe if you stay inside the temple. Even a king is no match for Dalathik's flames."

"But..." His expression was conflicted. "Yala needs our help, doesn't she? That's why she let the prisoners out of jail before she came to the temple."

"She did what?" Kelan nearly tripped over his own feet. "She can't have. You're mistaken."

"I saw them walking to the docks." He pointed vaguely down a side street. "I don't know if Yala's the one who let them out, but it seems like the sort of thing she'd do. I don't want her to get into trouble."

"Then go back." His head throbbed with exhaustion. "Look... I'm sorry. You don't deserve to be punished for your old leader's crimes, but following me around isn't going to get you anywhere except dead."

Kelan didn't wait for a reply. He picked up speed, gliding for long enough to lose his quarry, and then slowed to a walk again.

He didn't need any more deaths on his conscience.

33

Yala and Niema came to land in an open space in front of the seafront. While Yala had expected to see some remnants of yesterday's army, the first person she set eyes on was Nanek, who sat cross-legged on the wooden pier as though he was waiting for someone.

Oh, fuck. Had he come here to reprimand her for letting Yalian die? She was surprised he'd survived the battle himself, if he'd made it to Amanar, and if he'd seen the former king's arrival.

If so... he'd know King Tharen would soon arrive in this harbour.

Yala climbed off the dead war drake. At her approach, Nanek rose to his feet with surprising gracefulness for someone who spent most of his time in the water.

"Are you going to Amanar?" said Nanek. "You're too late. The army has left."

"All those monsters can't have vanished into thin air," Yala responded. "Besides, we're not going to Amanar. We're going to destroy the Temple of Death."

"Why?" The usual sharpness of his voice bit with a pained edge. "What would be the point? It's far too late to stop Tharen."

"I already heard that at least twice today," Yala said. "I've made up my mind."

"Then you'll die for no cause, as Yalian did."

"She'd spit on you if she heard you say that." Yala didn't know that for sure, but she did know that Yalian had offered her life up to give Yala a fighting chance of making it through Mekan's army to the island. "If we close the Void, the king can't summon anything without a lot of inconvenience."

"Without a blood sacrifice," corrected Nanek. "Of which he's more than capable."

"I didn't claim otherwise," said Yala, "but that'll get in the way of his attempts to paint himself as a hero."

That didn't mean he wouldn't toss that plan aside as casually as he'd turned on his own army, but offering a mass sacrifice to Mekan would be slower, messier, and would make the public decidedly less well inclined towards him. Destroying the temple and the island wouldn't stop Laria's doom, but it would win them valuable time.

"You gamble with lives so casually," said Nanek. "I'd expect no less of a soldier."

"That island is a poison to Disciples and non-Disciples alike," Yala retorted. "I'm not the one making the choice to sacrifice my people on an altar. Don't blame me for the actions of someone who you could have put an end to years ago."

"Also, you're wrong," Niema said to Nanek. "Yala's already survived the island once."

Surprise flickered in his eyes. "Then you were lucky."

"I was," Yala agreed. "We would have gone there yesterday, but my friend was injured in the battle. I'm sorry for Yalian's death too. I didn't know her well, but she helped us."

Nanek's mouth pinched at the sides. "Yes. She was willing to guide you to the island, to her own detriment, in the end."

"You've known of the island for years." Yala's patience thinned. "You knew what King Tharen was doing there. You might at least have *tried* to stop him. You can control the oceans, can't you?"

"You overestimate the reach of our powers." His tone mingled hostility and exhaustion; for a moment, he looked as tired as Kelan had when he'd shown up at the inn. Doubtless he'd swum through the night to get here. "We didn't know the former monarch was on the island, not at first. Rumours have circulated around that part of the ocean for as long as we have lived near Laria's shores, and most of us had no desire to go close enough to investigate. The island sits on the cusp between our two nations, after all, and anyone who might venture into the area risks being targeted by Rafragorian soldiers."

"You must have seen the fire," Yala said. "When the island burned."

"You were responsible for that?" His gaze sharpened. "How can that be? You're no Disciple of the Flame."

"My friend was—" She broke off, not wanting to discuss Dalem with him. "The point is that I watched the island burn, and that temple shouldn't be standing any longer, but here we are."

"We thought the island destroyed at first," said Nanek. "Following the fire, the smoke faded, and so did the rumours. They didn't start again until a few years later, when our Superior noticed signs that the temple was active again."

"Didn't your Superior warn the rest of you?" Niema asked.

"Yes." His eyes clouded. "He picked a group of those of us he trusted the most to keep an eye on the island and report to him of what we saw. It wasn't long before we were caught."

Yala's heart jolted. "You've met him. King Tharen."

Not the king, she thought, giving herself a mental shake. Alive or not, Tharen hadn't been king for a long time.

"Yes," Nanek said after a short pause. "We recognised him as the monarch right away, though he didn't initially admit to his former status. When he did, he claimed to have been exiled for a crime he'd never committed."

"By the Disciples of the Flame?" Yala guessed. "Is that how he lured over some of your people to his side?"

"Not at first." His hands curled into fists. "After our first encounter, we took a report back to our Superior, who urged us to be careful and to avoid setting foot on the island in the future. Not everyone took that advice. Then several Disciples went missing."

"They joined him?" asked Niema.

"Or they were sacrificed," Yala added. "I assume he needed willing victims."

Niema blanched. "Was he already summoning the dead? How did he learn when he didn't have those books with him?"

"You probably don't need them when you're inside a Temple of Death," Yala said. "What you *do* need are sacrifices. What did he do, hire your people to ambush passing boats?"

Nanek's scowl said yes. "He mostly targeted Rafragorian ships, so nobody in Laria would suspect, but it wasn't long before our people figured out what was going on."

You didn't tell anyone else, though.

Nanek looked up at her. "I know what you're thinking. That we should have told Laria's authorities. If we had, the Disciples of the Flame would have seen to our deaths as well as his."

"You're Disciples of the *Sea*," Yala said. "Last I checked, water puts out fire."

"The gods are more complicated than that, as you should know." Nanek stiffened. "There are some Disciples of the Flame behind you."

Yala tilted her head. "Good. They're here to help us."

Or so she hoped.

"Help you?" he echoed. "They'll as soon turn you to ashes as they would have done to the king."

"We have a mutual enemy now." Yala watched the robed figures approach out of the corner of her eye. "Why did *you* come back, out of curiosity? Were you hoping to get here before the king did?"

He slid into the water without answering. The Disciples of the Flame continued to walk, giving the war drakes a wide berth.

The woman who Yala had spoken to in the jail reached them first. "If you want us to help, you haven't told us how we're supposed to get to the island."

"You have two options," Yala told her. "Borrow a war drake from the king's paddock or take a boat."

"We don't have to do as you ask," said an older male Disciple. "Both those methods put us at your mercy."

"I'm asking you to trust me, yes," she said. "And I'll trust you not to set me aflame in return. Isn't that a fair exchange?"

"Fairness has nothing to do with it," the woman argued.

"I thought your deity taught you to be self-sacrificing," she said. "You offer a tribute, and He gives you abilities. I offer freedom, and you destroy the island."

"You know nothing awaits us in Laria but death," said the female Disciple. "You mean for us to die on the island instead."

"Would you rather die at his hands?" Yala asked. "We've also established that you're willing to go as far as to commit regicide for the sake of keeping the peace, but that you weren't able to carry out the final act. Why not come with me and finish the job?"

"Destroying the island won't bring about Tharen's end," said the male Disciple.

"No," Yala agreed. "I don't know what the king is going to do with his newfound power, but it's safe to say it'll be worse if the island is left unchecked and the Void inside the Temple of Death remains open."

The trouble was, when they'd decided to kill King Tharen, they'd acted on the orders of their Superior, not because they'd thought they were making the right choice. She didn't command the same respect, though they might have been more inclined to say yes if she'd been someone other than the person who'd had them locked up for murder. Moreover, Danir and Mieren were the more active and determined of the group of conspirators and the most likely to have taken independent action against the island, but their brashness and tendency to violence had cost them dearly in the end.

A younger Disciple stepped forward. "I'll come. I want the boat, not a war drake."

"Your choice," said Yala. "I'm not responsible if Mekan's army shows up in the water."

"They're as likely to come from the sky," said the female Disciple. "I'll take the boat too."

They must dislike flying. That or they assumed Yala intended to turn on them while they were in the air. It'd take much longer for them to reach the island by boat, undeniably, but Yala knew better than to think she and Niema would be able to succeed in their mission without their help. Like it or not, they were stuck together until the island was obliterated.

This time, Yala would wait and watch until every handspan had burned to ashes.

———

Kelan walked until his legs ached and he wished he'd taken a wagon, but there was little traffic that day and fewer people. When he neared the docks, he spied two winged shapes rising into the air. *Yala and Niema.* If he flew fast, he might be able to catch up to them, but it'd be a fine thing for his dwindling strength to give out halfway across the ocean and send him falling into a watery grave.

Otherwise, there were fewer soldiers present on the seafront than he'd expected and certainly not enough to defend against King Tharen's imminent arrival.

"Kelan," Lakiel called. "You aren't going after that Yala and Niema, are you?"

"Does it matter?" He frowned at his fellow Disciple. "I thought you were staying at the inn."

Had he come to apologise? Unlikely. Lakiel was far too proud to ever consider such a thing.

"I've already sat out one battle." He fidgeted. "And I wondered if you were planning to do something foolish."

"I'm out of favours from the god of the sky," Kelan responded. "I thought someone ought to watch for the former king to show up."

"You really think he's coming."

"Have I ever been wrong?"

"Frequently. You have the worst sense of judgement of anyone I've met."

Kelan sighed. "I *saw* the king. So did everyone else. The people of Amanar knelt before him as though he was a Superior. The others will back me up when they eventually get here."

"Kelan!" called someone else. "There you are."

He spun around. A few Disciples of the Flame came out of a side street, led by the novice he'd sent away, who seemed to have picked up some friends on the way.

"You didn't walk out of your temple, did you?" he said to them.

"We had to," Yachim said. "Our Superior was lying to us."

"I told you you'd be safer in there." *Did I start a mutiny?* Superior Shralin deserved no less, but they would find themselves in even more trouble when King Tharen did arrive in the city, and they'd picked the worst possible place to follow him to.

"Kelan, what did you do?" asked Lakiel.

"Nothing, if you can believe it," he said. "Their Superior nearly started a fight with another Superior on their doorstep. I imagine your faith starts to waver when you witness that kind of thing."

Lakiel groaned. "You're unrepentant—who *is* that?"

Kelan followed his gaze to the glittering ocean, where a boat had appeared in the distance, approaching at such a speed that it might as well have been flying. "Shit. I think our wayward monarch might have beaten our fellow Disciples to the capital."

"Kelan." Lakiel groaned again when Kelan glided into the air to get a better view. "You aren't going to fly out there, are you? Do you ever learn?"

"Yes." It was a miracle that the god of the sky listened to his whispered prayer, but he didn't have much choice but to put himself into debt to his deity again. "If I had to guess, Yala is on her way to the island, and she'll appreciate anyone who keeps his attention off her while she destroys that temple of his."

"Did she tell you where she was going?" he asked. "She's proven to be unstable, at the very least."

"Why did you follow me if you only wanted to criticise my every action?" Kelan kept both eyes on the boat. *Definitely moving too fast.* The Disciples of the Sea had helped the king in his journey, but he couldn't tell how many accompanied him nor if the army had come with the monarch.

"Would it surprise you to know that I don't want you to die?"

That got Kelan's attention. "I thought you hated me."

"So did I." Lakiel averted his eyes as if startled at his own nerve. "You're—oh, fuck."

"What?" Kelan looked up, surprised at his profanity, then he saw the boat was much closer than it'd been beforehand. A large wave rose beneath it, propelling the small vessel towards the shore.

The Disciples of the Sea.

Kelan flew higher, praying to his deity not to forsake him. The wave drew closer, higher, the boat appearing to glide atop its edge.

The king stood on the deck, imperious, facing the capital he'd come to reconquer.

Smaller waves crashed onto the piers, swept boats into the water, chased guards away from the docks. A gust of wind struck, and Kelan felt the moment the sky god let him go, sending him plummeting into the path of the oncoming tide.

———

Niema flew at Yala's side, occasionally doubling back to check on the Disciples of the Flame to make sure they hadn't fallen too far behind. They'd climbed into a single boat, and some of them did appear to have some knowledge of how to sail, but their slow progress grated on Yala's nerves. She wore a scowl and snapped whenever anyone tried to ask her a question.

Nanek must still be nearby, but he'd declined to show his face to the Disciples of the Flame. Niema glanced at the sea anxiously every few minutes, and when the water began shifting around the Disciples' boat, she assumed he was responsible.

At the rocking of the boat, a younger male Disciple jumped to his feet and shouted up at them, "What is this? Are you trying to drown us?"

The sea churned, waves beating at the boat, and Niema's heart sank. *That's not Nanek.*

"Shit." Yala twisted in her seat. "We have company."

Niema followed her gaze. Movement stirred on the water in the distance, nearer to the capital than to their own location. *Is that the king? Or Mekan's army?*

The Disciples of the Flame kept shouting, but she could do nothing but watch them cling to the side of the boat to keep from being flung into the water by the roiling waves.

A head bobbed in the water behind the boat. *Nanek.* He must be trying to help, but they were bound to believe the worst. Sure enough, one of the Disciples gestured towards him. Flames exploded in the air, and Nanek ducked below the surface to avoid being struck.

"Stop!" Niema shouted. "He's on your side!"

Mist swept in around them, and shadows filled the water. The next wave hit the boat head-on, and the Disciples vanished into the haze.

34

Yala's first sight of the island was through the sickly mist that seemed to rise out of the very ocean itself. The Disciples of the Flame had been swallowed up by the wave in the same instant that the mist swept in, stealing her vision.

The island. Her heart pulsed in tandem with the tingling in her fingertips and the shadows seeping through the war drake's wing-beats. It became harder to remember that she'd come here for a reason other than answering the call of the shadows that whispered her name.

"Yala Palathar, welcome home."

"Yala." Niema hissed her name. "Yala, the Disciples of the Flame need our help."

"They're dead." She spoke without conscious thought, her attention focused on the blurry scene gradually revealing itself through the fog.

The temple's ruins clustered at the edge of an overgrown plaza. Open jungle filled the rest of the island, giving way to narrow beaches. She could trace every fingerspan without opening her eyes.

"Yala!" Niema flew closer, her living war drake's wings clipping

Yala's steed's, desperation etched on her face. "You aren't thinking. The island... it's affecting you."

"It's affecting you too." The mist clung to Niema's skin and outlined her war drake's wings in a ghostly halo. "Didn't your Superior loan you some of her power?"

"I don't know what she did, but I can't close the Void if I can't see where it is." Niema gestured ahead. Smoke seeped through the cracked flagstones leading up to the wide stone staircase at the temple's entrance, but there was no gaping hole leading down to the island's interior.

They flew closer. The claw stirred against Yala's leg, and her heart shivered with something like pleasure.

I'm home.

Yala seized that thought and flung it into the abyss. *Focus.*

The temple hadn't changed in the years since her last visit; the jungles destroyed by fire had long since returned to their former extent, and the thick greenery might conceal any number of horrors. As she flew over the flagstones, she glimpsed movement on the staircase leading up to the palace doors.

Niema leaned over her war drake's side. "They're human, I think."

"Don't count on it." The figures stood upright on two legs, but she hadn't forgotten those assassins whose bodies had rotted while they still drew breath.

Yala's war drake descended, and she got a better look at the nearest figure, who was female, long-haired, and clearly alert from the way her eyes followed Yala's approach.

The woman moved forward a couple of steps, and one arm fell off, trailing sinew and muscle. Niema gagged behind Yala.

"Charming," Yala muttered. To the woman, she called, "Seen an army of the dead anywhere?"

The woman staggered down another step, viscera streaming from her rotting arm. "You're one of us. Did he send you?"

"I assume you mean Tharen?" Had he abandoned these people on the island to die? They were already halfway there and hardly in any shape to fight, so she guessed that must be the case. "No, we're here to find the Void."

She gestured downward at the flagstones, recalling how they'd split open to expose the island's innards and a hole leading down into Mekan's realm. Mentioning that they'd come to destroy the Void would not endear her to anyone, but there was little the woman could do to harm either of them in her current state.

"The Void is everywhere," said the woman in reverent tones. "It is within us all... including you, Disciple of Death."

The shadows between Yala's fingers thickened, and an itch grew on the side of her face near the scar left by the void drake's claw. A similar itch started to creep up her shin near the larger wound the void drake had inflicted during her last escape from the island.

"Come with us." A second figure tottered into view. This one, an older man, had a gaping hole in the side of his face through which she could see the planes of his skull beneath stringy grey muscle. "We will take you to Him."

"Yala," Niema hissed. "Don't listen."

The war drake descended, and its claws touched down on the stairs in front of the dead or dying Successors. "Where would that be?"

"Inside His temple, of course."

Is that where the Void is open? Yes, the Void lay beneath the whole island, but she could hardly rip apart the flagstones with her bare hands to reach Mekan's beating heart. If some remnant of Him lurked inside the temple, that would be a much quicker way for her to reach the source of this.

"Come with us," said the man. "You will be transformed."

"I can't say I'm keen on that idea," Yala commented. "Whether with a knife to the chest or rotting from the inside out, dead is dead. Personally, I prefer the quick way."

"One must dance on the edge of death to be truly transformed." The woman grinned, exposing rotting gums.

"Right." Yala rolled her eyes, but she swung a leg over the dead war drake's side.

"Yala." Niema's mount landed beside Yala's. "Yala... please listen. I don't know what Superior Kralia gave me, but I can't—if you die—"

"I won't." Yala climbed to the ground. This steed, at least, wouldn't flee at the sight of Mekan's beasts, though there was a question as to whether a dead war drake fuelled by the Void would survive the island's end.

Of course, that was working under the assumption that Superior Kralia had given Niema the key to destroying the Void and hadn't been trying to trick them both.

I don't want her to die either. That, above all, stopped her from walking into the temple without a thought. Her own death would leave scarcely a ripple on the world. Niema's, though... she mattered. To the enclave, yes, but to the world at large. The world didn't need another soldier. It did need people like Niema, willing to try to enact change in ways that nobody else would dare.

"Wait outside," she told Niema. "I'll see what's going on in there. If I think it's survivable, I'll let you know."

"Yala." Her beseeching eyes sought out Yala's, pleading with her to stop. "What are you doing? I don't understand."

"I'm not sure I do either." Yala reached for a spear from the sack she'd tied to her steed and used it as a cane to climb the rest of the short distance to the temple's entrance.

Not a single drop of sunlight penetrated the caved-in roofs, but the visible carvings on the walls of the entryway brought a shiver of familiarity. With a jolt, she remembered that she'd left the journal with Kelan at the inn, but she didn't need to look at Mavilangran's words to know what she would find within the temple.

The room—the main chamber, she assumed—was dominated by stone statues. Serpentine tails lay in shattered ruins across the floor. Broken wings framed the doorways. Carved faces with pointed teeth sneered at her amid the ruins.

Statues of Mekan.

Behind her, the woman let out an excited noise like the cry of a bird. "This way... it's this way."

Yala peered through the gloom and made out a doorway ahead of

371

the woman, who beckoned with her one remaining hand. Yala followed, extending her spear to feel her way across the uneven floor past the pieces of shattered stone. Mekan's serpentine face watched, unseeing, from the decapitated head of a statue. Was that what He truly looked like or an interpretation by His worshippers? The latter, given what she'd seen inside other temples, but the thickening shadows around the pitted eyes gave the impression of life where none existed.

The tingling in her fingers intensified, making it increasingly hard to keep a firm grip on her spear. Her leg, by contrast, grew numb, and she was barely limping when she entered the room off the main chamber.

Near-total darkness awaited on the other side. Her ears picked up shuffling noises, some from the woman she'd followed, others less clear. A void drake or a similar beast would make far more noise, so she continued to move forward, cursing the lack of visibility.

Gradually, her eyes adjusted. She glimpsed a large blocky form on the floor—an altar—and several stooped figures standing around its edges. Her steps stuck to the floor, and a coppery smell filled her nostrils. Blood. This must be where they made their sacrifices.

"Lie down," the woman rasped in Yala's ear, making her jump.

"What?" Yala didn't move. Shifting shadows resolved into figures standing behind the altar, and as her vision further adjusted, she made out their features.

And recoiled. They weren't human at all. Their form was humanoid, certainly, with two legs and two arms, but their bodies were thin and skeletal and covered in what appeared to be black scales. Their eyes, pitch-black, gleamed in the darkness, focusing on Yala.

"Come here," they rasped, their voices merging into one. "Complete your transformation."

Gods. Transformation? Would the woman rotting behind her eventually resemble one of those beasts? Was that Yala's fate if she lay upon the altar, or would they simply slit her throat and leave her to bleed into Mekan's waiting maw instead?

"Isn't this what you want, Yala Palathar?" Mekan whispered through the voices of the dead. *"All your pain will cease, and you will truly be one of mine."*

"I'll be subject to your will, you mean." Revulsion choked Yala's throat like bile. "I don't think so."

She held up her spear defensively as one of the figures moved closer to her, its claw-like hands reaching out.

Yala stabbed with her spear, but it bounced clean off the creature's scaly arm. The woman behind her seized her arm in a frailer grip.

"Don't struggle," she rasped in Yala's ear.

Yala stomped on her foot. Bone and skin gave way; the smell of rot intensified. Baring her teeth, she wrenched her arm free of the woman's hand, and then she ran.

The pain in her leg returned as she ran out into the main chamber, but fury and desperation spurred her onward until she reached the doorway. Niema stood on the threshold, her body as rigid as a statue, eyes closed as though to repel Mekan's rotting influence by sheer force of will.

"Yala." Her eyes flew open. "What—?"

Footsteps echoed behind her. Yala hefted her spear. "Niema. Time to go."

"What *are* they?" Niema retreated out of the temple, gasping at the sight of the figures following Yala. Their scaly bodies looked even more unnatural in the light—or what passed for it in the misty outdoors—and their facial features had shifted, becoming reptilian.

"The Successors," Yala said. "That's the end goal of the transformation. I want no part in it."

"Come closer, Disciple of Death," He whispered through the mouths of the dead. *"At last, you are home."*

"No," she snarled back. "No, I'm fucking not."

Yala gestured with a hand, and the dead war drake launched into flight, its claws reaching towards the monstrous semihumans. Even its sharp claws made no impact on those thick scales, though the distraction gained her enough time to hurry downstairs towards her mount.

One of the monstrous humanoids grabbed her shoulder; twisting, she drove the spear into its face until the sharp point found its pitted eyes. Like the other beasts, the eyes were its weak spot; her spear drove through flesh into what was presumably the brain, or what was left of it. The thing crumpled on the spot, its head leaking fluid.

Descending the last few steps, Yala leapt onto the dead war drake's back with a lunge that caused agony to tear up her leg. The pain brought a rush of clarity, a reminder that she was alive, and the creatures inside that temple certainly weren't.

A tremor resounded below, rumbling underneath the stairs. Niema whistled to her war drake, beckoning with an urgent hand. The flagstones had begun to shake, the darkness within the island preparing to expose its rotting core. Yala forced herself to stay close to the ground until Niema had safely mounted her war drake and then launched upward, while the scaly humanoid monsters gathered on the temple's stairs to watch the island open like a rotting flower in bloom.

"There it is." The Void. After everything, after Dalem's sacrifice… nothing had changed.

Rage bubbled inside, swamping any remnants of the force urging her to answer Mekan's call, and she gripped her spear until the wood creaked in protest.

How could she have believed a few mere flames had been enough to bring an end to Him?

"Come closer, Disciple," Mekan whispered. *"Don't you want me to take away your pain? To transform you into what you can truly be?"*

"No," she answered, scanning the island for any signs of a weak spot, any signs that Niema might be able to draw out something living amid the wasteland of death.

"You're destined to die. That is your tragedy. If not on the battlefield, you'll wear away, piece by piece, until you'll wish you'd answered my call."

The rasping voice and Mekan's laughter reverberated through the very island itself.

Kelan returned to consciousness with a heaving cough. He lay on the pier amid shattered wooden beams. His heart jolted when he spied a body lying nearby. Lakiel.

His fellow Disciple of the Sky lay on his back, not moving.

"No." Kelan crawled over and gave him a shake. Lakiel still didn't stir.

Fuck. He wouldn't have been here if not for me.

"Wake up," he snarled, pressing on his chest. Lakiel didn't stir. Fuck. *Fuck.*

Drawing back his fist, he punched his fellow Disciple in the midriff. Lakiel jerked upright with a gasp and spat water everywhere.

"Did you just hit me?" Lakiel wheezed, pushing up onto one elbow. "Some gratitude for saving your life. What happened?"

Good question. The seafront was a wasteland. A single boat remained the right way up without so much as a scratch on it, bobbing against the pier, deceptively serene. "King Tharen is already here."

He must have taken his followers with him, because not a soul remained on the boat, and the Disciples of the Sea were nowhere to be seen either. Nor did Kelan see any of the Disciples of the Flame who'd so unwisely followed him. He hoped they'd had the sense to get as far away as possible.

Lakiel glided beside him, his gaze on the rooftops. "Is that a war drake?"

"Where?" He squinted, spying a winged shape descending above the upper city. They were too far to make out its features, but the black scales trailing shadow brought the echo of a familiar pain in his shoulder.

A void drake.

Kelan ran. He breathed a prayer to the god of the sky, but he scarcely managed to glide for a handspan before his feet hit the ground again. Lakiel had better luck, overtaking his pitiful glide, but Kelan knew in his heart that they were far too late. The rest of their people were trapped in the upper city with that monster.

"No." Lakiel swore with each breath. "Is the army back? Why is there only one of those beasts?"

"I imagine our former king wanted to make an impression." Kelan broke into a run, though his legs were shaking from his near drowning and bone-deep exhaustion.

They encountered few people on the streets, and the murmur of noise in the background centred around the upper city. Atop the city wall, the guards had ceased their patrolling and stood in groups to watch whatever was occurring inside the upper city. The back gates lay open, unguarded.

Once inside, Kelan and Lakiel walked the short distance to the back entrance to the palace grounds. That would be the former king's eventual destination, Kelan guessed. With each step, the murmur of voices grew louder.

Lakiel snagged his arm, gesturing up. The void drake had stopped mid-flight, hovering directly above Ceremonial Square.

Ah. Maybe the king does have one last stop to make before the palace.

"I think Superior Shralin might be having regrets at not listening to us," he murmured.

"Where *is* Yala?" Lakiel hissed. "More to the point, why is nobody attacking that monster?"

"Yala's trying to stop this from getting even more out of hand than it already has," he replied. "Trust me, there's little she can do here, given that that monster's owner is the one who sent her to the island in the first place."

"This is madness." Lakiel overtook Kelan and glided down a side street. "What of the Disciples at the inn?"

And the ones returning to the city? Guilt twisted in Kelan's chest. They didn't deserve to pay for the Disciples of the Flame's crimes, but it was anyone's guess as to how the former king would apportion blame for his exile. Certainly, no other Disciples had come to his rescue.

At Ceremonial Square, Kelan finally glimpsed the king's entourage. Tharen had acquired more followers since Kelan had seen him last, dressed in plain clothing that might belong to civilians or soldiers and wielding short swords and spears like the city guards. The Disciples of the Sea weren't present as far as Kelan could see, but he couldn't imagine they spent much time on land.

Superior Shralin's tremulous voice drifted from somewhere in front of the temple. "Your Majesty... it is an honour to witness your return."

Really. He could only imagine how Yala would react if she'd been able to hear this performance. Kelan halted just out of sight of the square, in the temple's shadow, where he could watch without being seen.

Lakiel halted his glide, his head tilted to the sky. "Gods. Isn't that monster going to attack?"

The void drake hadn't budged since they'd begun their journey from the docks. Had the king given it orders to hover above the city until he needed it to strike down his enemies? Kelan hadn't thought it was possible even for a Disciple of Death to control one of those beasts, but it was clear there was a great deal he didn't know about what the king had been doing for the past few years.

From the front of the temple, King Tharen's voice rang out. "Those who attempted to have me killed must surrender."

"They already have," Superior Shralin replied. "They're in the guardhouse. I would be happy to show you."

"Not enough." King Tharen's tone put him in mind of a Superior exerting their might. *Shit. Is he that strong a Disciple of Death now?* Or was this all an elaborate bluff? He hadn't openly used his powers except for whatever he'd done to subdue that beast.

"I apologise, Your Majesty," Superior Shralin murmured. "Please, let me know if there is anything we can do. We would be more than happy to pledge ourselves to your service."

That can't be good.

Superior Shralin must know he had little choice but to throw himself at the king's feet and beg for mercy, but he hadn't allowed the other Disciples of the Flame to have a say. What of the ones who'd fled, attempting to follow Kelan? What of the Disciples of the Sky?

A grating noise from his right-hand side drew Kelan's eye to the palace gates, which had begun to swing open. Drums beat, thumping beneath his feet.

It's starting.

———

After her disastrous visit to the king, Viam had returned to the infirmary. Part of her knew she ought to be preparing for King Tharen's inevitable arrival, but she couldn't bring herself to move away from Brenat. She didn't know what else to do other than listen to her friend's breathing and hope that she awakened before the palace erupted into chaos.

Raised voices outside the door. Shouts of *King Tharen* echoed back and forth.

"Brenat." She carefully shook her shoulder. "Wake up."

Brenat's good eye cracked open. "What…?"

"He's back!" someone shouted. "King Tharen is back?"

Brenat sat upright. "Fuck me."

If she'd been Saren, she might have made a crude joke, but this wasn't the time. "I'm sorry… I have to get out of here."

"Why?" Brenat groaned. "Ow, my head hurts. What do you mean, you have to go?"

"The former king is coming back to claim his throne," Viam whispered. "How do you think he'll react when he finds the mess his son has caused?"

"What?" Brenat ran a hand through her tangled hair, her uninjured eye widening. "Shit. Didn't you say he was a Disciple—"

Viam lunged and put a hand over her friend's mouth. "Please don't say it. *Please.*"

Brenat's breath was hot on her hand. "Aren't *you* a Disciple of—?"

Viam pressed harder for an instant and then let go, not wanting to hurt her. Brenat seized her wrist before she could pull away, and when she rose upright, their lips crashed together. The breath escaped Viam's lungs, and she clung to Brenat, gasping, "Not the time."

"Yes, it is." Brenat gave her a gentle push. "Do what you have to do."

Viam's eyes brimmed with tears. Blinking furiously, she joined the growing crowd leaving the infirmary, formed of those well enough to walk. Other soldiers ran up and down the corridors, and commanders relayed orders through the barracks.

Assemble in the grounds. Wait for the king.

When she spied Commander Sranak, Viam ducked in the opposite direction. She was too recognisable to go unnoticed, but if she could get out of here before the king showed up—

Beating wings overhead drowned out the soldiers' shouts. Viam ran out of the nearest exit, hoping against hope that Yala was back— that she'd come to her rescue—but the shadow above the grounds didn't belong to a war drake. Pitch-dark scales covered a beast with long spikes jutting from its wide, leathery wings.

Viam's blood turned to water. *A void drake... here.*

She tried to run back into the building but was promptly caught in the crush of soldiers lining up in the grounds.

"Everyone outside!" shouted one of the commanders. "King's orders."

But which king? The question died on her tongue along with the others.

Not everyone shared that reticence. As she watched, a young novice waylaid a passing commander. "What is that monster in the sky? Are we under attack?"

"It's safe," said the commander. "The king has brought his followers to defend Laria against an imminent threat. He has also asked all Disciples of Death to present themselves to him at once."

He wanted the Disciples of Death. Did he mean her squad, or—? No. There weren't any others as far as she knew.

Drums began to beat, drowning out the pounding footsteps of the assembling soldiers. Cheers drifted over the wall from the palace grounds, joyous cries.

"King Tharen has returned!"

35

Niema gripped the war drake's back, watching Yala hovering perilously close to the growing hole forming in the island's centre. Despite the vibrant greenery at the edges of the square, the sense of life pulsing from below tasted sour on her tongue. Pain throbbed in Niema's chest, and she swallowed bile.

Yet it was the sight of the Corrupted people, who might have once been the Successors, that truly shook her to her core.

That's what Mekan does? That's the transformation?

No wonder Yala had turned away at the last moment. And thank Yalet she had.

Yalet... that was why Niema was here. She had to close the Void somehow.

Extending her senses, Niema reached outward, seeking anything living that might lie beneath the veneer of decay. Yet the entire island was a gateway to the Void, and it was no wonder that Dalathik's fire hadn't been able to entirely destroy it. The jungles had burned, but the temple had remained, and now, every handspan of the island heaved with horrors. The jungles were thick, not with life but with the half-dead creations of Mekan's, and the temple stairs crawling with scaled humanoids.

The stones cracked open, expelling a void drake. Wings unfurling, the beast flew upward towards her and Yala. Niema whistled a command, and the void drake slowed, landing on the stairs amid the monsters that had once been human.

Maybe the void drake had been a war drake at one time, before it had undergone the same transformation as those humanoid creatures.

An idea occurred to her. She whistled, this time directing her command at the beings on the stairs. The Successors ceased their movements, their scaly bodies going slack.

A mixture of revulsion and vindication seized her. *I can control them too.* But her powers had a limit. She couldn't stop an entire army.

"Yala. I'm going to close the Void." Taking in a breath, Niema began her prayer to the god of life.

As soon as she stopped whistling, the void drake shook off her command and took flight. The figures on the stairs, too, began their advance again.

Yala swore. She brought the dead war drake into a dive to intercept the void drake. The beasts' claws tangled in a grim frenzy; when Yala began to overbalance, Niema ceased her prayer and whistled another command. The void drake ceased its attack, descending to land on the Void's edge.

"I can't do two things at once," she said. "I'll need to keep its attention off me while I close the Void, but I don't know how."

"I'll do it." Yala moved a hand, and the dead war drake's claw mimicked the motion. "Get ready."

When Yala flew at the void drake and moved her hands, her mount's claws seized the other beast around the neck and squeezed. Niema began her prayer again, but she'd hardly uttered a word before Yala shouted. More large claws reached out of the gaping hole of the Void, grabbing the dead war drake's legs and pulling downward.

"Let go." Yala twisted in her seat, stabbing with her spear, but she was outnumbered. One of the claws seized the spear straight out of her hand.

Niema ceased her prayer to whistle a command, but while the void drake's attack halted, the other beasts paid her no attention. There were too many. *We're going to die here.*

Yala's hands streamed shadows, gesturing furiously as her steed tried to shake off its unwanted attackers. Niema whistled, louder, and the claws released her. Yet more emerged from the abyss, clawing their way out of the Void to reach for living prey.

"What *did* your Superior give you?" Yala grunted. "Was it a trick, or is she not strong enough to stop them?"

I don't know. The stench of death was overwhelming, but she trusted Yalet, and that trust bolstered her. She recalled the burning sensation nestled in her chest, the glow that had sunk somewhere deep inside her.

Niema reached towards the sensation, envisioning the green light her Superior had passed to her, and tried to call it out of her body and into her hands. A glow bloomed, but not as bright as it should be. Was there a specific prayer she was supposed to speak? How could she think clearly with Mekan's forces grasping at her heels?

A loud splash came from somewhere below, and Yala twisted around in her seat. "What's going on?"

Niema's gaze landed on the strip of sand visible beyond the jungle. While the dead had yet to make it to the beach, a figure had half emerged from the ocean, a distinctly human shape pulling himself out of the water. *Is that—Nanek?*

Another wave splashed, surging up the beach and into the jungle. Yala's eyes widened. "Nanek? He survived—but does that mean—?"

As the wave receded, a boat bobbed into view. Flames ignited, held in the palms of Disciples who were soaked through to the skin but very much alive.

"Nanek saved them." How they'd got here through the fog and confusion was a mystery—and now that Niema counted their heads, at least one or two were missing—but when the boat bumped against the jungle's edge, the Disciples stepped out onto the sand.

The murmur of a prayer reached her ears. Flames spiralled upward, and the outer rim of trees burst apart. Screeches and cries rose up from the jungle, presumably from Mekan's monsters, and the flames swiftly roared towards the island's centre, devouring everything in their paths.

Niema's attention went back to the Void, into which some of Mekan's monsters had already fled. Smoke billowed above the jungle as the flames advanced, unyielding, and when they reached the plaza, the stones began to close. The same grating noise that had announced the Void's opening filled the air.

"Even if it closes up again, the temple will still be there," Yala said. "Even Dalathik's fire can't melt stone."

Neither can Yalet. But that wasn't the point. The god of the flames devoured all, His flames leaving no mark as all living and dead beings alike were swallowed up. The god of life, though... Her domain revelled in creation, not destruction.

Niema reached for the glowing light within her chest and called to mind a prayer, a simple one she'd learned early on in her training as a Disciple. The prayer uttered when a forest fire finally extinguished itself or when trees rotted away to make room for new life.

As Niema began to pray, light blossomed from her palms, calling life not from the island but from within herself or from the gift her Superior had given her.

"Bring life," she murmured. "From the ashes."

The light exploded outward, above the blackened remains left in the wake of the Disciples' flames. The temple itself trembled as the light washed over its dark walls, seeking out crevices in the gloom.

Trees sprouted in the ashes left around the plaza. The jungle crept in around the temple, swamping the flagstones, greenery rising up the temple stairs as though to chase the remnants of Mekan's beasts away from this world.

She prayed for those beasts, too, praying that they were set free from the half existence between life and death and that new life would bloom in their place.

When her prayer finished, Niema could no longer sense the Void. Not even inside the temple. The life she'd called had infiltrated its walls in a way that no other deity was capable of, and Mekan had fled from its influence.

All lay still.

———

Yala felled the last of the dead, watching the greenery creep over the temple's entrance. The remnants of the scaled human-like figures fell beneath a carpet of grassy brightness, and she thought she heard Mekan shout in fury as His temple was defiled.

Niema glowed, her very skin incandescent, until it hurt Yala's eyes to look upon her. She scanned for the Disciples of the Flame instead, but their boat had vanished, and so had Nanek. *I hope they got away,* she was surprised to find herself thinking.

Eventually, the glow faded from Niema's skin, though a faraway look lingered in her eyes. "Is... is it over?"

"I honestly don't know." The mist had faded, exposing thick jungle that might have been untouched for generations. Had Niema really caused all *that* to grow out of nothing? "What did you *do?*"

"I prayed for new life to grow from the old," she said. "Even this island isn't solely Mekan's domain, or else no living creature would exist here."

"Including His followers?" From what she could see of the serpentine monsters who had once been the Successors, the greenery hadn't spared them either. They stood or lay amid the ruin, and a closer look revealed vines creeping outward from inside the black pits of their eyes. "Good thinking."

I can't believe that worked. The temple was still in one piece, and she hadn't *seen* the Void close, but her instincts told her that Niema spoke true.

"I can't sense Him," Niema added as though she'd guessed Yala's thoughts. "I can't sense anything dead... not in the unnatural way."

Yala grunted. "That's good enough for me."

"If someone were to make a big enough sacrifice, it might open again," Niema said. "But the same is true of the Temple of the Earth. I think... I think this is it."

Then what now? Part of her had almost revelled in the notion of her life coming to an end here on the island. Not only would it be a fitting end, but she wouldn't have to return to the chaos she'd left behind in Laria. When, though, had her life ever been that easy?

"I know," Niema said. "This isn't truly over. I wish we'd destroyed the army as well."

The army. Had they been hiding in the Void? Yala hoped so, fervently, but there seemed no good reason for the king to dismiss his army before he'd reclaimed his throne.

When he did so, of course, the first thing he'd do was reassemble the old army. Whether that included her or not, her fate would end on the battlefield.

I can't go back. A part of her wondered what would happen if she simply let the wind carry her where it would, soaring like a Disciple of the Sky over the open sea. Like Kelan. *Gods. He's back in the capital, and so are Saren and Viam. I can't leave them. I promised I'd get them out.*

Yala's gaze skimmed over the beach, landing on a body. A human one.

The female Disciple of the Flame.

Niema noticed, too, and flinched. "What—happened to her?"

"Is she dead?" Yala flew lower, glimpsed a long spear sticking out of her chest. Blood leaked onto the sand. "That wasn't Mekan."

Nearby, the Disciples' boat lay upside-down in the water, surrounded by a halo of blood. Yala watched, bewildered, as another body floated towards them, his head half detached as though teeth had bitten through his neck.

Water splashed, and a sea drake cut through the surface of the water. Upon its back sat a long-haired man wielding a spear and undoubtedly alive. Several other sea drakes, also equipped for war, gathered behind him.

"Shit. It's Rafragoria."

At least ten soldiers, armed with spears and bows, surrounded the boat. A sopping-wet Disciple of the Flame attempted to surface, but an arrow hit him in the side of the head, and he fell back, his ear trailing blood.

Spotting Yala and Niema, the Rafragorians began to shout and point. Yala recognised a few words she'd learned during her time in the army.

Laria.

King.

War.

Death.

She didn't need to hear the rest.

"I know where King Tharen's army of the dead went."

"No." Niema sounded faint. "No. We're not on their side! We stopped the dead!"

A spear flew, piercing Yala's steed through the neck. It didn't leave a mark on the dead war drake, but her steed's body tilted alarmingly to the side, and she realised too late that she'd never grabbed a fresh weapon.

A second spear hit its tail, shaking the bones. Yala held on tighter, shouting, "We didn't send that army! We're not with the king."

A futile effort. To the Rafragorians, all Larians fought for the same cause. If Laria had been beset by an army of the dead sent by a rogue Rafragorian empress, she would have reacted the same, yet that knowledge did little to temper her desire to avoid sharing the Disciples' fate.

Yala leaned sideways, attempting to grab the bag of spears from between the dead war drake's ribs. As she did, Niema's war drake let out a howl as an arrow lodged itself into the meat of its thigh. Niema whispered a frantic prayer, perhaps an attempt to heal its wound, but the war drake's flight path tilted sideways.

A sea drake reared up out of the water, its teeth closing around her steed's leg with a sickening crunch. The war drake screamed.

"Fuck." Yala managed to grab a spear and dropped in the air to reach her target. She jabbed at the sea drake, and her spear sank into the vulnerable flesh of its neck, causing its grip to break on Niema's mount.

The war drake's leg was freed, but rivulets of blood dripped into the water. An arrow whipped past Yala's face. She lifted her chin, blood sliding down her cheek, as the soldier took aim again.

She flew upward, but he'd aimed higher than she'd thought. The arrow slammed into her upper arm. Yala grunted with pain, her hands slipping on the spear.

The sea drake rose upward again, its neck gushing blood, and its rider hurled his spear at Niema. She howled, blood spraying from her ankle.

"Niema!" Yala gasped. "Get away. Fly…"

Yala stabbed, her spear sinking to the hilt in the sea drake's neck. This time, the beast sank, and the other soldiers moved in to help the rider while the beast thrashed out its last breaths.

The dying sea drake's tail lashed upward, striking the front of Yala's steed. Its skull fractured, and she lost her grip on the shadows holding the fragile bones together.

The next spear hit her in the chest. The point burrowed into Yala's shirt. Numbly, she looked down, suspended for a heartbeat before she fell.

In death, she expected to hear Mekan's voice, but all noise was drowned out by a whistle that vibrated through her very bones.

"Stop!" cried Niema. "STOP!"

———

What have I done? Niema watched the Rafragorians freeze in the midst of their attack, stilled by her command. Not a spear flew, not an arrow left its bow. Even their steeds had stopped moving, the death throes of the doomed sea drake fading to silence.

"Leave," Niema ordered. "Leave us. *Now.*"

Blank-faced, the Rafragorians retreated, their steeds gliding smoothly over the water. Niema watched with the unreal sense of slipping over a boundary that she hadn't known existed. She'd used her abilities on humans. Humans who were on the run from the dead, who'd been attacked by her own country…

Yala groaned, snapping Niema out of her horror-struck trance. She lay sprawled atop the broken bones of her war drake, and blood clouded the water around her. *Gods. She's badly hurt.* Niema's ankle burned with pain from the blow she'd taken to the ankle, but Yala... the spear in her chest had snapped off at the end, and blood blossomed to the surface.

Niema reached for the remnants of power Superior Kralia had loaned her, but not so much as a twinge responded. Her hands glowed, but with her own power, and it wasn't enough.

Help me.

Niema reached for Yala's hands in a futile attempt to pull her out of the water. Pain rippled up her palms as they brushed against the grey-tinged ends of Yala's fingers.

Niema gritted her teeth and ignored the sting of Mekan's touch, this time managing to keep her grip. Yala slumped forward, and several minutes of painful struggle followed as Niema pulled her over the war drake's front. The position was bound to make her injury worse, but there was no help for it, nor for the shattered ruin of the dead war drake in the water.

Yala groaned again.

"Sorry," Niema whispered. She uttered a quick healing prayer, but her own pain made her dizzy, and the war drake's leg continued to trail blood too. She didn't have enough resources to heal all of them.

They would die, she was sure, before they reached Laria's coast. No option remained but flight, and so she gave the command, and the island vanished behind them.

Soon, Niema's world was reduced to beating wings and whispered prayers and Yala slumped over the war drake, every breath ragged enough to be her last. *Please...*

Another winged shape appeared ahead of them, and Niema's heart plunged. *No. Not now.*

She whistled, but their adversary moved in unison. A rider sat upon its back, commanding the beast to match their flight, like a mirror image waiting to meet them.

Superior Kralia.

36

As the king's entourage crossed the square to the palace grounds, Kelan retreated into the side street. The drumbeats and the thunder of footsteps indicated that Tharen had wasted no time in calling together what was left of his army.

Lakiel lingered near the mouth of the street nearest to the square. "I have to find my sister."

"I'll wait here." A lie. Kelan wanted to see what was going on inside the palace grounds, but his whispered prayers to Terethik went unanswered.

Since he was unable to see over the wall, he made his way to the war drakes' paddock and peered around the corner. The gate was closed but unguarded, though heavy footsteps pounded on the other side. From the barracks, he guessed. Through the gap, he spied soldiers moving, but he couldn't tell if they were following orders.

A lighter, faster pair of footsteps came running down the alley between the paddock and the fence circling the palace grounds.

"Kelan." Viam stumbled to a halt in front of him. "Help me."

The thump of boots behind the fence continued, interspersed with drumbeats. Kelan pictured the king's retinue making their way to the barracks, where the soldiers awaited them... except for Viam.

"Please," she added. "He... the king... he asked for all Disciples of Death to turn themselves in. I have to warn..."

"Yala?"

"No, Saren. He might be in danger too," she said. "I don't think he's ever *used* his abilities, but that doesn't necessarily matter, does it?"

No. It didn't. He gestured for her to come closer, making up his mind.

"I've overused my abilities," he told her. "I can't fly for long, but I might be able to get us over the wall to the outer city."

The nearest stretch of wall happened to run around the back of the Temple of the Flame, but the Superior would be a tad occupied at the present time. They stuck to narrow alleys as they made their way towards Ceremonial Square, but all eyes were on the palace, and the alley behind the Temple of the Flame was deserted too. The sheer wall would be impossible to climb, so Kelan whispered a prayer to the god of the sky. He beckoned Viam over to him and positioned himself behind her, hands closed around her upper arms like when he flew with Yala.

Just give me this, Terethik. Please.

His feet left the ground. Holding his breath, he drifted upward and glided over the wall.

Nobody stopped them. He heard what might have been a shout, but the guards' attention was on the palace instead.

Kelan landed, his feet stumbling on the ground, and released Viam.

"I don't think I'm going to be able to fly again," he said. "We'll have to find another way out of the city."

Unless Yala comes back, he thought. Yala and Niema had taken both war drakes with them, and while he understood why they both needed to go to the island, Yala surely hadn't intended her friends to end up hunted down by the king's guards while she was gone.

Viam ran ahead unsteadily, the wound in her arm bleeding through its bandage. Kelan followed, slower, not wanting to push his luck. When they reached Yala's house, Saren opened the door before Viam could knock.

"Tell me it's not true," he said.

"It's true," Viam said. "The king is looking for Disciples of Death. We have to leave."

"Where the fuck do we go?"

Oddly enough, they both looked at Kelan. "Don't ask me. I can barely fly."

"Nalen," Saren said. "Yala mentioned asking him to help, but—the Undercity is the first place the dead will infest if His Majesty unleashes monstrous hordes of the dead upon the city."

"He only brought one void drake," said Viam.

"Only." Saren laughed humourlessly. "One's enough. He's come to take back his crown, by force if necessary."

Kelan had no better ideas, so once Saren had grabbed his belongings, they left for the Undercity. Guilt assailed Kelan when he thought of his fellow Disciples inside the upper city, but there was nothing he could do. They hadn't broken any laws, and with the guards distracted, they'd have a better chance of getting out than his own odds of sneaking out of the city in the company of a Disciple of Death.

Nalen waited at the entrance to the Undercity, bearded and broad and armed with twin swords. "Yala told me to expect you here."

"Me?" Kelan frowned.

"She inferred that you'd do something unwise that'd catch the wrong kind of attention." He nodded to Saren and then Viam. "As for you, she wanted to make sure that her squad was taken care of if she didn't come back."

"She's coming back," Saren insisted. "She has to."

"She can't die," Viam whispered.

She can. Yala wasn't immortal. She might be lying dead on that island, or worse... turned into one of Mekan's followers.

"Dead or not, she gave me instructions," said Nalen. "She asked me to offer you shelter, but I can't guarantee your safety. *He* claims otherwise."

"Who?" Kelan peered over Nalen's shoulder at a slight figure who might just be on the cusp of adulthood, draped in a reed-woven garment not unlike the one Niema had worn when he'd first met her.

391

Dark hair curled on either side of his pointed face, and a birthmark on his chin painted him as a Disciple of Life. "Who are you?"

"I'm Hachim," said the boy, twisting the hem of his garment in his hands self-consciously. "Niema might have mentioned me if she talked of the enclave."

Niema. "You're in her enclave? Does that mean you came with Superior Kralia?"

"I followed her." He hung his head. "I came for Niema, though."

"Did Niema tell you what Superior Kralia did to her?" He didn't recall her mentioning the enclave members by name, at least when he was listening, but this boy must have expected a warm reception if he'd followed her all the way here.

"Yes." He bit his lower lip. "I understand why she left the enclave, but Superior Kralia promised not to harm her again. She's offered to help."

"This is a pleasant diversion," Saren said, "but while being recruited into His Majesty's army of the dead isn't on my plan, as far as I'm concerned, going into the jungle with your creepy Superior is no better."

He blinked. "How did you guess that was what I was going to ask?"

"It's the obvious place to hide," Viam said. "Outside of the city, far from the king and his army."

"I'm not putting my fate in the hands of someone who can overturn the will of anyone who disagrees with them," Saren said flatly. "Tell me why I should agree to this."

"Because," said the Disciple of Life, "if all goes to plan, Yala will be there soon too."

———

Yala returned to consciousness to find a wooden roof above her head and the sounds of the jungle all around her. Birds chirped. Kekins chattered to one another. Trees rustled.

She closed her eyes for a long moment and then opened them again. The scene remained intact. Was she back in her jungle cabin?

Was it possible that the last few months had somehow been some kind of detailed hallucination? No… impossible.

Yala turned, and a sharp and unfamiliar pain stabbed her in the chest. More twinges ran through her upper arm and leg when she struggled to sit up, raising a hand to shield her eyes against the sunlight lancing through the hole in the wall that passed for a window.

"Yala." Niema hurried over, her hands aglow with green light. "Don't move. I healed most of the damage, but you'll be sore for a while. I couldn't do much while we were flying, and it took more than a day to get here."

"Flying?" Yala croaked. "You brought me to—?"

"I'm sorry," Niema whispered. "I didn't know what else to do."

Yala forced her body into a sitting position, though pain rippled up her chest. The cabin was larger than she'd initially thought, comprising two rooms connected by a closed door. Another sleeping mat lay across from hers, occupied by a frail-looking elderly woman.

"Sorry," Niema said again. "I didn't know where else to bring you. That's Ekim. She's from my enclave."

The old woman didn't stir. Noise sounded outside, leaves brushing against the window, and the door creaked inward.

Superior Kralia entered. Yala scrambled back, reaching for anything she might use as a weapon.

"I have no intention of doing you harm," said the Superior.

"She doesn't," said Niema. "You were hurt—really hurt—and my war drake was injured too."

"The former king will not be able to find you here," added Superior Kralia. "However, your friends will be glad to hear you're awake."

"What friends?" Yala's arms trembled from the effort of holding herself upright, and she fell back onto the sleeping mat. "What have you done?"

"It wasn't her," said Niema. "Hachim—he followed me to the capital. He must have shown up after we left for the island, and he didn't know where to find me."

That made no sense to Yala. Gritting her teeth, she pushed herself onto her elbows and spied her cane lying across from her. With a painful effort, she lurched to grab it and used the wooden stick to push to her feet. "Who brought this here?"

"You should rest," Niema objected.

Not while she's in here. Yala glowered at Superior Kralia, who withdrew from the cabin, saying, "Your friends are here too. I shall let them know you're conscious."

She withdrew. Yala watched, becoming conscious that someone had removed her drakeskin gloves but left her other battle-stained clothes. Her hair clung to her face, tangled and damp with sweat, and dried blood caked her arms. Rivulets of perspiration ran from under the bandages around her chest. Her weapons were gone, but her weapons belt hung from her waist, as did the pouch containing the void drake's claw.

"I... convinced her to let you keep it." Niema followed her gaze, confirming her guess. "I told her that you wouldn't summon Mekan's beasts."

"And she believed you?" Yala snorted. "I'm hardly in any state to attack anyone, mind."

Then she heard voices, an unlikely combination. Kelan, Viam... and Saren?

"What are they doing here?" Her voice was hoarse from underuse. "Who convinced them?"

"Hachim. He's been showing them around the enclave." She darted outside, while Yala trudged to the doorway and leaned on the frame for balance, gripping her cane in both hands.

A minute later, Niema returned, accompanied by a male Disciple of Life who couldn't be older than seventeen. Behind him walked Kelan, Saren, and Viam, a sight utterly incongruous with their surroundings. The latter's drakeskin trousers were less out of place than Saren's silk shirt and Kelan's blue cloak, but she hadn't thought to see a single one of them in the forest.

Upon catching sight of her, their group descended on the cabin. Niema reached the door first and all but steered Yala back to her sleeping mat with surprising force.

"You don't want to reopen the wound," she insisted. "I healed most of the damage, but that spear went in deep."

"I felt it." Her skin itched, a reminder that she needed to wash away the blood, but she needed answers more. "What *are* you all doing here? Do any of you realise this is the same place where Niema was sentenced to death and left to be eaten alive by Mekan's monsters?"

No doubt Superior Kralia would be within hearing distance, but Yala didn't bother lowering her voice. She had no intention of masking her opinions on the Superior's treatment of Niema.

"No," said Saren. "Why does nobody ever tell me anything?"

"You don't listen," Viam corrected. Her arm was still bandaged, but her wound looked better than the last time Yala had seen her. "We didn't have a choice. The king... Tharen ordered all Disciples of Death to join him."

"Why?" Yala looked between them. "Is he claiming that status publicly?"

"I don't know, but it's pretty obvious he either wants to make us into an elite part of his army or kill us off to bolster his own standing with Mekan," Saren said. "I decided to take my chances with the jungle instead."

"Hardly a choice." Gods. Were they all indebted to Superior Kralia now? "Sorry I didn't get back to you in time. We were ambushed by Rafragorians."

"They're the ones who nearly killed you?" Kelan asked. "What were they doing near the island?"

"Fleeing from King Tharen's army." Yala caught Niema's eye, guessing that she hadn't told them all the details of their foiled escape. "At a guess, the army of the dead that mysteriously vanished from Laria was sent to another destination."

"King Tharen ordered the dead to attack Rafragoria?" Saren gawped at her next to an equally slack-jawed Viam.

"It's certainly a way to send a message that he's back," Kelan remarked. "Starting a war with Rafragoria before he even takes back his crown."

Through the window, Yala spied Superior Kralia making her way towards their group. In the jungle, she moved like part of the land-scape itself; flowers bloomed at her feet with each step she took, as bright as the ones adorning her headdress and the long garment she wore.

"I'm glad everyone made it here safely," she said.

No, you aren't. Aloud, Yala asked, "Why'd you keep me alive? I was completely at your mercy, and I was under the impression that you wanted all Disciples of Death to be eradicated from existence."

Niema took in a sharp breath. The forest itself seemed to hold still, waiting for the answer.

"I do," said Superior Kralia. "However, you may be the only person who can remove the former king from his throne before it's too late for all of us."

Yala stared back at her. Then she broke into laughter so hard that her wounded chest ached.

————

Later—much later—Yala and the others sat around a cookfire. Niema was relieved at Yala's recovery; while her wounds pained her, she'd been in a worse state when Yala and her Superior had reached the mainland after their flight from the island, and they hadn't been able to stop to fully heal her on the way. Superior Kralia had depleted her resources to give Niema a chance on the island, and Niema herself had lost much of her power in the fight and the ongoing drain of her own injuries.

Nevertheless, they'd made it to the enclave. All of them had. Niema couldn't quite reconcile the idea of sweet-natured and gentle Hachim making the journey to Dalathar alone—much less finding his way safely to the Undercity—but he'd managed to bring the others here.

That Superior Kralia had saved them all didn't erase the harm she'd done, however, nor did it remove the wedge between Niema and the rest of the enclave.

Hachim was the exception. He even sat with the newcomers to eat when his fellow Disciples were too wary of strangers to come near.

They ate bowls of vegetable broth and chunks of baked flatbread from the nearby village, and Niema found the tension seeping out of her bones until she could almost forget that the exiled monarch held Laria's throne and that Disciples of Death ruled the capital. The forest was serene, untouched by Mekan's rot. Or so it seemed.

Yala put aside her empty bowl and watched a bright bird sing in the trees above. "Pity you don't eat meat. The animals would practically walk up to you and wait for you to cut their throats."

"That wouldn't be ethical." Here above all, she felt a heightened awareness of every living creature. The enclave members most of all, their beating hearts resounding inside her own chest, while her awareness extended throughout the whole forest.

She hadn't brought death with her this time, or so she thought, but how long would that last? How long before Mekan's forces reached the jungle too?

Kelan slapped a buzzing bloodfly with a palm and grimaced when it sprayed blood on his sleeve. "Now I remember why I don't spend much time outside the city."

"Those things are a fucking menace," Saren agreed. He looked more peaceful than he did in the city, though it helped that nothing had tried to kill them for a couple of days. Unless you counted the bloodflies, anyway. "How long are we staying here?"

Everyone looked at Niema. Heat rushed to her face. "As long as you like. Yala needs to recover."

Kelan cleared his throat. "I can only stay a few days before I need to get back to Skytower. I assume my fellow Disciples of the Sky will head straight there, too, if they managed to get out of the city."

He'd had to leave them behind to help Saren and Viam escape. To help Yala. That must have been a hard choice to make.

"I hope they are," said Viam. "The king only asked for the Disciples of the Flame to surrender. They were directly involved in the plan against his life. Your fellow Disciples weren't."

Yala grimaced. "Yes, but I can't imagine he'll be thrilled to find the conspirators aren't in the jail any longer."

"You what?" Saren dropped his bowl, splashing soup everywhere.

"You *let them out?* After all the trouble you went to to get them locked up in the first place?"

Viam shook her head slowly. "Yala. Why?"

"I needed their help to destroy the island," Yala said. "It didn't quite go according to plan, though, and they ended up being killed by Rafragoria's soldiers."

"Good," said Saren. "I think. Gods, what a mess."

"I can't even blame the Rafragorians for attacking me." Yala fingered the hem of her shirt. "If there's anything left of their army, they're within their rights to raze this country to the ground."

"I have a feeling King Tharen's only just getting started," Saren said darkly. "He hasn't come back home to sit idly in his palace. He wants more."

"And we don't know how deep he is with Mekan," Viam murmured. "All the more reason to stay out of his way."

"We're not safe here." When Yala's eyes narrowed in suspicion, Niema added, "When I first returned from Dalathar, Mekan's creatures followed me into the forest."

Yala, Saren, and Viam exchanged looks. They were all Disciples of Death to varying degrees. There was no chance Mekan would fail to take advantage of that, even within Yalet's territory.

"Yes," said Superior Kralia, approaching their group. "They did."

Dread gripped Niema, banishing her brief sense of peace. "Then why did you let me bring the others here? Why take the risk?"

"As of yet, we're the only people in Laria with a full understanding of what King Tharen is capable of and what he may plan to do," said the Superior. "Mekan's forces have yet to appear in the jungle, though I have people keeping an eye out for them."

"We might know what he's capable of, but that doesn't mean we have any ability to stop him," Niema protested. "The Disciples of the Flame are the only people who might have challenged him, and they already surrendered."

Saren snorted. "We were never going to get any help from them."

"My Superior might help." Kelan eyed Superior Kralia. "If I were to ask her, would you agree to communicate? To join forces?"

"Yes." The answer was terse but firm.

"That's the plan?" Niema guessed. "You want us to find other allies among the Disciples?"

Superior Kralia inclined her head. "I'm sure you'll be able to collectively think of a way to do so."

She strode past their group. Niema held her breath until she'd vanished from sight. "I knew she'd have an agenda."

"What else is new?" Yala muttered. "Kelan, your Superior said we have an invitation to Skytower?"

"Yes," he said. "I can't say King Tharen *won't* find us there, but it'll be lower on his list of priorities."

Yala huffed out a breath. "Given that he has at least one void drake, I won't rule anything out."

No. The void drake obeyed *him,* and Niema didn't understand why. Had he accessed a power like the one she'd gained when she'd healed Yala and become something between a Disciple of both Life and Death at once?

Niema hadn't dared to mention to anyone that she'd used her abilities to stop the Rafragorians from attacking. How could she look her fellow enclave members in the eye and say she was any better than Superior Kralia? Even Hachim, who'd followed her despite her transgressions, despite her position on the knife's edge between life and death.

"If we don't run," Niema said to Yala, "what should we do?"

"What else?" Yala flashed the ghost of a smile, lifting a hand half smothered in shadow. "We'll drag him into hell with us."

ACKNOWLEDGMENTS

It's that time again! Firstly, I'd like to offer a massive thank you to everyone who's supported *Death's Disciple* and the whole series over the past year. It's been wonderful to see the support build with each book release and to see the Kickstarter surpass both previous campaigns. Thank you to my backers, and thank you to all the bloggers and reviewers who've championed the series, too!

I also owe a huge thanks to the behind-the-scenes team, in particular my lovely editor Sarah Chorn and my fabulous cover artists at Deranged Doctor Design, and to my assistant Mary Fields for staying on top of my chaotic schedule and making everything run so much more smoothly.

Finally, thank you to my patrons over on Patreon and to everyone who's supported the three Kickstarter campaigns for the series. I'm heartened to see this level of traction for my dark and weird fantasy series, and I'm very excited to continue sharing my stories with you!

ABOUT THE AUTHOR

Emma spent her childhood creating imaginary worlds to compensate for a disappointingly average reality, so it was probably inevitable that she ended up writing fantasy novels. She has a BA in English Literature with Creative Writing from Lancaster University, where she spent three years exploring the Lake District and penning strange fantastical adventures.

Now, Emma lives in the middle of England and is the international bestselling author of over 30 novels including the Changeling Chronicles and the Order of the Elements series. When she's not immersed in her own fictional universes, Emma can be found with her head in a book or wandering around the world in search of adventure.

Find out more about Emma's books at www.emmaladams.com.

Milton Keynes UK
Ingram Content Group UK Ltd.
UKHW042140201024
449848UK00018B/116/J

9 781916 584105